PRAISE FOR CAT

WIFE BY WEDNESDAY

"A fun and sizzling romance, great characters that trade verbal spars like fist punches, and the dream of your own royal wedding!"
—Sizzling Hot Book Reviews, 5 Stars

"A good holiday, fireside or bedtime story."
—Manic Reviews, 4½ Stars

"A great story that I hope is the start of a new series."
—The Romance Studio, 4½ Hearts

MARRIED BY MONDAY

"If I hadn't already added Ms. Catherine Bybee to my list of favorite authors, after reading this book I would have been compelled to. This is a book *nobody* should miss, because the magic it contains is awesome."
—Booked Up Reviews, 5 Stars

"Ms. Bybee writes authentic situations and expresses the good and the bad in such an equal way . . . Keeps the reader on the edge of her seat."
—Reading Between the Wines, 5 Stars

"*Married by Monday* was a refreshing read and one I couldn't possibly put down."
—The Romance Studio, 4½ Hearts

Fiancé by Friday

"Bybee knows exactly how to keep readers happy . . . A thrilling pursuit and enough passion to stuff in your back pocket to last for the next few lifetimes . . . The hero and heroine come to life with each flip of the page and will linger long after readers cross the finish line."

—*RT Book Reviews,* 4½ Stars, Top Pick (Hot)

"A tale full of danger and sexual tension . . . the intriguing characters add emotional depth, ensuring readers will race to the perfectly fitting finish."

—*Publishers Weekly*

"Suspense, survival, and chemistry mix in this scintillating read."

—*Booklist*

"Hot romance, a mystery assassin, British royalty, and an alpha Marine . . . this story has it all!"

—Harlequin Junkie

Single by Saturday

"Captures readers' hearts and keeps them glued to the pages until the fascinating finish . . . romance lovers will feel the sparks fly . . . almost instantaneously."

—*RT Book Reviews,* 4½ Stars, Top Pick

"[A] wonderfully exciting plot, lots of desire, and some sassy attitude thrown in for good measure!"

—Harlequin Junkie

TAKEN BY TUESDAY

"[Bybee] knows exactly how to get bookworms sucked into the perfect storyline; then she casts her spell upon them so they don't escape until they reach the 'Holy Cow!' ending."

—*RT Book Reviews,* 4½ Stars, Top Pick

SEDUCED BY SUNDAY

"You simply can't miss [this novel]. It contains everything a romance reader loves—clever dialogue, three-dimensional characters, and just the right amount of steam to go with that heartwarming love story."

—Brenda Novak, *New York Times* bestselling author

"Bybee hits the mark . . . providing readers with a smart, sophisticated romance between a spirited heroine and a prim hero . . . Passionate and intelligent characters [are] at the heart of this entertaining read."

—*Publishers Weekly*

TREASURED BY THURSDAY

"The Weekday Brides never disappoint and this final installment is by far Bybee's best work to date."

—*RT Book Reviews,* 4½ Stars, Top Pick

"An exquisitely written and complex story brimming with pride, passion, and pulse-pounding danger . . . Readers will gladly make time to savor this winning finale to a wonderful series."

—*Publishers Weekly,* Starred Review

"Bybee concludes her popular Weekday Brides series in a gratifying way with a passionate, troubled couple who may find a happy future if they can just survive and then learn to trust each other. A compelling and entertaining mix of sexy, complicated romance and menacing suspense."

—*Kirkus Reviews*

NOT QUITE DATING

"It's refreshing to read about a man who isn't afraid to fall in love . . . [Jack and Jessie] fit together as a couple and as a family."

—*RT Book Reviews*, 3 Stars (Hot)

"*Not Quite Dating* offers a sweet and satisfying Cinderella fantasy that will keep you smiling long after you've finished reading."

—Kathy Altman, *USA Today*, "Happy Ever After"

"The perfect rags to riches romance . . . The dialogue is inventive and witty, the characters are well drawn out. The storyline is superb and really shines . . . I highly recommend this stand out romance! Catherine Bybee is an automatic buy for me."

—Harlequin Junkie, 4½ Hearts

NOT QUITE ENOUGH

"Bybee's gift for creating unforgettable romances cannot be ignored. The third book in the Not Quite series will sweep readers away to a paradise, and they will be intrigued by the thrilling story that accompanies their literary vacation."

—*RT Book Reviews*, 4½ Stars, Top Pick

NOT QUITE FOREVER

"Full of classic Bybee humor, steamy romance, and enough plot twists and turns to keep readers entertained all the way to the very last page."
—Tracy Brogan, bestselling author of the Bell Harbor series

"Magnetic . . . The love scenes are sizzling and the multi-dimensional characters make this a page-turner. Readers will look for earlier installments and eagerly anticipate new ones."
—*Publishers Weekly*

NOT QUITE PERFECT

"This novel flows extremely well and readers will find themselves consuming the witty dialogue and strong imagery in one sitting."
—*RT Book Reviews*

"Don't let the title fool you. *Not Quite Perfect* was actually the perfect story to sweep you away and take you on a pleasant adventure. So sit back, relax, maybe pour a glass of wine, and let Catherine Bybee entertain you with Glen and Mary's playful East Coast–West Coast romance. You won't regret it for a moment."
—Harlequin Junkie, 4½ Stars

NOT QUITE CRAZY

"This fast-paced story features credible characters whose appealing relationship is built upon friendship, mutual respect, and sizzling chemistry."
—*Publishers Weekly*

"The plot is filled with twists and turns, but instead of feeling like a never-ending roller coaster, the story maintains a quiet flow. The slow buildup of a romance allows readers to get to know the main characters as individuals and makes the romantic element more organic."

—*RT Book Reviews*

DOING IT OVER

"The romance between fiercely independent Melanie and charming Wyatt heats up even as outsiders threaten to derail their newfound happiness. This novel will hook readers with its warm, inviting characters and the promise for similar future installments."

—*Publishers Weekly*

"This brand-new trilogy, Most Likely To, based on yearbook superlatives, kicks off with a novel that will encourage you to root for the incredibly likable Melanie. Her friends are hilarious and readers will swoon over Wyatt, who is charming and strong. Even Melanie's daughter, Hope, is a hoot! This romance is jam-packed with animated characters, and Bybee displays her creative writing talent wonderfully."

—*RT Book Reviews*, 4 Stars

"With a dialogue full of energy and depth, and a twisting storyline that captured my attention, I would say that *Doing It Over* was a great way to start off a new series. (And look at that gorgeous book cover!) I can't wait to visit River Bend again and see who else gets to find their HEA."

—Harlequin Junkie, 4½ Stars

STAYING FOR GOOD

"Bybee's skillfully crafted second Most Likely To contemporary (after *Doing It Over*) brings together former sweethearts who have not forgotten each other in the eleven years since high school. A cast of multidimensional characters brings the story to life and promises enticing future installments."

—*Publishers Weekly*

"Romance fans will be sure to cheer on former high school sweethearts Zoe and Luke right away in *Staying For Good*. Just wait until you see what passion, laughter, reconciliations, and mischief (can you say Vegas?) awaits readers this time around. Highly recommended."

—Harlequin Junkie, 4½ Stars

MAKING IT RIGHT

"Intense suspense heightens the scorching romance at the heart of Bybee's outstanding third Most Likely To contemporary (after *Staying For Good*). Sizzling sensual scenes are coupled with scary suspense in this winning novel."

—*Publishers Weekly*, Starred Review

FOOL ME ONCE

"A marvelous portrait of friendship among women who have been bonded by fire."

—*Library Journal*, Best of the Year 2017

"Bybee still delivers a story that her die-hard readers will enjoy."

—*Publishers Weekly*

HALF EMPTY

"Wade and Trina here in *Half Empty* just might be one of my favorite couples Catherine Bybee has gifted us fans with so far. Captivating, engaging, lively and dreamy, I simply could not get enough of this book."

—Harlequin Junkie, 5 stars

"Part rock star romance, part romantic thriller, I really enjoyed this book."

—Romance Reader

FAKING FOREVER

"A charming contemporary with surprising depth . . . Bybee perfectly portrays a woman trying to hold out for Mr. Right despite the pressures of time. A pitch-perfect plot and a cast of sympathetic and lovable supporting characters make this book one to add to the keeper shelf."

—*Publishers Weekly*

"Catherine Bybee can do no wrong as far as I'm concerned . . . Passionate, sultry, and filled with genuine emotions that ran the gamut, *Faking Forever* was a journey of self-discovery and of a love that was truly meant to be. Highly recommended."

—Harlequin Junkie

SAY IT AGAIN

"Steamy, fast-paced, and consistently surprising, with a large cast of feisty supporting characters, this suspenseful roller-coaster ride will keep both series fans and new readers on the edge of their seats."

—*Publishers Weekly*

MY WAY TO YOU

"A fascinating novel that aptly balances disastrous circumstances."
—*Kirkus Reviews*

"*My Way to You* is an unforgettable book fueled by Catherine Bybee's own life, along with the dynamic cast she created that will capture your heart."

—Harlequin Junkie

HOME TO ME

"Bybee skillfully avoids both melodrama and melancholy by grounding her characters in genuine emotion . . . This is Bybee in top form."
—*Publishers Weekly*, Starred Review

EVERYTHING CHANGES

"This sweet, sexy book is just the escapism many people are looking for right now."

—*Kirkus Reviews*

An
Unexpected
Distraction

OTHER TITLES BY CATHERINE BYBEE

Contemporary Romance

Weekday Brides Series

Wife by Wednesday
Married by Monday
Fiancé by Friday
Single by Saturday
Taken by Tuesday
Seduced by Sunday
Treasured by Thursday

Not Quite Series

Not Quite Dating
Not Quite Mine
Not Quite Enough
Not Quite Forever
Not Quite Perfect
Not Quite Crazy

Most Likely To Series

Doing It Over
Staying For Good
Making It Right

First Wives Series

Fool Me Once
Half Empty
Chasing Shadows
Faking Forever
Say It Again

Creek Canyon Series

My Way to You
Home to Me
Everything Changes

Richter Series

Changing the Rules
A Thin Disguise

Paranormal Romance

MacCoinnich Time Travels

Binding Vows
Silent Vows
Redeeming Vows
Highland Shifter
Highland Protector

The Ritter Werewolves Series

Before the Moon Rises
Embracing the Wolf

Novellas

Soul Mate
Possessive

Erotica

Kilt Worthy
Kilt-A-Licious

An
Unexpected
Distraction

Book Three
of the
Richter Series

CATHERINE BYBEE

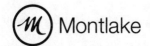

Published by Montlake, Seattle

www.apub.com

Amazon, the Amazon logo, and Montlake are trademarks of Amazon.com, Inc., or its affiliates.

ISBN-13: 9781542029568
ISBN-10: 1542029562

Cover design by Caroline Teagle Johnson

Cover photography by Regina Wamba of MaeIDesign.com

Printed in the United States of America

To Holly Ingraham
For keeping it real . . . always.

CHAPTER ONE

Jax hit the first wall with a running jump. Muscle memory kicked in as her legs wrapped around the thick rope to help her upper body heave hand over fist until she was at the top of the steep wall and hurling herself over the other side. She didn't see the pit of watery mud until she was already knee-deep and someone else on the team splashed into it on her left.

Her feet moved and her chest heaved with every gasp of air as she barreled to the next obstacle. Each year Neil managed to obtain access to a course that challenged her entire body. This one sat inside Camp Pendleton, just outside San Diego, and the team had been granted early access before the Marine base opened for a public mud run the following Saturday.

But for now, it was theirs.

She and Claire were partnered up, and currently Claire was sailing past her on the straightaway. Her best friend had serious speed. Jax could hold her own on a flat-out sprint, but she knew Claire could beat her with her eyes closed. The two of them had an advantage over the other teams when it came to the tight spaces, the sprints, and even some of the rope challenges. But when it came to brute strength, they needed to work together.

They had a strategy, one adopted from their years at Richter, where agility testing started before puberty and didn't end until you graduated.

It was simple . . . run fast, don't look back, reach for your partner if you arrive at the challenge first, and trust that they will be there.

They also may have done some recon on the course the previous week and spent extra time training.

The others on the team weren't nearly as competitive.

Well, Cooper and Sven seemed determined to win. In reality, they were the younger male members of MacBain Security and Solutions and actually stood a chance. But Jax still had her money on her and Claire.

Neil had flown in several members of the London team to partake in the fun. Three days of team building and healthy competition. The obstacle course was only part of one day. They had trigger time on a range, a swim in the Pacific Ocean, a paintball arena where they divided into two teams for an old-fashioned game of capture the flag. From there they all worked together to infiltrate a mock stronghold where Neil's senior members of his team, and a few Marine volunteers, acted as the bad guys with a hostage. The entire weekend ended with Jax's personal favorite . . . a skydive from fourteen thousand feet.

But Jax was getting ahead of herself.

This was day one, level one, of a handful of days that were sure to leave her tired, bruised, and smiling like a fool when it was all over.

There was mud . . . the kind that would stick in the crease of your ear for a week before you discovered it.

The scratches on her back wouldn't be found until she used a loofah to reach the hard parts.

They won . . . by 0.40 seconds.

Which was too close.

Sasha stood at the finish line. She tapped the stopwatch while her gaze moved between Jax and Claire as if the tip of her finger accused them of losing for cutting it so close. But the right corner of her mouth lifted ever so slightly.

They did win.

In the end . . . that's all that mattered.

Sven crossed the finish line, dove for the ground, and clasped his stomach. "Bloody hell."

Hands on her knees, Jax sucked in air but had enough reserves to laugh.

Claire shoved a bottle of water into Cooper's hands and then patted the side of his face with muddy fingers. "You owe me a massage."

"Remind me to send my kids to Richter," Sven said from his position on his back.

"Don't you dare," Jax warned.

The rest of the team started piling in, just as exhausted as the winners.

Lars and Isaac trailed the lot of them . . . walking.

Jax narrowed her eyes and took in the relatively clean state of their clothing.

"They're not even dirty," Claire said at her side.

"Don't rush, mates!" Sven yelled across the wide-open field.

The older members of the team sauntered closer . . . the only thing they were missing was a beer in their fists.

Sasha tucked the stopwatch away before Lars and Isaac crossed the line.

"Did you even try?" James, a member of the London team, asked.

Lars looked at Isaac.

Isaac glanced back.

They both shrugged.

Jax rolled her eyes and turned away. She had been surprised when they were at the starting line. In her time with the team, she'd only ever seen the two of them driving the vans and working surveillance from inside headquarters. They were good at what they did, they just didn't spend a lot of time running, jumping, or shooting at things.

A Jeep rolled up, kicking up dust that hadn't been wet down.

Neil stepped out, sunglasses shielding his eyes, his expression perfectly neutral.

The man's superpower was hiding his emotions.

He walked over to Jax and Claire. His praise was a tiny lift of the right corner of his mouth and a minuscule nod.

"Damn right!" Claire exclaimed with her shoulders pulled back.

"Don't get cocky," Neil told her.

Considering Neil was the closest thing to a father that Claire ever had, his words were expected.

"Too late," Cooper said at Claire's side.

Neil turned away, covering the smile on his lips with a swipe of his hands along his chin.

But Jax saw it.

Crazy how a tiny twinge of jealousy tickled the back of Jax's throat.

Envy of the respect Neil showed Claire was an unwanted emotion.

If anyone who knew Claire and Jax growing up was watching now, they'd remember that it was Jax that had all the family connections and money to keep her comfortable for her entire life. Claire was an orphan and destined for some nefarious clandestine existence, which was exactly what would have happened had Neil and his team not come along.

And here Jax was, pushing away the evil green monster because of the simple nod, smile, and reprimand Neil offered to her best friend.

"Time to celebrate our victory." Claire pushed into Jax's shoulder with the suggestion.

"Nobody's celebrating yet." Neil killed their joy with his next words. "You have thirty minutes to shower and report on the range."

Ten minutes later with the cold spray of an open shower pouring over them, Claire turned to Jax. "What do you think? Let the boys win?"

Jax rubbed the water out of her ears and turned the water off. "Wait . . . what?" Claire was one of the most competitive people she knew. Sasha taking a close second. Throwing a competition wasn't in their wheelhouse.

A slow smile spread over Claire's face. "Kidding."

Jax grabbed a towel. "Thank God. I started to think Cooper was taking the drive out of you."

She followed Claire out of the showers to the dressing room they had all to themselves.

"Bite your tongue," Claire chided. "Not a bad strategy to make them think that, though."

Jax liked how her friend's mind worked. "I can agree with that."

At the end of the day, Jax and Claire didn't have to worry about taking the gold behind the scope. Cooper and James took the lead with the rest of them close on their heels.

And with this being an all-expenses paid weekend—Neil was the sugar daddy for the team—Jax knew none of them would be pulling out their wallets.

With her blonde hair brushing her midback, Jax sat at one of several round tables in a bar in Oceanside. The community was known for its "newlywed and nearly dead" residents—and those that were transient because of the military base that kept the economy alive—so it was safe to say the mingling young people didn't live there permanently.

Not that Jax had an opportunity to mingle.

Sven sat next to James, the two of them yammering on about the day.

"What's next?" James asked.

"Team building," Jax offered. She looked around the room to find Claire and Cooper standing beside the bar. The way Cooper was looking at Claire suggested it wasn't going to be long until they sealed the deal and shared their last name.

Jax was happy for her bestie.

Cooper was one of the good ones.

"What does that mean?" James asked.

Jax shook off the image of her friend and addressed James. "The kidnapping. Which means tomorrow could start at any time and doesn't

5

end until we find and release the victim. So go easy on the tequila." She looked at James's glass and realized it was already too late.

He was new, so she turned to Sven. "Didn't you warn him?" she asked him in German.

Sven shrugged.

Another scan of the room and Jax took in Sasha and Neil standing away from the group, heads together.

"Does James at least know the safe word?"

Instead of answering, Sven turned to James. "What's the safe word?"

"The pussy 'I give up' word?" James asked. His British accent somehow made his use of the word *pussy* less abrasive.

"Yeah."

James sucked down a shot of tequila. "I don't need to know."

Jax pushed aside her martini and looked James in the eye. "Kiwi."

"The hairy fruit. Got it." James stared back.

Jax sighed and looked at Sven. "You need to cut him off."

Sven turned to James. "You might want to take it easy, mate."

"I sober up on a dime."

She hoped that was true. The previous year it took all of them to unscramble the maze Neil had put in place to find the victim.

She pushed Sven's shoulder and stood from the high perch she'd been sitting on. "Deal with your friend. I'm going to mingle."

Because what was learned the night before the previous year's kidnapping had been crucial to finding the victim in the time slot they were given, Jax decided to make eye contact with more than a handful of the team members.

She pushed up next to Lars and eyed his long-neck beer. "I see you're not worried about getting nabbed tonight," she told him.

"It's beer."

"You mean what you called *water* when you were in the service?"

He nodded and took a drink.

She turned her back to the bar and kept her gaze moving around the room. "Any idea who the victim will be this year?"

"Neil never tells us till the last minute."

Which meant as a senior member of the team, Lars would not be a victim but someone to watch once he left the bar. "Keeps you guessing," Jax suggested.

"He likes it that way."

Jax bumped against his arm and moved along. The majority of the London team were making the most out of the open bar. The same thing had happened the year before, and it was one of them that had been taken.

Claire stepped beside her, a tall glass with a lime and a skinny straw in her hand.

"Club soda?" Jax asked.

"Duh . . ."

"Any idea who it's going to be?"

Claire shook her head. "Not Isaac."

Jax glanced toward the bar, where Lars and Isaac were snuggled up with their beers. "Lars is on the kidnapping team."

"I figured as much. But what part?"

Jax shrugged. "Who knows?"

"I wouldn't be surprised if Cooper or I were the victim."

The thought had crossed Jax's mind, too. Mainly because with their relationship, it made them more vulnerable and less focused. Or so it was assumed. Jax thought the two of them actually worked better together than separate.

"I say we take turns sleeping tonight," Jax suggested. "There's no way Sasha and Neil will ignore the tracking devices we have in our phones. You know she's going to nix that app as soon as we leave the bar."

"Defeats the purpose of the exercise anyway."

Jax removed her phone from her back pocket and opened up the tracker she used for her best friend and Cooper. Even if they didn't all work in the same location and at the same danger level, the fact that they lived under the same roof made tracking each other a must-do.

Each of their names popped onto her screen, showing them all in the bar.

She slid the phone away. "Let me know when you want to head out. I'm going to keep circulating."

"Will do."

Within thirty minutes, the bar had completely filled, and the team members that tossed caution to the wind were well past the point of sober. No matter how much they thought they'd sober up when told to, Jax had her doubts.

"Can I buy you a drink?"

The question came from her left.

One look told her he was in the service. Military haircut, thick chest, clean-shaven, boyish smile. Younger than her, if she had to guess. Since the night was met with suspicion, she couldn't help but wonder if he was a guy in the bar hitting on her, or part of the pending ruse.

"Hello," she said with a smile.

"I'm Wess."

"Jax," she said.

Wess looked over his shoulder to a group of guys standing at a high-top table nearby.

The guys lifted their beers as if approving.

"Friends of yours?" she asked.

"Yeah. How about that drink?"

She let Wess buy her one beer, which she drank out of the bottle.

She watched the team as they slowly left the bar, while maintaining a conversation with the recently-turned-twenty-one Marine. He was cute enough. Held his side of the conversation enough. Old enough, although she was four years older in age, and quite a bit older in life experience . . . and since she was not willing to leave with him, she eased her way out of the conversation before tipping the last of the beer back.

Claire and Cooper found her as they were headed out. "You about ready?"

"You're leaving?" Wess asked, disappointment on his face.

"We have an early day tomorrow," Jax told him.

Cooper lifted his chin. "I'm Cooper, this is Claire."

Wess was polite, shook Cooper's hand.

"Give us a few minutes. Meet you outside," Jax encouraged her friends.

Wess set his beer down as the others walked away. "Any chance I can see you again?"

She lifted her hand, palm out. "I'll give you my number. Like I said, I live in Tarzana. It's not exactly down the street." And she wasn't entirely sure she was interested enough to make the drive.

He handed her his phone and she typed in her number. Under the contact information she typed "Hot Blonde in Bar."

Wess laughed, and when he took the phone from her, he slid his fingers along her wrist. "Enjoy your team-building weekend."

"Thanks for the beer." She set the empty bottle on the table and turned to walk away.

The guys Wess had come to the bar with had walked closer, blocking her way. "You're leaving? The party is just getting started."

Wess pushed his buddy's shoulder. "She has to work tomorrow."

"On a Saturday?" The shortest of the group of three was the most vocal. "Sounds like you're getting blown off, Wess."

"If he was getting blown, he'd know it," Jax said, purposely leaving the word *off* out of her sentence.

The three of them howled.

Jax looked over her shoulder to find Wess blushing. Yeah, he was a little too young and innocent for her taste.

Too bad . . . he was cute.

"If you'll excuse me, boys." She moved to push her way through them.

"Men, not boys. Fighting for your country." The short one was letting the liquor speak for him.

"Ease up, Mendez."

Jax did a quick look around, caught a glimpse of Sasha on the other side of the bar.

"The men I've known in the Marines never boast." Jax put a finger to Mendez's chest and pushed him back for her to squeeze through. "The boys, on the other hand, always do."

"Ouch!"

"Ohh . . ."

Mendez put a hand to his chest with a smile. "The Barbie has claws."

She walked past them. "Be careful out there."

She heard one of them whistle.

It seemed to take forever to make it to the exit.

The cool ocean breeze put a nip in the air that hit her the second she stepped outside.

She looked around, expecting to see Claire and Cooper by the entrance.

Jax rubbed her bare shoulders and peered through the dark.

She stepped into the parking lot to make her way to where they'd parked the car.

The lights that were working in the back of the lot flickered. She couldn't help but wonder if the ones that were out were a sign of neglect or by design for Neil's team.

An itch on the back of her neck brought up the hair on her arms as she walked in the dark lot.

The car wasn't there.

She pulled her phone out of her back pocket to text Claire.

The moment she pressed Claire's name she read the last text.

I'm going to stay for a while and catch a ride with Sven.

Jax read the message twice.

A message she hadn't sent.

Which could only mean one thing.

The footsteps beside her shot her to full attention, right as a bag went over her head.

"Damn it."

CHAPTER TWO

Even though Jax knew she wasn't in any real danger, that didn't stop her nerves from firing as her "kidnappers" forced her into a van and sped off.

The rules were pretty simple.

Make no real fuss if abducted in public since they didn't want any Good Samaritan getting the wrong, or right, as it stood, idea.

Once she was secured where they wanted her, she could do whatever she needed to in an effort to get away. Though in the years she'd been doing this drill, no one kidnapped had escaped on their own.

When someone on the team used the safe word, it meant they tapped out.

The goal was to work together to release the victim, not to get hurt.

"You okay back there?" It was Sasha's voice.

The bag over her head was unnerving, but Jax decided to close her eyes and pretend it wasn't there.

"I'm taking a nap," Jax informed her.

Someone laughed.

A *male* someone.

"I thought for sure it would be Claire or Cooper," Jax said.

"Not this year."

"Is Neil with us?" she asked.

"Nice try. I'm the only voice you get to hear." Sasha's words were spoken in Russian.

Jax found herself listening more intently with the language change.

"If you were actually being abducted, perpetrators would watch your body language to see if you understood. It's always best to hide your knowledge as long as you can," Sasha told her.

Jax had heard that before, but never thought it would apply to her.

She kept her hands on her thighs as the van bounced down the road. She'd paid attention to the turns until she was fairly certain whoever was driving was going in circles.

"When we get to the location, you'll be put in a room with a change of clothes. Everything comes off, even your earrings. The simulation is that of a full body search." Sasha switched to German, a language Jax was one hundred percent fluent in. She made a point of not moving even a finger when Sasha spoke. "From there you'll be in a room, a single chair, hands behind your back. This is meant to make you think. If at any time you feel truly trapped, use the safe word. We'll put you in an adjacent room with a bed and food to wait out the team."

Jax sucked in a breath. If memory served, the last two years they'd found the victim comfortably in a room watching TV and eating popcorn.

Jax leaned her head back and closed her eyes . . . for real this time.

Eventually whoever was driving stopped the van, and she was led out into the cold, damp air.

She smelled the ocean, stronger than being a half a mile offshore.

Although she tried hard to keep her balance, Jax found herself stumbling even with someone on each side keeping her from falling.

None of them spoke.

They stopped, and the sound of a beeping keypad preceded the noise of a metal gate opening.

Then they were walking slowly, descending in elevation, her shoes gripping the surface. Once the ground leveled, it moved.

The soft lapping of water and creaking of ropes told her they were on a dock.

Motion sickness had never been something Jax was burdened with, but she felt a little nauseous walking on the moving surface while she was unable to see.

As soon as she was on board the vessel, she was put in a cold space and told to wait.

Once Sasha was out of the room, an intercom crackled. "You can take off the hood, change your clothes. Leave everything behind . . ." Sasha hadn't stopped talking and already Jax took off the hood that had covered her head. Even with the dim light, there was comfort in seeing the world around her.

"There's a restroom to your left. Use it. When you're done, put the hood back on and stand facing the door with your hands behind your back. In the real world you would fight. You would get hurt. You might even escape. But most times this is where the victim is debilitated enough to make it impossible for them to get out on their own."

As promised, she was placed in a room, hands tied behind her back and sitting in a straight-backed chair. They replaced the hood with a blindfold.

As soon as she was alone, she started working on getting the blindfold off.

Not seeing what was around her was freaking her out more than she would have expected. The slight sway of the ship wasn't helping.

She shifted in the chair, quickly realizing that even though her hands were tied to the edges of the chair, she had some give as the rope slid up and down.

In what felt like a half an hour she managed to get a tiny gap in the bottom of the blindfold so she could see the floor.

But the room was dark. Her field of vision was next to nothing.

If she had shoes on, and those shoes were hiding some kind of sharp device . . . she might be able to kick her feet back and remove it with her fingertips.

She found a slight laugh on her tongue. The next time she planned on getting abducted she'd have to be wearing said shoes with said knife.

For a moment, Jax considered trying to stand and walk with the chair on her back to determine if she could see anything in the room. But Sasha had said the room would be empty, so what was the point?

Instead, she tried to relax and let her body listen.

When one sense was turned off, the others were known to turn on.

She quieted her brain and took in her surroundings.

The space was quiet, the boat gently swayed. A soft hum of power, maybe from a refrigerator or something like it, came from just beyond the room. Every once in a while, it felt as if the boat pushed up against something. The dock.

She listened for footfalls or voices. Within the hour she was rewarded with someone moving outside the door. Heavy feet with a slight limp.

Lars.

The man had an old injury that plagued him.

Another set of footsteps, softer. Could be Sasha's. Although Neil, as big as the man was, had been known for being light on his feet when he needed to lurk.

Out of nowhere, she heard laughter. Far off, but voices that carried. The laughter moved closer.

She could scream . . . but would she if this whole thing was real?

No. Not with people in the next room who could kill her screams . . . literally.

Time ticked slowly.

Never once did she consider falling asleep. Even though the whole thing was fake.

She couldn't.

Why was that?

Loud footsteps moved close, and the sound of the door opening changed the air slightly.

"Time for room service?" she asked. The sound of her own voice felt strange to her ears.

A second set of footsteps, lighter.

The smell of mint gum filled her nose.

The feel of hands on her shoulders was followed by something heavy being slipped over her head.

A weighted vest.

"Time for me to swim with the fish?" she asked.

No one spoke.

She heard tape unrolling before she felt it being strapped on to whatever they'd put around her.

Someone pushed her chair into a different position.

Four hands, but another set of footsteps.

The limp. *Lars.*

Then, just when it seemed as if everyone was walking away, someone took the blindfold from her eyes.

Jax blinked several times, her vision attempting to adjust to the minimal light in the room.

She was facing the wall.

When she swiveled her head, all she saw was the shadow of one person walking away.

On her chest was a pretty decent simulation of a bomb.

The reason for the safe word was now revealed.

She closed her eyes at the sound of the door shutting behind her. *This isn't real.*

Richter had trained her to think under pressure, not to give up.

It was time to start thinking.

∼

"Is she still awake?"

Neil moved his head and acknowledged Lars's words as he walked into the room.

In front of Neil were three screens. One was directed at Jax, complete with a monitor of her vital signs, which she likely didn't realize they were monitoring. The second was of the perimeter of the ship they were on . . . and the third was with the mole they had in the team that was closing in on their location.

"She's tough."

"That's Richter," Sasha said, as if their alma mater was enough of an explanation. "Although I don't think Jax spent much time in isolation for insubordination like me or Claire."

The fact that the German boarding school had once isolated students who broke the rules in a way that would at all mimic what they were simulating made Neil want to shoot something. Jax was an adult. A licensed private investigator, but more to the point, an operative in his company. This was something she signed up for.

The school she was forced to attend when she was a child was not.

"How far out is the team?" Lars asked.

Neil looked at the monitor, saw the team putting on their vests. The ones that worked like laser tag. A fatal "shot" meant the member was out. On either side. "Twenty minutes."

Neil glanced at Jax's monitor once again. "First time in three years our objective held out."

He was proud.

Damn proud of the girl.

"Let's suit up."

~

When someone says the phrase "All hell broke loose," one never imagines how silent that hell can be.

There is a feeling that surges in the air when that hell is starting to fall.

That is what being isolated in a room with a simulated bomb strapped to her chest gave her.

A feeling.

Hell was footsteps.

Quiet, rapid footfalls and energy swirling around in sweeping colors.

The windows in the room were blacked out, but a tiny bit of light suggested the sun had started to rise.

Jax would swear it was midday by the state of her bladder.

She had been about to cry uncle for the sake of a bathroom when hell moved.

Her heart started to pound.

It wasn't real . . . but that didn't stop her from thinking about what she needed to do to make sure there wasn't a simulated black toe tag on her when this exercise was over.

Much as the night had been uncomfortable, she was better for it.

She opened her mouth and screamed. Unlike earlier when she heard voices, now was when the team needed to find her and know she was alone.

What better way to reveal that?

And if there was someone assigned to her side, they'd be there . . . not out running around on the deck of the ship.

"Here! I'm down here!"

People running.

Grunting . . .

"Bloody hell. I'm out!" someone yelled.

A timer on her chest blinked to life. "Holy shit."

That, she was not expecting.

Two minutes.

"Hurry!" she yelled at the top of her lungs.

18

Fifteen seconds passed before the door to the room burst open.

"One minute forty seconds and we all blow," she yelled.

"James!"

Claire rushed to Jax's side. "Really?"

"Minute thirty." Jax kept her eye on the clock.

"James!"

The room filled and finally James made his way front and center.

He dropped to his knees, a smile on his face. "Easy stuff." He withdrew a pocketknife and flipped it open. His fingers pushed through the multiple wires, then he looked around the back.

He nodded a few times, picked at the wires.

"I hope you sobered up."

He looked up at her. "Hours ago."

James started cutting while everyone watched.

Four wires later, with twenty seconds on the clock, and the work was done.

Jax felt her shoulders slump while the team started to cheer and pat each other's backs.

~

The team was riding on a high.

The day before had fueled them like any team-building weekend should, and now they were taking on altitude for their jump.

They found their place in line.

No obligatory seatbelt needed.

This was for fun.

A way to end the weekend.

A reward for a job well done.

Cooper was poised at the open door, first to make the leap.

A quick twist and he kissed Claire before jumping out of sight.

Claire disappeared next as Jax moved into position.

The world opened up under her.

Adrenaline pumped and excitement filled her lungs.

A tap on her shoulder and she lunged forward.

Air rushed past.

Her eyes found Claire in the free fall.

Jax held out her arms and legs, her eye on her watch, calculating the altitude. They had a full minute of free fall.

The fun part.

The coast of California spread out under her, the line between land and sea nothing but strips of white, shimmering on the shore.

The horizon was dotted with clouds, and the crescent shape of the earth always made her wonder how anyone ever thought the earth was flat.

She laughed at the freedom.

Screamed at the excitement.

Nothing made you feel more alive than jumping out of a perfectly good airplane and risking death.

The timer in her ear made her reach for her chute as the earth plunged closer.

The world stopped.

Like that of a cartoon character hitting a rock canyon, the fall ended, and the harness strapped to her legs that kept her tied to the chute promised to leave a bruise in the morning.

"Whoo hoo!" she yelled.

"I love this!" Jax heard Claire calling through the silence.

It always amazed her how loud the jump was until the chute was pulled.

She tugged on the levers, swinging right, then left.

"Better than a roller coaster."

"Yeah, baby!" someone above her chimed in.

Jax looked up, never once worried her chute wouldn't open.

The team dotted the sky.

She maneuvered through the air . . . their target in sight.

Only instead of an *X* it looked like something else.

She turned herself around until it came in clear.

CLAIRE, WILL YOU MARRY ME?

Jax knew it was coming.

Not this . . . not exactly this . . .

But Cooper had been working up to popping the question for months.

Jax couldn't see Claire's face but knew she must have seen the question written on the ground.

"Well done," Jax whispered to the silence around her. Her heart filled with excitement for her best friend.

She slowed down enough to hit the ground running.

When she stopped, she witnessed Claire and Cooper kissing in the middle of the field.

"I take that as a yes," Jax heard someone say behind her.

Jax turned to see Sven gathering his chute as the others reached the ground.

They descended on the happy couple.

Claire turned to Jax. "Did you know about this?"

"Not a word."

They both turned to Neil.

Claire's semiadoptive father stood to the side. "I think Cooper had help."

Jax held back while the team moved in to congratulate the couple. She couldn't be happier for her friends. But even as that thought entered her head, she knew their marriage would mean a complete change in all of their lives. They were roommates, all three of them, but marriage would change that. As it should.

The image of what that life looked like left Jax slightly . . . empty.

Swallowing that thought, Jax pushed forward and pulled Claire in for a hug.

Thirty minutes later, with champagne in hand, a toast was given and Jax's phone rang.

Her brother's name on the screen caught her off guard.

She answered and put the phone to her ear as she walked away from the group. "Harry?"

"Hey, little sister." His voice sounded strange.

"I'm in the middle of something. Can I call you back?"

"Are you at a party?"

Jax smiled. "I just jumped out of a plane."

"You just what?"

The connection wasn't great. Or maybe it was the noise in the room. "A plane. Skydiving."

"No wonder Mother takes so much Xanax."

That, Jax had heard before. "I'll call you back in an hour."

"Sure, but, uh . . . I need you to come home."

Home was London.

And not a request Harry ever made.

"Is something wrong?"

"Not yet . . . but . . ."

Jax shook her head . . . his words difficult to hear.

"Is anyone ill?"

"No. Call me back when you're not risking your life for fun."

She laughed. Her brother had never ridden a bike without a helmet, let alone jumped out of a plane. "Give me an hour."

Jax tucked her phone away.

"Who was that?" Sven slid up next to her, an easy smile on his face.

"My brother."

Sven's grin faded. "You have a brother?"

"Crazy, right?" Jax didn't talk about her family.

"Everything okay?"

"I don't know." The thought of going home didn't give her any warm-and-fuzzies. In fact, it always made her squirm and look for a distraction to prevent the trip. Pushing her family out of her mind and putting them into the little box hidden under her bed had always been a gift. So, when the laughter in the room grew, Jax's attention returned to the celebration at hand.

She walked over to Claire and wrapped her arm around her shoulder. "You're getting married!"

CHAPTER THREE

"I can't believe you're leaving." Claire leaned against the doorway, her arms crossed over her chest.

"It's only for a couple of weeks. Less if things get sticky." She shoved another sweater into the plastic bag she'd suck the air out of before closing the suitcase. It was spring in the UK, which meant rain with bouts of warm, the occasional hot if she was lucky, but guaranteed cold most of the time. It made packing a bitch.

"It always gets sticky," Claire said.

"I know. But Harry never makes requests. I have to go." Jax looked up to find Claire frowning. "Stop it, you're making me feel guilty."

"I just got engaged. I want to go shopping."

"Is this you whining?" Jax asked, laughing.

Claire stepped in the room and plopped on the bed. "Yes."

Jax stopped pushing clothes into bags, shoved the suitcase aside, and sat beside her friend. "Okay, how about this . . . join me in a week. Sweet-talk the boss, get sexually exhausted with your new fiancé, and then join me in Europe."

"And stay at your parents' house?"

Jax cringed. "God no. Only if we have to. Ask Gwen if we can crash at the Harrison house." Gwen was Neil's wife, and the Harrison house was a family property occupied primarily by staff.

Claire looked at the ceiling as if it held the answer to going to Europe the following week.

"It will be awesome. Maybe we take a quick trip to Milan and try on some Italian wedding dresses."

Claire shook her head. "I can't afford that."

Jax pushed her shoulder and stood. "I said try on . . . not buy. Besides, you find *the dress*, I snap a picture and tell Neil and—"

"That's manipulative."

Jax held a pair of slacks in her hands and stopped to stare. "Is Neil walking you down the aisle?"

Claire paused, and a smile spread from ear to ear. In a heartbeat her eyes swelled with moisture. "Yes."

"Is he or is he not loaded?"

Claire shrugged. "I think so."

Jax rolled her eyes. "He will buy you *the dress*."

"We haven't talked about it."

She went back to packing. "Talk about it. And then join me." Jax looked at the time. "The guys are picking me up in thirty minutes. Help me get this together." She was jumping on the same flight the London team was taking back home. The private plane that Neil, the questionably loaded boss, was paying for.

Twenty minutes later her bags were downstairs, and they were waiting for the van filled with testosterone.

"Call me the second you know more about what's going on with your brother," Claire said.

"Harry is never cryptic." He'd told her there was some significant family drama and he needed his sister and her covert skills. All that did was spark questions that he didn't want to answer over the phone. When he said that their parents weren't going to approve, Jax stopped asking questions and committed to going. Harry didn't buck their parents often, so the fact that he did now gave her enough joy to request time off and jump on a plane.

The van pulled up and Jax turned to hug her friend. "One week. Then we'll make Europe our wedding planning oasis."

"Sounds great."

A sharp knock on the front door broke up their hug.

Sven and James stood on the other side of the door. Their eyes went straight to the two bags at her side. "Only two?" Sven teased.

Jax frowned. "There are five more upstairs."

For a hot second Sven looked worried. She walked past the two of them. "Kidding." She didn't even pretend like she was going to carry the luggage as she marched toward the van.

~

Heathrow never ceased to be a bitch.

The only thing that made it tolerable was arriving on a private charter. Even thinking about that reminded Jax just how privileged she was.

No matter how long it had been since she'd set foot in Europe, London especially, she found her spine stiffen, her chin lift, and her shoulders pull back. It was the stance expected of her when she arrived.

Jax personified it.

"You're sure you're okay?" Sven asked.

"I'm brilliant." Even her accent snapped together like Lego bricks for a toddler.

"Do you see your brother?"

"He'll be here." Jax pushed past her irritation that the reason she flew to London on a moment's notice wasn't waiting for her the second she stepped off the plane.

"I'm wrecked," James said at their side. "We leaving or not?"

Sven gave her a final glance. "You sure?"

"Would you ask that if I had a pair?" she asked him with one final flair of the dramatic.

Sven twisted his head side to side. "All right. You need something, you know where we are."

Jax offered a two-finger salute as Sven and the others walked out of the airport and into awaiting cars.

She looked left.

Then right . . .

"Damn it, Harry," she said, her words a whisper.

She could take a cab.

Find a hotel.

The last thing she would do is show up at her parents' unannounced.

Minutes swept by.

Anyone she recognized was long gone before she started to move.

She kept scanning the men, and occasional woman, holding signs with names.

The drivers for the rich. Not an uncommon way for Jax to travel.

Harry told her he'd pick her up at the airport himself, but the brat wasn't there.

Resigned to the fact he wasn't coming, Jax tugged both pieces of luggage out of the line of people. Once she'd moved away from the crowd, she unzipped her purse and reached for her phone.

"Miss Simon . . . Miss Simon?"

She turned to the man calling her name.

The first thing she noticed was the paper with her name on it. Then her eyes scanned the man.

Tall, early thirties, if she had to guess, strong jaw, eyes hidden by sunglasses. He was wearing a damp trench coat. "You're Jacqueline Simon, right?"

"Harry sent a car." It wasn't a question . . . more of a complaint.

"He had an unavoidable distraction, I'm afraid."

Jax shook her head and let her expression show her disappointment. "Are you at least driving me to his flat?"

The man shook his head. "He's arranged a room at the Connaught."

"Damn it, Harry." She zeroed in on her phone once again.

"I take it you're not happy." The man's British accent chipped his words.

"Brilliant deduction." She pressed Harry's number and put the phone to her ear. "Where's the car?" she asked as the call rang through to Harry.

The driver lifted his hand to the exit.

Jax used her one free hand to grab the smaller roller bag while he managed the larger one.

Harry took his own damn time answering the phone as she followed the driver out of the airport into the car park.

~

Harry had warned Andrew that Jacqueline was a fireball of energy and wit. But so far all he saw was a ticked-off female with her claws out.

"Goddamn it, Harry. Was it too much for you to pick me up after a ten-hour flight?"

Andrew was happy he wasn't on the other end of the line.

He approached his car and clicked the button, unlocking the doors while Jacqueline continued to yell at her brother.

She left her roller bag at the boot and helped herself to the back seat.

"Uhm . . ." Andrew started to suggest she take the passenger seat and then realized how this all looked.

Jacqueline Simon thought he was a paid driver.

Wasn't that fabulous.

Instead of correcting her, he wrangled her bags in the back of his car and circled around to the driver's seat.

". . . I know the Connaught is a nice hotel. That isn't the point."

Andrew adjusted the rearview mirror, managed a better view of the woman in the back seat.

The picture Harry had given him didn't do her justice. Her long blonde hair was swept up in a simple ponytail. Jacqueline didn't appear terribly out of sorts for such a long flight. Her deep blue eyes sparkled, her makeup looked perfect, her traveling outfit unwrinkled. Perhaps she'd changed clothes before getting off the plane. Even though the flight from the West Coast to Great Britain wasn't the worst trip, it still left you feeling pretty hammered. Jacqueline wore it well.

He pulled out of the garage and wound his way to the airport exit.

"Tomorrow . . . you're serious?" She pulled her cell phone away from her ear, glared at it, and mouthed a few choice words.

Andrew chuckled as he maneuvered onto the motorway.

"Tea? Good God, you sound like our mother. Why not happy hour?" She paused. "Fine. But you owe me a proper bender after putting me through this. Oh, don't worry, I'll make use of the martini bar with or without you."

Andrew lowered his sunglasses to look at her without the shade. A woman who enjoyed martinis . . . nice.

Harry failed to say exactly how beautiful his little sister was.

And older. The way his friend had described the woman was more like a girl. One spending time in America to find herself.

The woman in his back seat was completely settled in her skin. Not a backpacking teen on a gap year.

"I will. Cheers." She disconnected the call with a dramatic sigh and leaned her head back.

Andrew opened his lips to comment.

He didn't get a word in and she was back on the phone. "Hey . . . yes. No. The son of a bitch didn't even come to the airport." A pause in the conversation. "You've met my mother, it's an accurate statement."

Andrew couldn't stop himself from laughing.

Jacqueline looked up, saw him in the rearview mirror, and frowned. The next words out of her mouth weren't in English. Russian, if he had to guess. Not that he understood a word. And then, as if she sensed his concentration on her, she offered a slight smile before turning toward the window and continuing to talk.

While she rattled on in a language he didn't speak, red lights stacked up in front of him.

Traffic heading into the city was thickening up, which put his foot on the brake more than the gas.

His favor to Harry was moving out of the friendship zone and into the "you owe me" zone.

His phone rang.

In the mirror he saw Jacqueline glance his way.

On the third ring he looked to see who was calling.

Harry's name flashed.

Instead of using the speaker function, Andrew picked up the phone and put it to his ear.

"This is going to cost you."

"I know it. Are you driving?"

"I am." A glance told him his passenger was still on the phone having a conversation of her own.

"Jax is with you?"

Jax . . . Was that her nickname? It fit. Much better than Jacqueline. "Yes."

"Does she know you're talking to me?"

"You're paranoid."

He heard his friend sigh. "You have no idea."

"You owe me."

"I know . . . Handful, I warned you."

As if she understood he was talking about her, Jacqueline looked up and caught his gaze. "I'm driving. Traffic bites."

Harry sighed again. "I owe you a night in a pub—"

"A weekend."

"That, too."

A nasty look from the back seat. Not that it mattered, traffic was at a dead stop.

"Keep an eye on her," Harry said.

"Not hard when traffic isn't moving."

"No . . . I mean . . . make sure she's settled at the hotel. I can't have her grabbing a ride to my place."

Andrew moved his head from one side to the other. The tension in his neck was threatening a decent headache in the morning. "You do remember I don't work for you."

"I know . . . it's a lot to ask. My morning was shot to hell." His friend's voice was stressed.

The silence from the back seat had Andrew glancing in the mirror.

"I'll do what I can." But no promises.

"Thank you. I really do—"

Andrew disconnected the call, tossed the cell on the passenger seat.

"Important call?" Jacqueline asked.

"Annoying call."

She nodded a few times and looked out the window. "Sometimes you're better off ignoring the phone and pretending you never got the message."

"The real thorns just keep ringing." The crush of cars inched up to twenty kilometers per hour before the red lights had Andrew hitting the brakes again.

She shook her head and released a long-winded sigh. "I see traffic is just as lovely as ever."

"No worse than LA."

Jacqueline caught his gaze in the mirror. "You've been?"

The words *many times* were on the tip of his tongue. But considering she thought he was a driver and not Harry's friend, he thought better of elaborating. "Who hasn't?" he said instead.

"I suppose."

"How long have you been in the States?"

"Six years."

"You like it there?"

She smiled. "The weather in California beats England every day of the week."

"That wouldn't take much." And as if Mother Nature wanted to add her exclamation point to the subject, the sky promised more rain before they pulled up to the hotel.

"Why did you move? School . . . work?" Harry was light on details about his sister, and Andrew wasn't a fan of silence in a car.

"Yes. Both. School, then work. Now I only come back when I have to."

He smiled. "When those annoying phone calls are from family."

"Did I say this was about family?"

Andrew picked up speed. "No. You did say something about tea and your mother. I assumed," he lied.

She leaned her head back. "I guess I did."

He kept silent for a few minutes and that's all it took. Her eyes were closed and her face had lost the tension he'd seen on her since the airport.

Yes, sir . . . Harry's baby sister was seriously hot.

Way too wound up for his taste, but hot.

Andrew drove in silence. A frequent glance to the back seat, a slight pull under his belt . . . and a quick change of thought.

As he maneuvered off the motorway and skirted the edges of Mayfair, Jacqueline's eyes opened.

She blinked several times. "We're here already?"

"You fell asleep."

"Oh . . ."

Ten minutes later, he pulled up to the hotel, where a uniformed doorman, complete with top hat, opened the back door for Jacqueline to step out.

Andrew played the part of hired driver and popped the boot before stepping out to help gather her luggage. The doorman took the suitcases from him with a smile. "We'll take it from here." The man turned to Jacqueline. "Checking in?"

She gave him a smile as she reached into her purse. "Yes. Jacqueline Simon."

"Very good." The man walked away with her bags.

Andrew turned and found her reaching out.

At first, he thought she wanted to shake his hand, then he saw the money in her palm.

It took serious effort not to laugh.

And since he couldn't deny her tip without explanation, he took it. "Thank you."

"You're quite welcome." She turned toward the entrance to the hotel.

Andrew thought of Harry's request to keep an eye on her. "I suppose you'll likely sleep soundly until the morning."

She glanced over her shoulder. "Oh, God, no. I plan on running up a significant bar bill for my brother to cover in payment for his absence."

Andrew painted on a smile. "Right."

She waved with her fingers and started up the steps.

He ran a hand over his face and lost his smile the moment she was out of sight.

So much for going home to his flat and coming up with ways to poke back at his friend.

CHAPTER FOUR

The Connaught sat in a wealthy section of Mayfair. To be fair, all of Mayfair was wealthy, but when a century-old hotel was surrounded by the finest stores London, Paris, and Milan had to offer, and cars worth a quarter million dollars were parked on the street, the wealth wasn't overlooked.

The hotel itself was quintessential London. Rich wood banisters and ornate ceilings. Paintings depicting fox hunts and large country estates filled the dark walls. The occasional chairs and tables on each floor weren't picked up at a budget furniture outlet but likely made exclusively for the Connaught.

The fact that Harry sprang for a suite should have eased some of the bitter taste left in her mouth over him sending a car . . . but it didn't.

In less than an hour of her arrival, she'd showered, changed, and worked her way to the ground floor. With no intention of actually leaving the hotel, she didn't bother with a coat. She wore slacks, high heels, and a blouse that accented her curves. Her long blonde hair flowed down her back and she knew without checking that her makeup was spot-on. Stuck in a hotel and not having to work did have its perks. A few drinks and a one-night stand sounded just about perfect. And if word got back to her brother, or her family . . . all the better.

She followed the sound of people talking down a long hall to the hotel's martini bar. They offered other libations, but when a cart was

An Unexpected Distraction

brought to your table and martinis were custom made for each customer, you found yourself ordering the twenty-five pound apiece drink. The lights in the bar were dim and the natural glow from outside was minimal since the sun had set.

Jax did a quick sweep with her eyes and an assessment of the clientele.

Several couples. A party of four . . . all businessmen, by the way they were dressed. And considering what she was looking for, much too old and dignified for her taste. A couple of stragglers at the bar. She stepped around a corner long enough to see a few other patrons. Nothing terribly entertaining, but that wasn't going to stop her from having a couple of drinks.

Instead of taking a seat at one of the tables, she leaned against the bar and waited for the bartender to look her way.

"Good evening."

"Hello." Why was it her British accent came out whenever she was back in the UK? A simple greeting and she was reminded that this was where she was born . . . where she spent her off time when away from boarding school growing up, and where she returned for holidays and the occasional distress call from her brother.

"What can I interest you in tonight?"

She opened her mouth to find her words spoken by someone else.

"The lady would like a martini, the most expensive one you have, if I'm not mistaken."

She turned to the voice and found her eyes colliding with her driver.

He'd taken off his coat and tie and released the buttons at the top of his shirt. His light brown hair was ruffled, his easy smile contagious.

Jax returned his grin and took note of his casual stance. The drink in front of him was half-empty.

"Miss?" the bartender addressed her.

"The gentleman would be correct."

A bar menu was placed in front of her.

35

"They have an extensive selection of bitters," her driver told her.

"Is that right?"

"Lavender?" the bartender suggested.

"Flowers . . . no." Jax glanced at the menu. "Something earthy."

The bartender reached over the bar with a small vial in his hand. "How about this?"

One sniff and she was sold. She told him her preference for vodka, not gin, and then turned to the man ordering for her.

"I'm pretty sure each drop of bitters is five pounds. Should help pump up that bar bill for your wayward brother."

She laughed. A flirty one she used when in a bar attracting the opposite sex. "I'm surprised to see you in here."

He shrugged, picked up his martini. "You were my last . . . *obligation* for the night. Traffic was especially fun and that martini you mentioned sounded too good to pass up."

She saw a slight twitch in his left eye. "What is your name?"

He sipped his drink as she asked, set it down, and slowly tilted his head. "Andrew," he reported.

"Do your friends call you Andy?"

"Not really. When I was young . . . playing cricket."

"You were on a team?" she asked, surprised.

"Yes . . . no—" he stuttered. "Not really."

"Which is it?"

The bartender finished making her cocktail and set it in front of her. "Shall I start a tab?"

"Absolutely." She gave him her room number and picked up her drink. "To bad traffic and good drinks."

Andrew clinked his glass to hers.

One sip and she understood why the Connaught was known for its martinis. "This is perfect."

Andrew nodded toward an empty seat away from the bar. "Would you like to sit down, Jacqueline?"

"Only if you call me Jax."

He had tiny dimples when he smiled and the notch in his chin softened. "I can do that."

"So, Andrew . . . Andy," she started as she took the empty seat. "Who may or may not have played on a cricket team when he was younger." He wasn't old. Early thirties was her guess. Close to her brother's age without the receding hairline. Clean-shaven, tall, fit . . . her type if she were being honest with herself. "Did you decide on a drink in this particular bar because I told you I'd be here?"

Jax already knew the answer but wanted to see if he had the balls to admit he had.

The grin on his face gave him away. "One hundred percent."

Jax tossed her head back with a laugh. "Then you won't mind if I let my brother pay for both our drinks tonight."

"Music to my ears."

~

Jacqueline . . . *Jax* Simon was the polar opposite of her brother.

Harry was a poster child for the reserved British businessman climbing the corporate ladder to prove he wasn't there because of his father's influence . . . when everyone knew he was there because of his daddy's clout.

Jax was the young, sexy rebel sister living far away from her family's influence sitting now in a bar flirting with the driver who gave her a lift from the airport.

When she'd walked into the room, he had to look twice.

Her travel outfit and conservative makeup were gone, but while she wore slacks, and not a provocative skirt of some sort, the blouse she wore made it a little hard to not look at the space between her ample breasts, which she clearly wanted to show off. Long blonde hair and full lips she painted in a shade of red that screamed confidence. Not one conservative bone in her body.

Harry's sister . . .

That's what Andrew kept saying to himself as they finished their first drink and she casually ordered another. He already knew he'd be calling a taxi to make his way home.

Jax was the handful Harry had warned him about.

What Andrew wasn't expecting was that he'd be attracted to that handful.

As their second drink arrived, Jax was telling him about Harry's interruption in her week.

"Jumping out of an airplane! You're serious?"

"You've never been skydiving?" she asked as if everyone plunged out of a perfectly good airplane.

"I prefer to stay inside the aircraft."

"Missing out," she said with a shake of her head. "Neil always says . . . the best things in life are on the other side of fear. I'm certain he is quoting someone else, but he *is* right."

"Who is Neil?"

"My boss. Well . . . technically." She was sipping her second cocktail.

"Technically?" Andrew wondered if this Neil was an attraction of hers.

She shook her head, then nodded. "Yes. He's my boss. He's also Claire's dad . . . sorta."

"Sorta?"

Jax set her drink down, put both hands in the air. "Claire is an orphan. Neil stepped into the father role even though she isn't technically adopted." Jax air quoted the word *technically*.

"Claire is your best friend," he clarified as he lifted his cocktail to his lips.

"More like a sister." Jax laughed. "Sister from a different mister. If only one of my parents had stepped out, then maybe I could claim her as the real thing."

The second Jax's words registered, Andrew sucked in a breath and his martini shot down the wrong pipe.

He instantly started to cough as the alcohol burned. The jarring shook his whole body and his cocktail splashed from the glass.

Jax reached for his drink as he tried—unsuccessfully—to stop the coughing fit.

She shoved a glass of water into his hand as tears started to pool in his eyes.

Patrons in the bar turned to stare.

Finally, the sensation that he was going to choke to death subsided and he managed to wash the fire away with water.

"Are you okay?"

He looked at his shirt, glad vodka was a clear liquid. "Better."

A waiter walked over with a handful of napkins. "Can I get you anything?"

Andrew waved him off. "I'm quite all right." He noticed Jax's hand holding a napkin and dabbing at the spill on his pants.

She pulled away. "Sorry."

"That's all right, too."

Their eyes caught and his body stirred.

Jax sighed. "Appears you need another drink."

"You sure your brother won't mind?" Even as Andrew asked the question, he knew he'd eat those words. Eventually Jax would know that Harry was his friend and Andrew was at her side acting as a nanny. Not that Andrew disliked the job.

"Harry owes me." She captured the attention of the waiter and ordered another round.

"Is it really so bad your brother didn't pick you up at the airport?"

She leaned back, crossed her legs. "It's cold. Something our parents would do. He called and asked me to come. He didn't elaborate as to why. I jumped."

"Do you jump often?"

"No. And Harry doesn't ask. I thought something serious was happening. The entire flight over was a constant question I expected answers to the second I landed." She waved a hand Andrew's way. "Then he sends you. No offense." Her smile was gone . . . and so was the anger. Replacing it looked dangerously close to hurt.

"None taken."

"I'd like . . . for once . . . for my family to act out of character and at least pretend that my presence is appreciated."

Andrew felt the knife in his own chest at her words.

Jax swallowed a generous amount of her drink and looked him in the eye.

She pasted on a smile. "I'm sorry. Too deep for a barroom conversation."

He sat forward, placed a hand on her knee. "It's okay. I asked."

She sucked in a breath, placed her hand over his. "It might be a good idea to order food with the next round."

"How many rounds are you planning on?"

Her eyes were already glassy. "I'm not working tonight, and I seriously doubt anyone is trying to kidnap me."

With those words, Andrew realized Harry's baby sister was tipsy and certainly needed food.

~

Jax walked into a closet. The need to empty her bladder sat on the edge of desperation and pain.

The closet wasn't right . . . but damn, she needed to go.

Someone would see her. Find out.

The space itself was familiar. Not her closet, but a foyer closet like the one at her parents' house.

She couldn't pee in her parents' closet. Jax would never be able to show up in her childhood home again if she did.

Jax jolted awake.

The room was dark, unfamiliar.

And that last drink had been a mistake.

Much as she'd like to go back to sleep, her bladder told her to move . . . and quickly.

She stumbled to the bathroom, still aware that the alcohol hadn't completely left her system.

The toilet came into view. She turned and sat.

The wide rim of the bowl had her catching herself as she sunk way too deep. She stood, realized the toilet seat wasn't down, and corrected her problem.

Jax leaned her head against the cold marble of the wall, thankful for dreams that made you wake up before you wet the bed.

She sat there long after she was finished. The room was a little spinny.

Water.

Hydration would be her best friend by the time the sun came up.

With the lights off, she finally started to move, washed her hands, and made her way to the minibar in the suite. She reached for the refrigerator and noticed a bottle of water on the counter, next to it a foil pouch containing a pain reliever. Without thought, she opened the acetaminophen, popped it in her mouth, and chugged the water.

Plastic bottle in hand, she walked back to the bed, glanced at the clock, and tucked herself in.

Now this was the cloud she wanted to relax in.

The next time she opened her eyes light filtered in through the blinds.

A slow move of her head to the left . . . then the right.

London. She was in London.

The reason for her location made her moan.

London equaled stress.

And drinking.

Her head was right on the edge. The middle-of-the-night medication and water had been the right call. But her stomach wasn't going to accept anything anytime soon. Even the thought of much-needed coffee made her wince.

It was six in the morning. Which sounded perfect, but her body still needed a year of sleep. She rolled over, buried her head in the pillow, and took a deep breath.

Cologne.

The bar.

The man . . .

Andrew.

Her eyes popped open and she scrambled to a sitting position.

Jax's hand grasped the side of the bed, certain there wasn't a person beside her.

Nope.

She looked at the pillow. The one with his scent.

She remembered his face . . . cheek against the pillow and lips smiling.

Did she?

Her blouse was still on. So was her bra. The snippet of memory was of opening the door to her room and encouraging Andrew to come in.

That's when the fuzzy became a void.

They'd been drinking, it was getting late. Jax remembered being consciously drunk, oxymoron that it was. Somewhere between the martini lounge and her room . . . regret for the last drink, for maybe the last two drinks, set in.

She'd invited Andrew to join her.

An image of him lying next to her . . . then the midnight bathroom need.

Her slacks were at the foot of the bed, her panties on.

Never in the history of her life had she let herself get that drunk without a wingman.

Not knowing exactly what had happened had her hyperventilating.

Ignoring the time in the States, Jax found her cell phone and called Claire.

"Hey."

Claire's voice alone grounded her.

"What the hell am I doing here?"

Claire sighed. "That bad, huh?"

"I don't really know."

"What?"

Jax swung her legs off the bed and sat on the edge. "I don't know what's going on with my brother."

"How is that possible? You've been there for hours."

"I know." Jax rubbed her forehead . . . the headache she thought she'd avoided started to emerge. "He sent a driver. Harry said he'd see me today for tea."

"Tea . . . really?"

"I know. Worst part, he put me in a hotel."

Claire sighed. "I'm sorry."

"I know, right? I flew all the way here and I don't know what the emergency is."

"I'm sure whatever it is you can handle it."

Jax moaned. "I got drunk."

"I would, too."

"No . . . I got *really* drunk. With the driver."

Claire started to laugh. "Was he cute?"

Jax couldn't stop herself from smiling. "Is that relevant?"

"Would you do him if you were sober?"

43

"Yes . . ."

"Then yes, it's relevant."

"I don't know if I did anything."

Claire paused. "Really?"

"I remember coming up to my room, Andrew was there. I kicked off my shoes . . ." Jax looked around the room and saw her heels in two completely different places. *"Kiss me."* "I told him to kiss me."

"Did he?"

"I don't remember." In fact, she didn't remember anything after that moment.

"Wait . . . do you think . . ."

"No. I mean. I don't think so. We were both pretty hammered. And to be fair, I was willing."

"Still . . . if you were drunk—"

"He was a decent guy. Not the type to take advantage." At least that's how she remembered him.

"You need me there."

"I know." Although if she'd been working, she would never have put herself in the same position.

"For someone who should be hungover you sound good."

"I don't feel too awful, actually. I won't be ordering a heavy breakfast, but I'm okay."

"Do me a favor," Claire said.

"What's that?"

Jax heard Claire take a deep breath . . . let it out slowly. "Don't let your family drive you to drink yourself into oblivion unless I'm there."

Her best friend was right. "Last night will not repeat."

"Good." Claire yawned. "Call me in the morning."

"I will. G'night."

"Love you."

"Love ya back."

Jax disconnected the call and tossed her cell phone on the bed.

She glanced at the clock on the bedside table with a moan.

So many hours before teatime.

If she didn't find something to busy herself, she'd likely march into her brother's office and demand answers.

Jax kicked the covers off and swiveled to the side of the bed.

Shopping.

She was in London, and her best friend did just get engaged. Jax had a London bank account she only used when she was in Europe. Suddenly the thought of spending some of her trust fund made her smile. It wasn't something she tapped into for her daily life. Her job gave her more than enough to live on. Being independent from her family was important to her. They'd paid for her college education in the States, even though they weren't happy about her decision to study abroad. Or more importantly, at a school not of their choosing. But the moment she started earning a living with Neil's company, she stopped consistently using the account her grandparents and parents funded. Although she was steadfast in her conviction to be independent, she wasn't stupid. It was a sizable sum, which grew every year. She wasn't about to tell her family she didn't want the money. Instead, she simply didn't use it.

Well, outside of an occasional shopping spree when your brother interrupted your life and was making you wait for answers.

She pushed off the bed and headed to the shower.

Anger shopping had a nice ring to it.

CHAPTER FIVE

"You're an ass, Harry."

Andrew sat behind his desk, his phone on speaker.

"Let me guess, Jacqueline made your life hell last night."

The image of her sprawled out, face-first, on the hotel bed came to mind. "Your sister can certainly handle her alcohol . . . until she can't."

"Was it awful?"

No. It was entertaining and enlightening. Andrew knew Harry and Jax's parents were uptight, but now he had evidence to cement his opinion.

"I'm only calling to offer a warning. Your sister is understandably outraged."

"Jax doesn't get outraged, she just leaves." Harry paused and then returned to the conversation with dread in his voice. "Bloody hell, she didn't jump on a plane and leave, did she?"

"No, although now that I think about it, she did threaten to do just that." Somewhere between martini number three and one too many, Jax mentioned the plane would return to the States after the pilot's required downtime. "I wouldn't put her off any longer."

"I carved out my afternoon so I could break the news to her."

Andrew shook his head. "You couldn't just tell her over the phone that your—"

"No, I couldn't. It's a little more complicated than that."

"You'll have to explain that to me."

"I will. But not when I'm at work. Thanks again for watching out for her. I owe you."

Andrew smiled. "Remember that when you get the bar bill."

Harry offered a strangled laugh before saying goodbye and hanging up.

A rapid knock on his open office door prompted Andrew to look up. "Hey, Dad."

"Glad to see you made it in." Kicking the can close to his sixtieth birthday, Andrew's father was a slightly heavier, grayer, and more jovial version of himself.

"That favor Harry asked of me took more time than he led me to believe."

His father walked into the office with readily available advice spilling off his tongue. "Friends and favors are important."

"I have a feeling Harry will need more before the week is out."

Lloyd *Andrew* Craig took a seat and leaned back in the chair. "Is everything okay?"

Harry had asked Andrew to keep the news to himself until the time was right. And in their corporate world, that made sense. "He asked that I keep the details to myself."

Lloyd nodded a few times. "I'm happy to know my son can keep a secret. If there's anything I can do . . ."

"I know, Dad. Thank you." One of the many reasons Andrew and his father got along . . . the man didn't press and was always there when he needed him.

"All right, then. I'd like to go over the Alabaster account before today's meeting."

Switching into work mode, Andrew signed in to his computer and started his day.

$\sim$

Jax shopped up until the last possible second in order to arrive within ten minutes of tea with her brother. Ten minutes late, that is. On purpose. Showing up on time or early smelled of desperation. Any later and her brother might think she'd left and bugger off himself.

Dressing in the way she wanted to be perceived, Jax wore a slim-fitting skirt that stopped just below her knees, a matching jacket, and a silk shirt. A perfect overcoat in case the weather didn't cooperate and sensible heels that she could run in if she had to. She looked like any other accomplished businesswoman in London. One with good taste and a bit more padding in her bank account that afforded her designer clothes.

She wanted to look like a woman whose time you didn't waste, not a baby sister to be fed white lies as to why a driver was sent to the airport to pick her up.

Jax walked into the drawing room at the Brown Hotel, where afternoon tea was in full swing. She approached the attendant and gave the woman her name. With a smile, the hostess swept her through the dining room, past dozens of patrons quietly talking and picking at the many finger foods stacked on tiered trays. English tea was serious business for locals and tourists alike. Knowing what was to come, Jax had skipped lunch in anticipation of tiny sandwiches and cakes. Much as she had scoffed at her brother's suggestion of tea, she liked the idea better than fish and chips at a pub.

She spotted Harry before reaching the table and took a deep breath.

He stood as she approached. "You look smashing." He leaned in, kissed one cheek, then repeated the gesture on the other side.

He looked like crap. Which she almost said but didn't, since the hostess was still within earshot. "Nice to *finally* see you," Jax replied, hoping he caught her dig.

He politely helped her with her jacket and then waited until she sat down in the small half-moon booth before taking a seat beside her. "I am sorry. Yesterday could not be helped."

The hostess left them alone, and Jax lowered her voice. "I would think my flying in from California on a moment's notice warranted a tiny break in your schedule."

Her brother actually looked sorry. And tired. His high-stress job was aging him . . . and quickly. "You're right. You're one hundred percent right." He sighed. "I'm so glad you're here."

She sat back, placed her hands in her lap. "Why *am* I here?"

Harry looked around the room. "Maybe we should order tea first."

"Harry!" His name was a warning.

He cleared his throat. "Champagne might be a better idea."

"Are we celebrating something?" Her brother didn't look in a celebrating mood.

He wouldn't meet her eye. "Definitely champagne."

"Harry. Fess up."

Finally, he looked at her. What came out of his mouth she wasn't expecting. "Our parents are getting a divorce."

Her thoughts froze. The word *divorce* was so far out of her parents' vocabulary she wasn't even sure they could pronounce it.

A waiter walked by and Jax lifted her hand to gain his attention. "Champagne . . . please."

"A glass or a—"

"Bottle." Her brother finished the man's sentence.

They sat in silence until the bubbly arrived and both took a hefty drink before either tried to talk.

"What the actual hell, Harry?"

"I know. I was just as shocked as you. More so when Dad showed up at my door."

Her glass stopped halfway to her lips. "He did not."

"He most certainly did. With a suitcase."

"Mother kicked him out? My God, what did he do?"

"I'm fuzzy on that."

"Our father shows up at your door, you ask, and the fuzz is cleared up." She couldn't wrap her mind around this. "How long has he been on your couch?"

"I have a spare room."

"Not the point." Sometimes her brother's literal nature frustrated the crap out of her. The man was brilliant with numbers . . . metaphors, not so much.

"A week. I thought maybe they had a tiff. Things would settle and he'd go home."

"He didn't."

"No, he didn't," Harry said. "I called Mum, asked her what was going on. She told me to ask Dad."

"And he said?"

Harry shook his head. "That he needed a little time and for me to keep things quiet."

"No one knows?" Jax found that hard to believe.

"No. Well, you and my friend—"

"No one at the office?" she interrupted.

"We drive separately to work. Dad leaves earlier than me . . . no one is the wiser."

The waiter arrived with the tiers of pastries and sandwiches and topped off their glasses. While the man worked, Harry and Jax kept silent. Not that the waiter would have any idea of who they were, it just didn't feel right speaking in front of a stranger about their parents' marital dispute.

"Why?"

"I don't know."

"Ask."

"I have," he said through clenched teeth. "He will not answer."

"How childish." And uncharacteristic. "What exactly did you want me to do?"

Harry set both hands on the side of his plate and paused. "Talk to Mum."

Jax felt that coming. "What makes you think she'll talk to me? You have a better relationship with both of them than I do." Which they both knew was fact.

"Maybe she won't . . . but you're an investigator, or some such thing."

Yes, she did have the PI license in the States, although investigating marriage issues was not part of her skill set. She was better at tracking down kidnappers, murderers, and members of organized crime. Although she didn't divulge those details to her family.

"You *are* an investigator, right?" her brother asked in her silence.

"I am, yes."

"So, investigate."

"Or . . . we could wait until they tell us."

Harry shook his head, eyes wide. "No, no . . . I'm not waiting." He lowered his voice to a whisper. "Dad is driving me mad. I want to know what is going on so we can fix it and send him home and I can get back to my life."

Jax smiled and actually felt sorry for her brother. "Since when do you have a life?" He was a workaholic, just like their father.

He tilted his glass back. "Very funny. I'll have you know I have a girlfriend."

Now that was good news. "You do? That's awesome."

"Not when your father is in the spare room, it's not."

Jax could see how that might suck. She grinned at her brother and took one of the sandwiches from the plate. "Okay."

"Okay you'll find out what's going on?"

"I will. If I ask you to do something on your end, no questions, just do it." Because if her father had done something truly awful to get their mother to kick him out, it would likely be hidden at the office. Which meant she'd start at the family home to rule out any clues there, and that couldn't be accomplished over a polite dinner or tea with her mother. Once the house was cleared, the office would be next.

Jax groaned. "I'll check out of the hotel tonight, throw Mother off guard when I show up."

"She'll hate that."

"I'll hate it more."

Harry grinned, reached out a hand and touched hers. "Thank you, sis."

"Don't thank me yet. Even when I find out what's caused this separation, there is no guarantee they will kiss and make up."

"I don't think our parents kiss."

"Harry!"

"Right. Yes. Kiss and make up. Please, God."

Jax lifted the sandwich to her lips. "So, tell me about the girl . . ."

~

Jax drove up to her childhood home and hesitated outside before turning in. The English Tudor sat on several acres and boasted seven bedrooms, nine bathrooms, servants' quarters, and a small cottage for the groundskeeper and his family. The house had been in her mother's family for three generations.

The surrounding area had been built up over the years, dividing property and making the estate, well . . . less stately, but there was no mistaking the grandeur of old money. And her mother and father personified that by their attention to old customs and rules of living. The Queen herself would be hard pressed to find this family outside of her liking. Routines were kept, from mealtimes to weekly tea with friends.

The rigid nature of Jax's life growing up didn't feel terribly strict at the time. Then at the age of twelve, she was sent away to Richter, a military-style boarding school six hundred miles away in a different country, where the rules were even more unbending.

Jax followed the rules. The first two years, she pleaded to her parents to find a school closer to home. But her request was never heard. Then she met Claire.

Her best friend was a year older than her, and because of that seemed so much wiser. As they grew closer, the need to go home gradually faded. Twice she forced her parents to sponsor Claire's holiday away from Richter. She threatened to not return for Christmas if they didn't allow her friend to come. Of course, the threat was only that. A threat. When they sent for her, she was forced on the train without Claire.

Jax's act of rebellion took place on Boxing Day. A second round of Christmas was underway for her parents and their friends. They were going to show off their bright daughter, who was fluent in three languages and learning a fourth, getting high marks, and wouldn't she be the talk of the town, if that were still a thing?

Jax left.

Not ran away, per se, but left.

Because her parents' routines were run by a clock and nothing else, Jax woke early, called a car, and returned to Richter. She left a note in her father's study saying her best friend needed a holiday, too. And since they didn't have it in their hearts to listen to her request, she'd performed her daughterly duties and they could enjoy the rest of their holidays without her.

The following year they let Claire join them.

Jax remembered the first time Claire saw this house from the very spot Jax was parked.

"It doesn't feel like home anymore," Jax said.

They'd told the driver to stop at the street and let them out.

They held one bag each and stood staring at the house.

"And Richter does?" Claire asked.

Jax shrugged. "Sadly."

They both started up the long driveway. "One day, when we've graduated and found amazing jobs, we'll get a flat together."

Jax loved when Claire talked like this. "In Berlin?"

"Maybe. Or London."

Jax moaned. "Too close to here."

Claire laughed. "New York."

"I like that idea."

"The world will be ours, Yoda."

Jax nudged her best friend's shoulder with hers. "I say we find my father's liquor cabinet and drink to that tonight after everyone is in bed."

They were both all smiles when the housekeeper met them at the front door.

Jax put the car in drive as the memory of that day, so long ago, faded away.

She parked the rental car just past the front steps and popped the trunk. Taking the smaller suitcase, so there was no mistaking she was here for an evening nightcap and then gone, she climbed the stairs.

This was her family home, and she did still have a key . . .

Jax considered knocking.

She tried the door and found it unlocked. Not uncommon until after dark.

One step into the foyer and the usual tension started to gather in her shoulders. "Hello?" she called out to the empty space.

Footsteps from the back of the house sped up as they approached.

Angela, the housekeeper her parents had employed for as long as she could remember, slowed her pace once she saw who it was. "Miss Simon. So lovely to see you." Her easy smile went flat. "Were we expecting you?"

"No. I was in London—"

Slower footsteps descended the grand staircase, and Evelyn Simon, Jax's mother, approached. Her mother had perfected an unemotional expression. One that was without a smile or a frown. Not happy, not sad . . . just there. The common observer wouldn't think the woman had a worry in the world.

But to their family, this unemotional expression was filled with unspoken words.

"Jacqueline."

"Hello, Mother."

Evelyn's gaze moved to the suitcase. "This is quite unexpected."

Instead of offering a simple excuse, Jax decided on a direct approach. "Seems to be a lot of unexpected visitors just decide to show up these days. I would have stayed with Harry but—"

"No, no. It's quite all right." Her mother's interruption in front of Angela spoke volumes.

The staff didn't know the real reason her father was gone.

Angela reached for Jax's bag. "Is this your only bag, miss?"

"There's another in the car. I can get it."

"Don't be silly, Jacqueline." Evelyn took the last few steps and greeted her with an emotionless kiss to each cheek.

Angela walked out of the foyer and into the drive.

"We have to talk," Jax whispered.

Her mother lifted her chin. "Considering I wasn't expecting you, that talk will have to wait."

Not a complete denial of said conversation gave Jax some hope. It was then she looked long at her mother's face.

She looked . . . older. At sixty-two, she had the face of a woman ten years younger. Easy to do when money wasn't a concern and medical spas sold you on the latest and greatest product or procedure that promised the fountain of youth.

Jax had inherited her blonde hair from her father and her blue eyes from her mother.

Her mother was beautiful. There was no question about that. While Jax looked a bit like her mother, everyone always said she took after her father's side of the family. Her paternal grandmother's childhood pictures looked nearly identical to Jax's.

Now, as Jax looked into her mother's eyes, she saw a flicker of something new . . . and sad. "Are you okay?" she asked, all formality aside.

"Of course."

"Mother, you don't have to pretend . . ."

Evelyn looked up sharply as Angela returned with a suitcase in one hand and the packages Jax had procured on her shopping spree in the other.

"Let me help you with those."

Her mother used the distraction to stand back and lay the foundation of Jax's future lies. "Your father is on a business trip. I'm sure he will miss not seeing you."

Their eyes met.

Jax nodded in a silent agreement to keep up the ruse in front of the staff. Her mother had her reasons, and while Jax didn't have a lot of respect for some of her parents' choices growing up, she wouldn't make waves about that now in the current crisis.

"I'll get settled and maybe you and I could have a nightcap," Jax suggested.

Evelyn sighed; her expression said a denial was next. "Not tonight. I woke terribly early this morning and was about to retire."

Far be it from Jax to point out that the sun was only just now going down. "We'll catch up tomorrow."

Angela started up the stairs and Jax followed.

The familiar path to her designated bedroom was a comfort. Inside, the space seemed smaller. Considering it was twice the square footage of her room in the Tarzana home she shared with Claire and Cooper, the seemingly tighter room was all in her head. Her childhood was here. The time before Richter. She looked to the corner windows where a table once stood with a massive dollhouse. A toy that was likely stored in the attic along with anything else worth keeping. Although why keep it? It wasn't like Jax would go out of her way to bring her family around for any length of time when the day came that she had one.

Angela walked into the adjoining bathroom for a moment and then returned.

"Can I get you anything? Are you hungry? I'm sure there is something—"

Jax stopped her. "I don't want to bother anyone. I'm capable of cooking my own meal."

Angela frowned. "Your mother—"

"My *mother* is who you work for, not *me*. Believe it or not, I don't have anyone cooking my food or making my bed in California."

The housekeeper relaxed. "It truly is good to see you."

"You as well. How are your parents?"

Angela smiled at the mention of her family. "My mum complains about her joints and my dad brings her a shot of brandy. So about the same, I'd say."

That sounded like love to Jax's ears. "We should all be so lucky to have that in our lives."

"You're still so young. You'll find it."

Jax wasn't really looking. "I'll see you in the morning."

Angela offered a tiny nod and left the room.

Once she was alone, Jax dropped her weight on the edge of the bed and willfully slowed her breathing.

Her mother's greeting was just as she expected . . . polite and cold. The kind of hello one extended to your best friend's aunt you didn't really know but had met a time or two.

And it hurt.

Jax forced the melancholy from her heart . . . and for some strange reason thought of the previous night.

Andrew, a man she knew for less than an hour after arriving in London, had stuck around long enough to share a drink with her. Granted, she'd felt an attraction. The kind that was mutual.

But there were a couple of moments she remembered, before she'd had that third drink, where he'd actually listened and seemed to care.

Why she confessed to a stranger that she'd like her family to give a shit she was actually there, she couldn't say. Maybe because she didn't think she'd ever see the man again. Maybe because a driver from a service dropping her off at one of the most expensive hotels in London must think she had everything, when in fact she didn't . . . and she wanted him to know that. Why?

Jax squeezed her eyes shut.

It wasn't him she wanted to hear the words . . . it was her.

She'd never been able to articulate the actual feeling of being left standing at a platform waiting for her family and being met by a hired hand.

Jax hadn't asked her parents to meet her . . . not once . . . since she moved to the States. Thinking her brother would behave differently because his request had seemed so desperate was her mistake.

Andrew had listened.

Jax wanted to thank him for that. Maybe when she had a grip on what was going on with her parents, she'd find out the service Harry used and contact the man.

But for now, the sandwiches from tea had worn off and her mother had an amazing cook. Maybe she'd be lucky and find leftovers that didn't come out of a pizza box.

CHAPTER SIX

The sound of rain pelting the window woke Jax out of a deep sleep. She rolled to her side and curled under the covers. She missed this sound. Even though she didn't covet the overall weather in and around London, there were times she would like nothing more than to spend a day filled with rain and fog, bundled up next to a warm fire.

She opened her eyes slowly and looked at the light coming in from the window. Dawn was trying to cut through the fog, but it looked as if the clouds were going to win. "Why can't this be a happy place for me?" she whispered to the empty room.

But she knew the answer.

It didn't bring her joy, outside of the sound of rain and the familiar sights, because of the people residing within the space.

She remembered saying once that it wasn't that her family were awful people, she just didn't know them that well. And up until now, she could blame them for that fact. She had zero control of where she was sent to school as a child. Zero control of her parents' involvement in her life growing up. All that bled into her adulthood. And Jax was happy to let their relationship continue within the parameters her parents had set.

If she knew them better, maybe she'd understand.

If they didn't open up to her questions . . . well, she was an investigator.

Jax stretched her arms over her head and wiggled her toes in the opposite direction as ideas began to form in her mind.

She'd give both of her parents an opportunity to talk. Ask the questions and see where they led. If they treated her as if she was a child barely able to grasp the concept of where babies come from, she'd put the education they gave her to use. After all, what was the point of being sent to a military-style school where scaling walls and shooting targets were her physical education, and hacking computers and learning four languages were the goals of math and literature. And that was primary and high school. What she learned in the three years it took her to graduate from the university felt trivial next to the skills she learned working with MacBain Security and Solutions. Or more importantly, with Neil's team. Some of which also graduated from Richter.

So yes . . . she'd ask her parents the hard questions.

One way or another, Jax would find the answers.

She smiled for the first time since arriving at her family home. She didn't think her parents had any juicy gossip or hidden skeletons, but it would be fun trying to find them. Who knows . . . maybe she'd unearth a logical reason for her being sent to Richter in the first place.

An hour later, dressed in jeans and a bulky sweater, she made her way to the kitchen.

"There you are. I heard you'd arrived last night."

"Good morning, Letty."

The cook of the house had never been her mother. It had always been Letty. The woman dusted her hands on her apron, walked around the island, and opened her arms.

Jax stepped into them and paused. It was the first hug she'd had since arriving.

The thought caused emotion to catch in the back of her throat.

"You don't eat enough," the woman said as her hands patted Jax's back as if she were counting her ribs.

"I'm sure you'll fix that while I'm here."

Letty stood back and peered closer. "I was surprised to hear of your visit. Your mum didn't tell us."

Jax looked beyond Letty to the dining porch on the opposite side of the room. Her mother sat with her back to the two of them, a teacup in her hand. She was far enough away to hear voices, but likely not catch every word being said.

"Mother didn't know."

Letty lifted one side of her lips with a sly smile. "That's new."

"Seems to be a lot of *new* around here," Jax whispered.

"It's good you're here, then." A wink was all Jax needed to know Letty knew something.

She stepped away and toward the coffee machine.

"I can bring that to you."

Ignoring her, Jax poured her own cup. "You spoil me."

Letty went back to what she was doing. "What can I make you?"

"I'm sure whatever you've already done is fine."

"Biscuits and jam, clotted cream, and eggs Florentine."

Just the sound of that made her mouth water. "Mother only has oatmeal and tea in the morning."

"A waste of my good cooking. So be a dear and don't complain."

Jax shook her head. "Oh, I won't."

Letty nodded toward the breakfast room. "Spend time with your mum. Today is her ladies' luncheon."

And as routine was what ruled Evelyn, she wouldn't miss it even with an unexpected visit from her only daughter.

Jax fortified her spine before entering the room. "Good morning."

"I wasn't sure you'd be up this early. Jet lag as it is."

Jax took the seat opposite her mother and set her cup of coffee on the table. "I've already had time to adjust to that."

"How long have you been here?"

"Long enough to talk to Harry."

Evelyn took her time sipping her morning tea.

"He's concerned." Jax kept her voice low.

"He's inconvenienced."

For some reason, the comment made Jax laugh. "That, too."

Another sip of tea and a gentle hand putting the dainty cup down . . . "What's between your father and I is our matter, not yours."

"True, in any other circumstance. But when your dad comes to crash on your couch and you fetch your little sister from five thousand miles away, it becomes *your* matter. All of our matters, in fact."

Footsteps paused their conversation as Letty walked in the room and brought a plate of fresh fruit. "Thank you," Jax said.

Her mother only smiled.

Alone again, Jax lifted her coffee cup and wrapped her hands around it. The heavily glassed room had a slight chill as the rain and fog permeated the space. Light colors for the furnishings and plenty of potted plants . . . it brought the outside in and was the perfect place to start your day.

"Marriage has its ups and downs."

That was a start.

Jax waited for her mother to say more.

Seconds ticked by.

"That's it?"

"What more is there to say?"

The woman was aggravating. "You kicked Father out."

The accusation had her mother looking directly at her. "Is that what he said?"

"Is that what happened?"

"We had a disagreement. He left."

"You encouraged him to leave." Jax purposely asked her questions and stated her assumptions rapidly to see where her mother would fumble.

"I didn't stop him."

"You wanted him to leave?"

"Your father . . ." She stopped, narrowed her gaze. "This is an inquisition."

"This is your daughter asking why her father is not at home."

"This is your mother telling you it's not your business."

Jax expected nothing less from her mother. She hit her with the bottom line. "Do you want a divorce?"

That's when it happened. A rapid blink of the eye, a sharp inhale, and a pause a split second too long. "Don't be ridiculous."

Letty walked in again, her hands full with breakfast. She left and returned twice more with everything they needed before either of them spoke again.

"I want to help," Jax said.

"And I'd like to enjoy my breakfast without getting upset." With that, Evelyn lifted her spoon as if doing so ended the conversation.

For the next thirty minutes they ate breakfast, engaged in polite conversation that Jax promptly forgot, and ignored the elephant in the room.

When the dishes were cleared, and Jax's coffee cup was refilled, her mother scooted her chair back. It was then Evelyn asked the question Jax was waiting for. "How long do you plan on staying?"

"Trying to get rid of me already?"

A blink . . . a look to the side. "You're always welcome."

Not really. "I haven't decided. Claire will be flying over, and we plan on doing some wedding shopping."

"Is she getting married?"

"She just got engaged."

"That's lovely." Evelyn stood and turned to walk away.

"Maybe you'd like to join us . . . when Claire gets here."

"When is she coming?"

"About a week."

Surprise was quickly hidden by a fake smile. "Don't you have a job?"

"A flexible one. My boss believes that family is the most important part of life." And sometimes that family was the one you chose as well as the one you're born to.

"Do let me know your plans. You know my dislike for surprises."

"I will be home for lunch but not dinner."

"Seeing old friends?"

Jax shook her head. "And who would that be? My friends from Richter don't live here."

Evelyn ignored the cut. "I'll be out at lunch and back tonight. If you're not too late, I'll see you then."

"Have a nice day."

Jax heard her mother talking with Letty, likely giving her the count for meals, and then she was gone.

The entire encounter was a repeat of her childhood. Her mother was accommodating, but distant.

And a shitty liar.

~

She'd checked out of the hotel.

Andrew looked at his cell phone after disconnecting the call with a frown.

Where was she?

He had managed to go two days and two nights since meeting Jax and had only thought of her every few hours.

Every.

Few.

Hours.

What started out as a favor to his friend ended up being a distraction Andrew couldn't shake.

It was easy to see that Jax had set out to get drunk, if only to forget that there wasn't a family member to meet her at the airport. She'd opened up early in the night . . . a glimpse of what she was thinking. Then she tightened up almost as swiftly.

He'd helped her into her room and knew the alcohol was talking when she'd asked him to kiss her. He left her sitting on the bed, told her he needed to use the restroom. When he walked back to her side, she was sprawled out, fast asleep.

He could have left then.

Instead, he pulled off her shoes and her dress pants, ignored the phenomenal shape of her long legs, and tucked her in bed.

She woke briefly with a flop of her hand on his face.

Then passed out.

He lay there for over an hour.

Not because of some perverse need to watch an intoxicated woman sleep, but to make sure she wasn't so drunk she'd get ill and harm herself.

And now he couldn't stop thinking about her.

He could flat out ask Harry for her phone number. Which would be met with questions. Or he could lie and say she'd left something in his car . . . which Harry would encourage Andrew to give to him to return to her.

Andrew didn't have anything of Jax's to return.

The thought of buying something wasn't out of the question.

Or . . .

Andrew could plop himself into the mix of the Simon family drama and play middleman.

Then he could see Jax.

Make sure she was okay.

With no more thought to the subject and knowing full well Harry told him not to stop by his place without warning, Andrew shed his office attire, pulled on more comfortable clothes, and left his home.

Harry lived close by, but the rain had him driving to his friend's place.

Knowing full well he was interrupting, Andrew laid his knuckles to Harry's door and knocked.

Noise beyond the door warned him someone was coming before it swung open.

"What?" Harry answered.

Not the greeting Andrew was expecting, he took a step forward, inviting himself in. "Great to see you, too. I thought you'd like a night at the pub." Andrew turned to see Harry's father in the room and acted surprised. "Mr. Simon, what brings you here?"

Before Gregory had a chance to speak, Harry did so for him. "My father just stopped by."

Andrew moved forward, extending a hand. "You look well." He looked like pure shit. Tired eyes, sloped shoulders . . . his tie askew, and not in a way a man wore it right before he took it off.

They shook hands, exchanged pleasantries.

Andrew turned to Harry, noticed the same haggard look on his face. "I thought we'd go out, have a pint . . . but maybe I should have brought some with me."

Harry offered a strangled smile. "You can see I have company."

Instead of giving in to the lie being offered, Andrew took a different approach. "What do you say, Mr. Simon? I'm sure the Mrs. wouldn't mind if you took a night out with your son."

For the span of about ten seconds, no one said a word.

"Brilliant idea."

"It is?" Harry asked his dad.

The father patted the son on the back. "Been a while since you and I sat in a pub."

"I'm not sure we've ever sat in a pub together."

"Long past due, then," Gregory said. "I'll give your mum a call."

Once he walked out of earshot with his pretend phone call, Harry rushed out his words. "What are you doing here?"

"Helping you out. You don't want him staying here forever, do you?"

"Obviously not."

"Then make it uncomfortable."

Gregory returned. His formal coat was off, and he was shrugging into a light jacket. "Ready?"

CHAPTER SEVEN

Jax wasn't sure exactly what she was seeing.

She'd parked across the street from her brother's flat and watched as her father arrived, then her brother . . . and then Andrew.

At first, she thought maybe he was there picking up her father or brother, but then she saw all of them leave on foot and head north.

She abandoned the rental car, pulled the collar of her coat high around her neck, and put her sunglasses on, even though it was cloudy and gray.

As she passed the car Andrew had arrived in, she snapped a picture of his plate with her cell phone and sped up her pace to keep from losing them. Not that she needed to worry. They ducked into the closest pub, which was only two blocks from her brother's residence.

Jax walked past and weighed her options.

She pulled her cell phone from her pocket. Her number was in Neil's database, so she wasn't surprised when James picked up her call from the local office and used her name.

"How are you doing, Jax? Finally figure out what the family emergency was all about?"

"My parents are sleeping in separate houses."

James laughed. "Sounds like the perfect marriage, if you ask me."

He might be right about that. "I'm going to need a few things while I'm here."

"Whatever I can do, mate."

"I need you to run a plate." She gave him Andrew's license number.

"Got it."

"I'll drop in later."

She ended the call and watched as the pub slowly started to fill.

London pubs were small as a rule, many dating back a couple hundred years, so waiting for the place to be packed so she could avoid being seen was necessary.

Not that she planned on staying hidden forever. Just long enough to see if she could figure out how Andrew fit.

Low ceilings and dark wood with enough liquor to pickle the livers of the entire block, the Cock and Bell was close to standing room only.

Jax spotted her family at the far end of the bar. Her brother and father both had their backs to the door, and Andrew had full view of the tavern, and therefore her. As he was currently laughing at something that someone said, he hadn't seen her.

The noise in the space was loud enough to keep her from eavesdropping on their conversation, but from the look of it, Andrew appeared to be very comfortable with the men in her family.

Was he a friend?

If so, why didn't he say something about that friendship when he picked her up at the airport?

She thought back on their first encounter. She'd been so busy looking for Harry, she didn't notice that Andrew had approached her.

"What can I get for ya?" The waitress circulating the crowded floor walked up to her.

"A pint. Hard cider."

The woman offered a toothy smile and walked away.

Jax looked up and saw Andrew's gaze fall on her.

So much for staying hidden for long.

His eyes narrowed.

She placed a finger to her lips, a silent signal to stay quiet, and nodded toward the bathrooms. Without checking to see if he would follow, she turned away so that all Harry or her dad would see was her back if they looked.

"Good to see you again," Jax heard him say before she turned to look at him.

"Imagine my surprise to see the cabbie drinking with my family."

His eyes widened along with his smile. "That was your assumption."

"That you didn't correct."

He rolled his eyes. "Technicality."

"Who are you?"

He opened his mouth and she stopped him. "I'd avoid any *technical* lies this time around." She glanced at her watch. "In about thirty minutes I'll know just about everything there is to know about you down to your last credit card transaction. Choose your words wisely."

"My credit card?"

"I'm waiting."

Andrew shifted from one foot to the other, arms folded over his chest. "Harry, my friend, asked me to pick up his *handful* baby sister at the airport and then watch over her to make sure she didn't show up unexpectedly at his flat and stumble on her father before he could talk to her."

She tried to find a weakness in his story. "Oh."

"Yeah, *oh*!" He moved aside so someone could walk past to the toilets. "Now, what are you doing here?"

"Confronting my father."

"In a pub."

"I went to Harry's, but you guys were leaving."

He took her elbow and moved her to the side as more people shoved past them. "Your confrontation will have to wait."

"Why?"

"Gregory doesn't know I know what's going on."

"What? Why?"

"He thinks I showed up to ask my friend to join me here."

"Is that all you're up to?"

Andrew looked at the ceiling. "A harmless beer or two."

There was more to his story than that. "I'll be sure and keep up the ruse." She moved toward the bar.

"You're staying?"

"I'm going to find out what's going on with my parents, with or without them telling me."

He grinned. "Like their credit card transactions?"

"Exactly." She turned away. "And I'm not a handful."

Her comment was met with a short laugh. "You passed out."

"And woke up without pants on." They made their way to her brother and dad, dodging other patrons en route.

"I thought you'd sleep better. I didn't do any—"

"I didn't say you did." She stopped walking and turned to look at him. "Just don't expect another peep show."

Andrew didn't have time to respond before she turned around and found Harry staring at the both of them.

"Showtime," she whispered.

Harry's eyes grew wide.

Jax placed her hand on her father's shoulder as she came up behind him.

He swiveled in his seat, his smile radiant . . .

Until it wasn't.

Jax swallowed back the disappointment of seeing how her presence made her father feel.

Surprise, she could handle.

Elation would be ideal . . .

That wasn't what she saw.

"Oh . . ."

At least he was at a loss for words.

"Hello, Father."

"Jacqueline?"

She lifted her hands in the air. "Surprise."

He blew out a sigh and stood. His eyes fell over her shoulder where she knew Andrew was standing. A kiss to the cheek, an attempt at a hug. "I wasn't expecting you."

Jax glanced at her brother. "Harry and I thought it would be a nice surprise. Right, Harry?"

"Surprise . . . right, yes." He looked at the both of them. "Surprise."

Her father kept looking over her shoulder. "You know Andrew?"

Jax waved a hand in the air. "I've known Andrew for quite some time, right?" she turned to him and asked.

"We go back a long way," Andrew said with a grin.

"I hope you don't mind me barging in on boys' night out."

Her father and Harry were both silent.

Andrew spoke up. "Of course not. We needed a little estrogen in the mix."

She felt his hand touch the small of her back as he reached around her and picked up his beer sitting on the bar.

"How long have you been here?" her father asked.

The details weren't important. The fact that her father had no idea she was in London, on the other hand . . . was. Why hadn't Harry told him? "Not long," she said.

A strangled smile crossed his face. "You look tan. Have you been traveling?"

The waitress walked up beside Jax and handed her the cider.

"Add that to our tab," Harry told the woman.

"I spent some time in Bali for work."

"What kind of work happens in Bali?" Harry asked.

"A little of this. A little of that." Her family never asked details about her job and she wasn't about to tell them she was shadowing an assassin to make sure he was retired. "Boring stuff."

"I've never been to Indonesia," Andrew said.

"It's wet. Beautiful. The people are lovely."

Her father lifted his drink, talked over the rim. "I thought your work kept you in California."

She shook her head. "We have an office here, remember? Before the holidays I was in Budapest."

"I didn't realize," Gregory said.

"You've never asked."

Silence stretched between them.

"What is it you do again?" Andrew questioned, as if he had already been told.

"I work for a security company. Investigations."

"International?"

"Sometimes," Jax told him.

Andrew smiled, looked at her with narrowed eyes.

"Fascinating."

Her father reached for the inside pocket of his jacket, glanced at his phone, and set it on the bar. The opportunity to dig into her father's personal life was just too easy to pass up. "Are you going to make me stand here all night, Harry, or give up your seat?"

Harry scrambled to his feet. "Sorry, sis. I kinda forgot you were a girl."

She looked at her chest and laughed. "Boys don't grow these."

Her brother blushed.

Andrew chuckled.

Her father missed it.

Jax pulled out her cell phone, glanced at it, and then set it on the bar.

"When I called Jax last weekend, she was jumping out of an airplane for work," Harry told Andrew.

"You're kidding," Andrew said as if he didn't know.

"What investigations require skydiving?" Gregory asked.

"Team-building weekend. Spent time at a Marine base." She sipped her drink, watched her dad's reaction. "It reminded me of Richter."

The mention of Richter stopped her father from asking more questions. At least that's how it appeared when he closed his lips and looked her in the eye.

She was about to recount a memory of Richter in order to quiz her father once again on why she was sent there when a man approached her brother. "Hey, Harry. Haven't seen you around here lately." He extended a hand, which her brother took.

Jax used the distraction to reach for her phone, purposely picking up her father's.

"Been busy."

"You work too hard, mate."

"He works just hard enough," Gregory said.

At that point Harry introduced his friend Sheldon to all of them. The man's smile lingered as he looked her way.

Jax stood. "I'll be right back."

The men moved aside, and she walked toward the restrooms.

Alone in a stall, she powered on her father's phone and found it password protected.

With enough time, she could hack in, but decided on an easier option.

"Hey, Siri."

The phone dinged.

She told the phone a series of numbers to make a call.

"MacBain Security and Solutions."

Jax put the phone to her ear. "I need another favor."

Five minutes later she left the restroom and went back to the party.

She sat down, put the phone on the bar, and pushed it toward her dad. "Sorry, I grabbed your phone by mistake."

Her father took it with a smile and returned it to his pocket. "They all look alike."

"That they do."

Sometime later, with half her pint down, the men were on a second round and Jax was ready to go. She wasn't going to learn anything else with the crowd that was gathering. Her time was better served behind a computer. And by picking up a few toys to put into play.

She pushed her drink aside and stood. "I'm calling it a night."

"You just got here." Andrew sounded disappointed.

"I'm still a little jet-lagged."

Gregory stood. "This was quite a surprise."

She looked at him straight on. "Make time in your schedule. Lunch maybe." It wasn't a request, more of an ultimatum. "We have a lot to talk about."

All her dad did was nod.

Jax accepted Harry's hug, whispered in his ear. "Call me."

"Good to see you."

Andrew stood aside, put his beverage down. "I'll walk you out."

Outside the bar, the cold, damp London air snapped her spine straight.

"Where is your car?"

Jax pointed across the street and up toward her brother's place. "I'm capable of getting there on my own."

"I would suspect anyone who jumps out of airplanes and plays on America's military bases is capable of more than crossing the street."

"Then why are you out here?"

The light turned green and they started walking.

"I want to help."

"Help with what?"

"Your investigation. That's why Harry asked you to come, isn't it?"

"Is that what he told you?"

"He told me he needed family reinforcements to get his dad to move out of his flat."

That sounded like the words her brother would use.

"I have a feeling my father is going to be just as helpful putting this to rest as my mother."

"He didn't seem excited to see you."

"Thank you for pointing that out."

Andrew paused his step. "I'm sorry. That was insensitive."

She stopped, turned to look at him. "I'm pretty sure I remember telling you my family was cold. Back when I thought you were a driver who didn't know them personally."

"Right. I'm sorry about that, too."

Jax started walking again. "I tipped you."

He followed. "I'll pay you back."

They crossed another intersection, and she slowed her pace as the rental car came into view.

She wondered if there was a way for Andrew to help her. "Do you work with my dad?"

He shook his head. "No. I'm in finance, but with the private sector. Hedge funds have no appeal to me."

"There's more money in it." Jax stopped at the car.

"And less quality of life. Look at your brother, he doesn't have any hair left."

"True."

Andrew reached out his hand.

She looked at it.

He wiggled his fingers as if asking for something. "Your phone. In case you need backup."

"There's an entire team here in London."

He pointed to his chest. "But only one of me."

That sounded like a line. But she handed him her phone anyway.

He pressed a button to power it on, then turned it toward her so it would open.

A sly smile sat on his lips as he put in his phone number.

When his phone buzzed, he silenced it quickly, obviously pleased with himself.

"Was this about me getting ahold of you, or you getting ahold of me?"

"Yes."

Jax narrowed her gaze, saw the same attraction she had the night they'd met. "I'm not here for that."

"I don't know what you're talking about." His eyes twitched. His smile grew.

Instead of calling him out, she reached for her keys.

He opened the door and waited for her to get behind the wheel. "Petrol," he said.

Jax looked up at him, confused. "What?"

"My last credit card transaction was at the petrol station."

It was hard not to smile. "You're an interesting man, Andrew."

He leaned down with a knowing smile. "You have beautiful legs, Jax."

She was blushing . . . she could feel the heat in her cheeks.

He closed the door and stepped back.

Jax drove away without saying goodbye, knowing full well she'd see him again.

CHAPTER EIGHT

"This is not going to wrap up quickly."

Jax spoke into her earbuds to keep at least half the conversation away from prying ears. Not that she needed to worry. The household was asleep by the time she made it home.

After leaving the pub she drove straight to the London office and "borrowed" a few items to help move things along.

"It doesn't sound like it," Claire said on the other end of the line. It was late for Jax and midday for her best friend. She'd already filled Claire in on everything that had transpired . . . or more to the point, everything that hadn't happened.

"I need another set of eyes," Jax mused aloud.

"Then get them."

Jax fiddled with a few mechanical eyes that sat on her desk. The ones she borrowed. "I'm working on it."

"I've done some research on divorce."

"Counterproductive when you're planning a wedding."

"Actually, I think that might work in our favor. Let's look at the reasons people say *fuck this*."

"Infidelity," Jax said quickly. She'd already thought of that. And the reason she'd put a trace on both her father's phone and her mother's.

"Right. Who would be most likely to step out?" Claire asked.

She closed her eyes. "It's hard to think that either of them would."

"Good thing I know your parents and I have an opinion. Your dad."

"He certainly has more of an opportunity. My mother is surrounded by staff or women from her clubs."

Claire laughed. "Your mom isn't out of the question. Eventually someone might have a pool boy that looks her way."

"There aren't that many swimming pools in the UK."

The laughter on the other end of the line grew. "Tennis instructor, then."

Jax rubbed her eyes. "I can't see it, but okay . . . let's assume one of them did."

"I'm going with your dad."

"Why?"

"He moved out. And neither of them are talking about it. Your mother would be embarrassed, and your father wouldn't want the world to know."

Jax couldn't find fault in that. "Incompatibility and lack of communication are the leading causes of divorce."

"True. Very, very true. But your parents are exactly the same."

"That doesn't mean they communicate."

"Lack of communication leads to infidelity."

"You really think that's it?"

"I just don't want you to be surprised if someone is sending dick pics—"

"Oh. My. God."

"I'm serious. You're tapping their phones and messages, right?"

"Of course."

"Then don't be shocked. I'm the voice of reason. You know it."

"I hate it."

"I could be right."

"I know and I hate that, too," Jax said.

Claire paused before she spoke. "Are you ready to go down this rabbit hole?"

Jax weighed her answer. "I feel I must." She closed the laptop she'd been looking at during their conversation and lowered her head. And then she switched languages from English to German. "I don't know my family. This is my opportunity to find out what makes them get up every morning. What makes them sad."

"What made them send you to Richter," Claire replied in German.

Yes . . . there was that. "Maybe if I knew them better, I'd understand."

"Then it's a journey that needs to be," Claire said . . . in English.

"You sound like Gwen." Gwen was Neil's wife.

"She's the closest thing I have to a mother, so I'll take that as a compliment."

Jax sighed. "If only my mother had someone like Gwen in her life. Someone she'd open up to."

"Maybe she does. Who is your mom's best friend?"

"I have no idea. I'm here during the holidays and occasional birthday. The parties are full of people with a place. A place in the company my father works for, the place where my mother has lunch. People of influence."

"Gwen has influence."

Jax paused. "What are you suggesting?"

"Maybe I ask Gwen to come with me to England so we can wedding shop. Maybe we bring your mom to the Harrison estate and let Gwen do what she does best."

"And what's that?"

"Act royal and real at the same time, which tends to open people up."

Gwen was technically *Lady Gwen*. Her brother, a duke. And Jax's mother ate that shit up.

"I like where you're going. Do you think Gwen will oblige?"

"I'll ask."

"Reinforcements. I need reinforcements."

"Unless you want to spend the next year in London unraveling your parents' drama."

"No one wants that. The only redeeming part of any of this is Andrew."

"Who is Andrew?"

"The driver."

"What?"

"The driver . . . who wasn't a driver. He was a friend of my brother who I assumed was a driver."

"The cute guy who put you to bed?"

This called for an explanation. "The cute guy who made sure I got to my room and was safe before he left me . . . untouched."

"Awww, that's so sweet. Much better than the other perverse explanation of your first night in London."

"He offered to help."

"Hmmm, I need to meet this Andrew person."

"It's not like that."

Claire flat out laughed. "Sure it isn't."

"He's in finance. A numbers geek. Someone my parents would love." And if there was one type of man Jax stayed clear of . . . it was a person her parents would approve of.

"Ouch."

"Exactly."

"But when he was a driver, he was cute and *drinks in a bar* worthy."

That stopped Jax cold. "I don't know if he'll be around when you get here."

"If he is into you, he'll be around."

Jax rolled her eyes. "It's late. I'm going to bed."

"Talk about diverting the conversation."

She laughed.

"I'll talk to Gwen, get back to you."

"Talk tomorrow."

~

"You got in late last night," Evelyn pointed out when Jax joined her in the breakfast room.

"I interrupted Harry's evening with Dad."

Evelyn looked over her teacup.

"I wanted him to know I was aware of your situation and was in town."

"How did that go?" her mother asked.

"Uneventful. He wasn't in a position to talk."

Letty brought in a tray of fruit, halting their conversation.

Once the cook left the room, Jax started in again. "Much like it is here."

"I prefer to keep my personal life . . . personal."

"You don't really believe that Letty and Angela are oblivious, do you?"

Evelyn released a long-suffering sigh, set her cup down. "Is it going to be like this every morning with you?"

Instead of answering, Jax tried a different approach. "I'm worried, Mum."

The use of *Mum* must have caught her mother off guard. She lost some of the tension in her shoulders and attempted a smile. "I'm okay."

"I don't believe you."

Evelyn chuckled. "That's nothing new."

"You're here alone now."

"I'm not alone."

"Letty goes home at night. She and Angela both have their days off. You leave the front door unlocked. I know you think it's a safe world out there, but it isn't."

"I'll start locking the doors."

Jax sat forward.

Letty walked back in the room. "I've been telling your mum to lock the doors for years."

"I've been ignoring you for years," Evelyn argued.

Letty placed two croissants down. "You'd think after last month you'd at least try."

Jax stopped the coffee halfway to her lips, noticed her mother's back stiffen. "Last month? What happened last month?"

"Letty . . ."

Even though her mother's tone was a warning, Jax didn't let the subject go. "Mother!"

"It was nothing."

She turned her attention to Letty. The look in the cook's eyes said differently.

"Your father said it was a bum."

"Said what was a bum? What happened?"

Evelyn shook her head when Letty started talking. "There was a man who came around to the back of the house and was looking in the windows, knocked over a chair, busted a pot."

All of Jax's nerves started to fire up at the same time.

"Angela saw him and screamed. He tripped over himself running off. Never saw him again," Letty said.

"Just because you haven't seen him doesn't mean he isn't out there." Jax turned back to her mother. "Why didn't you tell me this?"

"There's nothing to tell. A bum looked in the windows and ran away."

"Or a man was casing the house and is waiting for a better time to come in or—"

"Your father said—"

"He's not here!" Jax's voice rose enough to end the argument and chase Letty from the room.

Silence stretched like a sour smell in a confined space.

"I want you to put in an alarm system."

"You mentioned that before. I don't think it's necessary."

"Before, it was a precaution, now it is warranted. I have to assume you didn't call the police."

"Of course not. He was a scared rabbit."

Jax would grill Angela later on those details. "You can either let me occupy my mind with something I can do about this situation, allow me to put an alarm system in, or leave my mind free to ask you more and more questions every day to chip away at your stubbornness and get the information I seek about you . . . Dad . . . everything."

Her mother hesitated. "It sounds expensive."

"It's part of what the company I work for does. And besides, I'll make Father pay for it."

"Why is that?"

"Because him not being here is why you need it. Not that you need to worry about the cost. Still . . ."

Evelyn actually smiled. A devious smile Jax had never seen on her mother's face before.

"It's settled. I'll have a team here today and present the bill to Father tomorrow."

Her mother reached for one of the French pastries. "I would hate to see something happen to the staff should someone break in. Though I really don't think we have to worry."

Yes!

Jax opened her mouth and her mother stopped her.

"And nothing more about your father and I."

"What if he says something to me I think you might want to hear? Seems only fair since Harry and Dad are drinking beer at the pub every night." Jax wasn't sure they were drinking every night . . . in fact she doubted it, but poking her mother felt like the right move. "Married couples shouldn't have secrets . . . right?"

Evelyn sat with that for a few seconds. "I would rather hear news from you than someone around town."

"Brilliant."

Her mother pushed her half-eaten croissant aside and dusted the crumbs off her hands. "Enough about me. Are you seeing anyone?"

Jax told her mother what she wanted to hear. "I was dating a lawyer."

Evelyn's eyes lit up. "That's hopeful."

Jax shook her head. "He was dating me to level up, I was dating him because he was good in bed."

"Jacqueline!"

She laughed. "What? It's true. He was painfully dull in every other way."

"Please tell me you're at least a little selective in who you sleep with."

"Don't worry." She was a lot pickier than she ever led her mother to believe. "What about you? Did you date a lot before Dad?"

"I wouldn't say a lot. Enough, I suppose."

"Let's hope you can avoid dating again. Let me tell you, it's rough out there."

Her mother grinned. "You're beautiful and in the prime of your life. You can have any man you want."

"Oh, I have them . . . I just don't want to keep them."

Her laughter suggested she was teasing, and before long, her mother started laughing, too.

"Speaking of men. Do you know Andrew? Harry's friend?"

"Andrew Craig?"

"Yes. What's his story?" The digging Jax had done spelled out the basics . . . no criminal record, only a couple of speeding tickets. Owned a flat close to her brother's. Worked in finance as he'd said . . . and yes, his last credit card purchase was at a gas station. But who was he outside of that?

"Nice boy, good family. He went to school with your brother."

"Define *nice boy*."

"Why? Are you interested?"

Jax shook her head. "No. He's too . . ."

"Right."

"Really, Mum, I'm not—"

"I've not heard anything about the women in his life. And I find that rare in your age group. He was offered a job at your father's firm but didn't take it. Instead, he works with his father, making arguably less money but I'm sure doing quite well. That is my definition of *nice boy*. Not that you're interested."

They sat in silence, sipping coffee and tea.

"He is cute," Jax admitted.

"And tall."

They were both smiling. "Big feet." Jax hadn't ever looked at his feet, but the comment made her mother laugh.

That, in itself, was rare.

"What am I going to do with you?"

Jax shrugged. "You can't send me off to Richter again. I'm much too old for that."

Evelyn looked down and sighed.

This was likely the longest conversation she and her mother had ever had. The last thing Jax wanted to do was ruin it. "I'm going to call the team. It's going to be noisy in the house for a few hours." She pushed away from the table.

"Be sure and put in the expensive equipment. I wouldn't want to have to do things twice."

"Will do."

Jax left the breakfast room and smiled at Letty as she walked past the kitchen.

~

Two hours later the house was brimming with technicians installing the alarm system, complete with audio and visual inside the main walkways and around the entire perimeter. As a rule, Jax didn't normally take part in installations, but she did know the home and its weaknesses.

Three sets of service personnel showed up at the same time . . . upstairs, downstairs, and on the grounds.

Jax sat with Angela, recording her description of what she remembered about the day the man was caught checking out Casa de Simon.

"He ran pretty fast once he got on his feet, so he wasn't that old. I didn't get a good look at his face. He had a beard, like a lot of men do these days. Scruffy."

"Dirty?"

"Hard to say."

"Race? Weight?"

"Caucasian. Normal weight, I guess."

"How was he dressed?"

"It was raining. He had a long coat. Didn't see much else. Truth was, I was just as scared as he was."

The whole event lasted a few seconds. Her father had been in the house and had seen the tail end of the man as he jumped a hedge. According to Angela they locked things for a week or so, but soon went back to their old ways.

"If you remember anything else, let me know."

Angela offered a nod and left to chase after one of the many workers making a mess of the house.

Jax followed to find her mother staring at the parade of employees.

"This is a bit much," Evelyn said at Jax's side.

"They're all here at once to get it done in one day."

"Our neighbors will think something's wrong."

"Something *is* wrong."

Evelyn offered a pretty decent eye roll. One that made Jax proud. "Then tell the neighbors I gave this to you as a gift for your birthday and you couldn't say no . . . although you wanted to."

With the front door wide open, Sven walked in and straight up to them. "Hello, Jax."

She opened her arms for a hug. "What are you doing here?"

"Special request from Neil." Without further explanation, he turned to her mother. "You must be Jax's older sister."

"Oh, please." But her mother was smiling.

"Laying it on a bit thick, don't you think?" Jax laughed. "My mother, Evelyn. This is Sven, part of the London team I've told you about."

Sven shook his head. "No." He stood back, looked between the two of them. "I do see where Jax gets her beautiful eyes."

"Aren't you charming," Evelyn said.

Sven moved to her mother's side. "See, Jax. I'm charming."

"You're a playboy and flirting with my mother. Now what's this about a special request from Neil?"

Sven looked at one of the men carrying a toolbox up the stairs. "Because this is your family home and personal, he wanted to make sure someone objective looked at the whole picture."

That was to be expected.

"Neil is your boss, right?" Evelyn asked.

"Yes."

"That's very kind of him to offer special care for someone he doesn't even know."

Sven laughed.

Jax moved around her mother and took ahold of Sven's arm. "I talk about my family all the time. I'm sure he feels he does know you."

Jax did not need her mother to know that Neil completed thorough investigations on all of his employees and, in turn, their families.

"Right. Well and good. Now . . . show me around the place."

"Oh, Sven." Evelyn stopped them before walking away.

"Yes, beautiful?"

Jax pinched his shoulder.

"Letty is preparing lunch for everyone. How many do you suppose that will be?"

Sven muttered off numbers while looking at the ceiling. "Eleven . . . twelve. Men."

Her mother blushed. "I'll tell her to prepare for twenty-four."

Sven glanced at Jax. "Your mother's nicer than you."

Evelyn giggled as she walked away.

Jax stared after her, wondering who the woman was.

"Are you showing me around the place or what?"

"You're incorrigible."

Sven laid a hand to his chest. "It's a gift."

CHAPTER NINE

Neil sat in his office at headquarters watching the footage coming out of Jax's family home. Much like the video, the audio came online slowly, which he kept at a low volume until the install was complete.

A slight knock on the door preceded it opening and Sasha pushing her way inside.

"Hello."

He motioned for her to come in and shut the door.

"Thanks for coming." The woman didn't technically work for him, so she was under no obligation to show up when he requested it. Yet he knew she'd be there.

Sasha wore slim, black jeans, a dark blue button-up shirt, and a black leather jacket she had draped over an arm. A slight variation of the black spandex she was known for, but a signature look nonetheless. "What's going on?"

He motioned toward the monitors on his desk. "Jax's mother agreed to a security system."

"Did something happen to prompt it?"

Neil shrugged. "Hard to say. Housekeeper reported an uninvited visitor in the back of the house last month. No break-in. No damage. Ran off when noticed and hasn't returned."

"A month ago." Sasha didn't look impressed.

"That and Jax's brother called her home because Dad left the wife and is now staying with the brother."

"Divorce?"

"Not yet."

Sasha shrugged. "Regardless, there needs to be a system in place, considering what we get mixed up in."

Neil couldn't agree more. Especially with the recent case where some big names in organized crime were put behind bars. And retired assassins were on their list to monitor. Neil didn't like any of their team to spend time in homes that didn't have the basics of security.

Sasha cut to the chase. "Why did you ask me to come?"

"Do we know why Jax was sent to Richter?"

Sasha stared and stayed silent.

"Could it have anything to do with the recent split of the parents? I don't care about the gossip. I care about the safety of my team." Neil glanced at the screen, saw Jax walking through the hall of her parents' home.

"There's always a chance her parents sent her to Richter for the education," Sasha said, her voice flat.

"And her brother to a local boarding school in England? Why? Neither parent attended Richter. Nostalgia doesn't fit."

"You want me to look at the files." The files referred to the thousands of documents and private information about the students attending Richter and their families. The secrets that made the parents desire a military-style boarding school where they knew their students would be safe and, perhaps even more importantly, be able to take care of themselves should their past return to haunt them.

"Much as I don't like opening Pandora's box, Claire and Gwen will be flying to Europe this week and will be in the middle of the family drama. Call me controlling, but I want to know what the drama is and, more importantly, if there is a threat."

"You *are* controlling." But Sasha was smiling.

"Then you'll do it." He'd do it himself, but most of the files were in German.

"I will."

"You must believe I have a point."

"You always have a point. The question is what do we do with the information when we obtain it. If there's a threat, we move . . . but if it's family gossip, secrets that aren't ours to tell?"

"Then we let Jax discover it on her own."

"I can live with that." Sasha looked closer at the monitors. "Where else is Jax digging?"

Neil leaned back in his chair. "Taps and locators on both her parents' phones. A complete overhaul of this house, and she asked for a team to be available to jump on her brother's. She's requested a personal search on an Andrew Craig, which came up boring as hell. And she borrowed a few toys from the London office."

"Weapons?"

"No. Just tech."

"Let me know if that changes." Sasha turned to leave.

"Thank you."

She acknowledged him with a lift of her hand as she walked out of his office.

~

Jax stood in front of one of three control panels scattered throughout the house. One was off the garage, one the front door, and the final one was in her mother's bedroom.

Her mother, Letty, and Angela were lined up and watching.

"Tell me what you know about alarm systems," Jax said to her mother.

Evelyn looked at Letty, shifted from one foot to the other. "You set the alarm and if anyone breaks in, it goes off. Someone calls the authorities."

"Yes. Every basic alarm system does that. But first, the company will call the home to determine if it's a false alarm. They ask for a code word, and if you don't deliver it, then they call the police. All of which takes time and delays. My company, or the one I work for . . . we have a different level of service. We have cameras inside the house and out. When your alarm goes off, even for a routine entry, the cameras are automatically turned on at headquarters. You press in the code on the keypad, the alarm is turned off within a minute, and the cameras go back to standby within five minutes."

"Are the cameras truly necessary?"

Sven took that moment to walk down the stairs, and Jax used the opportunity to *show* rather than *tell* her mother why cameras were key.

"Got a second?" she asked Sven.

"Anything for you, Jax."

Jax turned, set the alarm. Then she motioned for him to follow her out the front door.

"Where are you going?" her mother asked.

"Stay there."

Jax pulled Sven by the hand and closed the door between them and her mother.

"Do you have a pistol on you?"

"Of course," he said with a laugh.

She made a motion with her fingers, which prompted him to deliver it from behind his back.

Jax removed the magazine and unloaded the chamber and returned it to him. Then she stood with her back to his front. "Show my mother why cameras are necessary."

Sven sighed. "You just want me to get close to you."

The two of them waited for the beeping of the leave command to stop before moving. "Make it believable," Jax told him.

Jax felt his gun in her rib cage and opened the front door.

"Don't hurt me!" she cried as they pushed through the entry.

The alarm sounded, a voice from the box told them to enter the code.

Her mother, Letty, and Angela scrambled out of the way as Sven shoved Jax toward the control panel. "Turn that bloody thing off."

Jax noticed the moment the three women saw the gun. "Don't hurt me, you can take whatever you want."

The alarm still blared in the house.

The noise was deafening.

"Don't worry, lovely . . . I'll take everything." His voice was sleezy and perfect.

"Mother, what would you do?" Jax yelled.

Sven moved closer, leveled the gun at Jax's head.

"Put in the code. Put in the code," her mother cried.

Jax pressed the code and stopped the alarm.

The room went silent.

Sven moved closer, the gun still leveled. "Well done, kitten." He pressed the weapon to Jax's cheek with a purr.

With a classic disarming move, Jax shifted her weight, jabbed at Sven's groin but didn't hit, and twisted the weapon from his hand.

Sven, being a good sport, didn't volley, and Jax aimed the weapon at him.

The three women stared and collectively sighed.

"Now, unless any of you can do that, cameras are necessary." Jax returned the magazine to the gun, chambered a round, and handed the weapon back to Sven. "Thank you for the demo."

"Anytime, love."

Jax leveled her gaze at her shocked mother. "You turn off the alarm, the cameras turn on, and the team is put into motion."

"What happens then?" Letty asked, her eyes round with shock.

"As expected, the authorities are notified. But so are we. And if we're first, we neutralize the threat."

"Neutralize?" her mother asked.

Jax shrugged.

"Oh, my," Angela whispered.

Jax continued her explanation of the system. "For the next several days, the videos are live twenty-four seven. To determine routine, patterns, and the like." And so it went on.

Once she was finished with her tutorial, her mother and the two others were nodding and smiling. It was then that Angela spoke up. "What about Mr. Simon, ma'am . . . should someone warn him before he comes home?"

Jax glanced at her mother.

Letty looked away.

Evelyn shook her head. "Don't be daft, Angela. We all know that Mr. Simon left with more than a suitcase and a week's worth of clothing." She paused. "Not that he's a threat." Evelyn looked directly at Jax. "But he isn't expected without an announcement."

And in that moment, Jax felt the first hint of a bond with her mother.

The first in her entire life.

~

Instead of waiting for the evening, when her father and brother were done with the workday, Jax decided an office visit the next day would work to her advantage. It would keep any discourse to a minimum and give Jax the opportunity to make her face known at the office. That way, when she needed to have an excuse to be left alone in her dad's work space, there would be fewer questions or concerns.

Wearing linen pants, a silk blouse, and heels high enough to make most men look her in the eye, she walked into the high-rise complex twenty minutes shy of noon. According to the tracker on her father's phone, he was at his office.

The double glass doors of the modern space welcomed her, as did an attendant at the front desk.

The greeter was a man, midtwenties, well dressed, with an earpiece pressed to his left ear. He was speaking into a phone, and acknowledged her with a smile but continued with the call. "Absolutely, I'll put you through."

He turned his attention to her. "How can I help you?"

"I'm here to see Mr. Simon."

"Senior or junior?" He looked down at an event calendar, likely checking for her appointment.

"Senior. Though if he is busy, I'm happy to speak with my brother."

Her words tore his eyes away from the book and up at her.

"You're Mr. Simon's daughter?"

There were absolute truths about who knows what is going on in life.

The butler always knows who did it.

The maid always knows who is pregnant.

The groundskeeper always knows whose car is parked in the drive . . . that maybe shouldn't be parked in the drive . . .

And the secretaries spend time with ancillary staff for happy hour and divulge corner office gossip after a few drinks.

It was just the way of things.

Creating friendships, or in this case, trust, with those at the front desk was ideal.

Jax extended her hand. "Jacqueline Simon." She lowered her voice. "Jax, actually, but Dad and Mum hate the nickname."

The man pressed his palm to hers. "Peter." He smiled. "I don't think I've seen you here before."

"I live in California. I'm not here often. I was in the city and thought I'd surprise my father for a few minutes. With any luck, he doesn't have a lunch meeting."

Peter looked at his book with a grin. "His schedule looks open to me."

"Brilliant. Now, if you'll just point me in the direction of his office . . ."

Peter lost his smile.

She whispered, "You point. I'll pretend you were in the bathroom and I let myself in."

He sighed, pointed. "Down the hall to the end. Make a right . . . his office is the last one on the corner. Can't miss it."

"Thank you."

Before she could walk away, he whispered, "Is that Chanel?"

Jax shook her head and whispered back. "Gap," she lied.

Bonding with the reception staff secured, she walked through the office.

Her chin was high.

Determination with each step.

Some employees glanced up from their desks.

Most ignored her.

Her father's name was on the door Peter had indicated.

Gregory's personal secretary sat at her desk and looked up when Jax approached.

"Can I help you?"

Jax pointed toward the closed door. "I'm Jacqueline. Mr. Simon's daughter. I'm trying to surprise him."

The woman's lips parted, a denial on her next breath.

Jax didn't give her time to respond before walking through the door.

Her father stood with his back to her, his frame in front of a large window overlooking the city.

"Hello, Dad."

He turned, his expression guarded.

"I'm sorry, Mr. Simon. She just walked in."

Gregory attempted a smile.

He sucked at it. "It's quite all right." As if to emphasize the point, he walked over and air-kissed one side of Jax's face, then the other.

"I was hoping to catch you for lunch."

Her father swallowed, glanced at his secretary. "I have a client lunch today."

The woman blinked a few times. "Yes. A Mr. Brodeur. A new client."

"Brodeur. But I can be a little late. Be sure and let him know I'll be tardy," Gregory told his secretary.

None of this rang true in Jax's head.

Then again, the conversation she needed to have with her father was anything but comfortable.

Once the other woman, who her father didn't bother introducing her to, left, Jax moved to the space in front of the window where her father had been standing. "Lovely view."

"I like it."

She looked over her shoulder, took in the room. Modern, or at least more so than anything she'd ever seen in her parents' personal spaces. "Isn't it strange that I've never been in here?"

"It isn't as if you have a need."

"Father-daughter day . . . bring-your-kid-to-work day . . ."

Instead of coming up with an excuse, her father changed the subject. "Why are you here now?"

Jax moved to one of the chairs on the other side of his desk and waited for him to take a seat.

"What happened? Between you and Mother?"

He sighed, sat down, and lifted a pen, looking at it as if it held the answers. Jax reached into the side pocket of her purse and removed a small microphone with a transmitter. The bug might be overkill, but from the look on her dad's face, he was going to add to his lunch lie, or not say anything at all.

And eventually, Jax wanted to get on with her life instead of keeping the company of a family who lied about appointments instead of taking her to lunch.

"I'll tell you the same thing I told your brother."

Jax waited.

"It's personal."

She laughed. And continued to laugh until she covered her lips with her palm. In doing so her purse slid from her lap and onto the floor. Reaching down, she placed the bug on the underside of her father's desk and controlled her mirth as she settled back into the chair.

"I don't understand your humor."

Jax swallowed, stopped laughing, and looked him in the eye. "It's *our* family. It's not personal? It affects all of us. Hence the reason I'm here."

"Exactly why are you here?" he asked.

His question rang cold.

So did her tone. "It's not exactly for the invitation or hospitality."

"You know you're always welcome."

"Am I? Really? When was that, exactly? Before I was in a training bra and sent off to Richter?"

"Richter was a good school."

Arguably. "Why Germany?" Jax couldn't help but ask the personal questions.

"You speak German, don't you?"

"That's ridiculous."

Gregory sighed, placed both palms on the table. "I don't want to fight with you."

Jax pulled back her argumentative tone, placed her hands in her lap. "We can avoid the fight for now. Divert the questions." She leaned forward, placed one arm on his desk. "But eventually you'll have to answer my questions because Richter was a good school. They taught me many . . . many things."

He cleared his throat. "Sending your daughter off to boarding school is different than a son. We wanted to keep you safe."

Safe.

The word stuck out. She'd heard it many times in the past.

"Safe from who?"

Her father looked away. "Safe. Just safe. Nothing more, nothing less."

Liar.

The phone buzzed on his desk and his secretary chimed in. "I'm leaving for lunch, Mr. Simon. Don't forget your appointment."

"Thank you, Miranda."

So that was her name.

Jax stood, taking the cue.

"How long do you plan on staying?" her father asked.

Her normal response would have been with a quick exit. The weekend . . . midweek . . .

"Not sure. I'm actually enjoying myself. Meeting new people." Her mind immediately moved to Andrew. "My company has a London-based team. Claire's getting married . . . Maybe I'll ask for a transfer." She'd never considered it. But saying the words evoked the strangest look on her father's face.

"That's a"—he cleared his throat—"surprise."

Jax swallowed her disappointment that the mere mention of returning home offered nothing more than *surprise.*

"I'm sure it is." She stood, took two steps toward the door, her father at her heels, and stopped. "Oh, I almost forgot." Jax reached into her purse, removed the security bill, and handed it to her father. "Now that you're no longer living with Mother . . . she wants to be *safe*, too. I encouraged an alarm system, and hired my company, since there is no longer a man in the house warding off the bad guys. Like the one Angela ran off last month with her screams."

"Angela spooks when cats are fighting in the neighborhood."

"A six-foot cat in a trench coat is a little more of a threat. Any idea who it could have been?" She watched his eyes to see if he knew.

He blinked. Shook his head.

"Did it ever occur to you to call the police?"

"Not really."

"Why? I would have." She wouldn't have had to. Not with the people she worked with. But her father didn't know that.

"Bums end up on doorsteps in London all the time. They're told to move along, and they do."

"Mother's house isn't in the heart of the city, though, now is it?"

"Our house."

She tilted her head to one side, squinted her eyes as if weighing the comment. "I'm there now. I'll keep her safe."

Her father stood taller, lifted the bill to eye level before dropping it on his desk. "I'll take care of it."

"Good. Be sure and look at the fine print for the monthly service. I'd hate for my boss to have to ask."

"No worries."

She reached the door, stood to the side, and waited for her father to open it. "Enjoy your lunch with Mr. Bassett." Jax purposely used a different name.

"As much as one can with a work meeting."

No correction on the name.

Her father kissed the sides of her cheeks, and Jax walked out of the office.

Half tempted to stalk her father and prove he didn't have a meeting, she instead turned and walked down the streets of the busy business district.

She had a lot to process. The lies, the truths . . . and the parts that hurt the most.

Three blocks and two turns later, she found herself in front of an address she'd only looked at on paper.

She removed her cell phone from her purse, dialed a number, and lifted it to her ear.

"Jax?"

Just hearing her name, the way she preferred to hear it, made her smile. "Where are you?" she asked.

"Are you okay?"

Why did his simple question make her tear up? "Where are you?"

"At the office. You don't sound okay."

"Isn't it lunchtime?"

"It is, but I'm—"

"I'm out front. Do you want to grab a sandwich?"

"I'll be right down."

CHAPTER TEN

Andrew tried to play it cool as he darted from his office, pressed the button for the lift several times as if that would make the thing move faster, and finally made it to the ground floor of his building. A quick scan of the lobby and he moved through the glass doors to the outside.

Jax stood with her back to him.

Long blonde hair, slim frame . . . tall. Yup . . . that was her. "Fancy meeting you here." His tone was light. Completely opposite of the excitement brewing inside.

She turned, and the sadness in her eyes shot through him.

"Hi."

"Oh, boy." He opened his arms and, for reasons he couldn't say, she moved into them.

Her cheek rested on his chest; her arms hesitated before slowly moving around his waist.

Andrew hugged her tight.

She held him tighter.

"That bad?"

The busy occupants of the business district moved around them as if they were water in a stream and he and Jax were the massive stone in the middle.

Only when Jax loosened her grip did he let go.

With his hands on her shoulders, he looked her in the eye.

If he wasn't mistaken, she was on the verge of tears. What the hell had happened? "Are we talking? Walking? Eating? Or what?"

"I'm interrupting your day."

"That wasn't an answer to my question."

She attempted a smile. "I'm hungry."

"Martini lunch? Beer lunch?"

"Just lunch."

He could do that.

Andrew turned them around, a hand to her elbow, and directed them toward lunch.

"How did you know where I worked?" The question had crossed his mind, but asking the more important questions—like what had happened and why she was searching him out—didn't feel right. She'd open up when she was ready.

Jax placed a hand to her chest. "Private investigator."

"Oh . . . right. You really did do a search on me."

She looked away. "I did. I'm sorry. It feels like an invasion now."

He slid his arm into the crook of hers. "Did I come out okay?"

Her eyes inched toward his. "You're not a criminal."

"I stole a lot of hearts in primary school."

She laughed. "My investigation didn't dig that deep."

An Italian restaurant, which was a little pricier than the average in the business district, didn't have a line out the door. "This okay?"

"Perfect."

The next ten minutes were filled with small talk and ordering food.

She asked for sparkling water, not wine. Pasta and bread . . . and a side salad. The hungry part hadn't been an excuse.

Andrew followed her lead.

Only once the waiter left and she had a glass of fizzy water in her hands to fiddle with did Jax open up.

"I went to my father's office."

"Okay." He wasn't sure what the implications of that were.

"I've never been there."

"Really?"

"No. Not once. That's odd, right?"

"I work with my father. He's been taking me to his office since I was old enough to hold a pencil. Grooming me for the family business, if I'm honest."

"It's not a family business. But even so, my brother works there. I'm sure he had been invited before his employment."

Andrew knew personally that Harry had been mentored by his father. "Did you show interest in the world of finance?"

"When I was twelve? That's when they shipped me off to school."

"Not uncommon in Europe."

"To Germany?"

Okay . . . no. "I seem to remember something about that."

"There are fifty-two weeks in the year. I might have spent eight of those in my family home. Not *with* my family, mind you . . . simply at the house my mother now resides in alone. Surely there must be a school closer than Germany that offered an education."

Andrew opened his mouth to agree.

She cut him off. "Harry managed. Yes, he's a boy . . . and yes, there are a few years between us . . . but the difference isn't that great."

Six years older, just as Andrew was six years older than Jax. "Not that great."

"Exactly. You know what my father said when I asked him why Germany?"

"No."

"He said, 'You speak German, don't you?'" She paused, jaw dropped. "You've got to be kidding me. You send your daughter away to a school. And not just any school. Richter was . . . is . . ." She sighed. "It doesn't matter. Hire a tutor if you want your child to speak a different language. Don't send them away to a different country where they know no one, have no family . . . where the world was harsh."

He waited for her to quiet and pause. "You're just now asking these questions?"

"I've asked them my whole life. Only now I'm demanding answers. I'm ready for the answers."

"All because your parents split."

"Yes. United we stand . . . divided we fall. Something is going on with my parents, and it's not the obvious. Since Harry invited me to figure out what the hell is happening, I'm putting the skills Richter taught me to work."

Andrew found a laugh. "Exactly what will speaking German help you with?"

"I'm not talking about my language skills. Did your school feel like a prison?"

"Of course. Curfews, discipline if you were caught somewhere you weren't supposed to be. It was a boarding school. Not a hotel."

"Did you learn to shoot a gun?"

"What, at school?"

Jax looked at her hands. "What about hacking computers? Memorizing code? Did you run laps during physical education? Or did you scale walls and learn to take down someone twice your size in hand-to-hand combat?"

Andrew thought she was kidding. Then he looked into her eyes. "You're serious."

"You know what really kills me?"

He shook his head.

"I don't think my father knows even half of what I'm capable of. A third . . . a quarter. Yes, I've enhanced those Richter skills through the years. Took the military boarding school and powered that up with equipment and teamwork. Learned about investigations, fraud, criminal . . . domestic. Learned the legal parameters in the States and Europe. Maybe not all of Europe, but the places I'm put into action."

Andrew saw her monologue for what it was. Jax was processing the conversation and her grief over her father's words. "You don't believe your parents think you can find out what is prompting this split."

She shook her head. "My parents have zero idea what I'm capable of. Zero understanding of the evil I've helped take down. Whatever their little domestic squabble is . . . it's nothing compared."

The distant look in her eyes made him want to question the depths of what she'd been a part of.

Maybe another day.

"I can see how you'd want to prove them wrong."

She looked him straight in the eye, blinked a few times. "Good God, I sound like a whiny child."

That's not how he heard it. "You sound like a daughter who is tired of being underappreciated and underestimated. And you're at the point in your life where you're no longer going to put up with it."

Jax's gaze softened. "And whiny."

He made a gesture with his thumb and forefinger to show an inch between them. "Maybe a little."

"I'm pretty angry with my parents."

"I caught that when we were sharing martinis."

Jax had a beautiful smile. Full lips . . . bright eyes.

Their food arrived, and they waited for the waiter to leave before continuing.

She lifted her fork. "Thank you for being available on such short notice."

"I'm glad you called me. I was trying to come up with an excuse to call you."

"You were?"

"I suck at excuses and I'm a pretty terrible liar. I finally decided on the truth."

She brought a forkful of salad to her lips. "Which is?"

Andrew felt a little warm under her gaze. Or maybe it was nerves. "I think you're rather incredible, and I'd like to get to know you better."

She smiled through chewing her food, lips closed. Jax nodded her head and wiped her lips once she had swallowed. "What about Harry?"

"I already know Harry, and besides, I don't want to date him." Andrew purposely misinterpreted her question.

She laughed. "I live in California."

That was a bit of a problem. "But you have family here."

"Family that doesn't like me."

Andrew wasn't convinced of that. "Harry loves you. He's talked about you several times and never says a bad word."

"I don't want to mislead you . . ."

"You're not interested?"

She shook her head. "That's not what I said."

"You *are* interested." He put a bite in his mouth and enjoyed seeing the heat in her cheeks.

"I live in America. I don't see that changing."

"I'm not asking you to marry me, Jax. I'm suggesting we go out on a couple of dates. Maybe I can help you get to the bottom of what's going on with your parents."

Jax closed her eyes, blew out a breath. "That sounds so normal."

"And that's a problem?"

"Yes. No." She shook her head. "Yes."

He laughed. "Which is it?"

"I don't know."

"We can figure it out together." He put more food in his mouth.

Conversation stilled as Jax chewed on what he was suggesting in addition to her lunch.

"Wait . . . you don't have a return ticket, do you?" he asked.

She rolled her eyes. "No. I thought this would take a week, tops. Now I'm not so sure."

Andrew waved a celebratory fist. "Yes!"

Jax smiled ear to ear. "You're incorrigible."

"Determined."

She glanced away, and slowly her smile faded. "You know what's sad?"

"Oh, no."

Jax placed her hand on the table, halfway to him. "No, not you. Both of my parents have asked how long I'm visiting, but neither have asked me to stay."

Andrew placed his hand over hers and stroked her wrist with his thumb. "I, for one, don't want you to uncover what's going on with your parents in any timely fashion. In fact, I might even sabotage your efforts, or at the very least, distract your attention."

"Okay."

He waited for her to say more.

When she didn't, he squeezed the hand that still rested under his and waited for her eyes to look up.

In the moment their eyes met, a spark of energy traveled up his spine. "I should probably have my hand back so I can finish my meal."

Andrew looked at his fingers touching hers. "Life is full of sacrifices." He released her and went back to eating with more vigor.

Close to an hour later, they walked back to his office.

"Thank you for lunch."

"You said that when I paid the bill."

"I'm saying it again."

He turned to her. "Technically, this is already our third date."

"No. Harry paid for martini night. And I'm pretty sure my father covered the bill at the pub."

"You like to argue."

"That's because I'm good at it."

He looked up at his building, thought about some of the things she'd said at lunch. "Do you have a few more minutes?"

"Yeah, why? Don't you have to get back to work?"

"I do, but, ah . . ." He took her hand and tugged her toward the doors.

"What are we doing?"

"I have something I want to give you that's in my office."

"I can wait here."

He kept walking, Jax at his side. "That won't work, actually."

They reached the lifts and waited with everyone else returning from lunch. Inside he pressed his floor and melted with her to the side of the elevator. Either she'd forgotten he'd kidnapped her hand, or she didn't want to pull away. The confusion on her face said it could go either way.

The door opened on his floor and he led Jax out, excusing their exit to those inside.

The open center atrium of the building offered an airy feel to what was often a confined space. Live plants and a skylight helped remove the gloom that often shadowed London's climate.

"This won't take long," he said as he opened the office door and introduced her to his world.

Megan, the receptionist at the front desk, saw them, and it was then that Jax freed her hand from his.

"Megan, this is Jax."

"Hello."

Andrew kept walking.

The space wasn't huge and served only a dozen employees. He slowed his pace as he walked into his office. "Raylene is my assistant, but she's out for the rest of the day. Her youngest is sick."

"Nothing serious, I hope."

He lowered his voice. "Her son puked at school, so they sent him home."

"That would do it."

In his office, he purposely left the doors open. "My corner of the world."

She walked to his desk and ran her hand along the edge. "Is this an antique?"

Andrew looked at his work space and saw what she saw. Ornate carvings in finely polished mahogany. The kind of details not often seen with new furniture. "No. The antique is in my father's office down the hall. He had this replica commissioned for me when I agreed to join his practice." Andrew pointed out the places where practicality met the past, and cords from the computer and phone disappeared into the wood so they could be plugged in below.

"It's lovely."

"Traditional over modern."

Jax nodded, looked around. "Without the fussiness and clutter of London's past."

"That's about right."

"It suits you."

A knock on the door had them both turning around.

"I thought I heard an unfamiliar voice."

Andrew smiled and stepped to the side. "Dad, this is Jacqueline Simon. Jax, this is my father, Lloyd Craig."

"Simon? Harry's sister?"

"That's right."

His dad walked closer, extending a welcoming hand. "I see the family resemblance."

"A pleasure, Mr. Craig."

He shook his head. "We don't do formal around here. Lloyd is fine."

"Jax and I just finished lunch and I wanted to show her the office."

His father looked between the two of them. "Oh. I'll leave you to it. Be sure and tell your brother I said hello."

"I'll do that."

Once his father left the office, Jax turned to Andrew. "There was something you wanted to give me?"

"Yes. There is." He moved behind his desk, grabbed a pen and a piece of paper, and wrote down his home address.

Back in front of her, he pressed the paper into her palm.

She narrowed her eyes. "I did a background check. I already have this."

He nodded. "I thought you might."

Jax waved the paper in the air. "Then why?"

"That was an excuse. I wanted to invite you into my office. Let you know you're welcome to drop by any time you're in the city."

She narrowed her gaze. "I said yes to a date. And not even a date, but the possibility of a date. This is a bit—"

Andrew lifted both hands in the air. "Truth is, I don't want anything about me to be remotely compared to your parents. I'll pick you up at the airport. Ask how long you're staying and see if I can squeeze more time out of you . . . and show you where I work."

He noticed the pieces fall into place, and the worried lines in Jax's face softened. "And if dating doesn't work out?"

"We're adults. No reason we can't remain friends."

She paused, stood back. "You're different."

"Not the highest praise, but I'll take it."

Jax tucked the piece of paper in her purse and headed for the door.

"I can walk you out."

On the ground floor he turned to her once again, reached for her hand.

"You're getting rather comfortable doing that," she pointed out.

He kissed the back of her fingers. "You're squirming a little less every time I do it."

That had her pulling away.

He smiled. "I'll call you."

"I'll answer."

What more could he ask for?

Jax turned and walked away. Only after she glanced over her shoulder to see if he was still looking did Andrew head back inside.

CHAPTER ELEVEN

Two days later Jax sat in her mother's garden soaking up the rays of sunshine the day blessed her with. "When are you getting here?" she asked Claire over the phone. The original plan was for her to be there that evening. A text message had said they were delayed, and this was the first opportunity Jax had to talk to Claire since.

"I know, I know . . . Gwen had to have an emergency teacher's meeting at Emma's school, then Neil got involved. We're flying out day after tomorrow."

"Nothing serious, I hope." Considering Jax had been undercover at Emma's private school the year before because of a human trafficking ring in the area, her concern wasn't unfounded.

"She didn't elaborate. I'm sure if it was, Neil would have just yanked Emma out and brought in a tutor to homeschool her." Something the man had threatened more than once. His trust in people at large was slim at best.

"I can pick you up at the airport."

Claire informed her of their already booked arrangements with a promise to call to make solid plans once they were on British soil. "I heard you have your brother's and mom's homes online."

"Mother was easy. Harry barked at it."

"Men like their privacy over safety."

"I reminded him he wouldn't have any privacy until Dad was out, and the invasion of his privacy was needed to move Dad along." It took an extra day in Jax's timeline to make the security system at Harry's a reality.

"Have you learned anything yet?"

"From spying on my parents?"

Claire laughed. "Yeah."

"I've learned that my mother doesn't deviate from her schedule to even grab a cup of coffee, and my father has no friends outside of work."

"Does your dad know all the details of the alarm?"

"No. He thinks it's a typical system with one camera at the front door."

"And Harry?"

"He knows."

"Hmmm. I bet we have to mix the pot to get anything stirred up."

Jax nodded and watched two birds playing in a small puddle from the recent rains. "Exactly what I was thinking. We need to find a way to get my parents in the same place."

"Have they even talked to each other since you've been there?"

"Not that I can tell." Jax wasn't monitoring everything her parents were doing, just enough to find any pattern or unusual location or person that needed further investigation.

"We'll figure it out."

"With Harry and Andrew on Dad's end, and you, Gwen, and I on my mother's, we'll get to the bottom of this sooner or later."

"Andrew, huh? I keep hearing that name."

"He promised to help."

"Uh-huh."

"He also wants to date me."

"Really. Color me surprised."

Jax laughed. "Seems silly to even bother since I don't live here."

"You said yes anyway . . . didn't you?"

She sighed. "He is rather sexy . . . in a number-pushing kind of way. And thoughtful."

"When you say *number pushing*, are you suggesting he's twenty pounds underweight, with pale skin, button-up shirt, and a pocket protector?"

"My God. I have a higher bar than that. Andrew fills out a suit, not the other way around. Tall, warm skin."

"Warm skin?"

"Not pasty, as you describe. Warm . . . I don't know. You'll see."

"You know I will."

They both laughed.

"How do you feel about me asking Neil for a relocation for the next few months?" Not that Jax needed her best friend's permission, but she wanted her blessing anyway.

"I was waiting for that."

"Unless one of my parents opens up, this is going to take a while."

"Might happen."

Jax doubted it. "I think it would have by now. Besides, being here under these circumstances has opened my eyes to a few things. The main one being I don't know my family. And I don't like that. Not anymore."

"And then of course there's Andrew," Claire teased.

"It's comforting to have a male distraction."

Claire busted out laughing. "You've been in London too long . . . *male distraction*. Please. You're talking like your mother."

"Take that back." Jax was smiling.

"Has he kissed you?"

"He's held my hand."

"That's sweet."

"It is."

Claire took a deep breath. "Much as I'll miss you, I completely understand why you'd want to hang out there for a while."

"Thanks, Loki."

"Anytime, Yoda."

Jax hung up the phone and looked around the garden. Lush and effortlessly green with tiny flower buds popping up everywhere as the sun shined down.

According to the tracker Jax had on her mother, Evelyn was at a women's club she'd been a part of for years. A place for middle-aged housewives to get together and plan charity events. Jax had volunteered to join her mother but was denied. The excuse had been that it was a planned luncheon that Jax wasn't expected at.

Propriety was always taken into account with her mother.

Now, with both Angela and Letty off for the day and night, and Evelyn out of the house, Jax decided to explore. She'd scratched the surface of most of the rooms when they were setting up the security system. Digging deep when her mother, or the staff, was home wasn't possible.

Much as she would like to enjoy the rare sunny day, Jax headed inside.

She started in her father's study. Using a small video camera mounted to a headset, she pressed record and started opening drawers. The point wasn't to look at the details while she was searching, but to put all the information into a system that she could pick apart later without threat of being caught. Besides, she didn't know what she was looking for.

Infidelity.

Claire's assumption kept creeping into Jax's head.

With the camera facing the files as she pulled them out, Jax leafed through them one at a time without reading.

She went from one to another as quickly as possible.

After searching for hidden drawers in the desk and coming up empty, Jax moved to the wall of books and scanned the shelves. Some of the titles were classic literature, a scattering of popular fiction, but mainly books on finance and tax law. At least those were the titles that stuck out. Jax removed a couple of books at random and thumbed through them.

Boring stuff.

A credenza housed the usual suspects of extra paper for the printer, office supplies . . .

Jax eyed the printer paper and then turned back toward the desk.

There wasn't a computer or a printer in the space.

How had she missed that?

She remembered her father working from home all the time.

When he left, did he take the computer with him? And wouldn't her mother have need of it to pay the online bills? Or did her mother do things that way? Did her mom pay any of the bills herself?

Once her dad's space was completely exhausted without one secret revealed, she checked on her mother's location, which hadn't moved, and then relocated to her parents' bedroom.

She started with the bedside tables, told herself to be prepared to see just about anything, and was somewhat disappointed that she didn't find anything remotely sexual. Not that she wanted to envision her parents having sex, but she wanted to think that maybe they enjoyed it at some point. But nothing . . . no lubricants, condoms . . . toys. She thought of her bedside table back in California. "I'd give you a heart attack, Mum," she said to the empty room.

Jax found a few vibrant ink pens in the drawer and searched for paper. She seemed to remember her mother journaling long ago. With her eye looking for a diary of sorts, she moved around the room, opened a few drawers, and found her father's space, which was more than half-empty. The closet had a significant lack of clothes.

Yeah, there was no way Letty or Angela would have missed this.

Jax patted down the suits left behind. She fished a few business cards out of the clothing and put them in her pocket to look at later.

Did her parents have a safe?

She didn't remember one, but wouldn't they?

Jax looked around the walk-in closet for a place that might hide her mother's jewelry. A safe drawer, at the very least. She found a couple of small boxes, but nothing of any merit. Jax knew for a fact her mother had a decent amount of jewelry. An early memory of her wearing ruby earrings and a matching necklace at Christmas came to mind.

A renewed search for a safe of some sort had Jax opening drawers and running her hands along them in search of a hidden compartment. When she exhausted the closet, she moved to the bathroom, where everything was in its place.

Instead of looking behind every picture in the entire house, Jax decided the direct approach would be better. Her mother would have no reason to keep a safe in the family home hidden from her.

With the camera still rolling, she moved through the house in search of anything personal. She found several photo albums, which she took to her room to look through later.

The closet in the farthest guest room housed the door to the stairway leading to the attic.

She opened the door and released stale air from the space. The scent reminded Jax of secondhand stores and old costume shops.

The semifinished stairway led to an expansive area and a series of individual hanging lights with pull strings. There were two windows on each end of the attic, giving natural light to the room. As expected, there was dust and cobwebs, but it wasn't as if no one ever walked up there. Clear plastic storage boxes were stacked four high containing what looked like Christmas decorations.

Jax was moving past the holiday decorations when her phone rang. She looked at the name on the screen and smiled. "Hello, Andrew."

"Good morning."

"Is it still morning?" She glanced at her watch. Barely.

"Where are you? Your voice sounds like it's echoing."

She brushed a cobweb aside and walked over to old furniture covered in tarps. "I'm in the attic."

"What? Why?"

The dust on the tarp suggested it had been there for years. "Aren't all family secrets hidden in the attic?"

He laughed. "Most beautiful day so far this year and you're in a dusty attic."

She found the dollhouse that once lived in her room and unearthed it. She remembered it being huge, but maybe it was her smaller eyes that saw it that way.

"My mom is out, and the housekeeper and cook have the day off. Best time for me to snoop without anyone asking questions."

"Have you found anything?"

She ran her hand along the roof of the dollhouse. "Memories."

"Good ones?"

"Yeah."

"How long are you going to be?"

"In the attic?"

"Yeah."

She looked around. "It's a big space."

"Oh." He sounded disappointed.

Jax covered up the house and turned her attention to the man on the phone. "You could threaten me with a good time, and I might consider a change in plans."

"Now we're talking. I'm thirty minutes away from your parents' house. I was thinking a walk . . . maybe an old-fashioned picnic."

The image made her smile. "Do you have a picnic basket?"

"More like takeout in a bag. Almost the same thing."

"Tell you what. You get the takeout. I'll find a basket and a bottle of wine."

"You know that area better than me. Do you have a spot in mind?"

A spot and a way to get there. "I do."

"I'll stop for food and see you in less than an hour."

"I'm looking forward to it."

"Me too."

One more glance around the massive attic and Jax retreated. Trips to the space in search of her old childhood memories wouldn't likely raise red flags when everyone was home.

For now, the sun was shining, and spending the day in a dusty attic when someone wanted to treat her to a picnic didn't sound like the logical thing to do. Besides, when Claire arrived, so would her reinforcements. The search would take half the time.

Jax removed the camera headset and turned off the recording before heading downstairs.

CHAPTER TWELVE

"Bikes?"

Andrew had met her at the front door, walked right past the bicycles Jax unearthed from the garage.

"You know how to ride a bike?"

"Yeah, but it's been forever."

"It's like sex. You don't forget," Jax teased.

Andrew lifted his eyebrows. "Sex I remember."

"Let's start with a bike ride, England."

Ten minutes later, with their late lunch secured in a basket on the front of Jax's bike, they headed down the road. Considering Andrew had wanted to snag a casual date with Jax and shower her with his charm, instead, he was concentrating so hard to keep from falling he could barely stream two words together.

"How are you doing back there?" she called from in front of him.

"I'm still vertical. And I haven't crashed yet." *God, please don't let me crash.*

"You'll be a pro before we're back."

Only once they got off the main roads and found one where few cars traveled did Andrew feel comfortable enough to push up beside Jax. "You've obviously done this before."

Jax had her hair pulled back in a ponytail that sat high on her head. She wore a light shirt with a sweater over it and jeans rolled up with flat sneakers. She had the lightest amount of makeup on. She didn't need it. And the fact she didn't bother told Andrew that the woman was secure in her own skin. Another reason he liked her.

"This is my saving grace every time I visit."

"How so?"

Watching her ride without any effort at all helped Andrew relax his death grip on the handlebars. They weren't on performance bikes . . . these were meant for exactly what they were doing. Taking a ride in the country on their way to a picnic.

"When I was young, my first years at Richter, I'd come home for a holiday and couldn't escape. It wasn't like I had friends close by I could run off to visit."

"I'm sure you had friends."

"I did. Only none lived here. Don't get me wrong, before they shipped me off, I had plenty of friends. But after one year away and our schedules not working out when I did come home, suddenly I didn't fit in."

"Kids can be cruel."

"I dug my own hole. My first summer, I tried to blend in again and found myself speaking to them in three different languages. They thought I was showing off."

"Three?"

"German, as expected. But I didn't actually study German. Not in a classroom. Not really."

"I don't understand."

"Immersion. Halfway through my first year at Richter I was forced to take a language. German wasn't offered. I took Russian that was taught in German."

"Are you kidding?"

Jax glanced over her shoulder toward him. "Whenever I'm talking about Richter . . . I'm not kidding."

He was starting to sense that. "How is it possible to learn a language from a language you don't speak?"

"Easier than you think. And a lot of help from my friends. The lower-grade housing staff spoke to all of us first in German, then in English. By the time I was out of primary education and into the upper levels, I was one of the volunteers that mentored the new students coming in. When I came across words I didn't know in German while learning Russian, I asked."

"Sounds stressful."

"Kids rise to the expectations they're given. Anyway . . . when I came home that first year, none of my friends had a clue what was expected of me, and they thought I was showing off. At that point I had a hard time finding refuge when I wanted to get away from adults." She pointed to the road ahead of them. "So, I pulled an old bike out of the shed and took off."

"By yourself."

"By myself."

"Sounds lonely."

"It wasn't," Jax told him. "Crazy as it sounds, I enjoyed the solitude more than being around people who didn't understand me."

Andrew lifted one hand to his chest. "I can be an understanding guy."

Jax looked at him and started to laugh.

"What?" Offering the most pathetic, innocent look he could muster, Andrew was certain he'd ensure admiration for his effort . . .

Right as his front wheel hit a pothole. Next thing he knew, he was on his side in the middle of the road.

I fell.

Holy shit, I fell.

He started to laugh.

"Are you okay?" Jax was over him. Knees on the ground, hands on his face.

He laughed harder. Talk about ways of securing a future date. Falling off a bike you learned to ride when you were four.

"You must be okay."

He splayed out completely on the ground, and continued to laugh.

Jax sat back on her heels, the worry lines slimmed to a smile.

"You know, England, when a woman rushes to your side to see if you're okay, you can fake injury to gain her sympathy."

And because she called him England, and for no other reason, Andrew couldn't stop laughing even harder.

Until she was laughing right with him.

He'd been so worried about falling he'd forgotten to enjoy the ride.

Now that his dignity was on the side of the road, it didn't matter.

Andrew pushed up on his elbows and did a quick scan of his body. He was pretty sure his left knee was a bit banged up from the initial impact, but other than a scrape and a big bruise to his ego, he felt fine. *"A kiss to your knee and off you go."* His mother's words were clear as day.

"You're okay?" Jax was smiling at him.

He took the moment, even if it wasn't the right one. "I don't like to fake an injury to get what I want."

"You don't?"

He shook his head, sat up, and touched her face.

Jax licked her lips, and that was all the invitation he needed.

She met him halfway, and their lips touched for the first time in the middle of a back road after he'd fallen off a bike. And like the first time he'd kissed a girl, this was something Andrew knew he'd never forget.

Her lips were full, lush, and passionate. Nothing timid about her.

He felt her palm on the back of his head and he moved closer, opened his lips, and invited more.

A car horn blasted the moment.

"Get a bloody room," someone yelled as the car sped by, kicking dirt up around them.

They both scrambled back, looked at each other, and started laughing again.

Jax found her senses first and stood with her hand extended.

Grasping it, he felt her tug, and he tested out his legs.

"You good there?" she asked.

"I will ride another day."

~

A race to the finish, Andrew beat her by a hair as they reached the front door, both of them desperate for a bathroom.

"The advantage lies with the woman who knows where the bathrooms are," Jax said as they breached the door. She started toward the closest one.

"I can always find a rosebush, lady," he called back.

"My mother would kill you."

Jax heard Andrew suck in a breath.

She stopped midstride and turned.

"Yes, she would."

Evelyn stood in the entry to the family room, hands clasped in front of her.

"Of course I wouldn't . . . ," Andrew said.

"I should hope not."

Jax laughed, uttered the word *busted* before disappearing into the lavatory.

Moments later she found Andrew in the hall, smile forced, and pointed him toward the bathroom.

"We didn't know you were home." Jax led her mother out of the foyer and into the family room.

"Obviously." Her mother's tone was stern.

"Needing a bathroom isn't up there with being caught naked."

Evelyn turned. "Is that something I have to concern myself with?"

Jax laughed, shook her head . . . but didn't answer. "How was your luncheon?"

"The luncheon can wait. Is there something you'd like to tell me about Andrew?"

Jax shrugged her shoulders. "You tell me about your love life, I'll tell you about mine."

Evelyn narrowed her eyes, a slight lift to the edges of her lips. "You tricky little—"

"Ladies," Andrew said as he walked into the room. "Thank you both for forgiving my quick disappearance."

Evelyn looked him up and down. "Better than my roses?"

Andrew walked over, kissed Evelyn's cheeks. "Lovely to see you again, Mrs. Simon."

"I'm certain she's happy she didn't see more of you violating her flowers," Jax said.

When her mother laughed, the air in the room eased.

"It's a surprise to see you."

"Your daughter's enchanting, which I'm sure you must already know."

The word *enchanting* caught Jax off her center.

"She is that."

And now Jax was completely off her axis.

"Did you enjoy your ladies' luncheon?" Andrew asked.

"Sweet of you to ask . . ."

For several minutes they talked about her mother's lunch, her cause . . . Andrew mentioned a bottle of wine and their lunch.

While Jax stood and watched, her mother and Andrew carried on polite conversation in ways Jax had to force.

If she was truthful with herself, she'd admit jealousy.

She wasn't ready for that.

". . . anyway, I hope you don't mind our interruption to your day."

"Don't be ridiculous." Evelyn turned to Jax. "Why don't you offer our guest a beverage and I'll see what Letty has prepared for dinner."

Now *that* was out of character.

Andrew must have seen Jax's distress.

"That isn't necessary, Mrs. Simon."

Her mother turned before leaving the room. "You and my son are good friends, are you not?"

"Yes, ma'am."

"Surely you know this home is lacking male companionship."

Those words had Jax snapping her eyes to her mother.

Andrew paused before saying on a sigh . . . "Yes, ma'am."

"Then you'll stay for dinner. Perhaps replace a light bulb or two?"

There wasn't a light bulb even flickering.

"I'd be happy to," Andrew said.

With that, Evelyn left them alone and moved into the kitchen.

"What the actual hell was that?" Jax asked under her breath.

"Your mother likes me."

Jax moved up into his space, their bodies closer than when they'd actually kissed in the middle of the road. "There isn't a light bulb out in this house."

"That isn't why she asked me to stay."

Jax knew that . . . but still couldn't process it. "My mother doesn't do spontaneous."

"Maybe that's changing."

"Are you two going to whisper in the hall all day?" Evelyn called out from the kitchen.

Andrew laughed. "Lead the way."

Her mother had removed a bottle of white from the wine fridge and was currently arranging cheese, crackers, and olives on a platter.

"Andrew, be a dear and open that, won't you?"

If Jax didn't know better, she'd swear aliens had abducted her mother, and the woman standing in front of her was an imposter. Instead of calling her out, Jax removed three wineglasses and put them in front of Andrew to fill.

"Where did you two go on your bike ride?"

"Where didn't we go?" Andrew looked over his shoulder toward Jax as he spoke.

"Once Andy here decided to stay on the bike instead of falling off, he determined speed was the answer."

"You fell?" Evelyn asked.

"My ego was bruised, nothing more." He popped the cork free and filled the glasses, handing one to each of them. "To afternoon bike rides that end with wine and friends."

A dance with glasses clinking together and a chorus of cheers and Jax found her smile.

"Did you know that Jax is super competitive?"

Evelyn caught Jax's eyes. "That is not news to me. Her need to do more, do it better and faster, was a constant challenge when she was a child. And smart. Jacqueline is fluent in four languages."

"Five," Jax corrected her mother. "Claire and I took Spanish in college for shits and giggles."

Evelyn moved closer to Andrew, lowered her voice. "See what I mean?"

"Do you have occasion to use all those languages?" he asked.

Jax reached across the island and took a piece of cheese off the plate. "Sure. When Claire and I want to talk about boys or when we're taking down mob bosses who sell children." She popped the cheese in her mouth and looked up when the two of them became silent.

"Really?" Andrew asked.

She smiled. "Claire and I have been talking about boys for years."

"Not that. I can see that. But mob bosses?" His brow furrowed with the question, concern written on his face.

"Russian mob bosses." Jax chased the cheese with a sip of wine.

"You've never told me that," Evelyn said.

"You've never asked." Jax lifted the platter her mother had finished preparing. "Which room in this mansion do you want to take this to, Mother?"

"The sitting room. And this isn't a mansion."

And to prove a point, Jax headed toward the morning room only to hear Evelyn redirect her. "In the front of the house."

"Right," she said, smiling. "I wasn't sure which 'sitting room' you were referring to."

Andrew took the platter from her.

"And she's a smart-ass, I'm sorry to say," Evelyn chided.

"Such language, Mother." Jax actually thought her mother's comment was endearing.

Evelyn walked in front of them. "I suppose you have to take some bad with the good."

"Being witty is a virtue," Andrew countered.

"Then you're in for quite a time with this one."

~

"Your mother is delightful."

Evelyn had practically pushed Jax out the door to walk Andrew to his car. Her insistence was comical.

"Pretty sure that's a droid and my mother is locked in a closet somewhere."

Andrew laughed, and Jax followed him down the front steps to his car.

The decorative lighting scattered throughout the front of the house and the porch light helped keep them from stumbling in the dark.

"She does seem a bit different from the woman I've known all these years."

"Maybe facing being single and starting over has her loosening up." As the words left Jax's mouth, she realized it was the first time she'd actually considered how her mother must be coping with the split.

That is, if it was an actual split and not a fight that ended in apologies and expensive jewelry and flowers.

Andrew placed a hand on her shoulder. "You okay? You look like you just checked out there."

"What if they are getting a divorce? All this time I've been searching for the *why* and haven't even considered the outcome."

He stepped closer. "Maybe when you determine the *why* you'll have a better grip on the end result."

"Are your parents happily married?"

"Better than most. They laugh together. I catch them holding hands. Don't get me wrong, they annoy each other, too, but they fight fair."

"What does that fair fight look like?" Jax asked.

"It's not mean. So many people get hateful when they're angry."

Jax leaned against his car. "That's the problem. I don't think I've ever seen my parents fight . . . mean or otherwise."

"That makes this separation even harder."

"The arguments could have happened behind closed doors."

"True."

Jax blew out a breath. "I should let you go. You have a long drive."

Andrew didn't move toward the door to his car. Instead, he stepped closer to her. "You're worth the drive." His hand reached for her waist.

"What are you doing there, England?" she asked as she tilted her chin up in invitation.

"I was hoping to try that kiss again since we're not in the middle of an intersection."

"A back road, not an intersection." She licked her lips.

He stared at hers.

"See, competitive . . . not mean."

She leaned in closer, placed her hand on his arm. "Andrew?"

"Yeah?"

"Stop talking."

He was smiling when he brought his lips to hers.

Andrew took his time, lingered awhile before opening his lips to explore more. Jax normally liked to move a bit faster, but found his pace intoxicating. When he tilted her head and swept his tongue to meet hers, she melted into his frame.

There was a lot of his hard body touching her softer parts, and as his kiss went on, she had no problem envisioning the two of them with fewer clothes and more privacy.

He continued kissing her as if it was an art form. Unhurried, thorough, with attention to detail. A soft touch to her face, her neck, the closest he came to any more intimacy was a swipe of his thumb to the side of her breast.

That just about did her in.

She pulled him tighter, dug her nails into his back.

This was a night of first kisses, not hot, meaningless sex . . . although Jax knew she could be talked into that, if she were being honest.

Andrew started to pull away.

Jax took her time opening her eyes. "Wow, England . . . you're pretty good at that."

"You'll have to let me do it again sometime."

"I'm sure we can negotiate."

He frowned as he pulled away but kept hold of both her hands. "I had a fabulous time today. I'm certain my ass is going to scream at me tomorrow since I haven't been on a bike in years. But it was worth it."

"Remember that when you wake up and your leg is bruised from falling off."

He pulled her away from the car far enough to open the door. The light from inside invaded her senses.

"Call you tomorrow?"

"If you don't, then I'll know you're lying about having a good time."

Andrew leaned over, gave her another brief kiss. "I'm a terrible liar."

He slid behind the wheel and turned over the engine.

"Drive carefully."

"I will."

Jax stepped out of the way as he closed the door and put the car in gear. She waited until he reached the end of the driveway to turn and walk back into the house.

CHAPTER THIRTEEN

Jax was on her computer fast-forwarding through footage of her brother's flat.

It was up there with watching paint dry.

Actually, when watching paint dry there was always the possibility of a flying insect landing on said wet paint and the guess on whether the bug would be able to successfully remove itself from the sticky surface.

But yeah . . . boring.

Her father's routine did not alter even by a hair. The man didn't cook, nor did he clean. If Harry didn't prepare them a meal, or if her brother was out for the evening, Dad walked to one of three restaurants, all of which she traced from his phone, and returned straightaway. He poured himself a drink and retired to his room.

There was the occasional comment from Harry about not having a housekeeper and that his father could either hire one or help out.

Jax wasn't at all surprised to see a woman show up, maid uniform and all, with an armload of cleaning supplies. While Jax and Andrew had been pedaling around town, Gregory was dodging the cleaning woman as she buzzed around the flat.

When Jax's phone rang, she was happy for the distraction. The LA office phone number showed up. Assuming it was Claire with another delay, Jax answered complaining.

"Please don't tell me you're not coming."

"I'm not coming," Neil told her, deadpan.

"Sorry. I thought you were Claire."

"They are on their way to the airport now. How are things there?"

"Frustrating. Slow." She closed her laptop.

"It's always hard to see things you're close to," he advised.

She was happy to hear his words. "This is going to take a little longer than I anticipated." She took a deep breath, ready to ask for more time, or maybe an assignment in the local area to stay employed.

"I thought as much. As it turns out, I could use you on that side of the ocean for a while. If you're okay with it."

That was easy. "Yes! I mean . . . wait, did Claire put you up to this?"

"I don't share everything with Claire."

That didn't mean Claire didn't share things with him. Not that it mattered, the answer was still yes. "Did you have something specific in mind?"

"I received a call from Charlie."

That, she wasn't expecting. "Checkpoint Charlie?" Charlie worked at Richter. For the years she and Claire were in attendance, the man was the unofficial butler. The doorman and often the one they needed to sweet-talk to look the other way when they were caught doing something they weren't supposed to. He was the Deep Throat of Richter now, letting Neil know when there was something to be concerned about at the school. Neil wasn't completely convinced that Richter had changed its ways enough to no longer endanger the graduates of the school, so he took it upon himself to keep in contact with Charlie for continual updates.

"Yes."

"What did he say?"

"Sasha deciphered his message to mean that someone was offering financial compensation for four languages or more."

That alone wasn't a smoking gun. The school was known for multilingual students. "Sasha was concerned?"

"Sasha said the offer sounded too familiar to go without investigation. The enrollment of orphans is on the rise."

Damn, that did not sound good. "She thinks there's another benefactor." Claire had been an orphan with a benefactor. She'd been offered a five-thousand-euro bonus for every language she graduated with. The goal for the benefactor was to recruit her as his hired hand, often an illegal one. Many Richter orphans went on to work for government agencies all over the world. And some ended up as assassins with no way out unless they were dead. But that had all been blown up by Neil and his team the year before Jax graduated. The school lost half the students and staff that year. The headmistress went to jail for child endangerment, and the main benefactor, Pohl, suffered a mysterious death while awaiting trial . . .

Now Neil watched.

Took it personally since this future had been slated for Claire.

"I'm your girl. What did you have in mind?"

"We have some groundwork to do before we send you over there. Take time with Claire and Gwen. Maybe once Claire finds a wedding dress, she'll talk less about it."

Jax laughed. "I wouldn't bet on that."

Neil huffed out a breath. "Sasha is pulling in intel. We'll send it over and devise a plan. You're not going in blind."

"Sounds good to me."

"In the meantime, I'll let the London team know you're available if they need you."

"Thank you, Neil."

"It's not a favor. It's work."

Yeah, yeah . . .

Once the call was disconnected and watching the lack of excitement in her brother and father's life had her yawning, Jax decided to call the one person who would be happy with her news about staying in Europe.

Andrew answered on the second ring.

"This is a surprise."

"Am I interrupting?" It was a weekday and he was still at work.

"Never."

She laughed. "I could make you eat those words."

"I've seen *Fatal Attraction*. I don't think you're the type."

Her mind raced to find the film reference. "Isn't that an old movie?"

"It is. My mother made my father watch it when I was a teenager. It's about a man who has a one-night stand and the mistress is crazy, tries to kill the wife—"

"Ewhh. Wholesome family movies at the Craig home."

He laughed. "My mother told my father he wouldn't have to worry about the lover killing him, he'd already be buried in the backyard."

Now that sounded like something Jax would say. "Go, Mom!"

"I'm not worried."

"About your mom offing your dad?"

"No. About you making me eat my words."

Jax stood from her desk and stretched out her back. "I have better things to do in life than bother someone who isn't interested."

"That isn't me. What's up?" Andrew redirected the conversation.

She took a moment to answer . . . tried to find the words. "About that return ticket to the States—"

"No. No, no . . ." Andrew started freaking out.

Jax let him.

"What can I do to change your mind?"

She was silent.

"Jax?"

"Are you done?"

"Not by a long shot."

That made her smile. "My boss needs me here for a while."

"What?" Andrew's one-word question came out in a rush of air.

"In Europe. I'm available to the team in London, but there is work in Germany he is going to send me out on."

Andrew made a whooshing sound, half whistle, half sigh. "Okay. Good. Damn."

"Are you okay?"

"I am now. Germany isn't exactly down the street."

"Not across the pond either."

"True."

"I'd like to keep the Germany part out of any conversations that can get back to my parents." The words felt right as they were leaving her lips.

"Why? Wait, does this have something to do with your old school?"

"It does. But the *private* part of investigations suggests the least amount of people that know, the better." She stood by the window and watched misty rain fall from the sky.

"Aww, you like me."

She blinked a few times. "Excuse me?"

"You like me. You've told me something you want to keep from your family. You like me."

"Oh my God. You sound like you're twelve."

"I had more game when I was twelve."

She heard the smile in his voice.

If his adolescent game led to his current game, she wanted to thank that girl. "Did you learn to kiss when you were twelve?"

"Ten," he countered. "Her name was Susan."

"Really? Ten?"

"Yup. She kissed me on a dare. But from then on I considered myself quite the Casanova."

"Didn't he die of syphilis?" she asked.

"Nasty thought. I did contract mono when I was a teenager. I swear I had the same girlfriend at the time."

Jax couldn't stop smiling. "That didn't mean you were her only boyfriend."

"I figured that out." He paused. "What about you?"

"I'm not following."

"Where did you learn to kiss?"

"In the stacks at Richter, of course."

"Ahh yes . . . libraries are a solid choice for privacy."

He really was a joy to talk to. That, in and of itself, was new. "I've taken up enough of your workday."

"You've made my day."

That didn't suck to hear. "About Germany. I need that to be between you and I."

"I'm a bad liar, but I'm good at keeping secrets. Don't worry."

"I'll talk to you later."

"And not on an international call to the States."

She said her goodbyes and smiled at the phone long after he hung up.

It was the first time in her life she was excited to extend her stay in Europe. And there was someone willing to fight her over leaving.

She took a look around her childhood room, the window outside and the dreary weather beyond the pane of glass, and willed her shoulders to relax.

The need to talk openly made Jax long for the moment Claire landed in Europe.

~

Jax and her mother sat in the morning room, breakfast in front of them.

"I've always liked Andrew. I was surprised to see you two getting along so well."

"Why is that?" Jax asked.

Her mother stared over her cup of tea. "If for no other reason than your father and I would approve of the man. That alone usually makes you run in the other direction."

"That is very true."

They both smiled.

"Good man, solid job. Respectable family . . ."

"Good teeth."

Evelyn rolled her eyes. "Must you?"

Jax nodded. "I must."

That made her mother chuckle. "He seems to enjoy your humor."

"You mean my sarcasm."

"That, too."

The two of them had found a sort of canter. A serve and a volley . . . nice and easy. The stiff upper lip the British were known for had wavered.

"Are you sure you won't reconsider coming with us today?" Jax had asked her mother to join Gwen, Claire, and her on their bridal shopping expedition. So far, she'd been reluctant.

"It isn't your day to invite me. Besides, your friend doesn't care for me much. I'd just as soon avoid any awkward moments."

"That's nonsense." It was the absolute truth, but Jax wasn't about to tell her mother she was right.

The doorbell rang, signaling Claire and Gwen's arrival, and Jax got to her feet. "For what it's worth, I'd really like you to come."

Without waiting for her mother to answer, Jax headed toward the door.

Angela beat her to it.

Claire saw Jax and they both opened their arms. "I missed you."

Her friend's hug was warm and full and everything it should be. "You have no idea," Jax said.

Claire pulled back, paused.

For a moment neither of them spoke. Then their eyes caught, Claire's lips spread into a huge grin, and she shifted from one foot to the other in a little dance. "We're shopping for wedding dresses!"

Her enthusiasm was contagious.

Jax moved past her best friend to hug Gwen. "Is she driving you crazy?"

"Yes. I'm looking forward to you taking over," she said without an ounce of malice.

Behind them, Jax heard her mother clearing her throat.

Claire looked up and ran to her with arms open. Evelyn had no choice but to accept Claire's hug. "I'm getting married." The awkward hug was brief, and Claire's hand was thrust in the air, showing off her engagement ring.

"I heard. Congratulations."

Letty walked around the corner and Claire was off again, hugging and laughing.

"Did she have a lot of coffee this morning?" Jax asked Gwen.

"I cut her off at three cups."

"Good call."

Jax glanced at her mother, who waited politely for an introduction. "I find it hard to believe that the two of you have never met. Gwen, this is my mother, Evelyn."

"It's an absolute pleasure. Your daughter has been such a joy in our lives," Gwen said as she reached out and shook Evelyn's hand.

"I've heard a lot about you. And your husband."

They exchanged polite smiles. "Your home is stunning. I do miss the gardens of England when I'm away for too many months at a time."

"I seem to remember Jacqueline mentioning that you had a home here."

"It's a family home. More my brother's than mine, if I'm honest, though neither of us live here full time. The weather in California really is hard to pass up."

"As my daughter tells me often."

Claire bounced on her toes. "Are we ready to go?"

Evelyn took a step back. "You enjoy your day."

On cue, Claire mustered more excitement than she would have otherwise. "What? No. You're coming, right?" Jax knew it was half show since there had been no real affection between her mother and Claire through the years. But Jax had asked her to rally in the hopes that Gwen could work on opening up her mother.

"Please, Evelyn. Don't leave me alone with these girls. I haven't seen them this excited since the day Jax got off the plane for the first time in Los Angeles."

"I don't want to impose."

"I honestly assumed you were coming and made all of our reservations today for four. There's plenty of room in the limousine."

"A limo?" Jax asked as she turned around to look out the window by the front door. Sure enough, the black limo was parked with a driver standing by the door waiting for them to return.

"You can't shop for wedding dresses without champagne."

Jax conjured up a stuffy voice. "How silly of me."

Gwen laughed. "Please, Evelyn, if not for Claire, let it be a favor to me. Besides, I'd like to get to know the woman who raised such a delightful daughter."

"See, Mum, I'm delightful," Jax teased.

Evelyn looked between the three of them and sighed. "Give me a moment to retrieve my purse."

CHAPTER FOURTEEN

The drive getting into the city was spent hovering over bridal magazines with mimosas in hand. Having the time immediately after Claire's engagement announcement robbed from them, they were making up for it now.

They looked at everything, from wedding dresses to bridesmaid styles, colors, and textures. Flowers and venues.

"The one thing we know for sure is we want it outside," Claire told Jax.

"Have you picked a venue?" Evelyn asked.

"That comes down to picking a house. A formal venue doesn't make sense. Besides, we'd be limited on dates that way."

"I'm pushing her to use our place in California," Gwen told Evelyn.

"Trina and Wade have offered the ranch where Cooper and I met."

"A Texas wedding would be fun," Jax said.

Evelyn frowned. "Texas?"

"Wade and Trina are friends of the family," Gwen said.

"Wade is Texas royalty. Trust me, Mum, you'd approve," Jax explained.

"I've never heard of Texas royalty."

Claire waved off the conversation. "Cooper and I are torn about a destination wedding."

"It doesn't need to be decided today."

The closer they came to their first stop, the more excited Claire became.

They filed out of the limousine, ignoring the looks given by those passing by.

Inside the bridal salon, the four of them were met by the owner, an older woman who approached Gwen with a slight nod of her head. "Lady MacBain. So incredibly lovely to finally meet you in person."

Jax took in the moment of confusion on her mother's face. She'd purposely never mentioned Gwen's title and often forgot it was even there. Teenage rebellion stopped Jax from giving her parents anything to approve of. As far as she was concerned, titles meant nothing.

"I appreciate your flexibility, Beatrice."

"We are more than happy to accommodate you. Which one of you is the happy bride?"

"She is." Jax nudged Claire forward.

Beatrice extended a hand and started walking them away from the entrance. "Let me show you to your private rooms."

Evelyn moved beside Jax, lowered her voice. "*Lady* MacBain?"

"Courtesy title. Her brother's a duke."

"You've never told me this."

Jax looped her arm with her mother's. "You've never asked."

"I need to start asking you more questions."

She squeezed her mother's arm. "I'd like that."

The private room was large, with sofas, champagne, and snacks . . . the kind brought in from a French bakery. Indulgent, just as the occasion called for.

"Beatrice, this is Jacqueline Simon, the maid of honor, and her mother, Evelyn."

The woman shook their hands, hesitated in front of Jax. "You look incredibly familiar. Have you been in here before?"

"No. This is our first time."

"I know I've seen you before." She shook her head. "It will come to me."

"Everyone has a double somewhere," Claire announced.

"Let's get started. Claire, if you'll come with me, we'll get you into the proper undergarment to make it easier to get in and out of the dresses and actually see what they will look like without extra straps."

And they were off . . .

~

How's it going?

The text message came from Andrew two hours into shopping. Jax smiled at his question . . . and his attention.

Just as much fun as I expected. Claire is beautiful.

Has she found the right dress yet?

Jax watched her best friend standing on the platform looking at herself in the three-way mirror.

No. But she's narrowed down a style.

"What do you think, Jax?"

She looked up and put her phone aside. "You're right. The back is too low. You want it to be sexy, but not show off too much."

Claire nodded, looked at the phone Jax had just put down. "Is that Andrew you're talking to?"

"He wanted to know if you found the dress."

"That's sweet of him to ask."

"Who is Andrew?" Gwen asked.

Claire turned her back to Beatrice, who started undoing the buttons.

"A friend."

Her mother laughed. "Looked like more than friendship to me."

"Oh, do tell," Claire teased.

"Are you dating someone here already?" Gwen asked.

Evelyn nodded ever so slightly, the smile on her lips hard to miss.

"He is a friend of Harry's who picked me up at the airport."

"When are we going to meet him?" Gwen asked.

"We just started dating."

"What does that matter?" Claire stepped out of one dress while an assistant brought another.

"You'd love him, Gwen. Respected man, established . . . great family," Evelyn bragged.

"Good teeth." Jax couldn't help herself.

Claire laughed, and before long all of them were finding it hard to stop laughing. Or maybe that was the champagne.

"How about an informal dinner party so we can meet him? The staff at the Harrison house are absolutely bored."

Claire jumped on it. "That's a great idea."

"What do you think, Evelyn? The two of us can come up with a small guest list so Andrew doesn't feel under the microscope, so to speak."

"Which is exactly what he'll be," Claire said as she turned to Jax. "Have any of the guys met him?"

"No."

"The guys?" her mother asked.

"Like Sven . . . the London team we work with. And no. No one has had the opportunity to grill the poor guy. Like I said, we just started dating."

"No bow-chicka-wow-wow?" Claire asked.

"Oh my God, Loki, my mother is standing right here."

Claire pointed at Gwen. "So is mine."

Gwen turned and placed a hand on her chest.

The four of them paused.

"Do you know how much I love hearing that?" Gwen asked, her voice soft.

"You can't love hearing it any more than I love saying it."

The two women hugged, tears gathering in their eyes.

Beatrice fanned out the train of the dress she'd put Claire into, and Jax gasped.

"Oh, my." Evelyn stood to the side.

Claire turned toward the mirror, and Gwen placed her fingertips over her lips.

Claire swiped at a tear that had fallen down her cheek and turned to the side. "Oh my God."

Jax waited for her best friend's reaction before giving her own.

"This is it."

Jax rushed forward. "It's perfect." The beauty was in its simplicity. Sleek silk made up the foundation, with a minimal amount of woven lace etching the small sleeves that dangled over her shoulders and down the back. Its cascading train and just enough beading made it perfect and not overdone.

It was spectacular and flattered Claire in every possible way.

"It's stunning. You're stunning," Evelyn added.

"Neil's going to cry."

Jax and Claire both turned to Gwen, silent.

They then looked at each other. "If for no other reason than to see Neil cry, this is the dress," Jax said.

Claire turned to the mirror, placed a hand over her heart.

"This is the dress."

~

For the first time in Jax's life, tea with her mother wasn't a chore.

It helped that the tea on the table wasn't being drunk, but the champagne was.

They'd moved from wedding dress shopping to designing the maid of honor dress based on the cut Claire had picked for the main event. And because moving from one dress shop to another wasn't needed, the rest of the day was now open, and they decided on a whim to plan a dinner party.

"I say we invite a couple guys from the team," Jax suggested. "Sven was flirting with my mom."

"Sven flirts with everyone. No offense, Mrs. Simon."

"The man is a child. I may be newly single, but I'm not going there."

Her announcement made everyone pause.

Evelyn looked away, placed her hands in her lap. "I'm sorry. This day isn't about me."

Jax reached out, grasped her mother's hand.

"Claire's my best friend, Mum. She knows why I flew all the way here."

"I figured as much. Again, I'm sorry. I don't want to take away from your day."

"You're not. Honestly, I'm honored you trust us enough to bring the subject up." Claire was the best. Jax reminded herself to tell her when they were alone later.

Evelyn looked at Gwen.

Gwen, bless her all the way to Sunday, said exactly the right thing. "This means we remove Mr. Simon from the guest list." And to drill the point home, she scratched something on the pad she was taking notes on.

"No."

They all turned to look at Evelyn.

"Gregory dug his hole. If he chooses not to come, that's his choice." She turned to Jax. "Your father is a good man. He's made some bad decisions, but he's not a horrible person."

Jax closed her eyes, let what she saw come in clearly. "He cheated on you." Just as Claire suspected.

When her mother didn't immediately and undeniably denounce Jax's claim, she knew it was true.

Jax squeezed her mother's hand, felt comfort in the return pressure.

"It's your call, Evelyn. If you want Gregory to attend, we'll invite him. Or snub him, as he justly deserves." Gwen was poise and grace. Exactly the sounding board Evelyn needed.

Her mother looked around the table . . . making eye contact with all of them. "If we invite him, you mustn't treat him poorly."

"Kindness will stab him much harder than a knife," Gwen said.

Claire nodded Gwen's way. "What she said."

Jax glanced at her mother. "I have a lot of questions."

Her mother looked at her, paused. "I'm not ready to answer."

"I'll respect that," she said . . . meaning it.

Claire placed her hand on the table, palm up.

Evelyn looked at it before placing her hand in Claire's.

She then did the same to Gwen . . . and so on.

"There's a special place in hell for women who don't support other women. Whether you decide to forgive Mr. Simon or tell him to hit the road, we support you, but that doesn't mean we hate him."

Gwen looked at Claire. "I couldn't be prouder of you than in this moment."

"Jax was the first to teach me this. Sasha showed me what supporting women, even strangers, looked like, and you took it further and brought me into your home," she said to Gwen. "I am so blessed to be surrounded by strong women."

Jax was equally proud of her friends as they said the words she wanted them to without a prompt. Words that would resonate with her mother more because they came from others.

And as much as Jax was reeling from the truth that had been unveiled, she wasn't ready for the day to end.

"I have an idea."

Hours later, after they'd finished tea and shopped for needless things and sobered up with massages Gwen had arranged, they were back at Jax's childhood home, the four of them curled up in the family room, pizza from a box and wine from the vault, watching movies.

Never . . . in the history of ever . . . had Jax sat half-drunk in a room with her mother and enjoyed a chick flick.

They laughed, cried.

And eventually Jax and Claire scurried off where they could have some time alone.

In Jax's childhood room, they curled up on the bed and talked.

"Evelyn and Gwen are alone."

Without a pause, Jax removed her cell phone from her pocket and dialed the main London headquarters.

James answered. "Hello, doll."

"I need you to kill the audio and visual from my house."

"You sure? Looks like it's about to get good 'round there."

"Kill it, James."

A pause.

A click.

"Done."

"Thank you." She disconnected the call.

Jax hung up and looked at Claire.

"You okay?" Claire asked.

"My dad's an asshole."

"You don't know that."

"He cheated on my mother. He's an asshole."

"Yes . . . there is that. But we look deeper than that. Face value, your dad's a dick. But there may be more to the story."

Jax shimmied closer to where Claire was sitting. "What could possibly justify cheating?"

"I don't know."

"Me either."

They were both silent . . . foggy from the wine and the day. Jax rounded the focus back to Claire, where it was supposed to be. "Your dress is beautiful."

"Cooper is going to melt."

"I think he already did that."

Claire reached for her hand. "You're really going to stay here for a while?"

"I have to. For the first time in my entire life, my mother needs me. And she doesn't suck that much."

That made Claire laugh. "She's a different person."

"I know. Crazy."

Claire let out a long breath. "Living life without a family is awful. You deserve to get to know yours more."

Jax leaned her head on Claire's shoulder. "I'm glad you're here."

"Me too."

∼

"I don't care how you get him there. Just get him there. Tie him up and throw him in the car if you have to."

Jax was currently on the phone explaining the situation, and the plan, to Harry.

"I can't believe he stepped out on our mother."

"Well, get used to the idea, because that's exactly what he did. Now the questions are when and why. Are we talking one-night stand or a relationship? Is it still going on? Was it more than once? Answers that will determine if Mum would be crazy to try and work it out and if you should feel guilty for letting the bastard live with you."

"Has Mum shared anything?"

"Just the fact that he had an affair of some sort. She wasn't ready to say more and honestly . . . it isn't her shame. Dad should be the one to fess up. So, we put him in the hot seat by making him come to this dinner party. And whatever you do, don't let on that you know anything."

"I can do that."

"Good."

"How do you suggest I actually get him there, short of brute force?"

"Tell him I have an announcement to make. Something he won't want to hear secondhand."

"Do you?"

"In a matter of sorts. And bring your girlfriend. Mother wants to meet her."

Harry hesitated. "I haven't warned her about Mother."

"Mum has too many things on her plate right now to make your girlfriend uncomfortable. Besides, she's changing." Which made Jax think that maybe the split between her parents was for the better.

"I hope you know what you're doing."

"I do. And keep your eyes and ears open at the office. Listen to what others say about our father. Is there someone at the office that he spends a lot of time with? A woman?"

"His secretary. I can't see that. And she's married."

"So is Dad."

"Good point. Still don't think that's it."

"Has Dad been on any business trips lately? Consistently?"

"Nothing comes to mind. But I'll write down our annual events for you."

"That's a start."

They were both silent for a few moments. "I'm disappointed in him," Harry said with a sigh.

"Welcome to the club." She'd been disappointed in both of them for years. Only now there seemed to be some redemption going on with her mother. Her dad, on the other hand, had taken a giant step back.

"Jax?"

"Yeah?"

"I'm really glad you're here."

She closed her eyes. "Thank you, Harry. I need to hear that once in a while."

"I'll try and say it more often."

CHAPTER FIFTEEN

It was nice to see her mother smiling and meaning it.

They drove over to the Harrison estate with extra clothes. Gwen's family home was far enough away to warrant an overnight stay.

Even with a last-minute invitation, the guest list was reaching close to thirty people. Harry solidified their father's attendance by inviting two senior members of their team and their wives. Gregory couldn't say no.

Jax and Claire sat back and watched the experts in the world of entertaining flex their finishing-school muscles.

The staff at the Harrison house buzzed like a swarm of bees.

"Do all these people live here?" Jax asked Claire.

Claire shrugged. "Most of them. Someone has to make sure the toilets flush."

Jax had visited the estate a few times, but never had she seen it put into motion the way it was now.

It had been nearly a week since Claire and Gwen arrived, and just over two weeks that Jax had been in Europe. In years past, she'd be counting the hours for her return to California. But that anticipation wasn't in her this time around.

While Evelyn and Gwen scrutinized the seating arrangements, Jax and Claire brought Sven and James up to speed. The Harrison house, much like any property Neil's family frequented, was fully equipped with a security system, cameras, and audio. The main office would have eyes and ears on the event, not that there was any concern they'd be needed, but having the home wired for sound would make it easier to eavesdrop on the private conversations going around.

"Operation Stir the Pot. Our objective is to rattle my father without being obvious and see if anyone in adjacent cages responds. My brother and dad work with these men, have for years. The men won't talk, but their wives will." Jax showed Sven and James pictures of her father's colleagues and their wives. "This is Maxine, my mother's good friend. She knows my father has moved out, but not the details, according to my mother."

"We're really here to gather gossip?"

"Intel," Claire corrected.

"Gossip."

"My mother thinks this is happening to introduce Andrew to Claire and Gwen. And to meet Iris, my brother's new girlfriend. Gathering gossip is not on her radar."

James frowned. "You know, mate . . . the easier thing to do is just ask your parents what happened."

Jax nudged him. "Like that hasn't been done. Something isn't lining up, and I can't put my finger on it."

"Still surprised Neil authorized us to be here," Sven added.

"Well, he did. Suck it up, put on the nice clothes, and keep your ears open," Claire said.

"And enjoy the food," Jax added.

One of the maids approached. "Miss Claire."

"Yes?"

"You have a guest." The woman pointed toward the main hall.

The four of them walked out of the room they were in.

Cooper stood there with flowers in his hands.

Claire squealed and ran to him.

"Did you know about this?" she asked Sven.

"Not a clue."

The open front door was soon filled with Neil's frame.

Beside him was Sasha.

The looks on their faces put a stiffness in Jax's spine.

"What are you doing here?" Claire asked.

"You can't have an engagement party without the groom," Cooper announced.

Gwen walked around the corner. "Surprise!"

"What?" Claire asked. She glanced around the room. "An engagement party?"

"Now all of Neil's fuss is making sense," Sven said beside Jax.

Gwen moved to Neil's side, kissed him briefly.

Claire looked at Jax. "Did you know?"

She looked over at her mother, who pretended innocence.

"No idea," Jax said.

"We didn't think you'd keep a secret from Claire," Evelyn said.

"The party is in three hours. You must be exhausted from the flight."

"We arrived last night. We're good," Cooper told them.

Evelyn moved closer. "Introduce me to your friends," she told Jax.

Jax pointed to Cooper. "That's obviously Cooper."

"Congratulations, young man."

"Thank you."

"The big guy is Neil. My boss, so be nice."

Neil stepped forward, dwarfed her mother, and shook her hand. "Nice to meet you."

"And this is Sasha."

Sasha stood where she was, tilted her head to the side. "A pleasure."

"You look just as my daughter described," Evelyn said to Sasha.

"Don't worry, it was all good," Jax teased.

Gwen stepped away from Neil. "I have a few more things to look into before getting ready. If you'll excuse me. Evelyn?" she said with a nod. "Shall we get back to it?"

"It truly is a pleasure to finally meet all of you."

Once Jax's mother and Gwen left the hall, Neil turned to Sven and James. "We have things to go over."

The three of them exited the house, and Sasha stepped forward.

"Neil dragged you all the way here for a party?" Jax asked.

She shook her head. "I'm going ahead of you to Germany."

"To Richter?"

"No. We'll discuss this later. I understand you're aware of your father's infidelity."

"Yeah. Mother told us . . . wait. You knew?"

Sasha was quiet. "We assumed."

"I heard. That sucks, Jax. I'm sorry," Cooper offered.

"I'm still digging for details. Both of my parents are keeping their cards close to the chest."

"Eyes and ears open. We'll see how the night unfolds." Sasha looked up at the stairway. "I'll unpack." And she was gone.

Once she was out of earshot, Jax turned to Claire. "That felt odd, right?"

Claire nodded, nudged Cooper. "Do you know what's going on?"

"I was told I was going to see my fiancée, so I jumped on the plane. Neil and Sasha do what they do best . . . say nothing until they know everything."

Jax lowered her voice. "You know what . . . I bet they looked through the Richter files."

Claire's eyes lit up. "Of course they did. I would have thought of it myself, but I've been a little preoccupied."

"I wonder what they found?"

"Maybe they didn't find anything and that's why she's here," Claire suggested.

"One thing is for sure," Cooper said. "If it was anything dangerous, they wouldn't keep you blind to it."

Jax sighed. "And if it's not dangerous?"

"I'd tell you everything," Claire said. "But Neil hates chatter and Sasha doesn't gossip."

"They're going to make damn sure it's safe to send you into Richter. If there is a dangerous secret, it has to come out." Cooper placed a hand on Jax's shoulder, gave it a squeeze.

"Time to stir the pot." Jax fist-bumped Claire before leaving the two lovebirds alone.

~

Jax heard activity in the Harrison estate courtyard below and looked to see guests starting to arrive. Even though there were a lot of plates spinning in the air this night, she was most excited about seeing Andrew.

She checked her profile in the mirror one last time, slid on her high heels, and left the room.

As she passed her mother's, she noticed the door slightly open and the light still on. It wasn't like her mom to be anything but prompt, so Jax slowed and hesitated. When she heard her mother sigh, she rapped on the door and let it open. "Mother?"

Evelyn sat in a chair, her back rod-straight, eyes out the window. "I'm coming."

Her mother moved to her feet and turned with a fake smile.

Jax blew out a breath. "Wow. Look at you."

Informal dinner party meant cocktail dresses, not tuxedos.

For the first time in Jax's adult life she saw her mother as a woman. "This has Gwen's handwriting all over it." Evelyn wore a midnight blue slim-fitting dress that stopped just below her knees. The lace three-quarter sleeves said elegance and grace, and the square neckline screamed style. Her dark hair was in what Jax would call a lazy bun on the side. Youthful, without being young. Two pearl drop sapphire earrings dangled from her lobes.

Jax reached out, touched them. "Are these new?"

"Gwen insisted I borrow them."

"She was right." Jax stood back, took her mother in from toe to head. "Never go into a battle looking anything but your best."

"It's too much."

"It's perfect." Jax looked closer. "I have just one little thing to do." She walked over to her mother's cosmetics and found what she needed.

"What are you doing?"

Jax looked her in the eye. "Trust me."

Her mother closed her eyes and Jax dabbed on another layer of eye shadow.

Standing back, she admired her work. "Fabulous."

Evelyn glanced in the mirror, smiled. "That is better."

Jax smiled, held both her mother's hands. "Ready?"

Looking down, Evelyn lifted her left hand in front of them. Her wedding rings became the center of attention.

Jax saw the moment for what it was. Decision . . . crisis.

"Take them off."

Evelyn's eyes shot to hers. "People will talk."

"If someone mentions it, you say you left them by the sink when you were washing the dishes."

"I don't do the dishes."

"I'm going to forget the pretentiousness of that statement and remind you that everyone does dishes. And that isn't the point. Let me demonstrate." Jax cleared her throat. "You look lovely tonight, Evelyn . . . Whatever happened to your wedding rings?"

Jax adopted another voice. "Would you believe they fell off in the shower? The plumber is having a devil of a time retrieving them . . . Isn't that right, Gregory?"

Her mother found her smile. "You're entirely too good at that."

"Remember these words tonight. *Fake it.* I know you're an expert at hiding your emotions. Now maybe you let the ones you want to show stand out. Very few people in the room would even think to look at your left hand."

"But your father will."

"And isn't he the one you want to notice?"

Her mother squared her shoulders and removed her rings.

Jax presented her arm. "Ready?"

"I am."

The two of them walked down the hall and to the grand staircase.

Guests were arriving, and Gwen, Neil, Claire, and Cooper were inviting them in.

Jax's eyes immediately found Andrew as he first walked in the door. Dress jacket, turtleneck . . . sexy. He shrugged out of his overcoat, and Jax smiled as their eyes caught.

Her mother stiffened beside her.

That's when Jax noticed her dad.

His eyes traveled to the two of them, his feet shuffled.

Jax leaned in. "That one looks a little dodgy to me."

Her mother laughed and continued to do so as they met the bottom step.

Andrew approached them first. "Ladies. May I be the first to say . . . you're stealing the show."

Evelyn leaned forward. "You're biased," she told him.

"I most certainly am." He looked Jax in the eye. "Hello."

Before Jax could respond, he kissed her, on the lips, in front of her mom.

"Talk about liberties," she whispered when he straightened.

He then placed a polite kiss to each of Evelyn's cheeks. He said something Jax couldn't hear in her mother's ear and then stood back. "Thank you."

Jax squeezed his arm hard when he took his place between them and walked into the crowd.

~

Drop-dead gorgeous.

Sexy, stylish little black dress, high heels, and legs that Andrew hadn't stopped thinking about since he'd rid her of her slacks the night he'd met her.

That thought made him feel less than honorable, even though nothing had happened.

And the thing that hit him the hardest . . .

Jax stood by her mother.

Arm in arm, chins raised as they descended the stairs as if sharing a private joke.

From what Andrew had learned about Jax's relationship with her mother, it was anything but ideal . . . and yet there she was showing support in the best way possible without a care in the world.

"Maxine . . . you remember Jacqueline," Evelyn said to the first person who approached her.

"You've grown so much."

"Wonderful to see you again. Have you met Andrew . . ."

Polite conversation circulated as introductions were made.

When Jax turned to her father, Andrew felt her fingertips knead into his arm. It was the only sign of stress he sensed. "Hello, Father."

"Good evening. You look lovely." Gregory turned to Evelyn. "Like your mother."

Evelyn cleared her throat. "Have you met Lady Gwen and her gracious husband, Neil?"

Jax stood back as her mother moved forward and made the introductions.

Gwen was exactly as Jax had described, polite and poised. She said all the right things to Gregory. You'd never know she had knowledge of the man's indiscretion.

However, when Neil shook Gregory's hand, you could cut the silence with a knife.

Neil said nothing.

No one in a five-foot radius missed it.

And no one in that perimeter broke the tension.

"Andrew?"

He heard his name and found his parents walking toward them.

The moment between Neil and Gregory was broken, but not forgotten.

Andrew made the introductions.

Their hosts, then Jax's parents . . . and then Jax. "You remember my father . . ."

"I'm so glad you could make it on such short notice. Have you met my best friend, Claire, and her fiancé, Cooper? This is a surprise engagement party for them."

The moment of Neil's silence was pushed aside.

Though Andrew wouldn't forget it anytime soon.

The foyer was buzzing, and eventually Jax pulled Andrew and a handful of others toward the back of the house.

He lowered his lips to her ear. "Is Neil always that intense?"

"Pretty much. Loyalty means everything to him. He would just as soon cut off his own balls with a dull knife than cheat on his wife."

Andrew felt his pair recoiling at the image.

"He's your boss?"

"Yup."

He made a mental note to thank the man for giving Jax a job in Europe.

He was about to tell Jax how beautiful she looked when her friend Claire walked up to them. "You scooted by way too fast," she told him.

"Did you two meet?"

"Yes, when you were taking your own sweet time coming down," Claire teased.

"My mother needed some reinforcement."

All three of them looked around until they saw Evelyn standing with a few other people, a glass of wine in her hand. In the opposite direction, Gregory stood with a colleague. "Should be an interesting evening."

Claire looked up at Andrew and said, "So you're the one who poured Jax into bed after a night of martinis."

He felt his cheeks heat up. "I made sure she was safe and tucked in."

Claire narrowed her eyes, a tiny smile on her lips.

Cooper walked over, placed an arm around his fiancée. "Is she grilling you already?"

"Only slightly," Andrew reported.

Cooper nodded toward the far end of the room, where a bar had been set up. "How about a drink?"

"I'll take white wine," Claire called after them.

"A martini for me," Jax added.

He and Cooper walked away from the women. "You're the finance guy."

Andrew nodded. "Did everyone do a background check on me?"

"No. Jax did and we all looked at the data."

The honesty made Andrew laugh. "You have me at a disadvantage, then."

"Let me bring you up to speed." Cooper pointed out two men, late twenties, early thirties at best. Fit . . . alert. "Sven and James. They work here in the London offices. The knockout over there is Sasha." The woman he pointed to was exactly as Cooper described. Long dark hair in a thick ponytail at the nape of her neck. The dress she wore looked like it should be on a runway in Milan. "I wouldn't say she works with Neil. More of a consultant."

"Consultant?"

"It's complicated and would take longer to explain than we have time tonight."

"Are you all private investigators?"

Cooper laughed. "No. Security detail. With the occasional undercover work."

They stepped up to the bar. "A white wine, one beer . . ." Cooper looked at Andrew.

"Two vodka martinis."

While the bartender mixed their drinks, the two of them glanced around the room. "Who are all these people?" Cooper asked.

For the next five minutes Andrew pointed out those he knew. Which was several of them. It helped that he knew Jax's family and the people Gregory worked with.

"Where is Jax's brother?"

"That's him walking up to her now."

"He looks a lot older than his sister."

"We're the same age. Went to school together."

Cooper took a closer look at Andrew. "That's crazy."

They gathered their drinks and headed back to Jax and Claire, where Harry was introducing his date.

Andrew moved to Jax's side, handed her the cocktail.

"How are they getting along?" Harry asked, looking over their shoulders to his parents.

"On separate sides of the room, apparently."

Harry eyed their drinks. "I require a little fortification for the night." With that, he and his date headed toward the bar.

Andrew lifted his drink. "Cheers."

Jax, Claire, and Cooper all added their salutations, took a sip and a collective sigh.

~

When Gregory inched his way to Evelyn's side, Jax nudged Andrew in their direction. "If my mother looks uncomfortable, I'll make an excuse and pull her aside. Make sure my dad doesn't follow."

"I can do that."

"Go stir that pot," Claire said.

Jax laughed as she put her half-empty drink on a tray, and they walked away.

"What does that mean?" Andrew asked.

"Tell ya later."

They moved to her mother's side, putting themselves between her parents and the couple they were talking to. Jax offered her father a polite smile when all she really wanted to do was throttle the man.

"Very gracious of the MacBains to include us tonight," Gregory said.

Her mother's eyes traveled to Jax. "Claire and Jacqueline have been close friends since boarding school. When we started planning tonight, Gwen wanted to ensure that all the guests had people they knew in attendance. This little group just evolved. Isn't that right, darling?"

"That's right."

The woman her mother was talking to narrowed her eyes. "I don't think we've ever met your daughter."

"That's a shame. Paul and Lissa Grover, this is our daughter, Jacqueline. Paul works with your father," she explained. "This is Andrew Craig, Lloyd and Phillis's son."

"Have we met?" Paul asked Andrew.

Gregory answered before Andrew could open his mouth.

"Years ago, he and Harry came into the office. I tried to sway him over to our world."

Paul shook Andrew's hand. "Ah yes. That's right."

"I'm quite happy where I am, Gregory. But I did appreciate your endorsement."

Andrew abandoned his drink on a passing waiter's tray. Jax used the opportunity to place her hand on his arm. The movement was subtle but noticed.

Lissa winked at Evelyn with a broad smile. "I'm starting to see how this guest list evolved."

Gregory cleared his throat. "Jacqueline isn't in London very often. I'm sure she wanted to make the most of it."

"Quite true, Father. We wanted an occasion to finally meet Harry's girlfriend. Mother thought it would be a good idea to introduce me to a few of your close friends in light of the fact that I'll be staying in Europe for a while."

Jax looked her father in the eye. The polite smile was still in place, but a flinch of his eyes gave away his discomfort. "That's a surprise."

"Isn't it wonderful? Jacqueline has lived in California for years. It will be nice to have her home again," her mother said.

"I like to think I had a hand in that." Andrew placed his palm on the small of Jax's back and brought her attention to him.

"You certainly made it easy to say yes to the job transfer."

"Isn't that nice," Lissa said. "I remember when Paul and I married, seemed like everyone we knew was doing it at the same time. We went to three weddings that summer, remember, darling?"

"You took a job transfer?" Gregory asked.

"I did."

"Permanent?"

Jax glanced up at Andrew, then over to her mother. "We'll see."

The sound of someone tapping a glass brought their attention to their hostess.

Voices became whispers until it was silent.

"On behalf of Neil and myself, I wanted to thank you all for coming on such short notice. While Claire and Cooper's engagement might have been the catalyst for this evening, I can't help but look around the room and see how the young couples in this group are bringing some of us older ones along for the ride. We'll save the rest of the speeches for more formal events. For now, I'm told dinner is ready, so if you'll follow me into the dining room."

CHAPTER SIXTEEN

As dinner progressed, so did the tension between Jax's parents. Though they were separated during the meal, that didn't stop the daggered looks and occasional slight delivered by her mother.

"Am I the only one seeing your father sweat?" Andrew had asked at one point.

"I'd feel sorry for him if he didn't deserve it," she had whispered back.

When the meal finished, coffee was offered in yet another room of the house, this one with outside access that several people took advantage of. Their comfort was helped by the heaters that kept the area warm and twinkling lights that illuminated the space.

Every time Jax noticed her father try to intersect her mother, she jumped in to act as a buffer. Other than her mother, Andrew was the only one who noticed her effort.

"You're getting good at this," he pointed out as she headed off to intercept her father for the zillionth time.

"I learned about interception at all the college football games I attended in California."

Before she could walk to her mother, Evelyn made it to her. "I'm going to talk to him."

"You sure?" Jax asked.

"I've put it off all night. Weeks, actually. Here it will be brief and polite."

"He doesn't deserve polite."

Evelyn placed a hand on Jax's arm and smiled at Andrew. "You two try and enjoy your evening."

Jax tapped her finger against her leg, itching to hear the conversation.

When Evelyn motioned for Gregory to follow her outside, Jax took Andrew's hand and led him out of the room. "Where are we going?"

Jax pointed a finger up and proceeded to the staircase to the second floor.

The noise from the activity of the party faded as they doubled their steps leading to the bedrooms.

"You're serious?"

"The closer to the source, the more accurate the information."

"Privacy means nothing to you," he said, laughing.

Jax stopped at the top of the stairs. "My father should have thought about that before he slept with someone who wasn't his wife."

"Good point."

She walked into the room she thought would be above where her parents were standing outside. Without turning on the light, she pulled Andrew inside.

Jax walked straight to the balcony and quietly opened one door.

Noise from the party below filtered in, but so did her parents' voices.

With a thumbs up, she tilted her head to the side and encouraged Andrew to keep quiet with a single finger to her lips.

"Don't you think it's time to give Harry his space back?" Evelyn's voice drifted up, even though they both spoke in low voices. "Twice tonight I've heard him reference his privacy or lack thereof."

"If that's what you want, I'll come home."

Jax felt her pulse climb.

Andrew reached out and touched her arm.

Her mother's gasp was refreshing . . . as were her next words. "I don't think so."

"How do you expect me to keep this squabble from my colleagues if I occupy a separate residence?"

"This is a bit more than a spat, Gregory. Discretion is obviously your strong point. If you can keep an affair from your wife, you can certainly keep our estrangement from your coworkers."

"Be reasonable, Evelyn."

Jax shook her fist in the air. *Reasonable*. She mouthed the word to Andrew, who had taken on the role of shusher with a pursed lip.

"What I don't understand is why you told me at all, unless it's still happening."

"It isn't, I swear. It was nothing and a long time ago," Gregory said. "I want to come home."

"And I don't want you there. For the first time, Jacqueline and I are actually getting along, and I only see you getting in the way of that." Her mother's words felt right in Jax's ears.

"How can you say that?"

"You tell me. I couldn't help but notice tonight that when she and Andrew showed up together, you looked . . . uncomfortable. And when she said she was staying in Europe, you squirmed."

"I did no such thing."

Jax nodded to Andrew, who added his silent agreement.

"Anyone watching might actually think it was I who had an affair and you were the one questioning Jacqueline's parentage."

"That's preposterous."

"Perhaps, but that is how it looked. You've disappointed this family, Gregory."

Jax gave her mother a silent fist bump.

"You told Jacqueline about the affair," she heard her father say.

"I didn't deny it when she guessed the truth." Evelyn's tone was stern and to the point.

"How could you do that . . ."

"How could *I*?" Her mother's voice rose. "I suggest you get in your car and leave. Before I'm forced to make a scene."

"Evelyn . . ."

"I mean it, Gregory."

Footsteps faded, and Jax quietly closed the door.

"Can you believe him?" Jax asked Andrew.

"This from the woman who just eavesdropped on a private conversation between her parents."

"Privacy goes out the window when you break someone's trust."

"And your mother?"

He had a point.

"Collateral damage," she said, justifying her actions.

Andrew laughed.

Jax started for the door.

"We're going to follow him out now?"

She nodded.

"Won't it be obvious that we were up here listening?"

"You're right." Jax walked into his space and lifted her lips to his. "Kiss me."

Andrew caught on and reached for her. "You're wicked."

"You have no idea," she said as she closed the distance between them.

His touch might have been on cue, but that didn't stop him from putting effort into the moment.

Jax reached for his hair, gave it a little ruffling.

Andrew returned the favor.

She couldn't stop herself from laughing, and soon the lip-lock became less of a kiss and more of a sport to see who could look more taken advantage of than the other.

He pulled back and looked at her, and for a moment the comedy was gone, and they met in the middle for a kiss that had more heat.

A few moments later she stood back. "We have to stop."

Andrew wiped a hand over his lips. "Right." He blew out a breath.

She straightened her dress. "Ready?"

"No." But he headed for the door anyway.

"You're a good wingman," she said as they moved toward the stairway.

"Happy to be of service."

Jax glanced over, stopped him midstairs, and removed a smudge of lipstick off his lips with her thumb.

Someone below cleared their throat.

Gwen glanced their way before turning around. "We're happy you could make it, Mr. Simon."

Jax and Andrew reached the bottom stairs together looking only slightly guilty.

Her father stood staring at them, his expression lacking emotion.

"You're leaving?" she asked.

"I have a busy day tomorrow."

"Let me know when you're available for that lunch," she suggested.

Without committing, her father kissed her goodbye, shook Andrew's hand, and thanked Gwen again before walking out the door.

"That was quite entertaining," Gwen said. "Shall we?"

~

Andrew sat with Jax, Claire, and Cooper in the living room long after the last guest had left and Gwen, Neil, Evelyn, and Sasha had retired to their rooms.

"At the end of the day I think your dad's just an ass," Cooper said in summary.

A couple of hushed conversations had happened among the guests, but nothing anyone got a handle on.

"Do you think this did happen a while ago?" Claire asked.

Once Evelyn had gone to bed, Jax and Andrew had relayed the conversation they'd overheard.

"There is nothing pointing to something happening now. He goes to work, then to Harry's . . . the occasional restaurant."

"Why did he tell her?" Claire asked.

"Guilt?" Andrew suggested.

"Maybe, but why now?"

"And why would the guys he works with care? Seems he's working hard to keep this from them."

"Big money," Andrew offered. "Nobody likes instability when the person managing your bottom dollar is in the center of it."

"But people get divorced all the time," Jax said.

"Maybe the affair was with someone at the office."

Jax waved Claire's suggestion off. "I have a bug on his desk. Nothing is happening in that office."

"You bugged your dad's office?" Andrew turned to Jax and asked.

She looked at him, narrowed her eyes. "Have we met?" she teased.

"What about a client?" Cooper asked.

The three of them chewed on that in silence.

"That actually makes sense."

"Not to sound sexist, but most clients coming in are men," Andrew said.

"A wife of a client, then?"

Claire sighed. "That fits."

"I still can't understand why he said something to my mother in the first place."

"Men fess up when they're about to get caught. Read any tabloid and you'll figure that out," Cooper said.

"Maybe the woman is threatening to tell all. Maybe she's been blackmailing my father?"

"Have you looked at the bank accounts? Followed the money?" Claire asked.

"No." Jax cringed. "In my defense, we did just learn about the infidelity." But she chided herself for the rookie mistake.

Andrew ran a hand over hers. "I'm sure your mother would have noticed chunks of money missing from their accounts."

"I'm sure my mother doesn't know about all his accounts. I'll start looking tomorrow."

"Is that legal?" Andrew asked.

"Legal is relative," Jax said.

"Relative to what?"

"If you're caught," Claire said, laughing.

Cooper sat forward, rubbing his eyes. "I need to say this, Jax . . . because I see you going down this rabbit hole and I don't want you to get hurt."

"Okay. Go ahead."

"Let's say your dad had an affair with a client, or the wife of a client . . . he's been paying her to stay quiet. And either you find out who it is, or this woman comes out of the shadows . . . All the cards are on the table, what then? Does it really change anything? At the end of the day, this is your parents' marriage and their split. You and Harry get the fallout, and that sucks, but . . . it's no different for anyone else."

Jax knew, in the back of her mind, that Cooper had a point. "You're a hundred percent right. But . . ."

Claire looked her in the eye. "You can't move past it until you know all the facts."

Jax nodded. "Everyone we know that was sent to Richter had a secret. If this is the secret that prompted that decision, I have the right to know."

Cooper pulled in a long breath. "I can get on board with that."

Claire stifled a yawn. "I'm worn-out."

Andrew stretched his legs. "And I'm long overdue for getting myself home."

Jax squeezed his hand. "You can stay."

He smiled. "Tempting. But I'll leave that for another time."

The four of them unfolded from their seats.

"How long are you in town?" Andrew asked Cooper and Claire.

"A couple more days."

"If I don't see you before you leave, it has been a pleasure."

Andrew and Cooper shook hands.

Claire pulled him into a hug. "You passed the best-friend test," she told him.

Jax rolled her eyes. "I'll walk you out."

Cooper and Claire followed them out of the room, turning off lights as they went.

Outside, the fog had rolled in, making everything damp and cold.

Andrew stopped her right outside the door. "It's freezing out here."

She was wearing a cocktail dress minus the shoes that had been kicked off when the last guest left.

"You sure you don't want to stay?" It was after one a.m.

"Do I want to spend the night with you? More than you know. Do I want to do that in a house containing not only your mother, but your boss and your best friend?" He placed his palms on her arms and rubbed some of the cold away.

"I understand."

"Maybe midweek I can talk you into a night in the city. After everyone leaves."

She liked the sound of that. "I might be persuaded."

"Might, huh?" He moved closer, placed a hand to the back of her neck.

Kissing him, even in the cold, brought a flutter deep in her belly. Though he didn't linger.

"Get some sleep. You've had a long day," he urged.

"Text me when you get home."

He nodded, kissed her again, and quickly jogged down the steps to his car.

~

"The man is good at keeping a secret," Sasha reported to Neil the next morning while the house was being put back together after the party. "There isn't a money trail anywhere. Not that I could find."

Neil looked at the intel she'd acquired along with the translation of the files housed at Richter. "You're sure this is all the original document said?" He lifted the translation.

"'Indiscretions of the father that could compromise his job if they came to light,'" Sasha repeated the words on the paper verbatim. "Keep in mind, Neil . . . not everyone at Richter was there *because* of a secret, but the secrets of Richter were kept because of men like Gregory Simon. If he blew the whistle on the shady parts of the school, the secrets would be revealed. It was Richter's way of maintaining silence. Students like Claire made friends with students like Jax, and parents looked the other way when the Claires of the world were recruited to become assassins."

"Are you suggesting the Simons enrolled Jax in the school and then someone found out about the affair?"

"Highly probable."

"Who has that job? The investigator that researches the families to dig up the skeletons?" Neil voiced his question aloud while looking at the paperwork in front of him.

"There's only one person I can think of that could have that answer."

Neil looked Sasha in the eye. "Lodovica."

Sasha knew the former headmistress better than any of them. "She won't talk to me."

"She might talk to Jax."

"I can't imagine she doesn't know Jax works with us."

"It's worth a shot. Worst case, the woman keeps her mouth shut. Best case, she lets something slip," Neil said. "Another reason to send Jax to Germany."

"If Jax starts poking around and any of those wounds are open, someone is going to jump."

"We send her with backup." Neil held no faith that Richter had changed its ways. Not completely, anyway.

"What about Andrew?" Sasha asked.

"What's a numbers guy going to do to help her out?"

Sasha moved around the desk and to one of the floor-to-ceiling windows on the other side of the room. "We sent Jax to Richter last year, a fake fiancé on her arm. We send her in again, alone . . . anyone watching will know she's looking for dirt. If Andrew accompanies her, a real man in her life, with a name their investigator can research . . . suspicion decreases. Or who knows, maybe the current investigator for the school reveals themselves while searching for Andrew's secrets."

Sasha made sense.

She always made sense.

"No guarantee he will go with her."

Sasha smiled over her shoulder. "Men respect you. Ask him."

Neil sat in the chair behind the desk, thumbed through a few papers, and then reached for the phone.

Andrew answered in two rings. "Hello?"

"Andrew. It's Neil."

"Oh. Hello. This is a surprise."

"I won't take much of your time."

"Is everything okay? Jax?" Andrew's voice pitched higher.

"She's fine. I'd like to ask you for a favor." Asking for favors was out of Neil's wheelhouse. He told people what to do.

They jumped.

"Certainly, if it's in my means."

"I'm sending Jax to Germany on an assignment."

"Yes, yes . . . she mentioned that."

"I'd like you to join her." Neil looked up to see Sasha watching him.

"Why?"

"This situation with her parents has her preoccupied. If she learns something while she's away, I'd like to know she has . . . ah . . . emotional backup." *Emotional backup?* Where the hell had those words come from? Neil was convinced he'd been spending too much time in the company of women. "I want to know she's taken care of. I'm trusting you to do that."

Sasha hid a grin and mouthed the word *please.*

Neil shook his head. *Please* was not a word he was going to use in this situation.

"Of course. I'll make arrangements."

Neil smiled slightly. "I'll message you with my personal numbers and those of an emergency response team. Do not hesitate to use them."

"Emergency?" Andrew questioned.

"A precaution, Andrew. Nothing more. I'll send you the details."

"I'll keep an eye out for them."

"Thank you."

In the middle of Andrew saying goodbye, Neil disconnected the call. "Done."

Sasha started to laugh.

"What?"

"'Emotional backup'?"

"Shut up!"

Sasha kept laughing.

CHAPTER SEVENTEEN

Jax, Sven, Sasha, and Neil sat in the situation room inside the London office the day before Neil was slated to return to the States.

Sasha started the meeting. "In front of you is a list of every staff member, down to the kitchen help washing the dishes. They are divided into sections, new employees recruited after the change of management, and the previous staff that was cleared to stay. The next set of names are the current school board members. They are divided into appointed and voted in as well as who did the appointing. It is also noted if they have a student, past or present, in the school."

"Someone enlighten me on the significance of the school board," Sven said.

"When Jax and I were attending Richter, the board was primarily parents of students. Most of which wanted nothing to do with being on the board but were blackmailed into holding a seat. Their votes were paid for by threats of exposing whatever sin they'd committed. Therefore, people like Pohl were able to go in and harvest students like Olivia." Olivia was forced into a life of crime as a paid assassin because of Pohl. And she was someone they all knew very well. She was only able to retire because of Pohl's death.

"The board was displaced after Pohl and Lodovica went down. Is it re-forming? Or is there something else going on? Charlie suggested another benefactor is paying sign-on bonuses for students learning multiple languages. Who is he or she, and what is their angle?" Neil added. "This is an intelligence mission. We are only gathering facts that we can look at from afar and see if there is any validity to Charlie's concerns."

"Charlie wouldn't have cried wolf if nothing was going on," Jax said.

"Agreed. But I'm not sending two of you in to take the place down. Jax, I want you to interview Lodovica."

She wasn't expecting that. "In prison?"

"Yes. If she is truly sorry for her crimes, she wouldn't want them repeated. We want to know who she used, or who Pohl used to gather dirt on the families of the students," Sasha said. "Who discovered your father was having an affair?"

"You found that in the files, didn't you?"

Sasha looked her in the eye. "We did. But not a name. The files said exposure would compromise his employment. Your father wouldn't have volunteered that information, so who found it? Do they still work for Richter? These are the objectives of this mission. Are there orphanages funneling students in? Who are their benefactors?"

Neil stood from the desk he was leaning on, and walked closer. "Jax, you're in the spotlight. Sven will follow to see if anyone trails you."

"I go in alone, then?"

"Not completely. Andrew is coming with you," Neil announced.

Jax shook her head. "Excuse me?"

"I asked him to join you in Germany."

Jax looked at Sven, who seemed just as surprised.

"What exactly do you expect him to do?" she asked.

Sven laughed. "Hold your hand?"

Jax rolled her eyes.

"On the surface, yes. Your second trip back to Richter in a year will be questioned. And with a different man at your side. If something unethical is going on, chances are someone is going to look into both your backgrounds." Sasha waved a hand at Jax. "Your parents are in the middle of a split, it's only a matter of time before that is out in the open. You could have the excuse of wanting to know the name of the woman behind the affair. Spin that however you want. If someone is digging for dirt, they'll learn who you work for without too much difficulty. Hell, tell anyone who asks that you're an investigator. Throw them off. And when that eye is turned to Andrew, and maybe it's the same eye looking into you, then maybe we find who Richter's dirt digger is."

"What about Andrew's privacy?"

"I did the background check on him myself," Sven said. "The man has nothing to hide."

Neil lifted his hands in the air. "He already said yes to joining you."

"You asked him?"

"Yes."

"Seriously? When?" Jax honestly wasn't sure how she felt about this.

"This afternoon."

Neil wasn't one to ask permission, and taking his lead, she made sure her demands were known as well. "I'm not comfortable keeping anything about this from him," she announced.

"We wouldn't expect you to," Neil said. "This is a weeklong assignment. Get in, get out. Gather intelligence, plant the seeds for others to watch, and either return at a later date or send others in if you're compromised."

"A lot can happen in a week."

"If things heat up, we send backup or bring you home."

Neil handed them both envelopes. "You leave the day after tomorrow."

Jax glanced inside the envelope, saw two tickets for her and Andrew. Neil obviously didn't expect pushback from her.

He wasn't wrong.

"Any questions?" Neil asked.

"Only one," she said.

Once Sasha and Neil both looked directly at her, she asked, "Is there anything else in the Richter files about my family? My mother?"

"No. Nothing. I am personally looking for the mistress," Sasha told her. "To ensure that whoever she is, there is no threat to you or yours."

That made Jax feel better.

"The other woman always shows back up," Sven said.

Sasha placed a hand on Jax's arm. "I'll keep you informed. You concentrate on the Richter situation. We'll keep an eye on your family."

"Thank you."

~

"You know . . . you don't have to come." Jax had called Andrew the second she was out of the office and in the car.

"Is that your way of saying you don't want me to go with you?"

"No . . . yes . . . no."

"You have to stop doing that. Which is it?" His voice bordered on disappointment.

"I want you to understand what you're getting into."

He hummed into the phone. "I'm accompanying the woman I'm currently seeing on a business trip."

"It's more than that, Andrew. There is more to Richter and Germany and the whole mess than meets the eye. If you're with me when I'm there, chances are someone is going to want to know what you're all about, how you fit in . . . and investigate you."

"Let 'em. I have nothing to hide."

"Your privacy will be gone," she warned him.

"Says the woman who tracked down my credit card purchases . . ."

Jax squeezed her eyes shut and moaned. "I should feel guilty about that."

Andrew laughed. "But you don't."

"But I don't." She smiled.

"Jax, if you don't want me to go because you don't want *me* there
. . . I'll inform Neil. But if I'm not the problem, let's make the most
of it."

"You sure you want to do this?"

"Am I sure I want to spend the next week with the beautiful woman
I can't stop thinking about . . . in a different country . . . on someone
else's dime? Yeah, I'm sure."

Jax felt some of the tension in her shoulders ease with his insistence.
"I've seen the background check. You don't need Neil's dime here."

"I don't. But I'm not going to say no."

Neither would she. "All right. But I've warned you."

"You have. Now, let me get back to work so I can justify abandon-
ing ship on such short notice."

She hadn't really thought about his time off work. "Is it going to be
okay that you're leaving?"

"If I did this all the time, there would be an issue, but since that
isn't my routine, I'm fine. Besides, my parents both like you and your
friends, so my father will pick up some of the slack while I'm gone.
We're pretty good at tag teaming work at the office."

"Thank your father for me."

"I'll do that. Now be sure and pack something nice . . . maybe a
couple of somethings. I'm certain we can take a few hours off in Berlin."

"Okay, then. I'll see you soon."

"Looking forward to it," he said before hanging up.

Jax dropped the phone in her lap and placed her hands over her
face. "What am I getting myself into?"

~

The day before the trip to Germany was completely packed with activity and a bit of sorrow. Saying goodbye to Claire for an unknown
amount of time was harder than Jax anticipated. The two of them had

been inseparable since they met, with the exception of Jax's last year at Richter.

They both understood that the start of Claire and Cooper's marriage would end their roommate living arrangement sooner or later. Jax just thought they'd have more time.

She felt a tear slide down her cheek as she packed clothes in a single suitcase for the next day.

A knock on her open bedroom door had Jax turning around.

Her mother stood there, a soft smile on her face. "I thought I heard you sniffling. Are you okay?"

The fact that her mother asked brought a knot to the back of Jax's throat. She pushed the suitcase aside and sat on the edge of the bed. "I'm going to miss her."

Evelyn walked in the room and sat down. "It isn't forever."

"I know. It feels different. Even when I do go back, it won't be the same. And it shouldn't. They're getting married. College roommates eventually move out, move on."

Her mother took her hand and squeezed it. "Life is in constant motion. Even when you think you know what's going to happen, something completely different takes center stage. I never thought I'd have the opportunity to get to know you as well as I have in these past few weeks . . . and yet here we are."

Such an honest statement from her mother prompted Jax to open up. "I didn't think you wanted to know me."

Evelyn sighed. "I didn't exactly give you the impression otherwise, did I?"

"I always wondered if there was a reason. Did I do something . . . ?"

"My God, no. You and Harry were in boarding school, then he was off to college, and life became routine. I hardly knew what to do with you when you were home. Your independence after you were enrolled at Richter was unimaginable. Not at all like your brother. After a couple of years away, you'd come home and want nothing to do with us. A typical teenage phase you'd eventually grow out of." Her mother took a deep breath. "There were times I'd express to your father the guilt I had about not being there for my children day to day. He'd remind me that we both went to boarding school and it wasn't unusual. Your grandmother told me my feelings were normal, and eventually I stopped dwelling on it."

"Growing up outside of this house made it easier to leave," Jax said.

"I know. I assumed you'd eventually return. All the languages you speak and opportunities here in Europe . . . but no. California and beaches won you over."

"Claire was the reason I moved to America. She's the sister I didn't have."

Her mother laughed. "I'm well aware of that. Your father and I argued endlessly about her visiting."

"Why?"

"He said he didn't want to share you. To think I listened."

"I remember you being the one telling me no."

"Your father has never been good at confrontation. Good cop, bad cop? Besides, he was at work during the day, leaving me to break the bad news." Her mother's look became distant as she stared at the wall. "Or maybe he wasn't at work and instead fiddling with some woman."

"Oh, Mum."

She shook her head, faked a smile. "I'm sorry. I shouldn't be saying things like that to you."

"Oh, please. I've said worse." It was time for Jax to squeeze her mother's hand. "You know, when people asked me about my family, I'd tell them it wasn't that I didn't like any of you, but I didn't really know any of you."

"That's so profoundly sad."

"Perhaps. But now I can say I don't care for my father."

Her mother leaned on Jax's shoulder. "I don't know what to do with him. The betrayal is so deep. We've had a comfortable marriage. We like the same things. Raised two responsible adults. Out of nowhere he tells me about this other woman."

The more Jax heard her mother talk, the more ticked at her father she became. "Not that apologies fix anything, but he doesn't appear to be a man that's sorry."

"I know. He sent me more flowers during our happy . . ." Her mother stopped, let out an audible moan. "Or maybe they were guilty flowers after he spent time with her."

"What an awful feeling," Jax said. "Has he told you who it was?"

"No. He refuses."

"Then he's not sorry, Mum. If he can't be truthful about the whole sordid affair, he isn't . . ."

"You're right. I tell you, I've gone from sad to angry to sad again. Lately the needle is swinging over to hateful."

"Rightfully so."

Her mother let loose Jax's hand and placed both palms on the side of the bed. "Enough. I promised myself that I would not bad-mouth your father in front of you children, and here I am breaking my own rules."

"Good luck with that," Jax teased.

Evelyn stood, looked at the suitcase. "How long will you be gone?"

"About a week. Depends on what we find."

"What are you looking for?"

"Boring stuff. But you'll be happy to know that my language skills are why I'm able to work between California and Europe."

"Then it wasn't all a mistake."

Jax shook her head. "I honestly wouldn't change it for anything. Sending me to Richter wasn't a mistake. Not in my case."

"I'm thankful to hear you say that."

Her mother turned to leave the room.

"Oh, by the way . . . did I tell you Andrew is coming with me?"

Evelyn stopped, backed up without turning around, and sat on the bed. "No. You failed to inform me of that."

Jax grinned.

Her mother launched into a hundred questions, and Jax curled up in a ball and answered every single one.

CHAPTER EIGHTEEN

Andrew had led a rather relaxed life. His father was the sole breadwinner in the family and made enough to send Andrew and his older sister, now married and living in Edinburgh, to boarding schools when they were younger. Their college educations were completely paid for. Holidays when he was young took them all over Europe. The accommodations were comfortable but not extravagant. Being single, he afforded business-class tickets, especially for long flights, but as he sat in a first-class seat for a two-hour commuter flight to Berlin, Andrew started to see exactly how Jax lived her life.

"Neil is very accommodating," he said as they fastened their seatbelts while the other passengers filed onto the plane.

Jax tucked her handbag under the seat in front of her. "He doesn't always spring for first," she told him.

"No, sometimes he sends a private plane," Sven said from directly behind them.

"Sometimes it's coach."

Sven laughed. "I managed a lift on a cargo flight last year."

Jax looked over her shoulder and between the seats. "That's right. The leg from Indonesia to Western Australia."

"A cargo plane?" Andrew asked.

Jax smiled, turned back around, and nodded. "The occasional perks of first are happily accepted."

"Why a cargo plane? And how does one even manage a ticket?"

She leaned closer, kept her voice low. "Sometimes you don't want others to track where you're going."

Her comment led to a hundred more questions about what it was that she did for Neil. "Why would you—"

Jax placed a hand on his arm. "I'll explain later."

The flight attendant moved down the aisle, stopped at their seats. She glanced at the paper in her hand. "Miss Simon and Mr. Craig. Welcome aboard. Would you care for a beverage before we take off?"

Jax tilted her head closer to Andrew's. "We start every holiday with a mimosa, isn't that right, honey?"

"Every holiday . . ." That was new. He smiled at the waiting attendant. "Two mimosas."

Before Andrew could open his lips to ask, Jax whispered, "I'll explain that later, too."

"You warned me."

"I did."

He reached out and curled his fingers around hers. "Where did we go on our last holiday together?"

"Bali. I can't believe you forgot," she teased.

"Right. Hot and wet . . ." He remembered her definition of her time there.

"But the people were lovely."

"You're really good at this," he whispered.

"You'll catch on," she told him.

For nearly two hours they talked about their fake trip to Bali to the point that Andrew felt he'd actually been there. Moreover, he couldn't wait to go.

In Berlin, Sven pushed through the airport quicker since he didn't have to wait for luggage. When he told them he'd see them at the hotel, Andrew didn't think twice about it.

Jax kept steering the conversation toward pretend holidays they hadn't been on together and the tourist-type activities they could do while in Germany.

At the hotel, Jax became even more comfortable in the persona she was adopting. She spoke in German to the staff, even though most of them were fluent in English. Slipping between both languages seamlessly was impressive. Second and often third languages were common in Europe, but most of the people Andrew knew had taken French or Italian. The three years of French he'd been mandated to take gave him just enough ability to butcher the language years after he took his last test.

After they were escorted to their room, Jax immediately put the "Do Not Disturb" sign on the door and closed it behind the attendant. "You're a good sport," she said at the same time she unzipped her suitcase. "And better at spinning lies than you gave yourself credit for."

"I'm learning from the best." He crossed to the window and opened the blinds.

He heard a high-pitched noise behind him and turned to see Jax holding a small device that she waved around the room.

"What's that?"

She placed a finger to her lips and continued walking. She picked up the receiver on the bedside phone, then returned it. Jax kept walking and waving the device. In the bathroom, around all the lights, and the television.

Only once she turned the thing off did she start talking.

"It detects hidden tracking and listening devices."

"Bugs?"

"Precisely."

"You think someone could be spying on you . . . us?"

"Not now . . . but by the time we leave, perhaps."

Andrew shrugged out of his jacket and placed it on the back of a chair. "Why all the precautions . . . the fabrications on the airplane . . . all of it?"

"The rule of thumb when traveling for work is always appear as if you're traveling for leisure. At least in my line of work. Immigration isn't interested in tourists. Work visas are different."

"A flight attendant couldn't care less," Andrew said.

"True, but anyone asking her a question about the couple in aisle three is going to be given the information she received. They were on holiday and drinking champagne. Not a business trip. But that is not the main reason we set up a ruse while traveling. It's mainly for anyone who may have planted a bug in here. That person may find the flight attendant and ask questions. If we had talked of the objective behind this trip and she'd overheard anything . . . or someone in an adjacent seat overheard us . . ."

"Ah." The picture was starting to clear in his head. "And the cargo planes?"

"That's a bit stickier."

"How so?"

She took a seat in one of the chairs and placed the bug-finding device to the side.

"Sometimes the best way to go undetected is to take on a different persona."

"A different name?"

She nodded. "With matching identification."

"Fake passports?" Wasn't that illegal?

"On occasion."

"Isn't that ill—"

She lifted a hand in the air. "Sometimes the ends justify the means. Let me try and explain exactly what we're doing here, and I believe most of your questions will be answered."

"I'm listening."

"Tomorrow I'll be headed to the women's prison just north of here to visit the former headmistress of Richter."

Andrew had heard from Harry that the woman in charge of Richter had been imprisoned years ago but couldn't say as to why.

"Lodovica is in prison for her part in farming selected students into the employment of a man by the name of Pohl. Pohl offered jobs to these students that he pitched as secret spy work far outside of, say, British intelligence or CIA. Beyond Scotland Yard or the White House. Students like Claire, orphans, were his favorite recruits. He would act as the invisible benefactor for these students. He'd pay for their education at Richter. Orphans didn't have families, obviously, and less of a cushion upon leaving Richter. He'd give them bonuses when they left the school for every language they perfected . . . every special skill they dominated. Sounds innocent enough." Jax paused, lost any smile she'd had on her face.

Andrew felt his heart rate elevating in anticipation of how that all went wrong.

"Students took these jobs. One told me that the promise of spying for the good team and living a lavish lifestyle, especially after years of having next to nothing, was too good to pass up. Some of these students were recruited as young as eighteen . . . others stayed with Richter through an accelerated college education and left at twenty-one to work for Pohl." The more Jax spoke, the more monotone her voice became.

"What happened?"

"Within six months or less, the truth of their employment was revealed. Pohl wasn't working for a good team. In fact, it's hard to say if he had a team at all. Our belief is that he worked for the highest bidder. He'd put a gun in a recruit's hand, point at the person he wanted dead, and at the same time threaten someone close to his recruit."

Andrew swallowed . . . hard. "They killed people?"

Jax offered a single nod. "Kill or be killed."

"Jesus . . . The headmistress knew this?"

"She knew. Maybe not at first, but in the end there was no doubt. It was when Pohl attempted to recruit Sasha, years after she'd graduated, that the entire circus came undone. Claire struck up a friendship with Sasha when she returned to visit Richter while we were still students. When Sasha left, Claire ran away to follow her. When that happened, Pohl became unsettled, lied to the media about Claire's age, said Sasha had abducted her. And since he was Claire's benefactor, the authorities were put into motion. Fake passports were needed to get them both to safety until they could untangle the mess. This part isn't publicized, and I'm trusting you to keep it to yourself."

"That goes without saying."

"Neil and his team were imperative to uncovering all the truths. Like how did Pohl stay in a position to do what he did? That came down to the school board. Families with secrets that Pohl, and likely Lodovica, uncovered to ensure silence if board members became aware of students being turned into assassins. When it became obvious that the entire thing was unraveling . . . Neil, Sasha, and the team returned to Richter and uncovered a set of files with all the secrets Richter held. The ones needed to convict Lodovica and Pohl were revealed, while others have been kept silent."

"Why keep anything silent?"

"There are plenty of Sashas at the school as well. Her benefactor wasn't Pohl. In fact, not all benefactors have nefarious motivations behind their philanthropy. Sasha's benefactor kept her hidden at Richter, so Sasha's father didn't know of her existence. Russell Petrov would have killed his own daughter if he knew who she was. So, you see, not all secrets hidden at Richter are bad. They just are."

Andrew ran his fingers through his hair. "Good God, Jax. This is much deeper than a private investigator's skills."

"Sometimes. This mission to Germany is primarily PI work. But the nature of who we're investigating requires a certain amount of smoke and mirrors."

Andrew was starting to think the champagne on the plane should have been whiskey. "Why are we here?"

"The entire foundation at Richter unraveled, and a new board was quickly put into place, one overseen by an outside education organization. The military part of the school was brought aboveground and minimized to a fraction of what had been taught. Slowly, the school has been regaining its ability to educate students in the ways it is most famous for. Understand that governments all over the world employ, legitimately employ, Richter graduates. The skills learned there are not illegal unless a criminal mind is in charge. Since I left Richter, the change in administration has been on the right path. However, Neil received some intel that perhaps that is changing again. Therefore, I'm here to interview Lodovica, see if there is something she can reveal."

"And this Pohl person?"

Jax shook her head. "He's dead."

"Oh."

"I think Lodovica would be dead, too, if she knew who paid Pohl for the hits. Although I'm not asking her about Pohl. We're looking for who the school used to uncover the secrets that the families who send their children to Richter want to keep hidden."

Things did click into place, just as Jax had suggested. "Because if secrets are being collected, blackmail . . . looking the other way . . . it all happens again."

Jax winked at him. "Exactly. Sven and I are here to poke around, see if there is any truth behind Neil's intel. I will ask the questions. Sven will follow behind to see if anyone starts casing me."

"And me."

Jax looked away. "Now that you really understand the scope of what you're dealing with, I understand if you want to back out."

"Are we in any immediate danger?" Andrew asked.

"Immediate? No. But there is always a risk. I may not have been a part of the team that put people in jail, but I do work for them now. I tell people we're here on holiday, sweep the room for bugs, and tell an unlimited number of lies to stay under the radar."

"What can I do to help?"

Jax found her smile again. "Play the part of my devoted boyfriend while I search for the woman behind my parents' breakup. You see, my father's infidelity was hidden in the files of secrets. And I want to know who put it there and if there is more to the story."

"Is that the real reason we're here?" he couldn't help but ask.

Jax shook her head. "No, Jax Simon has a bigger mission of protecting innocent students from the next Pohl. Jacqueline Simon is on an emotional mission to determine family secrets and who else might know them, at least with the Lodovica interview. I don't think I'll take that approach at the school. Either way, the information revealed will give Neil what he needs to either move forward or continue to watch."

"Fucking brilliant." The whole thing.

"Thank you."

"I have another question."

"Shoot."

"Who pays Neil? Is the German board of education or—"

"No one," Jax cut him off. "I suppose if he needed help funding this assignment or anything to do with Richter, Sasha would kick in. But none of what we do in this situation is sanctioned by any authority. Richter is personal. To him . . . to Sasha."

"To you and Claire."

"Yes."

"Another question. What happens if you're caught with a fake passport?"

Jax laughed. "First of all, I don't have one of those on me right now. Second, that has never happened . . . Third . . ." She paused and took a deep breath. "In the six years I've worked with Neil, I've determined the man knows someone everywhere. Powerful someones. Bending a few laws to pull shitty people out of circulation is worth the risk of a free ride to the police station while Neil works to get you out. And no, that has never happened to me."

Andrew couldn't help but laugh. "I've always been told to avoid the back of a police car, but you make it sound like an honor."

She giggled. "I can spin anything if you give me enough time."

"You know . . . I thought you were intriguing when I picked you up at the airport. But I didn't realize the level of badass until today."

Jax placed a hand to her chest. "Flattery will get you everywhere."

"Now you're just teasing me," he said, laughing. Although he did notice there was only a king-size bed in the room.

She pushed out of the chair. "Today is an easy day. Not a lot of looking over our shoulders. We go out, I make a couple of phone calls to arrange a visit at the prison for tomorrow, and we do some sightseeing."

"And Sven?"

"We meet up at dinner. He has his own assignment today. But after the prison visit, he is always close, even if we can't see him."

Andrew rubbed his hands together. "All right, let's get the smoke and mirrors going, then."

"You're entirely too enthusiastic."

"Hey, I sit behind a desk all day determining projections on what the markets are going to do so my clients have a retirement. This covert mission is the stuff of unrealized childhood dreams."

"Calm down, Double-Oh-Seven. It isn't going to be that exciting."

Andrew cringed. "Don't pop my bubble."

Thirty minutes later they were headed out of the hotel, holding hands and ready to explore the city.

CHAPTER NINETEEN

With the phone calls and work put aside for the day, Jax and Andrew sat at an outdoor café in Gendarmenmarkt. They were sharing a bottle of white wine and enjoying the warm weather.

"This is what I miss about being away from Europe," she announced.

"Outdoor dining?"

"No, there is plenty of that in California, but not this." Jax waved a hand at the Berlin concert hall in the center of the square and the churches flanking it. The space itself dated back to the late 1600s, the historic building constructed in the 1700s and then completely refurbished after the damage from World War II. "The grandeur of old buildings and history that is preserved. America tends to tear down her history to make room for new and modern."

"I've been to California, there are a few places that offer a walk through time."

"Europe simply has more."

"It should. We've been around longer." He took a sip of his wine and set the glass down. "I like the fact that you're falling in love."

Jax snapped her attention Andrew's way. "I'm what . . ."

"With Europe," he added with a grin.

"Phew . . ." She blew out a breath. "Don't scare me like that."

Andrew leaned back, confidence written all over his face. "Are you afraid of that?"

"Falling in love?"

"With a person, not a place," he clarified.

"Hard to be afraid of something you've never experienced. What about you? Have you been in love?" She sat forward, played with the stem of her wineglass.

"I thought I was once. My last year in college."

"What happened?"

"Once the routine of classes was over and real life kicked in, we stopped working. It wasn't ugly . . . it just wasn't."

"Did she live with you?"

He shook his head. "Less than a suitcase full of things in my flat."

"I haven't even made it that far. The last man I dated was a lawyer . . . finishing law school, actually. My parents would have loved him."

"But you didn't."

She cringed. "No. He didn't respect my work or my decision to live without my parents' financial help."

"What did work?"

"Honestly?"

"Yeah."

"The sex was good."

Andrew started laughing, eased a bit . . . and laughed harder. "I somehow knew you were going to say that."

She sighed. "But . . . like anything, sex isn't enough, and we moved on."

"I'm glad it didn't work out," Andrew said.

Jax found his statement funny. "If my work doesn't scare you off . . . or my family drama, we might be good."

"Your job is crazy and the people you work with are beyond intense."

That didn't sound positive to her ears.

"But I'm in anyway."

"And if the sex is bad?"

Andrew sat forward, reached for her hand. "I don't think we're going to have to worry about that."

She moved closer, squeezed his fingers the way he was touching hers. "Is that cockiness or confidence I hear?"

"I'll let you tell me."

Yup, yup . . . and yup. Her body woke up with the hunger she saw in his gaze.

After kissing her hand, he reached for the bottle of wine and topped off both their glasses. "What do you want to do with the rest of the day?"

She had a couple of ideas.

Really good ideas.

Instead of revealing the images she had passing through her brain, they finished their wine and toured one of the two churches in the square.

They walked around the city, popped into a few stores, and shared one of those giant pretzels the Germans were known for.

When they passed two street performers, one playing a violin and the other a cello, Andrew pulled Jax into his arms and started to dance.

"What are you doing?" she asked, teasing.

"Shhh, I'm counting."

The small crowd on the street gave them room, and another couple, this one much older, joined the dancing.

"Look what you started."

"You have to make the most of live music when you hear it."

Jax relaxed in his hold and followed his lead. "You're pretty good at this." And he was. "Who taught you to dance?"

"My sister."

"Really?"

He spun her around, brought her back, this time closer. "I overheard her and her friends complaining that the boys at school would get a lot more dates if they learned to dance."

"She wasn't wrong."

"I know. I, being the smart child that I was, decided having an older sister was going to pay off."

Jax placed a hand on his chest and looked into his eyes. "Did it?"

The music came to an end, and those standing around started to clap.

"You tell me."

Caught in the moment, Jax relaxed in his arms as he brought his lips to hers. Through the cloud of his kiss, she heard the sound of someone whistling and a few claps added to the mix. Before the kiss became anything more than PG-13, Andrew pulled away.

He reached into his back pocket, removed a couple of bills from his wallet, and dropped them in the street musicians' bucket.

With his arm over her shoulders, they walked back toward the hotel.

"What are you thinking for dinner?" he asked. "Casual, nice . . . a nightclub with bar food?"

"That all sounds very tempting."

"You have a different idea?"

Keeping her eyes on the street in front of them, and without missing a beat, she said, "Room service."

Andrew walked faster.

Jax chuckled under her breath.

"It was the dancing, wasn't it?" he asked.

"Dance moves always fire me up."

He eased his pace and glanced her way. "You continue to surprise me."

"Let's circle back to that in the morning."

Andrew made a sound in the back of his throat and kept silent the rest of the way to the hotel.

They both smiled politely at the staff greeting them.

Jax wasn't sure if it was nerves or excitement, but her stomach started to twist in an anticipation she hadn't felt in some time. She knew when she agreed to having Andrew along on this trip that solidifying a physical relationship with the man was a foregone conclusion. At least for her.

She'd noticed him looking at the solo bed in the room, one she'd changed from two doubles to a king when she'd checked the reservations Neil made. Andrew had glanced at the bed, and she sensed his need to ask questions. Jax diverted that conversation and hit him with everything they were about to embark upon with her investigation. Instead of downplaying her role, or shying away from what his would be, he was excited.

That was rare.

The men she'd dated in the past either couldn't care less or felt emasculated in her presence.

Not Andrew. From the moment they met, he listened. More importantly, he heard her, understood, and asked questions. No one outside of Claire and the team did that in her life.

Even her family, although that seemed to be changing with her mother.

Jax was more than ready to take whatever they were doing to the next level. Curiosity about his confidence and cockiness did play a small part in skipping a formal dinner.

Inside the elevator he pressed the button for their floor, and when another couple jumped in at the last second, she heard him moan.

Jax attempted to hide her laugh and felt him squeeze the hand he hadn't let loose.

They waited through the extra stop.

Andrew pressed the close door button several times to prompt the elevator to respond faster. Only once they were approaching their room did he slow his pace.

He opened the door and waited for her to go in before him.

The door closed and the room grew silent.

She turned to find him looking at her, lips parted, his chest moving faster with every breath he took. The desire in his eyes was for her . . . all her.

Her purse dropped to the floor.

They both reached for each other at the same time.

His kiss boiled from the second they met. There was nothing shy about it . . . no sweet display in the town square for people to look upon and wistfully sigh. This was hunger, desire, and need all coiled up in a tight, combustible ball.

Andrew brought his hands to her face and kissed her so deeply she couldn't think.

She ran her hands down his chest, past his hips, and back up again. Jax playfully nibbled at his lip as he pulled away.

"I should be ashamed of all the thoughts rolling through my head right now," he said as he pulled her hair just enough to expose her neck to his kiss.

"Let's do those things and I'll tell you later if you should feel ashamed."

His teeth grazed the side of her neck as one hand fell to the small of her back and molded her to his frame.

"Brilliant idea."

He took hold of her hips and lifted her up.

Jax wrapped her legs around him.

His erection pushed against her clothing in all the right places as Andrew walked them to the bed and pressed her into the mattress. Her breath shuddered as sensation traveled through her body in one hot wave.

Andrew took delight in her reaction and pressed against her again.

She squirmed, dug her fingernails into his shoulders. "You're too good at this," she told him.

He muttered something she didn't catch, and his lips found hers again, gentler this time, but no less hungry. Jax explored the hard planes of his body as he filled one of his palms with her breast. Releasing her lips, he put enough space between them to pull her shirt over her head. "Incredible," he murmured.

His lips moved to where his hands had been, pushing the lace of her bra aside to touch more. Jax felt her nipples tighten, his bite just sharp enough to please.

She managed to toe her shoes off and tug his shirt out of his pants, but there wasn't enough of him touching her. Skin . . . she needed the man's skin on hers. "Too many clothes."

"The minute the clothes are off, I'm in you," he warned.

"That's the point, England."

He laughed and ran his hand down her flat belly, dipped under her pants, and grazed just a fraction of an inch shy of where she wanted him.

She lifted her hips and he pulled away.

"You're doing that on purpose."

"I." He kissed her stomach.

"Am." He unbuttoned her slacks.

Then he slid off the bed altogether.

Jax opened her eyes to see him tug his shirt off his back, kick off his shoes, and unbutton his pants.

She waited for the rest of the striptease, but he didn't deliver . . . Instead he moved back to her side and wiggled her pants from her body.

In a quick movement, Jax removed her bra and tossed it next to her forgotten shirt.

In nothing but a tiny pair of panties, she lifted one knee and curved her finger his way. "C'mere," she coaxed.

Andrew removed his wallet from his pocket, fished a condom from it, and put it on the side table.

"I'm on birth control," she revealed.

He placed both of his hands on her ankles and pulled her where he wanted her on the bed. "Good. You're going to need it."

That made her laugh. "Prove it."

With his hands tracing her legs, pushing at her knees when he got there, he said, "Oh, I will."

Jax leaned back and closed her eyes when Andrew's intentions became perfectly clear.

Warm breath touched the space between her thighs and her hips. Andrew's fingers coaxed the only clothing she had on to the side, and he was there. Exactly where she needed him. Lips and tongue, pressure and teeth . . . and holy hell he was good at this.

Jax lifted her hips to get closer only to pull back with the intensity he was bringing.

She felt his laughter more than she heard it. A vibration against the tight bundle of nerves at the apex of her thighs.

Her orgasm was coming too fast and too hard, and the more she tried to hold it off, the more Andrew surged in as if telling her he was the one controlling this and she was going there even if she didn't want to.

Just when she thought the intensity was fading, he did something, she couldn't even say exactly what, and she lost all control. Lightning-hot orgasm to end all orgasms that rolled through her in pulsating waves and left her dizzy.

"Holy shit," she whispered when she could talk again. Her eyes opened and Andrew was moving away, his smile radiant.

"Now that I know what you sound like . . . let me do it again."

He dropped his pants to the floor and reached for the condom.

The man was blessed, and preparing her had been the right call.

True to his word, his clothes came off and he crawled over her asking for entry.

"Kiss me," she said, as he pushed inside.

∼

Andrew met room service at the door, thanked them, but didn't let them in.

Wearing a bathrobe and a smile, he pushed the rolling cart into the room as Jax emerged from the bathroom. She crawled back in bed, bundled up in a matching robe, and pulled her long hair behind her shoulders.

"I'm starving."

He started with the wine, worked the cork free. "Considering all we've had today was breakfast on the plane, a bottle of wine, and a pretzel, I'm not surprised."

"There were olives and nuts with the wine."

"That's practically a meal. I completely forgot."

He poured the wine and handed her a glass.

She brought her lips to it, and he was lost in watching her. The softness in her face, kindness in her eyes . . . her unabashed zest for life. Making love to her had been a privilege like nothing he'd been blessed with before. Watching her now, sipping wine and wearing his scent, stirred something inside him he wasn't ready for. Or more accurately, wasn't expecting.

"You're staring," she said.

"I like the view."

She stared back, and her cheeks started to glow.

With a shake of his head, Andrew returned to their dinner. He rolled the cart to the side of the bed so Jax didn't have to leave her perch. He pulled a chair closer and sat on the opposite side.

"This was an excellent idea," she announced as she bit into a piece of bread.

"I've never been so happy to eat room service food in my life." Andrew tested the wine, was surprised at how good it was.

Jax closed her eyes and savored her first bite of the steaks they'd ordered. "I needed this. After that."

"Steak after sex, not a cigarette. My kind of woman."

She washed it down with the wine. "Tell me. Why hasn't anyone dragged you to the altar yet?"

Her question surprised him. "What?"

"You heard me. I mean . . ." She paused, blew out a breath. "You're sexy, fit, have a great job. You're witty and smart and not too full of yourself. You make love like a . . ."

Andrew held his breath, waiting.

"Never mind."

"No, no . . . you can't stop there."

"I can stop there because I'm not sure of the words to use to describe it."

As egos went, he felt his expanding to the size of the room. "Good words, I hope."

Jax rolled her eyes, cut into another bite of her steak. "If I say too much, your head will be too big to fit through the door."

She didn't have to say anything. Her cries when he tipped her over the edge did all the talking.

"I'm single for the same reason you are," he said.

Their eyes met.

He elaborated. "I hadn't met someone who I wanted to share my last first kiss with. Someone who is beautiful inside and out, funny and smart, and keeps surprising me . . ." He had to stop. The words he kept wanting to say described her.

As true as they felt, it was way too soon for any of that.

Jax kept staring before finally lowering her eyes to her plate. "If Mr. Lawyer made love like you do, it would have been a lot harder to walk away. That's all I'm going to say."

Andrew grinned, took a bite. A few seconds later, he told her, "I'm glad Mr. Lawyer fell short."

Jax's eyes grew big. "Me too."

CHAPTER TWENTY

The women's prison sat just north of Berlin's city limits. From the outside it didn't look a whole lot different from the surrounding buildings. There weren't electric fences or guard towers with uniformed correctional officers holding rifles on the inmates below. The Germans believed in and practiced rehabilitation with the incarcerated. And when it came to the female population, that became incredibly evident when you passed through the doors of the prison.

There were guards at the door that Jax identified because of the badges they wore, not because of how they were dressed.

The sound of children laughing filtered through the building, echoing in Jax's ears.

She'd done her research before walking in the door.

Linette Lodovica, former headmistress of Richter, was housed in a facility that resembled a community. Eight hours a day the inmates were mandated to work in one form or another. Mothers with small children could have their kids with them in the prison, so long as they followed the rules and didn't reoffend at any point while incarcerated. It was because of the children at the prison that the guards wore normal clothing and the space itself didn't have locking gates and barred cells. The rooms resembled small apartments, or dorm rooms like those at Richter.

Jax found it ironic that Lodovica left one contained building and life for a similar, albeit smaller, situation. One where she could not leave.

Her days in prison were numbered, however. The charges against her had been dumbed down to assault and false imprisonment with a sprinkling of coercion. Even those were hard for the prosecutors to prove, considering very few parents were willing to stand in court against her. Her dealings with Pohl would have pulled a bigger punch, but the man's own testimony was never heard due to his untimely death.

While Jax wouldn't mind knowing the truth behind the man's demise, she wasn't about to poke around, in light of the fact she knew people who would have had no trouble squeezing the trigger behind that scope.

Jax moved through a metal detector and went through the process of showing her identification and the papers approving an inmate visit.

A locker was provided for her purse and cell phone. She was allowed to bring in a pen and notebook, both of which were inspected before she was escorted to another room. The rules were given to her a second time. There would not be a wall between the two of them, no phones to talk through. A table would separate them, but no physical contact could be made. Fine with Jax, it wasn't as if she wanted to hug the woman. It was well past thirty minutes before Jax was escorted in to see Lodovica.

The visitation room housed several tables, a few of them occupied. Even with the inmates wearing normal clothes, not a government-issued blue jumpsuit, or orange, as depicted in many places, it was easy to separate the visitors from the residents.

Jax sat observing her surroundings as she waited for Lodovica to be brought in. As prisons went, this didn't feel like the hardship it was supposed to be.

One of the guards walked through a door with the former head-mistress beside her.

She'd aged.

Yes, it had been seven years since Jax had seen the woman, but she looked decades older.

The hair that had always been pulled back was now cropped short, just above her shoulders. More salt than pepper said that even if the woman could wear a normal pair of pants and a blouse, there wasn't a hair salon on site. She had always been thin, but Jax had most often seen her in a robe like that of a judge. A distinction of honor in her position as headmistress. Seeing her in plain clothes felt awkward.

Lodovica's eyes came in contact with Jax, and she hesitated.

For a split second, Jax worried the woman was going to walk away. No one was telling her she couldn't.

Jax held her breath and released it when Lodovica stepped closer and took her seat.

"Hello," Jax began.

"I was surprised to hear you wanted to see me. I half expected Claire or Sasha to be in this seat."

Jax softened her smile and reminded herself that in order to reach her goal of obtaining information from the woman, she needed to appear friendly.

"Sasha's enjoying her life in America with her husband."

"Yes, I'd heard she'd gotten married."

"You did? Who told you?" An innocent question.

Lodovica shook her head. "It doesn't matter. It pleases me that she found happiness."

"Claire just got engaged. We're planning her wedding." A little information to help Lodovica feel unthreatened.

"That I had not heard. I'm happy for them. Truly."

Jax lowered her eyes. "Miss Lodovica . . . Headmistress . . . I don't know what to call you." That was the honest truth. Headmistress Lodovica was how she'd addressed the woman from the moment she met her. Granted, as a student, she and the others had many names for the school disciplinarian, but none of them were favorable.

"Linette is fine, Jacqueline. I am no longer a headmistress and don't deserve a formal title in light of where we are sitting."

"How is it here?"

"That's not why you came to see me."

"No, but it is intriguing, isn't it?" Jax glanced around the room again, and purposely started to fidget.

"Jacqueline."

She offered a shy smile. "My parents have separated."

"That's unfortunate."

"I'm not really sure that they will stay that way . . . not that . . ." Jax purposely stuttered and hesitated. "I know about my father's affair."

Lodovica didn't so much as blink at the information.

"You don't seem surprised."

"I didn't know your parents well."

"But you knew their secrets."

She stayed silent, her eyes fixed without emotion.

"You knew a lot of secrets."

"Not as many as you may think."

Jax didn't believe that for a second.

With a forced smile, she tried a new angle. "Richter did teach me so many valuable things. I don't regret any of it."

"That's always nice to hear."

"It's because of that education that I know there is more to my father's infidelity than meets the eye. I know about the files, Miss Lodovica."

She looked away briefly, then back. Her lips remained sealed.

"I can't imagine you'd know everything that was in them, but if I knew who obtained the information, perhaps I could trace their steps and find out for myself what my father is hiding."

"Ask him."

"He won't answer."

"You're here for a name I do not have."

"Was it you who learned the secrets needed to keep the parents in line?"

"No."

"Then who? Brigitte?"

The mention of Lodovica's former lover brought a frown to the woman's face.

"She was guilty of many things, but spying on families was not one of them. You're seeking information I cannot give you."

"Won't," Jax corrected her.

Silence spread between them.

She lowered her voice. "My father's indiscretion was more than a drunken shag on a weekend away from home. I feel that here." Jax placed a hand on her chest. "Something about the whole thing feels dangerous to me. I would think a woman who professed to be sorry for her crimes would be willing to offer some help in stopping more pain for one of her students."

"I cannot help you, Jacqueline."

Jax narrowed her eyes.

She didn't truly expect the woman to answer differently, but that wasn't going to stop her from trying.

Jax lifted a hand to the guard and waited until she approached. With the notebook and pen, she wrote her name and phone number, handed it to the guard. "You can check it against the contact information provided. I'd like her to have this."

The guard looked at her notes and handed the paper to Lodovica.

Jax stood. "You have less than a year left. What will you do when you're out?"

Lodovica slowly brought her eyes to meet Jax's. "Mind my own business."

"That's safe, isn't it?"

"Give my regards to Sasha. Congratulations to Claire."

"I will." Though neither of them would appreciate it.

"And what about your wedding? Weren't you engaged?"

For a second Jax went blank, then she remembered her last trip to Richter. "That didn't work out."

"The next one, then."

Jax smiled, looked at the paper in Lodovica's hand. "If you remember anything."

She folded the paper, placed it in a pocket, and pushed her chair back. "Goodbye, Jacqueline."

"Good day." Not goodbye. Because as far as Jax was concerned, she'd see the woman again. The question was when.

~

In the movies, 007 was always a man and the busty blonde was the one on the sidelines waiting for the danger to pass while the man did the hard work.

How Andrew had become the busty blonde in this scenario was beyond him.

Jax had been inside the prison for nearly an hour. Each minute ticked by with a glance at his watch and a tap of his fingertips.

What the hell was taking so long?

He reminded himself that she'd walked into a public building . . . or at least a secure one, but the nature of Jax's work started to register when she wasn't in his presence.

It scared him, if he were being honest. From the things he'd heard to what he had seen so far, he knew she put herself in places with dangerous people.

Like the prison she was in right now.

Andrew leaned against the rental car, arms folded, staring at where Jax would walk out. He was tempted to go in and ask if she was okay.

When she finally emerged from the building, a weight slid off his shoulders like snow off a tin roof.

She picked up her pace as she made her way across the parking lot. "How did it go?"

"Better than I thought."

"She gave you a name?"

"No. Absolutely not."

He was confused. "How is that 'better than you thought'?"

Jax glanced over her shoulder. "Let's talk about it on the way back to the hotel."

He pulled out of the parking lot, and in the privacy of the car and away from the prison, Jax started to explain.

"Lodovica said she didn't have a name, but she does have a name, she simply didn't want to give it up."

"That wouldn't be surprising since it could incriminate her."

"Yeah, I'd have been shocked if she blurted one out. There is someone, but that isn't the surprise. Someone at Richter is talking to her. And more than that, someone is keeping her up to date about her former students. Mainly Sasha, and likely Claire."

"How did you reach that conclusion?"

"Last year I returned to Richter on an assignment. I had a decoy fiancé on my arm. The headmistress asked about my fiancé. The only time I pretended to have one was the one day at Richter. And she knew about Sasha's marriage. Other than a piece of paper filed at a courthouse, there wasn't any announcement of their wedding. It's not a secret that they're married, but hearing that in a German prison when Sasha and AJ live in the States with only a few trips across the pond every year . . . and most of those on assignments where no one really knows about it . . . How did she hear that? But it was when she said she 'had not heard' about Claire's engagement that I knew she had to have a source."

Andrew caught on to Jax's enthusiasm. "Then the interview paid off."

"In spades. Now we have a new lead to follow. Who is delivering information to Lodovica and why? How? We need the records of who has visited her, who she gets calls from."

"Is that public information?"

"I'm not sure if just anyone can access the information, but there is a record. Phone calls might be a little more difficult to find out. Especially if someone smuggled in a burner phone."

"A burner what?" The reference tickled the back of his mind, but he wasn't putting the pieces together.

Jax didn't answer, she just shook her head. "I doubt that. Too risky this close to her release, and really, what would be the urgent need for one?"

Andrew drove as Jax worked the details out loud. "What next?"

"I need to call this in. Get video on the prison, eyes if nothing else, especially after you and I go to Richter."

"Do prisons like being spied on?"

She started to laugh. "There are over seven hundred million surveillance cameras planted around the globe. Granted, a huge majority of them are in China, but over six hundred thousand live in London. And those are just the ones we know about. Last time I looked, Berlin was home to sixteen thousand, so if the prisons don't like being spied on, they need to move to remote parts of the country where no one is nicking bags on the streets."

"You're serious." He had no idea.

"Dead serious. Most of the time we want information, it's as simple as tapping into the system already in place."

"Is that legal?"

"Public street. If you damage property, I suppose there might be a law broken, but most of the time the recordings are in the cloud and not difficult to tap into."

"Tap or hack."

"Yes," she said with a little laugh. "Here's the thing. I always assume someone is watching. Probably because I've been on the watching end for quite some time. The foundation of Neil's company is security. And one of the ways you stay on top of that is to hire people that are good at getting past it. Ask a car thief their go-tos for stealing your shit and you figure out ways of protecting said shit. We learn ways to hack into systems and work to foolproof ours."

"Makes sense."

"Tapping or hacking . . . call it whatever you want. It was Richter that taught me those things. Anyway . . . clearly Lodovica has been watching and will know she's being watched, so we'll have to do so quietly. The real question is, Why has she been keeping tabs on us?"

"It was Neil's team that put her behind bars."

Jax nodded a few times. "That might very well be all there is to it. Her motivation won't become clear until she does something with the information. We're here poking the hive. If someone doesn't like that, we're likely to find out."

He turned down the street of their hotel. "Let me know when I need to start looking over my shoulder."

"That started the moment we got off the plane, but certainly now that we've been seen at the prison."

"I didn't go inside."

"Seven hundred million known global cameras, England."

"Makes me think twice about scratching my ass in public."

She laughed and removed her cell phone from her purse. "I'm inviting Sven to our room. We have things to go over and we want to be seen with him as little as possible."

He swiped his room key to access the parking garage and glanced over his shoulder. "You know what?"

Jax looked at him, the phone to her ear. "What?"

"You're bloody sexy when you talk all this spy stuff."

She pursed her lips, blew him a kiss. "Wait until I put on a disguise."

He looked forward to that.

CHAPTER
TWENTY-ONE

"I need you in Germany. Tonight."

He stretched his long legs up onto the window frame and felt the familiar burn in his gut. The call was both welcomed and feared. "This is your last token."

"Good thing the target is familiar."

"Who?"

"Details are in the vault in Berlin."

The line went dead.

He took one last drag off his cigarette and dropped his feet to the floor.

Freedom came at a cost.

A high cost.

~

The following day Jax and Andrew vacated the room at the hotel in Berlin for much smaller accommodations in a town closer to Richter.

Sven booked a room at an adjacent inn and arrived thirty minutes ahead of them.

According to Sasha, a local bar had been a good source of information when she'd needed some in the past. So instead of going directly to Richter, Jax and Andrew were taking the slow route in hopes of intercepting current faculty.

Out in the country, unlike in Berlin, the ability to speak English to nearly everyone diminished.

The proprietor of the inn was an older woman by the name of Hazel. Her smile offered nearly a full set of teeth, but was kind nonetheless.

Jax did all the talking since it appeared the woman didn't speak English. "We have a reservation under Simon," Jax said in German.

The woman looked at her log. "A king suite for you and your husband."

"My boyfriend," Jax corrected.

Hazel looked at Jax's hand, then narrowed her eyes at Andrew. "Then two rooms."

"One room is fine."

She didn't look up. "Two rooms for the unmarried couple."

Catching on, Jax placed her hand on the counter, shifted an occasional ring from her right hand to her left ring finger. "One room for me and my fiancé."

"What's going on?" Andrew asked beside her.

Jax clenched her teeth and whispered, "She won't rent us a single room if we're not married."

Andrew chuckled.

Hazel smiled. "The honeymoon suite for the couple who are here to elope."

Jax had to hand it to the woman; she satisfied her own beliefs with a lie and at the same time overcharged them for the room they requested.

After they signed the room agreement and gave the woman a credit card, Hazel pulled an actual key from a slot behind her. "I will show you your room."

With Andrew schlepping the bags up the stairs, the three of them walked single file up the narrow staircase to the third floor. "This inn has been in my family for two generations. I have eight rooms. The best one for you."

"How many guests are here now?" Jax asked.

"Only one other room is taken. This is a slow time of year. We have wine and cheese at four. Beer for your husband."

Jax glanced over her shoulder with a grin. Poor Andrew.

"In the morning, coffee and a light offering in the main room."

She stopped on the top floor and opened one of only two rooms taking up the space.

Again, Jax found herself surprised.

The room was as beautiful as you would expect at a boutique hotel in a more affluent area but at three times the cost. The vaulted ceiling and windows dotting an entire wall gave the room space and light. An oversized four-poster king bed sat in the center. A wardrobe stood to one side, a dressing table and small sofa rounding out the amenities. "You have a balcony. No smoking in my inn."

"We don't smoke," Jax announced.

"Wow, this is nice," Andrew said.

"Beautiful."

Hazel handed Andrew the key and turned to continue talking to Jax in German. "I used to have a restaurant downstairs, but it became too much after my husband passed. You will find we have a few in town, and two pubs for you younger kids."

"I'm sorry about your husband."

Hazel shrugged. "His own fault. He smoked."

Jax tried to cover a laugh.

"I'll leave you alone."

"Thank you."

Andrew said thank you in German, and Hazel winked before walking out the door.

Jax started laughing as soon as the door closed. "That woman is something else."

"We're married?"

"Boyfriend wasn't good enough, but she settled for fiancé en route to our elopement." Jax waved her left hand in the air. "Nice ring."

"I can do better than that," he said.

Jax crossed to the balcony and opened the French doors. The view faced the street, but the back of the room exposed the inn's garden and greenbelt beyond the fence. "There is only one other room occupied."

"That's a good thing?"

"Easier to see who belongs and who doesn't." Jax removed her cell phone and texted Sven.

Top floor facing the street.

It took only a few seconds for him to respond. Nice balcony.

She put a thumb in the air and walked back into the room, closing the doors.

"Was that Sven?"

"Yup." Out of habit, if nothing else, Jax removed her bug-finding device and turned it on.

Andrew followed her for a few seconds. "Why don't you show me how that works so I can take something off your shoulders."

Jax looked his way. "You just want to play with my toys."

Andrew walked close, mischief all over his face.

His hands reached around her, and both palms cupped the globes of her butt.

She giggled and tried to squirm away.

He held on tighter.

"You're making this difficult."

"I'm achieving my goal." He lifted her up and started walking around the room.

"What are you—"

"I'm helping."

With her legs wrapped around his waist, and one hand on his neck, she moved her device with half an eye on the monitor as Andrew waltzed around the room.

"You're nuts."

"You told that lady we were married, and I'm nuts?"

"Engaged."

He moved to the bed, plopped her down, and crawled on top of her.

Jax dropped the monitor on the side of the bed. No one knew they were there . . . yet.

Andrew kissed the side of her neck. "Can I play with your toys?" he asked.

She crossed her ankles behind his hips and squeezed her thighs. "Only if you let me play with yours."

~

They started their evening at four with Hazel in what she called the main room. The oversized living room had double doors that opened to the inn's garden. Like the rest of the inn, the room felt cozy and welcoming, the kind of place that Jax could see herself relaxing in for an entire weekend with nothing but a good book and a little sunshine.

Hazel brought in a tray of cheeses, nuts, and berries. She handed a bottle of white wine and a corkscrew to Andrew without saying a word.

"Does he want beer?" she asked Jax.

Jax translated.

Andrew shook his head. "This is fine."

Hazel nodded her understanding and left the room.

"This feels more like a bed-and-breakfast than an inn," Jax said.

"Makes me want to learn German and come here more often."

"We never stopped in this town, just drove by on the way to the train station or airport."

"You didn't come here with the other students?" He released the cork and looked around the room.

"I thought you were paying attention. We weren't allowed to leave Richter."

"Even when you were older?"

"No, a day pass was only granted when a parent or family member requested it."

Andrew stood and moved about the room. "Sounds like a prison."

"What are you doing?"

He lifted the bottle. "Unless Ms. Hazel wants us to drink out of the bottle, we need glasses."

The words no sooner left his lips than Ms. Hazel returned with a tray holding several glasses.

"Danke," Andrew managed.

She put the tray down in front of him and took a seat.

"I was telling Andrew that your inn is simply stunning," Jax told her in German.

"It is a lot of work."

Andrew poured a glass and handed it to Jax.

Hazel pushed an empty one his way and waited patiently.

It might be Ms. Hazel's inn, but she didn't do all the waiting on people.

Being a good sport, Andrew poured her a glass as well before taking care of himself.

"Your man is tall," she said after tipping back her wine.

"He is." Jax grinned, looking at Andrew. "She's commenting on how tall you are."

"Should I thank her?"

Hazel put her glass down and walked out of the room.

"Did I offend her?"

Jax shrugged. "I don't think so."

"Strange. I wonder if the other guests will come down."

She hoped so. It would be nice to see who was in the inn with them. But even if they didn't, Sven would likely notice someone coming and going. By now he'd set up a camera to keep an eye on the place when he wasn't there himself. "If there's no one by five, we'll head out."

"Sounds good—"

Hazel returned to the room. In one hand she had a box of what looked like light bulbs, in another, a step stool. She looked directly at Andrew and lifted the step stool toward him.

"I'm too short to reach. Your fiancé will have no problem."

The stunned look on Andrew's face was priceless. "She needs me to change a light bulb?"

Jax laughed. "She's asking quite nicely."

Andrew took a drink, set his glass down, and pushed off the sofa. "Okay, guess I'm fixing the inn."

Jax followed behind, glass of wine in her hand, as Hazel led the way.

"This is a first," he said over his shoulder.

"It's hysterical."

Hazel stopped in a hall leading to the kitchen and pointed.

A small chandelier hanging from the ceiling had two burned-out lights.

Andrew set up the stool and stepped up. One by one he replaced the lights.

"You're a good sport, England."

"This will be one of those things we talk about for years." He stepped down, folded the stool, and turned back to the main room.

Hazel made a clicking noise and nodded her head in another direction.

Jax coughed to cover her laugh.

Hazel walked with Andrew in tow and by the time the inn was all aglow, he'd replaced over a dozen lights in various rooms.

They knew he was done when Hazel took the stool from his hand, said thank you, and quickly walked away.

"Should I ask her if she has any leaky pipes?" he asked.

Jax looped her arm in his as they walked back to the wine and cheese. "Do you know how to fix a leaky pipe?"

"Something tells me my lack of knowledge wouldn't matter."

"Well . . . we aren't married, and she is looking the other way."

"What century is she living in?"

"Hers."

They both laughed.

Twenty minutes later, after Hazel retrieved her wine and left them alone, it became apparent they were not going to be joined by anyone else at the inn.

As they were leaving, Jax felt the need to tell their hostess they were going out.

Hazel shrugged, said the town was quiet and they'd be back early.

They walked into a predetermined restaurant, saw Sven sitting at his own table, and ignored him as they walked by.

The waitress spoke enough English to make polite conversation while taking their order.

"What drives the economy in a town like this?" Andrew asked.

"Richter plays a part. At least in housing some of the staff and then taking care of their needs. We passed the town that brings in food and does the laundry service."

"There's more to a school than food and towels."

"You're right, there's guns and ammunition and doctors on staff to treat injuries brought on by hand-to-hand combat."

"How much of that is still in play?"

"My senior year they removed all the weapons. They tried to hide it from the authorities, but the younger kids do what young kids do. They tell the truth. The school was put on a probation of sorts while it applied to reinstate weapons training."

"Did they get their permits?"

"Permission, yes. With the help of legitimate sources that recruit Richter students. But now they are limited to upperclassmen."

"How do they define *upperclassmen*?"

"Sixteen and up. And it isn't mandatory. At least the last time we checked."

"That's fair, I suppose."

Another couple was seated beside them, drying up the candid Richter conversation. Jax had already prompted Andrew on how the night would go.

She would talk of Richter just as any former student returning to visit her alma mater might, leaving out the extra information she knew only because of her position with Neil's team.

"The only boarding school I would ever consider for my children is Richter," she said loud enough to be overheard.

"I'm not sold," Andrew said. "You've talked a lot about it and not everything sounded remotely safe."

"There isn't a safer school. I know, I was there."

"My boarding school has incredibly high marks. And it's closer to home."

"How many languages do you speak again?"

"Two."

Jax faked a laugh, looked over his shoulder, and noticed the woman looking away. In French, she said. "My French is better than yours and I only took eighteen months of study."

"My French not bad," Andrew managed in French.

"Three years of French and he forgets the verb," Jax said, this time in German, her smile sickeningly sweet.

The man with his back to Andrew coughed.

"Now you're just showing off," Andrew teased.

Jax leaned forward, grasped his hands. "Just have an open mind when we visit tomorrow. It's important to me."

"I'm here, aren't I?"

Their meal arrived and they changed the subject.

~

The picture in his hand was tattered from the sheer number of times it had been unearthed from a hidden space sewn into his clothing.

She was eight now.

Innocent and beautiful, just like her mother.

Dark eyes, olive skin . . . what he wouldn't give to see her, even from afar.

He didn't dare take the risk.

One more assignment . . .

A few years to make it stick . . .

He kissed the picture, returned it . . . and peered through the binoculars at his target.

~

Andrew was getting better at this.

An hour later they sat in a pub, repeating the same conversation with a different set of people close enough to hear. The only difference was that Jax was making it look like she'd had a pint too many. She spoke a little louder, laughed longer, and touched him more in public than she had at any other time.

Finally, after what felt like hours, Jax recognized someone who walked through the door.

"Professor Müller," she announced quietly. "Tall, late forties, early fifties, dark hair, walked in with a woman in a green jacket."

Andrew slowly turned toward the door, looked over his shoulder. "What did he teach?"

"Russian. Mandarin, too, if I remember right. I just didn't take that."

"I honestly can't imagine that many languages rolling around in my head."

"Claire would know."

"She speaks Mandarin?"

Jax wasn't interested in answering his question. She leaned forward like she was going to kiss him. "I'm walking to the bathroom. When I return, I will 'notice' him and invite myself to their table and wave you over. Bring the drinks and follow my lead."

"You're the boss." Andrew kissed her before she left his side.

He lifted his beer and took a drink.

A stranger behind him tapped his shoulder. "Hey."

"Hello?"

"You know she's making fun of how you speak French," the man told him.

Andrew smiled, glanced toward the path she'd just used to walk away. "When you look like that, you can get away with just about anything."

The guy laughed, nodded. "You're right about that. You're a lucky man."

"I'll remind her of that later."

Andrew started to turn back around, hesitated. "Is my French really that bad?"

The guy shook his head. "How would I know? I don't speak French. She's giving you crap in German."

"I need to go back to school." With that, he turned around and awaited Jax's cue.

The music in the pub was a mix of pop hits in German and a few in English, which was easier on his ears. Straining to pick up words was more difficult than he cared to admit.

Out of the corner of his eye, he noticed Jax walking his way and then heard her voice above the noise in the room when she addressed her old teacher.

He waited to look up until he heard her calling his name.

Jax was waving her hand for him to come over.

He pushed his chair back, hesitated, then lifted his beer in the air. She nodded and he walked over.

"See, honey, I knew if we came in here someone from the school would eventually show up." Jax's smile was radiant.

"I see that. I hope we're not intruding," Andrew told the couple.

The professor's expression held no weight, but the woman he was with patted the table with a smile. "Of course not. I never have an opportunity to meet Noah's students."

"Professor Müller, Mrs. Müller, this is my . . . friend Andrew Craig. Professor Müller teaches Russian at Richter."

Andrew set the drinks down and reached out to shake the man's hand.

"Pleasure to meet you." The man's voice was even and, like his expression, devoid of feeling.

"The pleasure is mine. Jax has been talking nonstop about Richter. It will be nice to get someone else's opinion on the school."

"Noah's been teaching there for nearly thirteen years, I'm sure he can tell you what you need to know."

Andrew and Jax both sat. Jax pushed her chair closer to him and placed her hand over his on the table.

"I thought *friends* didn't sound quite right," Mrs. Müller said, looking at their hands with a grin.

Jax's smile grew. "Pay no attention to the ring. We're staying at the inn down the street. Ms. Hazel wouldn't rent us a single room."

"She's still doing that? Crafty woman."

"We think she's entertaining."

Andrew lifted Jax's hand, kissed the back of it. "The truth is, Jax won't let me talk about rings and tomorrows until I see what she wants for our children." This was the story they'd constructed, one that would be repeated when visiting Richter.

"*My* children. If you're not on board with that, I need to know now."

The professor finally spoke. "You want to send your children to Richter?"

Jax nodded. "I do. With all of Richter's interesting past, I still believe there is no greater education in the world. I would have stayed for my college years, but my parents weren't enthusiastic about the idea. Considering the drama my last year and the change in administration . . . you remember," she said to Noah.

"It was a challenging time."

"Which is why I'm not sold on it," Andrew told them.

"Professor Müller, please reassure him that Richter is safe, and the few bad apples have been pulled from the barrel."

That was when the professor attempted a smile. "If it wasn't safe, I wouldn't teach there."

As reassurances went, that one fell short.

"I told you." Jax squeezed Andrew's hand.

The couple looked at each other, and Mrs. Müller changed the subject. "Where did you go to college?"

"In California. I've only recently moved back. Before Andrew . . . I had another friend, an American . . . I brought him to Richter last year—"

"He didn't like it," Andrew interrupted.

"Americans don't understand boarding schools. It was appalling how little the first-year college students knew when I moved to the States. They could barely conjugate a verb in English, let alone another language." At that point Jax said something in Russian to the professor.

He replied and they both smiled.

225

"I'm sure that's an exaggeration."

"Yes, but the expectations were simply lower. I want my children to be able to handle themselves in a room full of educated people and feel safe walking down a dark street at night. I'm glad Richter transformed enough that the general public knows the military aspects of our education. I know people who have incredibly impressive employment after leaving Richter."

"Our alumni are highly sought after," the professor added.

"Thank you, Professor." Jax turned to Andrew. "See?"

"Your friend Claire doesn't feel the same."

"I'm telling you it changed after her senior year." Jax looked at her teacher again. "There aren't men like that Pohl person around anymore, right?"

A slight pause.

"I wasn't familiar with Mr. Pohl. And not party to anyone who encouraged his financial help with students."

Jax placed a hand on her chest. "Of course not. I hope you don't think I was suggesting you—"

Mrs. Müller tapped Jax's shoulder. "There were a lot of questions at that time. All the professors were under a microscope."

Noah sat forward, put both hands around the drink he had yet to taste while they'd been sitting there. "The institution has changed along with the administration, but the core values of Richter are still there. If you choose to send your children to Richter, they will have as bright a future as you do, Miss Simon."

With that, Jax lifted her glass in the air. "I can drink to that."

For the next thirty minutes, they kept the conversation out of the past of Richter and stayed on lighter topics. Jax glazed over the subject of her family life, alluding to some trouble she didn't want to talk about.

The professor lightened up a hair when Jax mentioned how she'd been hired by an undercover agency to help with a Russian crime ring, and how the language skills he had taught her were instrumental in her success.

By the time they left, Andrew had gone to the bar and paid for all their drinks. They both expressed their desire to see the professor the next day when they visited the school.

It was barely nine thirty and they were walking into the dimly lit inn, heading to their room. Once there, Jax walked around with her bug detector, checked out the space.

After she finished she started to talk. "You did pretty good tonight, England."

The truth is, he enjoyed himself completely. "Learning from the best."

Jax's phone buzzed. "It's Sven." She lifted the phone to her ear. "Yeah?"

Andrew shrugged off his light jacket and tossed it on a chair while Jax was on the phone.

"That was Professor Müller and his wife. Yup. Good. Okay. I'll buzz you in the morning." She hung up.

"Anyone following us?"

"Not that he saw."

Andrew sat on the end of the bed, removed his shoes. "Was he always that reserved?"

"Yes."

"Do you think he had knowledge of Pohl?"

Her sweater made it beside his jacket. "I'd like to think that the faculty that did know aren't there any longer. But I'm not that naive. I did get the feeling maybe he knew something about what might be happening now."

He sensed that, too.

"What now?"

"Nothing. We go to the school tomorrow, repeat the same mantra, see where it takes us."

"And if you feel something is going on?"

"Back to London. Reassess . . . recruit. I doubt we'll find a smoking gun tomorrow. We can hope someone will follow us, so Sven has a lead. This is the action part. The tedious part comes next."

"Which is?"

"Surveillance, research . . . background checking. Hours of computer time."

"In that respect, our jobs sound similar."

"I have better toys."

He reached for her. Brought her to stand in front of him. "Yes, you do."

Jax ran her hands through his hair. "Thank you for being here. It's not exactly a vacation—"

"People pay for mystery date nights. This is better."

She leaned down, kissed him. "It sure is. And one of us is on payroll."

"Score," he said as he pulled her down once again.

CHAPTER
TWENTY-TWO

It was a little like déjà vu.

Jax was returning to Richter, with a fake fiancé, looking for information.

Except this time, she made an appointment in an effort to be more visible. She wouldn't be trying to hide her true vocation, although she wouldn't volunteer any details. Any underclassman could do the legwork and determine who Jax worked for and where.

"You had guards at your gates?" Andrew asked after Jax had a brief conversation with said guard at said gate.

"Always."

Andrew looked around as they drove down the long, tree-lined drive. "Can't someone just jump the block wall?"

"Not without alarms going off." She glanced out the window. "I mean . . . it's been done, but not often. Sasha did it once when she was a student here. And again later, along with the team when they brought down Pohl and Lodovica."

They parked in the huge circular drive at the main entrance of Richter and emerged from the car together.

"It looks like a boarding school," Andrew said as he grasped her hand to walk up the steps to the front doors.

"Feels a little bit like home."

"Even considering . . . everything?" he asked.

Jax took in the large columns and high ceilings. "All that doesn't change the number of years I spent inside these walls."

Headmaster Vogt met them at the door. "You're back, Miss Simon."

"I am. Thank you for making time for us today."

"Always." He looked at Andrew and waited.

"Headmaster Vogt, my boyfriend, Andrew Craig."

They shook hands.

"Johan, please."

"Of course."

"Am I to assume that Mr. Kenner and your parents didn't get along?"

Jax offered a polite laugh.

"Who is Mr. Kenner?" Andrew asked.

Jax placed a hand on his arm. "Leo, hon. I told you I brought him here last year. After we visited the school, he met my parents. Which we'd told the headmaster about before it happened." She turned to the headmaster. "I'm surprised you remember."

"I remember details."

Andrew nodded his head a few times. "I've known the Simons for quite a few years. Went to school with Harry, Jax's brother."

"You're an Englishman," Johan concluded.

"I am."

That seemed to please him. "Come in. Welcome to Richter."

"Isn't it beautiful?" Jax asked Andrew.

"It is quite stunning." Andrew let his voice sound less than enthusiastic.

"Not as easily impressed as the American, I see."

"I, too, went to a boarding school. Most of them are all the same."

"Richter is different," Jax said.

They continued walking through the hall and out to the other side, which housed a courtyard.

"Yes, I remember Harry telling me about it. Not all of what he said sounded positive."

Jax sighed. "We've been over this."

"Your concerns are not unfounded, unfortunately. But I can assure you the darkness of Richter's past is exactly there . . . in the past. And really, that darkness was isolated to a very few. Regardless of what you may have heard, not everything was as it seemed," Vogt told him.

"How is that?" Andrew asked. "I read the papers. They alluded to parents being blackmailed and students being in danger."

They stopped on the fringes of the courtyard, where students walked between the buildings, books in their hands, a spring in their steps. Their uniforms in place, but never perfect out here unless . . . Jax noticed a boy look up, see the headmaster, and then straighten his tie. Unless someone of authority was about.

"All the parents had full disclosure of how Richter dealt with discipline. Even if some said they didn't when they removed their students from the school. Mr. and Mrs. Simon knew the rules. All parents signed papers agreeing to our terms."

Jax leaned closer to Andrew. "I can vouch for that."

"As for students getting hurt"—he huffed out a breath—"broken bones happen on every playground in every school. Concussions in sports, scrapes and bruises, papercuts, safety rules being disregarded in chemistry class. Show me one school that claims to be free of that and I'll cry foul."

Jax's enthusiasm radiated in her smile. "Thank you, Headmaster. I mean, Johan."

The man turned toward Andrew, looked him directly in the eye. "I think the real answer is standing right here. Jacqueline, a former student, is here considering Richter for her future . . . whatever that may be."

Andrew reached out his hand, grasped hers. "And I'm here giving it a chance. Please, show me around."

For nearly two hours, Johan walked them around campus, inviting them into classrooms. He discussed how things had changed in the school, and the things that hadn't. "We have no issues with cyberbullying or the evils of social media because the students aren't allowed on it. No Tinder, no Facebook, no instant access to online cheating on exams. We encourage parents to continue these disciplines when the students are away from school, and most of them agree. Weapons and hand-to-hand combat training have been limited to upperclassmen, as I'm sure Jacqueline has told you."

"She did mention that was different in her early years here."

"It was. In truth, we're petitioning to have the former methods reinstated," Johan told them.

"You are?" Jax asked.

"Parents can opt their children out. But we're finding that our graduating students aren't as competitive in some of the fields in which Richter once excelled."

Jax glanced at Andrew.

"Which fields?" he asked.

"Government jobs. Richter has a long history of funneling graduates to high-level jobs in governments all over the world. A valid point to consider when that has been the case here for decades. Obviously, our secrets weren't so secret."

"Your students are no longer getting those jobs?"

"Some do. Others are beaten out by stronger competition. We take that seriously here. The students are requesting we bring them into their military training earlier, and many parents agree. However, we have to go through channels to make that happen. Nothing to hide."

Jax had heard those words before.

Right from Johan's lips.

When someone said they had nothing to hide . . . they were hiding something.

Johan walked them through the library, the common rooms, the dorm she had been in with Claire. It was how she remembered it.

There was laughter and chatter. Yelling and whispering. Of course, in the presence of the headmaster those voices found a quiet place and the students straightened their spines. It wasn't any different than an adult adjusting their speed when they noticed a police car traveling close by.

They rounded out the tour back in the main hall.

They didn't see Professor Müller, nor did they get a glimpse of Checkpoint Charlie.

"If you're truly considering Richter . . . in the future, you might return when we have the work fair for our graduates. It happens every May."

"That's right, I forgot about that," Jax said.

"If you plan on staying locally, you'll want to book a room early. You'd likely not find one this year, but perhaps next. The accommodations in town are limited."

"I can just imagine what Ms. Hazel at the inn would charge," Jax added, making sure the headmaster knew where they were staying.

"Are you staying locally now?"

"We are." Jax felt bells going off in her head. "How many different employers come to recruit students?"

"Dozens. And if a student is interested in a company that isn't slated to come, we help them reach out in an effort to bring them here for an interview. It's a beautiful thing to witness students obtain jobs before they even walk out that door."

So long as that job isn't as an assassin.

"Have you seen enough, hon?" Jax asked Andrew.

"I have. This place is not nearly as intimidating as I first thought." Andrew reached out a hand. "Johan, thank you. I know you must be busy, and to do this twice with Jax is beyond the call of duty. If I have it my way, she won't bring another man on the tour."

Jax narrowed her eyes. "I haven't said yes to a question I haven't heard."

"You made it clear I wasn't to ask a question until after I came here."

She felt her cheeks heat up.

"I will leave you two to your argument," Johan said with a laugh. "Miss Simon, always a pleasure." He kissed each of Jax's cheeks.

"Thank you again."

He turned to Andrew. "Good luck. Perhaps we will meet again."

"It certainly is a possibility."

They got in the car and Andrew started to talk. "Well, that was—"

Jax leaned forward, pressed her lips against his. "Thank you so much for doing this," she said. She stared into his eyes and gave a tiny shake of her head. They'd been away from the car for two hours, and who knows what might have been placed inside.

Andrew seemed to understand. "Anything for you."

They kept their conversation light as they left Richter.

A mile away from the school, Jax encouraged him to pull over. "I can't find my reading glasses. They may have fallen out of my purse when it was in the trunk."

On the side of the road, Andrew cut the engine, and Jax removed her favorite traveling toy. She powered it up and waited for the lights to balance.

When one kept flickering, she tapped the side of the bug detector.

It didn't go out.

"Is it—"

She raised her hand, cutting Andrew off. Jax waved the device around, into the opened glove department, between the seats. The closer to the driver's side, the weaker the light.

She opened the door, stepped out of the car. As she walked to get in the back seat, the signal grew stronger. Back inside, the signal weakened.

"Can you open the trunk, hon?"

Andrew stepped out and joined her at the rear of the car.

Something was close.

The trunk was empty, not even a proper spare tire.

Look under the car. Jax mouthed the words to Andrew.

He got down to the ground. Jax retrieved a mirror from her purse and angled it to see the underside of the car.

"I found your glasses."

Jax looked over to see Andrew pointing.

"Thank goodness."

Ignoring the dirt on the side of the road, Jax dropped to her knees. A small black, classic GPS tracker had been magnetically placed on the underside of the car.

"Son of a bitch."

She left it where it was and let Andrew help her to her feet. To be safe, she circled the car again, had Andrew pop the hood. Her indicator only gave feedback at the known device.

Finally, she shut the thing down and turned to Andrew.

"That's a GPS. They can't hear us, but they know where we are."

"Holy shit."

She felt her spidey sense kicking in.

"Let's get back to the inn."

"We're leaving that on the car?" Andrew shuffled his feet side to side.

"Yes. They, whoever *they* are, are better off thinking we don't know it's there. Until we want otherwise."

He ran a hand through his hair. "It has to be someone from the school."

Jax shook her head. "This is the first time I checked the car since we picked it up at the airport." A mistake that the guys would be sure to give her hell about later. "That thing could have been placed back in Berlin for all we know."

Andrew suddenly reached for her, pulled her into his arms, and wrapped her close. "Jesus," he whispered.

Jax heard, and felt, his breathing shudder. "Hey."

He hugged her tighter. "It didn't feel real."

She understood that. It was one thing to *think* someone might be watching or listening . . . or tracking. It was quite another to *know* they were. The GPS device changed things.

Andrew placed his hands on the sides of her face and looked long into her eyes. "I . . ." He blew out a breath, kissed her hard, and then opened the door for her to get inside.

"What now?" he asked when they were back on the road.

"I have a feeling Neil is going to pull us out. Now that we know someone is tracking us, finding information will only lead them to an informant. And as strong and capable as I'm sure you are . . . you're not trained for this."

"I don't think watching Hollywood films qualifies me to do what you do." His nervous laugh gave away his fear.

"This is going to sound strange, but finding that thing was a good thing."

"How?"

"We level up our attention. Being alert keeps you on top of the situation and decreases your chances of becoming a victim. It makes you look twice when you feel someone watching you. When you're walking down the street and see the same person two days in a row, you stop and take notice. It's no longer an exercise to check for bugs, it becomes a necessity. Does that make sense?"

Andrew gripped the steering wheel with a nod. "Completely."

She lifted her phone. "I'm calling Sven, letting him know."

Jax watched Andrew's body language as she made her calls.

When she connected with Neil, the conversation took more time and started with a bit of humility.

"Talk to me" was how Neil answered the phone.

Jax skipped the small talk and put the phone on speaker. "Someone is tracking our car. It's unclear when it was placed. We just found it leaving Richter."

"When was the last time the car was clean?"

Jax squeezed her eyes shut. "When we took delivery of it upon arrival."

Neil made a noise but didn't comment.

"Lesson learned," she said.

"Good thing you weren't hiding where you were going."

"Sorry, boss."

He didn't harp. "What else do you know?"

She told him the facts and the feelings and the lead she thought they needed to follow next. "Vogt mentioned the job fair. Something I forgot about. When he did, he mentioned booking a stay in town early because the inns fill up. I think we need to tap into the local databases and pull names from the past and the future to see if there are any similarities worth a second look. There are only three inns in town."

"I didn't see a computer at Hazel's," Andrew interrupted.

"Oh, yeah, that's right. She has a physical book." Jax envisioned it sitting at the front desk.

"Then it won't prove a problem," Neil commented.

"If the others are the same, we'll need someone else to come in."

"One step ahead of you," Neil said. "Where are you now?"

"On the way back to the inn."

"Return, get the information you need, and pull out."

She knew that was coming.

"Copy that."

"Sven has extra protection. Make sure you're covered."

"Copy."

Neil cleared his throat. "One more thing."

"I'm listening."

"An article about your parents' separation was four pages into the financial section of the *London Report*."

Jax looked at Andrew. "What?"

"I just sent a copy to your inbox. Read it, digest it. Come up with a list of suspects on who could have leaked the story. We will do the same."

She was already scrambling to open the email on her phone.

"Will do."

"And, Jax . . ."

She paused. "Yeah."

"Distractions get you killed. I'll have a plane on standby in Berlin. Get back to London. We'll regroup. Ditch the tracker before leaving your current location."

Jax felt her nerves jumping. "Will do. My mistake won't happen again."

"I know."

She disconnected the call and leaned her head back. "Fuck."

"You okay?" Andrew reached over, grasped her hand.

"Fine." She dropped her phone in her purse, the article forgotten.

"You're not reading the newspaper?"

"Am I curious as to what it says? Yes, dying to know. But Neil's message was clear and completely on point. I'll read the article when we're in the air."

Because distractions are fatal.

CHAPTER TWENTY-THREE

This is real.

It was one thing to think of Jax's work as something she *did*, or *was* involved in. As if the dangerous parts were in the past. Flying off to Germany and playing with her spy toys was just that. Playing and fun.

Finding a motherfucking tracker on the car hit him in his solar plexus in a way he hadn't expected.

She was onto something.

Neil's voice kept ringing in his head.

"Distractions get you killed."

As excited as he had been about coming to Germany with Jax, he was ecstatic about getting the hell out of there.

With Jax.

Currently she was photographing Ms. Hazel's books while he played handyman after Jax volunteered him for duty.

With the woman pointing, and making her needs known, Andrew changed the air filters in the furnace and helped balance the hinges on a door that wasn't hanging correctly. He changed the batteries in smoke detectors in the tall corners of the inn.

It wasn't until Jax found them, a sign that she was done retrieving what she needed, that he stopped giving Hazel the opportunity to put him to work all day.

"Looks like you've been busy."

"Hazel needs a man."

Ms. Hazel snorted.

Andrew and Jax paused.

"You understand him?" Jax asked, in English.

Hazel shrugged.

"All this time we didn't think you spoke English."

"You don't ask," Hazel said.

"Well played, Ms. Hazel," Andrew said with a smile.

"Next time you come, I don't charge for room. I have list for you." She poked him in his chest, her toothy smile pleasant. "I have wine."

Jax stopped her. "We can't. My mother called. We have to get home."

Hazel's eyes narrowed, Jax went on to speak in German.

The two of them went back and forth a few times before Hazel nodded.

"I'll see you out when you leave," she said to the both of them before walking away.

"Didn't Mrs. Müller say she was crafty?" he asked.

"Neil should hire her."

Just the mention of the big man's name brought reality back.

"You have what you need?"

"Yes. Let's pack."

They took no time at all to put their things together and get them down to the car.

Ms. Hazel handed them a bag as she said goodbye. Thanked him, in English, for his help.

At the car, Jax reached under, popped off the tracking device, and tossed it in the bushes. She glanced across the street. "I'm going to grab something for the road. I'll be right back."

Andrew was hoisting a bag into the trunk. "I can—"

"It will only take a second." And she was jogging to the convenience store without another word.

He tucked their things away and got behind the wheel. The small town gave him a direct view of the market. But as the seconds ticked by, he felt his skin start to crawl.

Jax emerged and he released the breath he'd been holding.

She jumped in the passenger seat, put the bag in her hand on the floor. "Ready?"

"Yup. Is Sven close?"

"Oh, yeah. We'll meet at the airport."

Andrew backed out of the parking lot and onto the main road.

Jax reached down and lifted the bag to her lap.

From it she pulled out a pistol.

"What the hell—"

"Sorry, I should have warned you. It's just a precaution. This is the protection Neil spoke of."

"Is everything you guys say in code?" Because the word *protection* meant another set of fists, not a weapon.

"This is upsetting you," Jax said.

It was scaring the hell out of him.

He gripped the steering wheel. Took a breath.

"I know this is what you said you did. But I didn't expect . . ." What the hell did he expect?

She tucked the weapon in her purse and left it on the floor of the car. "This is only a tool, Andrew."

Get a grip.

Jax reached for his hand.

He took it.

The drive to the airport was one of the most stressful of his life.

And nothing was happening.

He saw Sven's car, off in the distance until they hit the busier roads.

At the airport, they dropped the car and left the key in a slot.

"Is that safe to bring in here?" he asked Jax, looking at her purse.

"Trust me. I have the documents I need."

He had no idea what that meant or if they were legal. Hell, he didn't want to know.

Jax stopped at a security desk and spoke to them in German.

She removed something from her purse and presented it.

The man looked at Andrew, his expression stoic, and asked a question.

Jax shook her head. "He wants to see your passport."

Andrew removed his passport and handed it over.

"Thank you. Follow me," the security guard said in English.

"What's going on?"

"Because of my protection, he has to escort us to the plane. Otherwise I would make every detector go off."

"Right, right." He felt better knowing the guard was with them, that someone knew about the gun. That feeling only lasted until they were led to a hall off the main part of the airport and into a private room.

"Routine," Jax said once inside.

She retrieved the gun and unloaded it before setting it on the counter.

"Thank you, Miss Simon. Your luggage, please."

They set their bags on a table and another guard came in.

They were scanned with a wand, the suitcases were opened and looked through. No one even paused at the bug finder.

Andrew watched them and kept silent.

"Everything is in order. I understand your plane is ready."

"We are waiting for one more agent."

"We have been notified," the guard said.

"Thank you."

They gathered their belongings, and Jax loaded her weapon again and tucked it away.

The whole experience was surreal.

And just when he thought he had seen it all, they were escorted to a door leading out onto the tarmac and an awaiting private jet.

"Holy shit."

The small plane held six plush seats, a small galley, and a bathroom.

And it was the first private plane Andrew had ever been on.

Jax poked her head into the cockpit when she boarded.

He heard her greeting the pilots and slipping in and out of German. From what it sounded like, one of the pilots wasn't completely fluent in English.

Not that it mattered, so long as he could fly the plane.

Andrew took in the space with a hundred questions on the tip of his tongue.

He turned around to see Jax staring. "Are you okay?"

He reached for her, pressed his lips to hers. It was there he felt balance. "I will be," he whispered.

Jax pulled their bags to the back and removed her laptop before securing them in a closet.

"You've been on this plane before."

"Not this one. But one like it."

"Do you know the pilots?"

"One of them. But they're vetted through the team."

Sven jogged up the stairs, tossed a backpack on the closest seat. "Hey, mate."

The complete calm of the man had Andrew's shoulders relaxing.

"Hey."

Like Jax, Sven ducked into the cockpit and said hello.

When he walked out, one of the pilots was with him. "I'm Tom. My copilot is Ely. Welcome aboard." He reached for Andrew's hand.

"I'm Andrew."

The pilot smiled. "First time in a private jet?"

"Is it that obvious?"

Sven and Tom both said yes at the same time.

"This is a self-service flight. Plenty of things to choose from in the back. Help yourself. Smaller aircraft tend to be a little noisier, and it will take us a bit longer to land at Heathrow. Just like British Airways, I'll let you know when you can take off your seatbelts and inform you if we're going to hit any bumps in the air. Looks good right now, so I'm expecting a smooth flight."

"Thank you."

"No worries. Enjoy."

He turned to the front of the aircraft and secured the door himself.

There was a collective sigh once the plane was off the ground.

~

"This is more than one token."

"You're asking to retire."

"I never asked." He had a debt to pay, he was paying it. That was all.

The voice on the line came close to laughing. "You and your family for this one assignment."

"I don't have a family."

Now they did laugh. "Everyone has family."

His left hand twitched. Why did he have the feeling his foot had just stepped in quicksand and he couldn't pull it out?

"One token. One hit."

"Two birds, one stone."

The pressure in his jaw threatened to crack his back teeth.

"Nothing comes around to us, or all deals are off the table. Loose ends are your problem. Do you understand?"

Which meant his contact expected loose ends.

"And if I say no to this assignment?"

"My token, my call."

That was how this worked.

~

Andrew placed his hand on her arm. "Read the article."

Sven looked up from across the aisle. "You haven't read it yet?"

"That bad?" she asked, the look on his face suggesting it was.

"Scandal is never pretty. Most of the time it's completely fabricated."

Jax opened the article Neil had sent and started to read.

> *It has come to the attention of the* London Report *that the long-term hedge-fund manager of JT Capital, Gregory Simon, and his wife of thirty-two years have separated. The news by itself is hardly worth the time of the* London Report *to share with its readers, except when the cause of that split is believed to be an affair Mr. Simon engaged in with a top investor's wife. What does this mean for JT Capital as the rumor mill flushes out truth from fiction? A slight dip in their market standing when the news broke has led to senior investors' concerns. It doesn't help that some of these investors are looking in their own backyards for the truth. In other news, a divorce between Gregory and Evelyn Simon is estimated to cost him north of forty million . . .*

Jax's gaze wavered. The rest of the article was facts and figures.

The first thought she surfaced was . . .

How was her mother?

How was the victim faring?

"Who spread this?" she asked before handing her phone to Andrew to read.

She paused.

"Have you talked to your mother?" Andrew asked.

Jax shook her head.

For the next two hours, the three of them combed over the facts and scribbled names on a paper. No one, including her mother, was excluded from the list.

From there they worked on when the GPS had been placed on the car and who had placed it.

They agreed that sometime between the meeting with Lodovica and the tour of Richter was the likely time frame.

But who? Did the former headmistress tip someone off that Jax was poking around?

Professor Müller?

Vogt?

The bottom line . . . . stirring the pot kicked up someone. And no matter who on their list was behind the tracker, that person had something to hide.

Which meant Checkpoint Charlie's tip was valid, and Jax and the others had a busy week or even months ahead of them.

"I don't think the article about your family coming out now is a coincidence." Sven tapped his finger against their list of names.

"I tend to agree with you, but my parents are living in two different places, and it's only a matter of time before someone important finds out. My father's timing for revealing his indiscretion has to be considered. Now that the cat is out of the bag, I'll lay pressure on him."

"I wonder how this is affecting Harry," Andrew said.

Jax felt a wave crawl up her spine. "You're right. If Dad is pushed out of JT Capital, will they fire Harry?" The whole thing made her ill. "What the hell was my father thinking?"

Sven leaned back, crossed his arms over his chest. "When the dick goes hard, the mind goes soft."

"I can accept that with a single man, not a married one. Look at the lives his crap is affecting. You make a vow, you stick with it. If something changes along the way, you own up to those changes before you act on them." The conversation was making her angry.

She'd managed to put her parents' issues aside while investigating Richter and exploring her new relationship with Andrew. But as the physical space between her and home shrunk, the weight of their drama pushed down hard on her shoulders.

"I'll check on Harry when we land," Andrew told her.

"Thank you. If he needs anything—"

"I'll let him know."

Jax leaned her head on Andrew's shoulder.

She enjoyed his closeness for a few minutes and let her mind rest. "Who are the top investors at JT Capital?"

Jax looked up at Andrew.

"If the paper is right, we might be able to figure out who the other woman was."

"I say we go straight to the office, bang out a few hours, and see if we can narrow anything down," Sven suggested.

"Agreed. I do need to get to my mother tonight. Make sure she's okay."

"Can I do anything?" Andrew asked.

"Just check on Harry. If you see my father, feel free to punch him." She glanced up. "Kidding."

Sven snorted. "She's not kidding."

CHAPTER TWENTY-FOUR

"It's a bloody shit show. That's what it is."

Andrew was afraid when he asked the question that Harry's response would be explosive.

"I thought as much. Is there any truth to an investor's wife?"

"If there is, my father is denying it."

"What do you think?" Andrew asked.

"I think he's a lying piece of shit. After that article came out, he's been sweating. I told him that if there was any truth to the rumor, he needed to distance himself from me. I do not want to be pulled out to sea if this ends up being true and they sack his ass."

Andrew couldn't imagine that conversation. In truth, he didn't think Harry had it in him to put his father in his place. "What did he say to that?"

"He turned it around, said he had worn out his welcome and would find his own place."

"He's distancing himself."

"Exactly. Fuck, Andrew. I'm on track to be on that top shelf, you know? This is going to drag me down."

"You don't know that."

"I hope I'm wrong."

"Can I do anything?"

"Yeah . . . when you see my dad, punch him."

Andrew laughed. The similarities between brother and sister were finally revealed.

"You're the second person today that's asked me to do that."

Harry sighed. "I suck. I didn't even ask. How is Jacqueline with all this?"

"Handling it better than you, I suspect."

"That's good."

"Have you spoken with your mother?"

"She seemed relieved for herself, and angry for me."

That was good to hear. "You'll be happy to know Jax is working double time to find out who the other woman is."

"I hope she's as good at her job as her friends say she is," Harry said.

"I've seen her work. She's good. She'll get to the bottom of this."

"I really don't want to start over with another investment firm."

"JT Capital can separate father from son. You'll be fine." Andrew squeezed his eyes shut, not believing his own words.

Harry shot off another obscenity as he continued to curse his father.

~

"You didn't cut your trip short because of me, did you?"

Before Jax dug into the pile of work in front of her, she put a call in to her mother. She sat in the surveillance room watching Evelyn walk through the house with the phone to her ear.

"No. We had a development that prompted our return. But I'm glad we came back when we did. How are you?"

"I'm fine. Really. It's the world that has learned of your father's infidelity. I already knew. It's Harry I worry about. Suddenly, working with his father seems like the bad decision."

Jax had already received a text from Andrew letting her know he was talking to Harry and would call later to fill her in.

"Do you think the papers have it right and that an investor's wife was involved?"

"I wouldn't put anything past your father at this point. I'm not even sure I care any longer."

Jax watched as her mother left the camera's view and moved into her bedroom.

"Do you have any idea, or even a best guess, who she is?"

"No. How could I? Gregory won't even tell me when this affair took place, only that it did . . . in the past. How long ago and how long did it go on? I don't care. I don't care! Who? When? How? Those answers change nothing."

Jax heard the distress in her mother's voice. "I'm sorry, Mum."

"No, I'm sorry you have to think about this at all. I know it's not possible that this situation doesn't affect both you and Harry, but I wish I could keep it from you."

Jax walked out of the surveillance room and stood in the hall. "You can't. I'll be home tonight, but probably late."

"Oh, I thought maybe you'd stay with Andrew."

"Not tonight. I want to come home, make sure you're okay with my own eyes."

She heard her mother sigh. "You're sweet to say that. I'll leave the light on for you."

"Mum?"

"Yes?"

"I have another question, please don't take offense." Jax took a deep breath. "Did you leak the story to the paper?"

She heard her mother laugh. "No. Although if your brother didn't work with your father, I might have. Now that this is out, I no longer have to pretend. But Harry is in the crosshairs, and that's most unfortunate."

"I'll see you in the morning, then."

"Drive carefully, my dear."

Jax stared at her phone, the conversation buzzing in her head. Somehow, in just a handful of weeks, she went from dreading a conversation with her mother to looking forward to it.

A few steps took her to the situation room. A huge magnetic whiteboard on a wall was slowly filling up with names and leads on Richter. A small portion was sectioned off for the quest to find her father's lover. Though that wasn't the priority, there was room to keep an eye on anything that developed.

Sven and two others of the team were huddled around a desk talking.

"What are you working on?" She walked over to them.

"Dinner."

"Best Thai food is across the street," Sven said. He passed her a menu and the paper with their orders written down.

After making a selection, she put the paper aside. Jax turned back to the whiteboard, and one by one the guys pulled out their wallets and started handing her money. "What's this for?"

"Newbie does the food run."

She opened her mouth to argue, but to them, she was new.

With her purse and their order in hand, she headed to the door.

"Ubon is the owner. If she's taking orders, tell her you work here. She always adds a little extra."

"Ubon, got it."

The days were getting longer, and it seemed some of the nice weather returned with her from Germany. Jax took her time getting across the street and into the small restaurant. There were less than a dozen tables, and only three of them were occupied. The smell of peppers and curry tickled her taste buds and made her stomach growl. It had been hours since she ate that morning before walking through the doors of Richter.

Jax gave the woman their order and asked if she was Ubon. The woman lit up with the use of her name and nodded several times when Jax explained where she worked.

They exchanged a few pleasant words before Jax took a seat to wait for their order.

She picked up her phone and started filtering through her personal email.

The longer she sat, the more tired she became. She'd need to get a ride home, where her rental car was parked. As her thoughts went there, she found herself wondering if finding an economical used car was in order. There was nothing practical about renting a car for as long as she'd been in possession of one.

Buying a car, even an inexpensive used one in England, felt like roots.

It felt strange to consider it, almost as if she were being unfaithful to her new American ways.

Which was silly. A car made sense.

"Your order ready," Ubon said.

With her hands full of white plastic takeout bags, Jax left.

Outside, the sun sat at just the right angle to make her squint as she studied the road before crossing.

A tingle up her spine had her looking twice.

A man, a few yards away, had been staring at her.

He was young, not much older than she was. Tall.

She glanced away, made sure no cars were coming, then back.

Yup . . . the man turned his head sharply and started walking in the opposite direction.

She crossed the street and put the man out of her thoughts. Whenever she was working a case, it was easy to see everyone as a suspect. But most of the time, the random guy looking at her on the street was just a guy looking at a girl.

But that didn't stop her from checking over her shoulder when she still felt eyes following her.

He was gone.

She walked through the doors of headquarters. "Dinner."

~

Jax fell into bed, her ear to the phone. "I'm exhausted."

"I'm fighting to stay awake," Andrew said on the other end of the line.

"I told you that you didn't have to stay up for me."

"I wanted to know you got home safely."

"I did. It's been a long day."

"It's hard to believe we were at Richter twelve hours ago. Did you have any revelations?"

She yawned. "Sorry . . . no. We have a lot of names. How's Harry?"

"Not having a good time. Paranoid he's going down with his father's ship."

"I knew this would bleed into his work."

"At this point, your dad still has a place at JT Capital. So long as the woman, especially if she was an investor's wife, stays hidden, this will blow over. Sadly, men cheating on their wives isn't the sin it should be, and the office isn't going to fire him. That's my father's take, anyway."

"And if the skeleton is revealed?"

"Could go either way."

"Really? I don't think so. If I was an investor and found out someone working for me was screwing my wife, he'd be gone. Or I'd pull out and that would get someone in the unemployment line."

"You're right. Your dad is screwed."

"No wonder he won't reveal a name."

"Makes me think the rumors are true," Andrew said.

"Me too."

She yawned again.

"You should go to bed."

Jax snuggled deeper under the blankets. "I am in bed."

"I feel a bit cheated I'm not with you. I thought we'd have at least a week."

"Be careful what you ask for. The commute to headquarters is gnarly at rush hour."

"And suddenly I like London traffic."

She laughed.

"I'll get you a key."

His words surprised her. "Isn't that a bit soon?"

"You don't want a key?"

"I didn't say that."

"Then I'll get you a key."

"Andrew!"

"What? I'm not asking you to move in, I'm giving you an option on nights like this where it's super late and you're exhausted . . . You've yawned three times in the few minutes we've been on the phone. It's an option."

Jax found herself hugging her knees into her chest and smiling. "I won't use it without telling you."

"I wouldn't give you a key if there was a risk of you walking in on something. I can't date two women at the same time. I don't have that gene. And considering everything going on with your dad, that would give me the Asshole of the Year award."

She laughed. "Okay."

"You'll take the key."

"I'll take the key. And you'll tell me if something changes and you want it back."

"I will."

"Because sometimes interest fades and people drift apart."

"And sometimes the glass is half-full. We're not your parents."

She cringed. "I'm going there, aren't I?"

"Yup, you are."

"I'll stop."

"It's okay," he said. "I'll keep it honest with you, and you do the same with me."

"I can do that." She sighed. "Do I get a special key chain?"

Andrew chuckled. "I'll see what I can do."

She yawned again, felt her eyes drifting. "You know what I really need?"

"What's that?"

"A car. I've been renting one since I arrived, and that's impractical at this point."

"Tell me what you're thinking, and I'll help you look. You have too many other things on your plate."

"You'd do that?"

"Are you kidding? The woman I'm dating who just a few weeks ago told me she wasn't staying in Europe is now looking at buying a car. I think my noncovert plan of keeping you here is starting to work."

"I'm still unsure of that future."

"I know. You told me. But a boy can dream. Now if you bring home a puppy, I know we're good."

The thought made her wistful. "I've never had a dog."

"Really?"

"No. Claire and I talked about it, but we never took the plunge."

"We'll start with a car. Now get some sleep. Give me a call tomorrow when you have a few minutes, point me in the direction you want to go, and I'll get on it."

"Thank you."

"Good night, Jax."

"G'night."

She plugged in her phone at the side of her bed and turned off the light.

She was getting a key to Andrew's house.

A house she hadn't even been in yet.

She couldn't stop smiling.

I wonder how he'd feel about a security system?

CHAPTER TWENTY-FIVE

He sat listening to half of a conversation and picking it apart.

Tapping the phone would have been easiest, but riskier. Right now, they didn't know he was out there, and they'd be lazy.

Andrew's voice changed when she was on the line. It was softer, lower . . . in love.

Pushing away the images the thought conjured in his head, he wrote notes.

"Your brother is going to have a heart attack or a stroke by the time he's forty if he keeps up at this pace."

Silence followed by laughter.

"You don't have to thank me. He's my friend."

Silence.

"Yeah? Huh . . ."

Silence.

"Any closer to finding who is filling the files now? . . . You think she'll talk to you?"

He sat taller. Listened harder.

"On the outside, Richter seems so completely normal . . . No, we're good. I'll see you then."

The call ended with a sigh.

"I'm falling fast for you, Jacqueline."

The words were a whisper to a disconnected line.

This was why he needed out. Knowing his target would soon be dead, leaving this man in despair mattered. It couldn't.

It can't.

He looked at his notes, circled the word *files*, and turned on his computer.

~

Jax spoke in front of a giant screen during the video conference with the California team. They could see all the faces of those at headquarters, along with their wall of suspects.

"I have gone over Lodovica's conversation a dozen times. Without a doubt, she has an informant at the school. Proven when she mentioned my fake engagement to Leo last year. She has a name of the person, or people, collecting secrets, but isn't telling. And she knew of my father's affair. My guess is she knows who the other half of that affair is, too. She'd also known about Sasha and AJ's marriage and seemed surprised to learn about Claire and Cooper's engagement."

"Sounds to me like Lodovica hasn't changed much in her prison years," Claire said.

Sven gave his opinion. "She could be guilty of talking to the papers or getting information to an outside informant."

"To serve what purpose?" Jax asked.

"Distract you," Neil said.

"Take you away from finding the informant."

"I also felt as if Lodovica gave up the information about knowing the ins and outs of our lives too quickly."

"She wanted you to know she has someone watching," Sasha said.

"Who are we looking for here? One person, two?" Sven asked.

Jax summarized who she believed they were after. "Who put the tracker on the car? Who is keeping Lodovica informed about her former students, and who at the school is talking to her? Is that the same person, or are we looking for two different people? Who is gathering secrets, and is that person using them for blackmail?"

"That could be four different people."

"Five if we add Daddy's mistress." Sven glanced at Jax, offered half a smile.

"He's a diversion," Neil said.

"I agree," Sasha added.

"How are we with the names at the inns?"

"It's taking time to get them into a database one at a time. It doesn't help that Hazel's handwriting is awful and her spelling of names, other than German, is completely off."

"Once that is uploaded, cross-reference names with those going in and out of the prison."

"This is going to take some time, boss," Sven said.

"We've got time. I want internal system checks moved from weekly to daily. Make sure a Richter grad hasn't hacked into our system."

"Copy that."

"We're done here. Give me an update tomorrow."

"Wait." Claire moved closer to the camera. "Jax, the lady at the dress shop called. She has three bridesmaid dresses that complement mine she wants to show us. Do you think you can get over there?"

Someone on Jax's left snorted.

"I'm going out later today to car shop. I'll stop by."

"Car shopping, huh?" Claire's smile dropped.

"It's practical."

"How is Andrew?"

"Enough chatter." Neil's voice rose above theirs.

The snorting behind Jax turned to laughter.

"I'll call you later."

Someone disconnected the feed without so much as a goodbye.

"'How is Andrew?'" James's voice rose an octave, mimicking Claire.

Without looking up, Jax said, "I will punch you. And it will hurt."

The laughter continued.

~

Jax was absolutely cross-eyed by the time Andrew picked her up at two.

He pulled her into his arms. "You look tired."

"I am." She snuggled close, lifted her lips to his.

He took them, made sure she felt his kiss.

Andrew opened the passenger side door for her before walking around the car and sliding into the driver's seat.

"Thank you for doing this."

"My pleasure." He turned over the engine.

She removed her bug detector and turned it on.

"You really think someone would bother with me?"

"Once bitten, twice shy."

She waved it around and called the car clean.

"Before we settle into car shopping, I have an errand to run for Claire."

"Where are we going?"

"You're going to hate it."

Jax had to give the man credit. He didn't so much as flinch walking into a wedding gown shop.

Beatrice met them at the door, her smile infectious.

"Miss Simon, thank you for coming."

"Claire said you had dresses to show me."

"Yes. Three absolutely stunning gowns. I hope you have a hard time picking the one." Beatrice glanced at Andrew.

Jax made the introductions.

"A man's opinion is always welcome."

"I can hardly wait."

They followed Beatrice toward the back of the shop. Jax leaned close to Andrew's side. "For an unmarried man in a bridal salon, you're not even sweating yet."

"Give me a few minutes."

She chuckled.

"Would you like champagne?" Beatrice asked once they were settled in a viewing room.

Jax shook her head. "It's not that kind of day. We're car shopping after this."

"Tea, then?"

"Sparkling water, if you have it."

Beatrice nodded and looked at Andrew.

"Make that two."

"If you'd like to get started, I have undergarments in the changing area. Did you bring shoes?"

"No, I didn't know I was coming."

"What size?"

"Thirty-eight."

"I'll be right back."

Jax put her purse on the sofa next to where Andrew had sat and slipped off her shoes.

"This is how women shop, huh?"

"You have a sister, don't act surprised."

Andrew winked and relaxed with his arms spread across the back of the couch.

"You look entirely too comfortable."

"You're about to take your clothes off behind that curtain, and I'm going to fantasize about that for a week."

Jax rolled her eyes but made a point of unbuttoning her blouse and slipping it off her shoulders before disappearing behind the curtain.

Andrew growled.

She looked at herself in the mirror, and the smile on her face brought joy to her heart. Andrew created that happiness.

"Here you are, Mr. Craig," Jax heard Beatrice say.

Seconds later, Beatrice joined her behind the curtain and helped her into the first gown. Like Claire's dress, this one hugged Jax's curves, had a low back and beautiful lines, and fell all the way to the floor.

Once Beatrice buttoned up the last hook in the back, she pushed the heels in front of Jax to slip into and then opened the curtain.

Andrew put his phone aside and looked up.

His smile softened and his mouth opened.

Jax beamed.

There was nothing better than the way a man looked at a woman with pure admiration and desire.

"Come over to the mirrors," Beatrice guided.

There, she fussed with the dress to pull out any wrinkles and pinched the sides while talking about alterations.

She grabbed a clip, gave Jax's hair a simple twist, and put it up in a loose knot. She pulled a few strands out to drape over the back. "The best way to show off this dress is with your hair up."

Jax turned around, looked behind her. "It's gorgeous."

"What do you think, Mr. Craig?" Beatrice asked.

Andrew cleared his throat. "Am I invited to this wedding?"

Jax laughed. "If you play your cards right."

"Then I love it."

Beatrice chuckled and grabbed a camera. "Let's take a few pictures and a video for the bride."

The sequence repeated for the next two dresses, and truthfully, Jax wasn't sure which one she liked the best and was glad she didn't have the final decision.

As Beatrice helped her out of the last gown, she started chatting.

"Remember the last time you were in here I mentioned that you reminded me of someone?"

Jax stepped out of the gown. "I do. Did you remember who that was?"

Beatrice beamed. "Addison Philips. Do you know her?"

"No." Jax reached for her bra and put it on.

"She was in last week with her friend who is getting married, and it hit me. I swear she's a spitting image of you. Could be your sister."

Jax smiled. Paused.

Everything went still as Beatrice continued to talk.

"Truly, they say everyone has a double, but . . ."

The room grew cold. "How old is she?"

"Around your age, I suspect."

"Addison Philips?" That name . . . Where had she heard it?

Beatrice hung the dress up and took the shoes with her as she walked out. "Yes. Uncanny. I will send these pictures to Claire."

Jax scrambled into her clothes in a rush to get out of there.

~

Andrew stretched his legs while waiting for Jax to get dressed.

When she emerged, the expression on her face had changed. "What's wrong?"

"I forgot about something." She grabbed her purse and his arm. "Thanks again, Beatrice."

"You're very welcome, dear. A pleasure to meet you, Mr. Cr—"

They were out the door.

"Where's the fire?"

"Addison Philips."

"Who?"

Jax all but jumped in the car, her fingers typing on her phone.

Andrew got in, turned in his seat.

She was reading, scowling.

"We're not shopping for cars, are we?" Andrew asked.

Jax slowly shook her head.

"Theodore Philips is an investor at JT Capital. *Was* an investor . . ."

The name sounded familiar.

And the dots started to connect.

Jax turned back to her phone. "Theodore's daughter looks like me."

"You think—"

She sucked in a sharp breath. "Holy shit."

He took the phone from her fingertips.

A family picture with a girl that looked almost identical to Jax stood to one side of the couple. Theodore Philips, according to the names on the bottom of the picture, was ancient. Well into his seventies and looked that way more because of the woman at his side, who had to be in her late forties, at best.

"What do you think?"

Andrew handed her phone back.

"That's crazy."

She dialed a number, lifted the phone to her ear. "Can you find an address for an Addison Philips?" Jax fished in her purse and removed a pen and paper. "Uh-huh . . . okay. Thanks. Nope. Okay."

She hung up and put the address into her GPS. "This is where we're going."

"You got it." He put the car in drive.

While he navigated, Jax read off what she could find about Addison Philips.

"She's a year older than me. Graduated from Oakman."

"A boarding school up north."

Jax kept looking at her phone. "She inherited her father's fortune when he passed away six months ago."

"That's why I knew his name. Yes, there was a bit of a stir in the financial sections." He couldn't remember the details.

"I think I found something." Jax skipped around the text. "Theodore Philips, dead at eighty-three . . . survived by Marion Philips and their daughter, Addison. And estranged son Richard Philips is fighting the will—"

"Yeah, yeah . . . I remember this. Harry told me about it. Said a kid inherited the shares."

"Hardly a child. She's older than me."

"It's a lot of zeros for someone our age," Andrew pointed out.

Jax blew out a whistle. "You're right about that."

"The half brother is fighting the half sister. Why didn't Theo give the wife the money? Looks like he skipped her completely."

They pulled off the motorway and onto the main road. The navigation moved them around the expansive properties and high fences. "Not sure what you think you're going to see."

"Me either, but I have to look."

The address led them to an estate that rivaled the Harrison house. But this one was open to the world. No huge gates to keep uninvited guests from wandering in. Hedges and trees framed the entrance and gave some privacy from prying eyes. But not much.

They parked a little way from the entrance and turned off the engine.

Silence from the country filtered into the car.

"Now what?"

Jax removed her seatbelt. "Stay here."

"What are you doing?"

"Poking around."

"You're serious."

Jax brushed her lips over his and got out of the car.

"What the bloody hell?"

Andrew's nerves started to climb.

This was ridiculous. Not one camera, not one alarm.

She looked up and down the street. The power lines must be underground.

Jax jogged along the road a little way and into the trees lining one side of the frontage of the property. Plenty of places to hide and get in without being seen.

With a plan designed in her head, Jax returned to the car.

Andrew was blowing steam. "Really, Jax? Anyone can see you."

"I'm looking for Fluffy. Damn mutt ran off."

He broke a smile. "You've never had a dog."

She opened up a satellite image of the area and directed Andrew to drive around to the back of the house. Unfortunately, another property abutted the Philips estate. Although that could come in handy.

"What now?"

She sighed, thought out loud. "I don't know. Maybe I'll gather some toys and come back later."

"Do I want to know what that means?"

"Ah, yeah . . . no."

"It could be a complete coincidence." Andrew gripped the wheel.

"I don't believe in coincidences. Think about it . . . my father, out of nowhere, tells my mother about his affair that he has insisted was 'a long time ago.'" She made air quotes. "Why would he do that? If Addison Philips is in fact my father's daughter . . ." The thought hit her. "My half sister, who has a striking resemblance to me . . . is now a legal investor at JT Capital and starts showing up at the office or board meetings."

"Or there's a legal battle over the estate and her parentage is questioned," Andrew added.

"Exactly. Big money and scandal sell newspapers, and when Addison Philips's image is plastered over them, questions might be asked. Dots will be connected. My father sees the potential fallout and owns up to my mother."

"Having an affair and having a child with another woman is a completely different thing."

Jax sat back in her seat, looked at Addison's picture again. She was beautiful. Wore her hair a little shorter than Jax with a slightly darker color woven in. "My grandmother used to joke that the boys in the family could be from any man, but the girls always resembled my great-grandfather. All our baby pictures look the same, just taken in different decades."

Andrew placed his fingers over hers.

"You might be onto something."

There was no *might* about it.

"What do you know about Oakman?"

"Good school. Private. My sister nearly went there."

"A contender for me if I'd been kept in England."

"What are you getting at?"

Her mind was spinning. "What is the likelihood of Addison's father bringing her around to JT Capital before he passed?"

"I'd prepare my daughter to take over when I was gone. We're introduced to those that are due to inherit all the time."

"I wonder how uncomfortable my father would be if I started showing up at his office on a regular basis?"

"Jesus, Jax."

"And I wonder if sending me to Richter . . . all the way in Germany, to keep me from being a visible part of his life was more to do with location than anything else? He said it was a *safe* place. But maybe that *safe* was just keeping his secret *safe*?"

"I might have to punch your father the next time I see him after all."

"Get in line."

~

A pair of binoculars brought into focus the address on the pillars leading into the estate.

A few clicks on the keyboard in front of him and he had a name . . . and a picture.

"You're making this entirely too easy, Jacqueline."

He put his car in drive and followed at a distance.

CHAPTER TWENTY-SIX

Instead of going back to headquarters, they went to Andrew's flat.

The lofty space was furnished with soft grays and blues and light wood tones. He had an overstuffed sofa and reclining chair in his main room, with a massive television filling one wall.

The art complemented the furnishings, and so did the lamps and tables. For a bachelor pad, it was well appointed.

"My sister helped," Andrew offered before Jax could ask.

"I like it."

He walked into the galley kitchen, which was open to the living room. "Something to drink?"

"What do you have?"

"Depends on if we're going back out."

Jax thought about that, put it aside for now. "I need to bounce this off the team. Make sure my personal involvement isn't getting in my way." She had the feeling it was.

"In that case . . . beer, wine . . . martini?"

"Martini."

Andrew walked over to the sink and started washing his hands.

"Do you have a laptop?"

"Down the hall, first door on the left."

Jax walked through Andrew's space, poked her head around doors. "You're very clean."

"Someone comes in once a week."

She found the laptop, unplugged it from where it sat on his desk.

"Do you work from home a lot?" She walked back into the kitchen.

"It's a bad habit, but yes."

"You're driven, nothing wrong with that."

"My father gives me a hard time about it." Andrew lowered his voice. "'Leave work at the door.'"

"Good advice."

She opened the laptop and it sprang to life. "You don't have this password protected?"

"I live here alone."

Jax rolled her eyes. "You have a lot to learn, England."

Andrew shoved ice into a shaker and closed the freezer door. "Good thing you're here to teach me."

Jax jumped onto the information superhighway and plugged away.

She started with Marion Philips. She looked enough like Jax's mom to suggest her father had a type.

Her marriage to Theodore Philips took place five years before Addison was born. Seemed like a typical older rich man marries young trophy wife situation. A third marriage for Theodore and a first for Marion. The articles were thin on details. A few society-page pictures early on at charity events.

The information dried up, outside of investment portfolio stuff that might interest Andrew and Harry, but stuff she couldn't care less about.

Andrew handed her the martini. "Cheers."

"Thank you." She took a sip, hummed. "Good."

He came around behind her and set his drink aside.

She started cross-referencing names. Her father's and Marion . . . Addison and Richard. Images popped up with articles attached. Addison was the daughter of a very rich man and therefore found herself in the spotlight on occasion. Mainly at her father's side. They looked close.

Jax jumped around the internet, pressed print more times than she counted to put the articles together later.

"What exactly are you looking for?" Andrew asked at the bottom of their first drink.

"I'm not completely sure."

"While you do that, I'll start dinner."

Jax looked up. "You cook?"

Andrew paused. "Four things . . . really well. The rest of it I fake."

"Am I getting one of the good things or the fake things?"

"You tell me once you take a bite."

Andrew moved around his kitchen with a towel over his shoulder.

Jax couldn't help but smile. How on earth had he happened into her life?

He turned his back to her, and she bit her lip at the sight of his butt. Nice . . . so nice.

Dragging her gaze away, she went back to the computer.

Every year JT Capital was a part of two major charity events. One during the holidays and the other in spring. One was for a childhood cancer organization, and the other was a stop-hunger event that hosted a silent auction and gave the money to the needy.

Society pages loved pictures of the rich and famous. The gowns and the glitter.

In what felt like the hundredth picture, Jax found it.

A photograph of her parents, and the Philipses. Standing in formal attire back when they were all a lot younger.

"I'll be damned."

"What?"

She turned the computer around and showed him the picture.

"That isn't proof."

"It proves they knew each other."

Andrew turned back to the steaks he was preparing.

Enough. She closed the laptop and pushed it aside. "What can I do to help?"

"How about another martini?"

"Coming right up."

Later, after their bellies were full and their brains were buzzed . . . and cleaning the dishes had been reduced to bubbles and soap, a slap on the ass, and sex in the kitchen, Jax and Andrew were curled up in his bed digesting the day.

"I wonder what she's like."

"If she is your sister, I'm sure you'll find out."

"I don't know about that. She looked like she was close to her father. Why would I ruin that for her?" In fact, the more Jax thought about it, the less she wanted to pull the woman into the scandal.

Andrew tucked her into his arms. "Let it go for tonight."

Jax closed her eyes. "Oh, shit."

"What?"

"I didn't tell my mum that I wasn't coming home."

"Text her. She'll see it in the morning." Andrew handed her the phone.

When she was done, she reached over him and placed it on the side table.

He stopped her from cuddling back in with a hand to her cheek. "Have I told you how beautiful you are? How much I love having you in my space?"

"No. You haven't."

Andrew flipped her over on her back, brushed her hair across the pillow. "You're beautiful, Jacqueline, and seeing you here . . . right here, like this with your hair spread out over my pillows and your lips swollen from my kiss . . . I've envisioned this from the moment you smiled at me over that first martini."

She ran her leg down the side of his. "That was a really good drink."

"It was." He laughed and brought his lips to hers.

Thoughts of cocktails and scandal disappeared, and all that was left was the two of them taking advantage of each other and enjoying every second.

~

"I found out who my father had the affair with," Jax announced to the team the following afternoon when the California team was online. "Her name is Marion Philips."

"I thought we agreed this was a distraction," Neil chided.

"And I have a half sister."

That changed his tune.

She presented the evidence she'd found and ended with the picture of Addison.

"That's pretty compelling," Sven said as the internet photographs were passed around.

"That's jacked," Cooper said.

"Damn, Jax. Have you told your mother?" Claire asked.

"No."

"Hold off," Neil told her.

"I am."

"James, Claire . . . I want the two of you to solidify Jax's findings. Jax, you and Sven find out who put the tracker on the car."

"I can help with Addison," Jax said.

"No. You're too close and won't be objective."

"I can be—"

"No." Neil's voice meant business.

Damn it.

"I'm going to call Lodovica," Jax informed them instead of asking.

"Why?"

"I want to determine if she knew about Addison."

"Jax!"

"Hear me out. The Richter files weren't complete. They only revealed an affair, not the outcome of it. Considering the size of the estate Addison Philips is about to inherit and the fact that there is someone looking for dirt, there is no guarantee Lodovica won't be tapped for that information. We need to know if she knew of Addison. If she didn't, fine . . . we go back to watching the doors of the prison and searching for clues. But if she did . . . we need to help Addison keep this secret."

"Why?" Neil's one-word question made Jax pause.

"Because it's not her fault my father slept with her mother. And from what I've gathered, Addison loved Theodore. She doesn't deserve to have her world shattered." Jax felt her body shake with the emotions crawling all over her.

The room was quiet until Claire spoke up. "And she's your sister."

Jax stared into the camera. "You're my sister."

"I don't—" Neil started.

Jax cut him off. "If Lodovica knew of Addison, what else does she know that we don't? One of the things she said during my interview was when she was released from prison she wanted to mind her own business. That statement rang true to my ears. If she is responsible for leaking the story, I want her to know that 'minding her own business' when she's out of prison will be a pipe dream."

"You're too close."

"One phone call and I'll back off and wait for the report."

"You will back off." Neil all but threatened her with his tone. "If you're being watched and you start poking around Addison, we won't have to worry about Lodovica spreading the rumor, you'll lead someone else right to it."

"One call."

"One call," Neil agreed.

~

It took twenty minutes to get Lodovica on the phone. Jax had the line tapped, recording the call for everyone else to hear.

"What do you want, Jacqueline?" No hello . . . nothing pleasant.

"How are you?"

"That's not why you're calling."

"You know about my father."

Lodovica sighed. "I've already told you I cannot help."

"Did you tell the paper?"

"What do I gain from that?"

That wasn't a no. "Why did you spare the details?"

Lodovica hesitated. "You're a private investigator now, correct?"

"Yes."

"You work with highly intelligent people with a wide range of useful skills."

"Your point?"

"I've made my point. Have a nice evening."

She hung up.

Jax wanted to scream.

"Simmer down, Jax," Sven coaxed. "We got what we needed."

"What the hell is her angle?"

James stood to the side, already in the process of uploading the conversation to California. "We're on it, Jax. Let us take it from here."

Sven came up behind her and rubbed her shoulders. "C'mon. Let's find out who tracked you in Germany."

One of the other team members poked their head in the door. "Jax, you have a visitor."

She pushed from the chair and walked into the situation room.

Andrew stood looking at the whiteboard, his back to her.

"What are you doing here?"

"Dropping something off." He waved to the board. "This is nuts."

She tried to see what he saw. "It's a lot of names."

He shook his head, turned around.

"Hey, mate." Sven waved as he walked by.

"Hello."

"I have a lot of work to do. I can't run off right now."

"I won't keep you." Andrew reached in his pocket and handed her a key.

One look at the key chain and she started to laugh. "'I love England'?" A cheesy dime-store souvenir with a British flag.

"You can't mix this up with your other keys."

"No, that won't be possible."

Sven looked over, spoke up. "Moving her in already?"

"Mind your own business, Sven."

"Hope you know what you're getting into, mate. This one is high maintenance."

"*This one* has a mean left hook, too," she playfully warned her coworker.

Andrew smiled. "You're back to your mum's tonight, right?"

"She's holding dinner for me."

"If it changes, let me know. I'll come home early." He kissed her quickly.

Sven walked over before Andrew could slip away. "Sorry, mate . . . eavesdropping isn't something I can help."

"Sven!" Jax warned him.

He waved a hand in the air. "You, ah . . . were with Jax when the GPS was dropped on your car, right?"

"Yeah."

"You were with her at Richter and at the prison visiting the headmistress, right?"

"You were there," Andrew pointed out.

"Right, right. I'm guessing you two have talked pretty extensively about what we're dealing with here."

"What's your point, Sven?" Jax asked.

"Who monitors your security system at your home, mate?"

"I don't have one." Andrew narrowed his eyes, catching on.

Sven nodded a few times. "Right . . . right. I knew that. Did the background on you myself. Theoretically, the guy who dropped the GPS could be in your flat right now sprinkling bugs and hacking your lines. Or maybe even waiting around for you to come home to learn what you know personally."

Jax pushed him aside. "Okay, you've made your point."

Sven winked and walked away.

Andrew looked around the room. "Well, hell."

"I meant to bring it up."

"I get it. I'm dating a woman who carries guns into an airport and takes down mob bosses."

"I don't want you to feel like we're invading your privacy."

He placed a hand on her arm. "And I want you to feel safe when you come home, ah . . . come over," he corrected himself.

"You sure?"

Andrew pulled her into his arms. "Now maybe you'll let me play with one of your toys," he whispered in her ear.

He was handling her job better than anyone she'd ever dated.

"Hey, Sven."

"Yeah."

"You book a time with Andrew. I'm going to let him borrow a bug detector for the time being."

"That's a banging idea. Glad you thought of it."

CHAPTER TWENTY-SEVEN

"I filed for divorce."

Evelyn delivered the information without preamble.

Jax put her utensils down, reached across the dinner table, and grasped her mother's hand. The news was jarring to hear, but not unexpected. "Are you okay?"

"It wasn't an easy decision."

"I can't imagine it was."

Her mother kept her eyes glued to the table in front of her. "I'm sorry, for you and your brother."

"Don't be ridiculous. You have nothing to be sorry about."

"I don't want you to hate your father."

Too late. "You're not responsible for my relationship with him. Don't put that on yourself."

"I want to shelter you from this."

"Good luck with that."

That made her mother smile and look up.

"I'm scared, Jacqueline."

She squeezed her mother's hand. "I'd be surprised if you weren't. But you're going to be okay."

"I wish I knew that for certain."

"Does he know yet?"

"No. I know if I call him, he'll try and talk me out of it. We'll argue and I'll be forced to have him served at the office. I want to avoid that, for Harry's sake."

Jax lifted her chin. "I'll call him."

"I can't ask you—"

"You didn't ask. I will call him tonight. When the papers are ready, we'll get them to Harry, and he can give them to Dad. Discreet. No fighting. I doubt he will want a scene."

"I wish I was stronger."

"It takes more strength to walk away than to let him make a fool of you." He had successfully done that and so much more.

"Harry told me he moved out."

Jax already knew that but acted surprised anyway. "Good."

Evelyn tapped Jax's hand and picked up her fork. "Thank you. You really are a godsend for me right now."

"Anything I can do, just ask."

Her mother shook her head. "Enough of that. How's Andrew?"

Jax was happy to change the subject. "He gave me a key to his place."

"Did he?" Evelyn didn't sound surprised.

"I think it might be too soon."

"Time doesn't matter when you're with the right person."

Was that what was going on? "How do you know when you're in love?"

Evelyn offered a wistful smile. "When the thought of life without them cripples you."

Jax winced. "Is that how you feel about Dad?"

"Not anymore, I'm sorry to say."

Jax quickly changed the subject back. "I'm not convinced the key is the right move."

"It's practical. You work late sometimes, and I'm not down the street."

Jax followed her mother's lead and cut into her chicken. "And when you start dating, you won't want me around all the time."

Her mother gasped. "The last thing I'm going to do is invite another man into my life."

"Like I invited Andrew? He's as unexpected as a sixteen-year-old's pregnancy."

Evelyn started to laugh and covered her lips with her hand to keep the food in. "Where do you come up with these things?"

"It's a gift."

~

Later that night, once her mother had gone to bed, Jax closed herself in her father's study and picked up the phone.

Fortifying her spine, she waited for her dad to pick up.

"Hello, Jacqueline."

"Father."

"I've been meaning to call you. Arrange lunch . . . or something."

"That wouldn't be advisable right now." Because she'd deck him if he came within five feet and no one was looking.

Hell, maybe even if they did have an audience.

"Later, then."

She didn't commit. "Mother filed for divorce."

Gregory was silent.

"She'd have called herself but was afraid you'd fight. The last thing she wants is for this to get ugly."

"It doesn't have to be this way."

"Arguing with me will do you no good. I'm better at it. When the papers are ready, she'll get them to you without fanfare. You owe it to Harry to avoid the argument and people looking too close."

"Jacqueline . . ."

She cut him off, her voice stern. "You owe it to *all* of your children."

Gregory was silent.

Seconds ticked away. "I do love you, Jacqueline."

She was entirely too angry with him to accept that. "Maybe some-day I'll believe you. That isn't today."

Minutes later, after she'd gotten off the phone with her dad, she was still staring into space.

She removed the key with the silly key chain from her pocket. Only this time, when she looked at it, she saw something different.

I love England.

At first, she thought of it as a passive way for him to drill in her desire to stay in Europe . . . now she saw the nickname she'd given him.

England.

I love England turned into something entirely different.

Jax knew she was diving into the deep end.

The question was . . . How deep?

~

Andrew had watched a few episodes of shows where a team remodels a home in a few short days, or a week. That was what it felt like to have the people Jax worked with flood into his home and wire it for sound. They came in, did their thing, and were gone. All that was left was a keypad and a feeling that someone was watching.

There were only two cameras, one on the outside of the front door, and the other facing the keypad itself.

Andrew had nixed the other ones Sven suggested. In the end, they agreed that two would be enough.

"You get used to them. In a month you'll forget that they're here," Sven had told him.

"I find that hard to believe."

"Let me know how you feel in thirty days. If at any time you want the interior audio and video cut, you say the word."

That was good enough for Andrew.

It did feel more secure, and now maybe Jax would use the key he'd given her.

When he'd come home earlier, with the bug detector in hand, he walked through his home wondering if it was possible someone could have been inside. Then he recalled how shocked he'd been when they found the GPS device on the car in Germany. The answer was yes, it was possible, and although he didn't have any reason for someone to track him, Jax did. And she was a part of his life.

His phone rang and he picked it up without looking at the caller ID. "Hello?"

"It's Harry."

"Hey, buddy. How you doing?"

"Dad finally moved out."

"That's great news. How is the office?"

"I haven't decided. You up for a beer?"

Andrew looked at the time. "Yeah. Meet at the pub by you?"

"Be there in fifteen."

~

Jax was looking over the surveillance recordings outside the prison doors. She'd watch the people walk in, most with their backs to the cameras, and then watch them walk out. All the time on fast-forward. On the way out, the street camera they'd tapped into gave them reasonably clear pictures of the staff's and visitors' faces.

With a zoom feature, they snapped images and cleaned them up with software. From there they found names and cross-referenced them with everything from the staff at Richter to those at Ms. Hazel's inn and the others in the town outside of the school.

So far nothing matched. They were coming up with a list of frequent fliers visiting the prison. While they did find a limited number of people who went in to visit Lodovica, there was no way to determine if a visitor seeking another inmate didn't visit her as well.

Everyone was a suspect until proven otherwise.

The routine and tedious work of filtering faces was enough to make you cross-eyed.

With the fast-forward feature in play, Jax noted the numbers of people walking into the prison. She could recognize the staff now and determine by the time stamp on the footage who was prompt when going to work and who was always tardy.

Jax found herself talking to the screen. "Well, Louisa, I see you were out partying last night. Late again."

A man followed Louisa in, a slight limp to his step. Jax made a note on her paper. Tan pants and wearing a fedora. Hats were common in Europe, and seeing someone wearing one wasn't a surprise.

"Hey, Jax, you want a coffee? I'm doing a run," James called out from the front of the room.

"Flat white," she told him. Jax loved the fact that she hadn't had a stale cup of coffee since she left California. There weren't pots of the stuff sitting around for hours waiting for some poor sap to come along and unknowingly pour a cup. She and Claire would make an American pot of coffee at home but always threw it out if it wasn't finished within the hour. In Europe, it was hard to even find a pot of coffee. It was Starbucks all day, every day. They did have an individual coffee cup machine in the office, but most of the time they went down the street to the French bakery to take care of their caffeine needs.

Jax rubbed her eyes and stretched her neck.

When she looked back at the screen, Tan Pants and Fedora was walking out of the frame.

She stopped the image and backed it up.

"How does Andrew like the new system?" Sven asked.

"He thinks all we do is watch his door all day long."

She'd backed up the recording too far, saw Fedora walking in behind Louisa.

Jax pushed the recording up, saw him walking out.

Something was off.

She backed up the images again.

Walking in.

Walking out.

Walking in, limp on the left.

Walking out, limp on the right.

Jax looked at it four times. "Hey, Sven. Come look at this."

Without telling him what she saw, she moved back and forth between the frames.

"He changed his limp."

She pushed in to get a clearer image of the man's face.

"I'll check the roster at the prison," Sven said, moving back to his computer.

Jax took a snapshot of his face, what his hat didn't cover, and moved the image to the software that brought it into view.

While the computer worked, she zeroed in on the man's hands, took a picture of them.

Next she looked at his shoes.

Once the facial image was done, Jax printed a copy and sent the digital to the database that cross-referenced with what they had already gathered.

The hat hid the man's eyes, but the side of his face, cheekbones, nose . . . lips. A good disguise could alter that . . . but maybe they'd catch a break.

"His hands are old," she announced when the image was enhanced. Sunspots and a lack of collagen gave the hands a spidery look, especially on the thin elderly.

He wore loafers. Slip-on brown shoes worn for comfort and ease, with style as an afterthought.

The computer flipped through pictures faster than Jax's eyes could catch.

She stood and walked away and stretched her back.

James returned with the coffee, and Jax warmed her hands on the cup before taking a sip.

A ping from her computer alerted her to a match.

Before she walked over to it, she heard three more chimes.

She lost the smile the coffee had given her, and she set the cup down. "Holy shit."

Jax looked up and over the monitor, met Sven's gaze.

"Checkpoint Charlie."

CHAPTER TWENTY-EIGHT

"We have a break in the case," Jax informed Andrew when she climbed into the passenger side of his sedan.

They were on their way to find her a car.

Again.

"Are we looking for a car or spying on another lost family member?" he asked, teasing.

Her smile was radiant. "A car."

Andrew pulled out of the parking lot and into traffic.

"Checkpoint Charlie is visiting Lodovica."

"Wait . . . what? I thought he was a good guy."

"He is. We don't know if he's trying to squeeze Lodovica for information or revealing some."

"The latter would be bad, right?"

Jax pulled her seatbelt over her lap and settled in. "I don't know. Claire reminded me that it was Lodovica who warned Sasha and Neil about the takeover at the school and gave them time to get in and stop it. In the end, Lodovica is serving time, but she didn't have to do that. She could have given her resignation and walked away."

"Why would anyone willingly go to jail?"

"Guilt? Remorse? Who knows?"

"The road to hell is paved with good intentions," Andrew quoted.

"Exactly. Anyway, it's a lead. Something solid to work with."

"Could he have been the one to put the tracker on the car?"

Jax shrugged. "In theory, but why would he? He knows we're there poking around. He prompted that. What would he gain from knowing where we were driving?"

"I'm glad I work with numbers. They're consistent."

"There is a job for every personality. You've been a pretty good sport with all of this."

"It's hard not to get wrapped up in it. You live an exciting life, Jax."

"Speaking of . . ." She reached into her purse and pulled out her cell phone. A few swipes later and she was showing him a picture of a man standing on a dark porch . . . *his* dark porch. "Do you know who this is?"

Andrew kept one eye on the road and the other on the phone. "No idea. Is that my place?"

"Yeah. The guy came to your door the night we installed the cameras."

"I don't remember anyone coming by."

"I watched the footage. You left, and about fifteen minutes later this guy showed up. He had a paper in his hand, knocked on the door, and called out the name Evan."

The worry washed out of Andrew's system. "Evan lives next door."

Jax put her phone away. "I figured as much. Better to check."

Andrew turned down a road littered with car dealerships. "What are you looking for?"

"I'm leaning toward a Jeep."

"Really? I thought you'd be more of an Aston Martin girl."

Jax tossed her head back and laughed. "My Double-Oh-Seven car is practical. An Aston is not."

"Are you still thinking used?"

"Yeah. Nothing too expensive."

"A new Jeep isn't that big of a difference. Why not get something with a warranty? I know you can afford it." And maybe if she had a brand-new car instead of something she could just walk away from, she'd be that much more inclined to stay in Great Britain.

"It's not about affording it."

"You don't like new cars?"

"I didn't say that."

"So, get a new car. You work hard."

"Andrew!"

He glanced at her, attempting to look innocent. "What? It's not like I'm suggesting you put a down payment on a house. It's a car."

She narrowed her eyes. "Why do I feel like we've had this conversation before?"

"I don't know what you're talking about." He turned in to the new-car dealership that sold Jeeps.

Two hours later, Andrew followed behind Jax's new four-wheel-drive Jeep Wrangler feeling a little like he'd won the lottery.

~

"You heard about Charlie." Jax was on a FaceTime call with Claire while Andrew took a shower.

"I did. I'm gonna be really pissed if he ends up on the wrong side of all this."

"What does your gut say?"

"Charlie's a good guy. I think he feels guilty for not doing more to stop shit from going down, and that's why he is still there. Think about everything we've learned from him over the years."

Jax felt the distress she could see on Claire's face. "I agree. What's your take with the headmistress?"

"She told you to use your skills. Use all of *our* skills. That doesn't sound like someone who wants to keep a secret."

"But she doesn't want to be responsible for telling us either."

"I'm guessing people would kill for the names in her head."

Jax curled up on Andrew's couch and tossed a blanket over her legs. "She wouldn't be of use to anyone dead. They'd have to threaten someone she cares for. And her lover isn't getting out of prison in this lifetime."

Claire paused. "I wonder if that is part of this. We're looking for whoever might be going around now to rekindle Richter's old ways. Who that person is, who they hired to gather dirt and secrets on new families coming in. But what if someone wants to cut to the chase and get to Lodovica? You know she's an encyclopedia of the Richter files. Tons of dirty laundry in her head."

"She's not the only one with that information."

Claire shrugged. "No one knows we have it."

"Charlie knows."

"He'd want to protect those secrets and keep the students safe."

"Would he want to keep Lodovica safe then? And how is she going to survive outside of prison? What stops a student used in this game from coming back and knocking her off?"

"Good question. It might be a case of keeping your friends close and your enemies closer."

"Maybe."

"I noticed you haven't asked about Addison."

"If there was something to tell, you'd tell me."

"Nothing earth-shattering. We'll have a report to Neil on Monday."

Much as Jax wanted to know, she didn't press. She needed to keep her head in the case, and not her personal drama. "Oh, I didn't tell you. I bought a car."

"You did?"

"That Jeep I was talking about last year."

"A new one?"

Jax cringed with her answer. "Yes. Don't hate me."

"I could never hate you. You have a life happening in England. You owe it to yourself to explore it."

The water turned off in the shower and prompted Jax to switch languages. German was their strongest second, so she went there. "I really like him."

"I know. I can tell."

"I think I might be falling in love."

"Yeah, I can tell that, too. He's one of the good guys, Jax. It takes a strong man to be with women like us. We're not easy."

"I miss you."

"I miss you every day. But I understand and I love you even if you stay there."

"Is that what I'm doing?" Jax glanced around Andrew's home, thought of the memories they were already creating.

"The good news is, we work for the same guy and he's always flying back and forth to London. It isn't like we're not going to see each other all the time."

Even FaceTime made the miles shrink.

Andrew walked around the corner, hair wet and a towel draped over his hips.

"Guess who just walked in the room half-naked?" Jax asked Claire, keeping with German.

"I'm guessing he has a nice body under those stuffy clothes."

"Big shoulders, tight butt . . . mmm."

"Are you talking about me?" Andrew asked in English.

"Yup!" She didn't even try to deny it.

"Okay, Yoda, I'm going to let you go before I get an eyeful," Claire teased.

"Love you."

"Love you back."

Andrew sauntered over, a huge smile on his face. "What were you saying?"

"Girl secrets."

"Secrets, huh?" He stood over her and shook his head, sprinkling water on her.

Jax squirmed out of his way.

He attempted to hold her down, but she managed to topple him onto the couch, and on the way she grabbed the towel. She was on her feet and running out of the room.

Andrew caught up with her in the bedroom, a playful tackle around her waist. Suddenly she was pinned to the bed, and their laughter melted when the kissing began.

~

Call it ADHD, the inability to follow orders, or the sheer fact that Jax couldn't sleep one more night without coming face-to-face with the woman she knew, in her heart, was her half sister . . . However it was labeled, Jax stood across the street from a café where Addison sat outside with a smattering of filled tables drinking coffee and looking at her phone.

The café was busy, making it easier for Jax to wedge her way to Addison's side.

Taking a chance, Jax ordered a coffee and a pastry and walked outside with a sign holding a number.

She walked up to Addison's table and paused. With her hair tucked up in a hat and her sunglasses shielding her eyes, Jax hoped Addison wouldn't take too close a look at her and notice how much they looked alike.

"Excuse me?"

Addison glanced up.

"Are you expecting anyone?"

She shook her head.

"I hate to ask, but would you mind terribly if I took a seat? Everything else is couples or . . ." Jax looked around, let the clientele do the talking for her.

Addison smiled, lifted her hand to the empty chair. "Absolutely."

"Thank you."

"Are you American?"

"No . . . yes . . . Born here. Spent the last six years there."

"I love America."

"You've been?"

"Yes. New York. Chicago. Los Angeles. Utterly fascinating to see women shopping in flip-flops on Rodeo Drive."

Jax couldn't help but laugh. "I live outside of LA and have more flip-flops than I care to admit."

Addison put her phone down and focused her attention on Jax.

"I'm Addison."

"Jax."

They shook hands.

"A pleasure."

The woman was older, by a hair . . . yet younger somehow.

"What took you to the States?" Jax asked.

"Family vacations. How did you end up living there?"

Jax considered lying and decided to stick to the truth. "My best friend from boarding school persuaded me to turn in London rain for Southern California's endless summers. It wasn't a hard sell."

"Yet you're back."

"I am. Family . . ."

Addison sighed. A sound that said more than words. "Welcome home, then."

And for reasons Jax couldn't explain, her throat tightened, and she pushed back tears.

"I don't believe anyone has said that to me since I arrived."

Addison stopped her coffee cup halfway to her lips. "That's terribly sad."

"In my parents' defense, they are getting a divorce and my brother was close to visiting Scotland Yard if my father didn't move out of his flat when I arrived."

Addison laughed, set her cup down, and continued to chuckle. "I'm sorry. A divorce isn't funny."

"My dad's a wanker . . . who knew? But my mother and I have never been closer. I'll take the good with the bad." It dawned on Jax once the words were out of her mouth that she'd just told her half sister that their dad was a dick.

"Parents aren't perfect, sadly." Her smile faded.

Jax reminded herself that Addison had just lost her father. And her mother had stepped out, too.

"No, they're not."

"Is your brother better now?" Addison shifted the conversation away from parents.

"There's still a risk of a misdemeanor or at the very least a lack of an invitation for a holiday, but all the felonies are off the table."

"Probably for the best."

"I agree."

They sipped their coffee and eased into a conversation about Brexit.

The longer the conversation went on, the more similarities Jax saw between the two of them.

The more Jax wanted to have a relationship with the woman.

~

It was late afternoon on Monday before the LA team was in the office and giving their report.

Claire started with the piece that Jax was most interested in. "We are ninety-five percent sure that Addison Philips is your biological half sister."

Jax closed her eyes and let those words sink in. She knew them to be true already, but to hear it confirmed made it more real.

"Theodore Philips married his third young wife despite naysayers raining on his parade. Gold digger and arm candy was the popular narrative. However, we didn't find anything ugly between the two of them. In fact, it was known that Theodore had undergone a reverse vasectomy in an effort for the couple to conceive a child. After several years of what seemed like they were trying, Marion got pregnant. We found one report saying Theodore's reverse vasectomy failed, and another one after Addison was born saying otherwise. Birth records show you and Addison have the same blood type, which in and of itself means nothing, but the family resemblance is a bit hard to deny. Outside of a swab to both your cheeks, we can call this what it is."

"Do you think Marion had sex with my father to have a child?" That's what it sounded like to her.

"Maybe. Possibly. Theodore made it perfectly clear that to avoid Marion being called a gold digger, he was leaving his estate to his daughter."

"Not his older son."

"He's a crackhead," James chimed in. "Total loser. His mother was absolutely a gold digger. Walked away from the divorce with thirty million and was broke in five years. Theodore paid for rehab several times for his son but eventually gave up. There is a stipulation in the man's will saying that if Richard can stay clean and sober for five years it's worth five million for him. But it doesn't look like Richard wants it bad enough. Instead, he's fighting the whole thing in the courts."

"What did Marion get out of it?" Sven asked.

"A daughter and a place to live. But not the house here. They have a second home in the South of France." James put an image on the shared screen.

"That's not a house. That's a villa," Jax said.

"She's not destitute. He gifted her money throughout their marriage, which she put into sound investments. The bulk of the estate is Addison's, but first she needs to go to court, and that is going to be a circus. Richard is claiming Addison isn't Theodore's daughter and says he has proof."

"Shit. How easy was it to find the vasectomy reports?"

"Not a walk in the park. But it's juicy news and Richard may have obtained it for a price," Claire told her.

"And if it's proven that Addison isn't his?" Jax asked.

"We got a copy of the will, sent it off to our lawyer. She doesn't think Richard has a chance, but because of the size of the estate and the people questioning it, it's going to be heard in court. When that media circus starts, Addison's photograph will be everywhere. And since JT Capital is the primary earner for her estate, it's going to get around the office."

"So, my father tells my mother about his affair before this can get its sea legs," Jax concluded.

"That's our theory." James patted her on the shoulder.

"It's also possible that the reason he sent you to Richter is because your parents gathered in the same social circles. Your resemblance to Addison even at a young age is rather remarkable," Claire told her.

Jax squared her shoulders and smiled at her best friend through the lens of the camera. "Well, I'm not sorry he did."

"What do you want to do with the information?" Cooper asked.

"Nothing. I'll stay out of my father's life, away from people who know him and the Philipses. My brother doesn't deserve to go down with the ship. My mother is going through enough. If she learns the entire truth, hopefully I can remind her of what is really important."

Neil's voice was a baritone of weight on the line. "For what it's worth, I'm sorry."

"Thank you, Neil. I know this whole thing wasn't a priority for the team and that you kept on it anyway. I appreciate it."

"Hey, we still don't know who was snooping around your mother's house. Our investigation wasn't completely unfounded."

"Just partially." But it was family. And that was something that Neil held close.

Cooper clapped his hands, breaking the melancholy. "In other news, Sasha paid our friend Lodovica a visit over the weekend."

"What? When?" She'd been watching the footage all day and hadn't seen her.

"Yesterday."

"What the . . ."

"Good luck picking her out of the crowd."

"She probably dressed as a nun for church services," Claire said, laughing.

That was a visual that had them all chuckling.

"Lodovica wants protection," Cooper announced.

"She's dreaming." Jax rolled her eyes.

Only Neil's face was stoic.

"You're not thinking of giving it to her."

"We're leaving it up to Sasha," Neil said.

"How can we even consider that? She's likely the one that called the papers and spilled the crap about my father."

"You pinned it yourself. Lodovica has a price on her head. If she can get out of prison and disappear, she can open up about what she knows. It's her only leverage with us."

"She also told me to use my investigative skills, as if she knows we can figure it out without her."

"We probably can, but how long will it take? How many Olivias will disappear while we're chasing leads?"

Jax couldn't believe what she was hearing.

"Sasha is on her way to Richter to talk to Charlie. Make sure their stories fit."

"What now? Is she or Charlie responsible for the GPS drop?"

"Not according to her, but she wasn't surprised."

"We're back at square one. Who dropped the device? Who is watching us? Who is opening up shop at Richter?"

"Answers the headmistress might have but won't share until we give her what she wants."

"Sounds like blackmail to me," Sven said.

"Or maybe she manifested all of this to make us think there's an issue to guarantee our help," Jax argued.

Claire paused, waved a hand at the camera. "She has a point. We have zero evidence of anything going on at the school. A tip from Charlie, who is visiting the headmistress in prison, and a simple GPS device on a rental car. Then Lodovica rattles the newspapers with some gossip to keep us engaged."

Jax pointed to her nose with one index finger and back at the camera with the other. "This!"

Neil growled. "If you're right, she won't have to worry about protection from others."

Neil did not sound happy.

They all waited for him to talk.

"Let's stay alert but bring it down a notch. Wait for Sasha's intel."

~

Once the conference call was over, Neil sealed himself in his office and tossed his com link on the desk. If Claire and Jax were right, and this whole shit show was just that . . .

He shook his head.

His gut said otherwise, but those two girls had valid points.

He pushed behind his desk and dialed up Sasha.

"Yeah?"

"Are you with him?"

"Standing by, waiting for him to show. Why?"

"I want to be a part of the conversation. We have a lot of smoking guns and no dead bodies. I want to make sure we're not chasing our tails just to give Lodovica a free ride once she's out of prison. I want to make damn sure Charlie's on the right side."

"You and I want the same thing."

"I know. Four ears are better than two."

"I see him."

Neil's spine straightened. He pushed the communication device in his ear to make it easier for him to hear and connected his phone. A few clicks of a mouse and the call was hooked to a recording device.

"Ready."

There was silence over the line, then a few clicking sounds.

Neil heard Sasha breathing.

"Hello, Charlie."

There were footsteps before a reply. "I was wondering who would end up at my door this time. I thought it would be Jacqueline. She left Germany before I had a chance to see her."

"She was being followed," Sasha said.

Neil listened closer, not making his presence known.

"I'm sorry to hear that."

"Any idea who it could be?"

There was a pause. "If this runs like it did in the past, it will be a hired hand. Someone gifted like yourself but working for the wrong side."

"We were led to believe that it was all shut down after Pohl's death and Lodovica's imprisonment. Once the board was disassembled."

"I'd hoped that was the case, Sasha. Now I believe differently," Charlie said.

The sound of him moving around the room had Neil closing his eyes.

"For someone who is so cryptic on the phone, you're sure quick to talk now."

Charlie laughed. "I'm tired. And I trust you above all others."

"Why are you visiting Lodovica in prison?"

He sighed. "Friends close and enemies closer. Truth is, I do think she's remorseful for her part. She also may have some idea who might have picked up Pohl's place, or at least know where to start looking. I keep hoping to catch her off guard."

"Any luck?"

"No."

"Did Pohl work alone?"

There was silence.

Neil finally let Charlie know he was listening. "Was that a yes or a no?"

"Neil," Sasha said as if explaining.

"I'm sure you investigated Pohl. What did you find?" Charlie asked.

"Nothing beyond him," Sasha said.

"You believe that?"

"No."

"Neither do I. Pohl cast his net over Richter slowly. He found the juiciest gossip, the most vile things that would send people to prison if they were found out. He then placed those individuals on the board to ensure their silence. It was only a matter of time before someone else came in to pick up where he left off."

"Are you suggesting the board is being stacked again?" Neil asked.

"No. But something is churning. I feel it. Just as I did before. And unlike the last time, I won't sit back and do nothing. Why do you think I stayed here? I could have retired when you left this school, should have when Linette went to prison. But if I left, who would be here to inform you and the others what is going on, so you could come in and stop it before it begins again? This is a good school. Fine students who move on to wonderful futures. It's the cancer that needs to be removed. We've been in remission, but the air is changing again."

"Who is involved? Vogt?" Sasha asked.

"I watch him above all others. I don't think so."

"Do you have a name?" Neil asked.

"He's shaking his head," Sasha told Neil.

"Watch the orphanages. Look for patterns. It may take years for this to evolve into what it was before. I don't have years. Less if those involved know I'm talking to you," Charlie said.

Neil heard the exhaustion in Charlie's voice.

Felt his sincerity.

"The London team is a few hours away if you ever need our protection," Neil offered.

"I appreciate that."

Neil tapped his pen on the desk. "One more thing."

"Yes?"

"Do you trust Lodovica?"

Charlie laughed. "I trust she will find a way to survive. I trust that if she does know something, she will be a target as soon as she is visible. I trust that she will always put herself first."

It was Sasha that let out a sigh in Neil's ear.

It looked as if Lodovica had managed to get his protection whether he liked it or not.

~

Andrew powered down his computer as the staff worked their way out the door. He was trying more and more to get out of the office at a reasonable hour. Now that there was someone in his life he wanted to spend time with, he felt it was important to enforce a work-play balance.

He walked to his father's office to see if he was walking out as well.

"Hey, Dad."

Lloyd was pushing his chair back. "Headed out?"

"I am."

"Date with a beautiful woman?"

Andrew shook his head. "She's working late tonight and headed to her mum's."

Lloyd pushed his arms into his jacket and tucked his cell phone into the breast pocket. He didn't carry a briefcase because he didn't take his work home with him. Something Andrew had yet to start doing. Maybe if he could persuade Jax to stay with him full time he'd give that a shot.

"You and Jacqueline seem to be getting along well."

Andrew felt his smile grow. "She's pretty amazing."

They started walking down the hall together as the janitorial staff worked their way in.

"When are you going to invite her over for dinner? Your mother and I didn't get to spend much time with her at that party."

The janitor pushed past with a rolling cart and excused himself when they needed to walk around him.

Andrew smiled at the man, met his eyes. "No worries. Thanks."

Hmmm.

". . . maybe this weekend?"

Andrew looked over his shoulder and shook off the feeling of someone walking over his grave. "Weekends are better. So far, anyway. I'll ask her."

He and his father walked out of the office and toward the lifts.

"How is Harry? Things simmering down?"

They talked all the way to the parking garage before going their separate ways.

~

"You heard Neil. Bring it down a notch."

Jax waved Sven out the door. "I'm working late tonight and having breakfast with my mother tomorrow."

"We don't work that way here. You can leave now and still come in late."

"I know. But I'm checking the orphanages." Jax clicked around the screen, pulled up another webpage.

"Trying to prove Charlie's tip is valid."

"Or prove it wrong. One way or another."

Sven swung his jacket over his shoulders. "Well, to me, *bring it down* means find a pub. It's been a dry few weeks."

"Have fun," she called after him as he walked away.

Even though most of the staff was gone, there were a couple of guys on surveillance watching the feeds from the homes they monitored. It was a boring detail that Jax avoided, but they all had to do it from time to time. Most of the staff in that room were new to the team, finishing school, or newly retired from the military and therefore rather used to long and late hours.

A little while later her stomach reminded her that she'd skipped lunch. And pad Thai sounded really good.

She poked her head into the surveillance room. "I'm headed across the street for Thai, you guys want anything?"

"I brought food."

"Pot stickers." One of the guys handed her cash.

She walked into the now familiar restaurant, greeted Ubon, and placed her order.

While she waited for the food, she patted her back pocket and realized she'd left her phone on her desk.

Considering they weren't allowed to have cell phones at Richter, she had certainly become dependent upon them for every quiet moment. Although she'd gotten used to unplugging when she was with Andrew. They made a point of leaving their phones tucked away when they were together and not checking their email while watching TV or going to bed.

"Miss Jack." Ubon never said her name right, and Jax didn't correct her.

"Thanks, Ubon."

"A little extra for you. Take home for your man," she said with a smile.

Jax stepped out of the restaurant and cursed the rain that had started to fall.

Someone walking toward her flipped open an umbrella and caused her to jump.

A taxi was parked half in a space and blocked her way.

Jax started to move around to the front when someone bumped into her side.

"Excuse me."

She was pretty sure someone jabbed her with an umbrella, and it was going to leave a mark.

"You need to be more care—"

The world started to tilt.

Her eyes saw double.

The last thing she remembered was the food sliding out of her hands and someone reaching around her waist.

Then the world went black.

~

"What does your gut say?" Neil asked Sasha once she'd left Charlie's side and was en route to Berlin.

"I put my money on Charlie. He's dead right about Lodovica. She knows something. Even if it's a starting point to find who Pohl worked for. That's who we need to find, and I don't think it's going to come easy."

"The question we might need to ask is, Should we make this our problem?"

Sasha let out a short laugh.

"Right. Forget I said that." Neil knew the words were full of shit before they even left his lips.

"Whoever put the tracker on Jax's car already knows we're involved."

"Unless Claire is right, and it was done by Lodovica somehow to keep us engaged to get what she wants."

"I'm going to stick around. Check out some orphanages. Let me know if something comes up."

"Copy that."

Neil hung up, rubbed at the tension between his eyes.

It was going to be a really long day.

CHAPTER
TWENTY-NINE

Andrew walked in his front door, smiled at the camera he knew was there, and said, "Hi, Jax."

He disarmed the alarm and pulled off his suit jacket. The rain had caught him off guard, and he started to strip out of his wet clothes.

He jumped in the shower and rinsed off the day.

Wearing a pair of lounge pants and a sweatshirt, he moved into the kitchen, picked up the pile of mail, and started sorting through it.

He considered making a cocktail but decided to wait for when he was with Jax. Martinis had become his new favorite, and that was all her. He loved how she nibbled at the olives and delicately removed the pit.

"You have it bad," he told himself.

He didn't care. Falling for Jax was the easy part, convincing her to stay was what took effort.

Although the Jeep was a pretty decent step in the right direction.

He walked over to his fridge and removed a bottle of water.

His eyes traveled to the front door and his spine shivered. The kind of tingling sensation you had right before you remembered something.

He walked to the door and opened it. It was getting dark.

Shaking his head, he closed the door.

That's when he remembered.

The picture Jax had shown him on her phone flashed in his brain.

And the image of the janitor pushing the cart in his office . . .

They were the same guy.

"I'll be damned."

He went to where he'd plugged his phone in to charge and dialed Jax's cell number.

It rang four times before going to voice mail.

"Jax, when you get this, call me. It's important."

He waited a good twenty minutes and tried calling her again.

Voice mail.

He called her mother's house.

"Hello, Andrew. How are you?"

"I'm good, Mrs. Simon. I'm trying to get ahold of Jax. She isn't answering her cell phone."

"She's not home yet, Andrew."

He felt his spine tingling again, this time growing cold.

"When she gets in, can you tell her to call me?"

"She said she'd be a little later. Did you try the office?" Evelyn asked.

"I'll call that now."

"I'll tell her you called."

"Thanks." He hung up.

Andrew went into his closet and pulled out a pair of jeans. At the same time, he dialed her office number.

"MacBain Security." The voice wasn't familiar.

"This is Andrew. I'm trying to get ahold of Jax. Is she there?"

"She stepped out to get some food."

He sighed. "Did she leave her cell phone behind?"

A few seconds passed. "Yeah, it's on her desk. Ubon's place is pretty popular. Gets busy this time of night. I'll tell her you called."

Andrew kicked out of his lounge pants and pulled on his jeans. "Thanks."

Her office wasn't that far, and after all the calls, and the image of the man in his office dancing in his head, he'd just as soon talk to her face-to-face.

Fifteen minutes later he was pulling down the street of MacBain Security feeling somewhat surprised she hadn't called him back.

When he saw her Jeep in the parking lot, he smiled.

He ducked under his raincoat when he jumped out of the car and ran to the building. The office doors were unlocked, the chime buzzing as he walked in.

The place was empty.

"Hello?" A man he didn't know walked around the corner.

"I'm Andrew. Looking for Jax."

"I'm Ben, she was getting . . ." Ben looked over at a desk.

Andrew followed his gaze and saw her coat on the back of the chair and her phone on the desk.

"She's been gone a while."

"Where did she go?" Andrew's breath started to pick up, his heart rate with it.

"The Thai restaurant across the street."

This didn't feel right.

Ben called out behind him. "I'm going to check on Jax."

They both walked out the door.

Andrew saw the lighted sign of the restaurant in question and doubled his step to get on the other side of traffic.

The place was crowded.

No Jax.

Andrew looked at Ben. "Where is she?"

Ben pushed his way to the front of the line. "Ubon. Did Jax come in?"

"Long time ago."

306

Andrew grew cold. He rushed out the door and looked up and down the street. "Jax?" he yelled.

The people walking by stared at him.

Ben came up behind. "What the hell."

Andrew was starting to panic, blood rushing to his ears and making them hum.

He ran a hand through his hair and looked at the ground.

He saw a takeout bag tied shut and a receipt stapled to the outside.

Picking it up, he looked inside. The containers were full and untouched.

Ben glanced at the receipt, ripped it off, and ran back in the restaurant.

When Ben returned, he was running, with a cell phone to his ear. "Neil. We have a problem."

~

Jax felt as if her eyelids were weighted shut with twenty-pound dumbbells.

The world spun and her body was limp.

She was higher than a fucking kite. She couldn't remember if she'd been drinking, and she certainly didn't do drugs, so that wasn't right.

It didn't matter. Nothing mattered. It felt so good to shut her eyes.

The next time they opened, she felt pain in her back and neck, like she'd been sitting at the same angle for far too long. Her brain was a little less dizzy, her eyelids lighter. She looked to the left, and again to the right. The space was cold, musty, and incredibly quiet.

Dark.

Maybe she was sleeping. It sure felt like a dream.

Except for the cold. That didn't fit a dream. The dizzy, yes . . . the strange location . . . that fit. But cold?

Wake up.

Her inner voice was talking to her, but her body wasn't listening.

She jolted awake with the sound of someone walking in the room.

For a minute Jax thought she was at home. Had fallen asleep in her father's study. Then she tried to move.

She pulled at her arms, felt a bind around her wrists.

Her butt was in a hard chair, her chest bound to the back. She wiggled her fingers, her hands behind her, feet tied to the legs of the chair, and Jax was still so fucking high.

What happened?

She thought of the bar in Oceanside, during the team-building weekend.

Was she dreaming?

She shook her head.

To her right she saw the shadowy figure of someone dragging something on the floor. They dropped whatever it was and turned to her.

"You're awake."

Jax opened her mouth to ask what was happening. What came out was "Waall chizen."

A hand reached out, slapped the side of her face a few times. Not a full-on assault, but not friendly either.

"Want to try that again?"

Even as she attempted to talk, all that came out was gibberish. Or a mixture of two or three languages jumbled in her head.

"You ladies enjoy the ride. We'll get to work when you can feel it."

She blinked and the person was gone.

Or maybe she fell asleep again.

Ladies?

Jax peered in the darkness.

The lump the man had brought into the room was the form of a person, curled up and lying on the floor.

Andrew followed Ben through the doors, his body in full panic mode, and raced over to Jax's desk.

Her purse was on the side, her phone in plain sight. Her coat. He picked it up and brought it to his nose.

It smelled like citrus from some kind of oil he saw her put on her neck.

Ben turned on the big screen and Neil's image jumped up, bigger than life.

Another person walked around the corner. "What's going on?"

"Jax is missing. Mobilize the team."

"Talk to me." Neil was rushing around in his home office gathering documents and shoving them in a bag while he spoke to the team on the monitors and had a phone to his ear with a separate conversation.

"She left for food. Didn't come back. Cell phone, purse, car . . . all of it is here. The bag with our order was on the sidewalk."

"How long has she been gone?" Neil asked.

"Twenty minutes."

"It's been longer than that," Andrew interrupted. "I called her at . . ." He pulled out his phone and checked his history. "Ten after six."

"Forty-five minutes," Neil stated.

"Jesus." Andrew turned a full circle. Panic overflowing in his system.

His cell phone rang in his pocket. He looked at the screen, didn't answer when he didn't recognize the number.

He dropped it on Jax's desk and pressed his hands to the flat surface.

Neil was barking orders and asking questions.

Andrew's phone rang again. "What the hell?"

"Wait!" Ben reached out and stopped Andrew from touching his phone.

"I don't know who's calling."

"Answer it," Neil said as he stood still in the frame.

Andrew slid the button over. "Hello?"

"Don't. Call. The. Police." The voice sounded electronic.

"Jesus. Jax? Jax?"

The caller hung up.

"Andrew?" Neil shouted his name. "Panic will get her killed. You sit your ass in that chair and wait for another call."

"What if they don't call? What if they hurt—"

"They won't. They want something, which is why they called. Trust my team."

"Neil."

"Trust me."

Andrew sat in Jax's chair before he fell down. He looked around the room, saw the pictures on the whiteboard.

"I think I know something," he said, his voice rising above Neil's, who was directing Ben.

"What?"

"Jax showed me a picture of a guy who came to my door shortly after you put in the system. I'd never seen him before. Until tonight. He was dressed as a janitor and at my office after we closed for the day."

"You're sure it was the same guy?"

"Positive."

"Were you in the office alone?"

"No. My father and I were walking out together."

"I want that picture uplinked to my side as soon as possible. I want a team to sweep Andrew's office, and all the feeds on Jax's family go live."

"You got it."

"Andrew?"

"Yeah?"

"I need you to write down every detail. What time you were leaving the office. What he was wearing. Did he say anything? Did he smell like anything?" Neil stopped.

"The car is ready." Gwen's voice came through the line.

Neil moved out of the camera's frame. "I love you, too," he told his wife.

When he came back on, he switched the feed to his cell phone and he was jumping in a car.

"I'll be back online in thirty minutes. Call if something develops." Neil hung up.

"We're not calling the police?"

"No."

He hadn't thought so.

"Tell me she's going to be okay."

"Jax will survive. The person who took her is an entirely different story."

~

There is a moment, right before you wake up after a decent bender, that you lie there and think . . . *If I just don't move, I can avoid getting sick.*

Every time Jax opened her eyes, the high let loose its grip, and the nausea and the headache took hold.

She did what she could to think past it and tried to stay awake. By the state of numbness in her hands and feet, she could tell she'd been sitting for hours.

Her breath started to hitch and rise as her internal fight to remain calm began.

This was not a simulation where a safe word was going to put her in a nice, comfortable room with a bowl of popcorn and a soda. And someone else was with her.

The person in the corner hadn't moved, but she could see enough movement to know whoever it was, was alive.

Jax swallowed hard, closed her eyes, and listened.

Quiet. It was hard to say if it was day or night. The room was damp, almost as if she were in a basement, and empty. Her abductor had a yellow light in one corner of the room, which she assumed was there to add light to a camera she couldn't see.

The space was primitively finished but there were no windows. Her back was to a wall.

Jax tested her bindings.

They didn't budge.

She pushed against them enough at her wrists to feel the cord cut into her skin. If nothing else, she'd leave her DNA behind for someone to find.

Panic tried to take hold, and she swallowed it back.

The team would know she was missing. They'd found her before, they'd do it again.

~

He watched two feeds, one focused on the women in the cellar, and the other on the street outside MacBain's offices. And he managed a couple of hours of sleep. Easy to do when you drugged your victims as heavily as he had.

This was not how he wanted this to go, but he was left with little choice. One token, one hit.

Two birds . . . one stone.

And his gut ached.

He'd been given his retirement token six months ago and told to wait for the call. When it came through, there would be no argument, no backing out. Do the job and walk away a free man. It seemed too good to be true. Staring at the camera, he realized it was.

Still, he was determined to make it work.

He had to make it work.

He once again removed the worn picture of his little girl and wondered if she slept with a favorite teddy, or a blanket with silk edging her mother had given her?

He'd missed so much.

This was almost over.

He kissed the picture and put it away.

CHAPTER THIRTY

"Why hasn't he called?"

Jax's office went from completely empty to brimming with people.

A live feed from the airplane Neil, Claire, and a host of others were on filled the giant screen.

Sasha had shown up first, but the others wouldn't land for another five hours.

"He will. Keep your cool."

They knew a man had taken Claire. Neil's team had downloaded video footage from one of those half a million cameras Jax had told him about. They cross-referenced those with their own, the ones surrounding their headquarters, and they saw the moment Jax was taken.

Andrew watched the footage over and over, and every time the lump in his throat grew bigger.

One minute she's looking across the street, the next she's startled by someone walking by with an umbrella. It looks as if she might have said something, then she takes a step and the bags she's holding fall to the ground. The man with the umbrella takes ahold of her. One step in the street and he pushes her in the back seat of a taxi and jumps into the driver's side. That's when they saw enough to know a man was behind the abduction.

The whole thing took less than a minute.

They traced the taxi through the city footage by the license plate until it hit a dead spot, a few blocks where no cameras were watching. Either the driver pulled over and changed the plates, or he abandoned the vehicle to climb into another.

Some of Neil's team were out there now looking for the taxi.

The others looked as if they were mobilizing for war.

That, at least, was comforting.

They had found bugs in Andrew's office. A place he never thought to look. He and Jax had talked many times over the phone while he was at work, so there was no way to know exactly what was overheard. Anything from Jax's biological sister to the secrets of Richter and the files everyone seemed to be so interested in. The only reason Andrew thought about any of it now was because Neil and the others encouraged him to write down anything that might have been overheard.

And now Jax was gone.

Each time the thought entered his head, he felt physically ill. She was gone and he didn't tell her just what she meant to him. He was too fearful he'd scare her off if he told her the depths of his feelings, and now it was too late.

Andrew looked around the room, squeezed his eyes shut.

Not too late.

Stay strong, Jax. I love you.

He swallowed his emotion and stiffened his spine.

She would be okay.

She had to be.

~

Moaning and movement brought Jax's attention to the other person in the room.

"Oh . . ."

"Hey," Jax whispered.

315

"What . . . ?"

It was a woman.

She rolled over, and Jax managed to see her face through her hair.

Jax's heart dropped.

No, no, no.

Addison Philips had her hands tied behind her back, her feet bound together. She looked as if she were trying to roll over and couldn't figure out why her hands weren't working.

"Addison?"

While lying on her back, Addison started to heave.

"No. Hey!" Jax yelled at the top of her lungs. "Get in here."

Jax attempted to move the chair, pushing her body weight against it. Anything to get over to the woman and keep her from choking on her own vomit.

She managed to move the chair two inches before her efforts rewarded her with a crash to the floor. The entire left side of her body took the impact, her head making a decent thud in her ears as it hit the ground.

The door to the room opened.

"She's puking," Jax yelled.

The man moved to Addison's side and rolled her over.

"Disgusting."

"What the hell did you give us?"

"Shut up."

Jax wiggled against the chair to no avail.

Addison coughed several times before quieting.

"Is she breathing?"

The man slid Addison over to a corner, through her vomit, and propped her up against the wall. "She's fine."

Jax closed her eyes and felt her adrenaline wane.

"You, on the other hand . . ."

She felt a warm trickle of blood down the side of her face.

The man heaved her, chair and all, back to an upright position. He grabbed her chin and moved it left, then right. "That's going to hurt."

His accent wasn't English, German, or Russian . . . but she'd heard it before.

"What do you want from us?"

Her abductor put both palms flat on Jax's legs and crouched down to her level.

Some of his features came into view. His face was familiar.

"She's leverage." He nodded toward Addison.

"What do you need from me?"

He patted her leg and stood. "All in good time."

He walked back out of the room, the door locking behind him.

"Addison? Are you okay?"

Silence.

"Fuck."

~

Dawn released fog over the city. And still nothing from Jax's abductor.

They received word that Neil's plane had landed and they were en route to headquarters.

At one point in the night, Andrew had leaned his head against the wall and exhaustion poured in. Forty-five minutes passed while he slept, but nothing had changed when his eyes opened.

Until Sven pulled the earbuds away from his ears and got everyone's attention. "There's chatter over the wire."

Sasha waved a hand. "Let's hear it."

A radio signal squeaked in the speakers in the room, the sound of police scanners Andrew had only heard on television filled the air.

Numbers were tossed out with a familiar address and the name Addison Philips.

"What are they saying?"

"Missing person's report on Addison Philips."

"You don't think . . . ," Andrew started to ask.

But the look on everyone's face said they all came to the same conclusion.

"This changes things," Sasha stated.

"Could work to our advantage," Sven said. "According to what they're saying, Addison was last seen in her home after Jax was taken."

"How long?"

"Two hours."

"Enough time to stash Jax somewhere and go get Addison."

A big-screen monitor held an image of the city, which they now expanded to encompass Addison's home address.

James typed into the computer, and the map started popping up circles and radii around the abduction sites.

"What if he's not working alone?"

"Then they could be anywhere, but right now this is what we have to go on. We need to get Jax on the phone."

The team had already told Andrew that when the phone rang, he needed to demand to speak to Jax. And the only question he needed to ask was *"How are you?"*

The abductor wouldn't let the phone call go on too long. But if he did, the next important question was *"How are you being treated?"*

They'd already attempted to call the number that had dialed in to Andrew's phone, only to find a disconnected number that was no longer in service.

Waiting became Andrew's nightmare.

~

The air in the room was stale and smelled like the underside of someone's acidy stomach. It was in a moment of complete silence that she heard the faint echo of a train. A horn, distant, and a rumble. Horns sounded at crossings. It was something. Not much, but something.

Geography, however, was not what was plaguing her.

It was the man holding her hostage.

He let her see his face.

And that never ended well.

It took a few minutes after he'd left them alone for Jax to recognize him. The man had shown up at Andrew's. Why? Was he looking to abduct him? Use Andrew as leverage?

Jax rolled the few words he'd spoken to her over her own tongue. His accent tickled the back of her head. Estonian . . . Turkish? *Time . . . time . . .* She said the word over and over in her head, attempting to hear the accent and pick it apart. Something about the vowels.

Then it clicked. *"I haven't seen you here before."*

Hungarian.

Budapest.

She closed her eyes, pictured the club in Budapest she'd been in last year. The place that was overflowing with people of questionable character. A safe zone where one could go to obtain information.

"A chardonnay?"

The bartender.

Jax visualized the whole scene . . . she and Leo walked into A Róka. She wore a revealing gown to keep eyes on her and off of Leo. The bartender who served them was the same man holding the ties now.

"What's happening?" Addison's voice was a whisper in the corner.

"You're okay, Addison. You're going to be okay."

"I know you." She looked closer.

"Yes, we met at the café."

"What's going on?"

"We've been kidnapped. Drugged."

"Oh, God. I'm tied up." Addison's voice lifted and started to shake.

"People are looking for us. Try and stay calm." Jax's voice wasn't as convincing as she'd like it to be.

Addison started to cry.

~

Neil, Claire, Cooper, and two older men Andrew had never met rolled into the building carrying long cases and determination.

Claire walked up to Andrew first and put her arms around him. "You okay?" she asked.

"No."

She pushed away. The fear in her eyes was below the surface, but it was there. "We will get her out of this."

Neil walked over, put a hand on Andrew's shoulder. "Underestimating her was this man's first mistake."

"I hope you're right."

Neil gave a single nod. "We're not here."

Andrew didn't understand.

"No one knows we're in the country, and it's staying that way," Claire told him.

"Just get her back."

"We will."

Andrew's phone rang, and everyone in the room stilled.

Neil put a hand in the air, and someone close by nodded.

"Andrew. *How are you? How are you being treated?*" Sven looked him in the eye.

He nodded.

"Answer it."

He couldn't press the button fast enough.

"Hello?" The phone was on speaker.

"You have thirty minutes to meet my demands." The voice was computer generated.

"I want to speak to Jax."

"The hidden files. I want them, all of them."

Sasha pushed forward. "What are you talking about?"

"Richter."

"We don't—" Sasha began.

"I will start shooting. Don't fuck with me."

Andrew squeezed his fists shut.

"They're not here. We do not have them in a database."

"Then you have a lot of work to do and thirty minutes to do it. I have two beautiful women here I will be happy to remove from the gene pool. One to prove I will, and the other to ensure my success."

Andrew brought his lips closer to the phone. "How do we know you haven't killed them already? Let me talk to Jax. We need to know she's okay."

The phone made a clicking noise. Then they heard him again. "Tell them."

"I'm fine, really. Tired."

"Jax, is that you? You don't sound good," Sasha asked.

"Should have taken that trip to Scotland."

"Jax, honey—"

"Enough. Thirty minutes. Ticktock."

He hung up.

"No!"

Neil clapped his hands, and everyone in the room started to move.

One of the older guys that came in with Neil walked to a whiteboard and wrote.

I'M FINE REALLY TIRED. SHOULD HAVE TAKEN THAT TRIP TO SCOTLAND.

"What is he doing?" Andrew asked Claire.

"Deciphering her message."

"What message?" Andrew asked.

The man at the board started underlining words, and explaining out loud. "*Fine* means one. We're dealing with one person, so far as she knows. *Really* . . . she recognizes him. *Tired* means she's in one place, they aren't on the move. *Should have taken that trip to Scotland. Trip* is train. She's close to a train track."

Andrew shook his head. "How do you know?"

"Let's narrow this field down," Neil tapped on the screen with the map.

Claire explained.

"We have different words for numbers. *Fine* is one. *Great* is two. *Been better* is three. If she used a combination of those words, we'd know it was four or more. *Really* means she knows who this person is. *Truly* would mean it's a stranger to her. *Exhausted* means they're on the run. *Tired* means they're stagnant. If there is something else, she can tell us the noise she hears. If she'd said she could use a *vacation* it means she hears an airport, but she said *trip*, and that means—"

"Train," Andrew caught on and finished for her. "She's close to a train track."

"Right."

"*Scotland* is the other clue, but what does it mean?" Cooper asked.

The team in the room started shouting out their thoughts.

"North."

"From what the footage from the street looked like, we have to assume she was drugged. There is no way to know if she has a clue where she is exactly."

"Still on the continent?"

"Could be." Cooper wrote it down.

"Cold and damp," Andrew tossed out. "Green."

"Isolated."

Claire walked to the board. "Basement. The one thing we don't really have much of in California."

"Good start," Neil shouted. "Lars, how are we on the files?"

"I'm on it."

"Isaac, where did that call come from?"

"Five minutes."

"James?" Neil called out. "*Ticktock*. You be ready."

James saluted the man.

"What does that mean?" Andrew asked.

Claire looked him in the eye. "We could be dealing with a bomb."

Andrew grew cold.

~

"You're the bartender."

"And you're the bimbo. Only not quite what you seem."

"Don't be offensive," Jax said. "Why the files? Why not just ask for money?"

"Money is not what I want."

That wasn't expected.

"How did you learn about Addison?"

At the sound of her name, the other woman in the room lifted her head.

"Your boyfriend isn't as good at finding things as you are." The Hungarian walked over to Addison, looked down. "You both led me right to her. With all the money, you'd think you would at least have a big dog."

"You're an asshole," Addison told him.

He grinned. "Yes. This is true."

"You followed us in Germany," Jax said.

"I did. I learned that your team is not as good as they seem. So here we are."

"You'll be hunted down for the rest of your life," Jax told him.

The man shook his head. "Nothing new."

Not good. Not good at all.

"You're going to kill us."

The Hungarian sucked in a long breath, released it slowly. "Probably. Many of you, if I can."

Jax felt her muscles tighten.

"You don't have to do this."

"Oh, but I do. I'm sorry. Really. Collateral damage is unfortunate. Now you both make peace with your maker . . . and each other. I have things to do."

~

They narrowed their search to a twenty-mile radius and were on the move.

Their team broke in two.

Neil looked over his shoulder at his team while Sven drove them to a central point to await the next phone call.

Sasha headed up the second team, James at the wheel.

Claire sat beside Andrew, who was holding up well . . . considering. The rest of them were dressed for business. Sniper rifles at their sides, bulletproof vests, black fatigues . . . they were ready.

The outcome ran in his head like a rolling camera. They'd find this fucker. Release Jax and her sister. And either end this miserable fuck's life or push him so far down in a cell he'd wish they had taken the shot.

"We're in position," Sasha reported over their headsets.

Lars sat in front of a motherboard and monitors with all of their locations being tracked. An uplink on the van would give them the juice they needed to narrow the cell signal once the call came through.

"This is the part about Jax's job that she doesn't talk about, isn't it?" Andrew asked.

Neil glanced over to see Claire pat Andrew's leg and smile.

No one commented.

Sven pulled the van off the country road. "This track follows all the way to Sasha."

Neil looked at his watch. "Two minutes."

~

"We're going to die," Addison said the second the Hungarian left the room.

"No, we're not." Jax's mind scrambled.

"How did this—"

"Shhh." Jax strained her ears. "Do you hear that?" It sounded like a car.

"No."

"We're in some kind of basement."

"It's a root cellar," Addison told her.

Jax took a look around the best she could. "How do you know that?"

"My grandmother lived on a farm. I went there as a child."

"Where does one put a root cellar? Next to the house?"

"My grandmother's was under a shed."

Jax glanced at the light in the corner of the room. "Hey!" she yelled at the camera.

"What are you doing?" Addison asked.

"I need to pee," Jax yelled.

"I don't think he cares."

Jax shook her head. "I don't think he's here."

That had Addison sitting up a little taller.

"Can you get over to me?"

Addison started to scoot, and for the first time since they both woke up, Jax felt in control.

CHAPTER THIRTY-ONE

The cell phone rang.

Andrew waited for a signal from Lars to pick it up.

"Hello?"

"I have the uplink address."

"I want to talk to Jax."

"Would you like to hear her scream while I shoot her sister?"

Claire grasped Andrew's arm. "What's the address?"

Lars wrote down a set of numbers, and Sven put the van in motion.

The computer-generated voice gave an uplink address.

Claire wrote it down.

"It's a large file, it will take time to download."

"Ten minutes."

"It's encrypted," Claire said to the caller. "It will show you three pages to prove it's there. You release a hostage and we'll give you the code for the rest."

The line went dead.

Andrew closed his eyes. "What now?"

Lars showed them a location, and Sven hit the gas.

~

"Bottom of my right shoe, by the heel, there's a small blade."

Addison scooted around to where her back was to Jax's, her fingers fiddling with her shoes. "Why do you have a knife in your shoe?"

"Long story. Can you feel it?"

"I think so."

"It should slide out the back. It's about two inches long."

"Got it."

"It's sharp, be care—"

"Ouch."

"Careful."

"I'm okay."

Jax managed to hop the chair a couple of inches to the left. "Can you reach my hands?"

Addison pushed to her knees. "Yeah."

"Start cutting."

"I'm going to hurt you."

"But we won't be dead. Just start hacking."

～

Their van arrived at the same time as the second team.

The farmhouse was in the middle of nowhere. From the look of it, it was abandoned.

"Stay here," Neil told him as they jumped out.

Andrew stood back while Neil's people fled the vans.

Lars handed Andrew a headset, and he put it on.

"Team Two in position."

"There is no heat signature inside," Andrew heard someone say.

"Team Three? Any noise inside?" Neil asked.

"Negative," Lars said beside Andrew.

"Does anyone else feel this was too easy?"

"Moving closer," Claire said.

"Hold up."

Andrew stepped out of the van to look at the scene.

Everyone was spread out, at least one team member perched in a tree.

"Where are the train tracks?" Sasha's voice called over the headset.

He looked around but didn't see any.

Andrew's phone rang.

"Answer it," Lars told him.

His hands shook. "Hello?"

"I don't take ultimatums." The abductor hung up.

"No!" Andrew looked at the house and started to run toward it.

Someone pushed him to the ground.

The sound of a gunshot came from inside the house.

Someone screamed.

"Hold your position!" Neil yelled. No headset needed.

Out of the corner of Andrew's eye, he saw Cooper grab Claire around the waist.

"It's a trap. Fall back."

"The signal is coming from due east," Lars announced.

Andrew scrambled to his feet, adjusted his headset.

Cooper reached the van with Claire, and Andrew followed their lead.

"Ben, what's your range?"

"Two hundred yards."

Neil made a circle motion with his hand. *"Stay behind. On my cue, pop the door."*

"You got it, boss."

Andrew jumped in the van, which moved the second the last of them were inside. "What's going on?"

"They're not in there."

"We heard a gunshot."

"With no vibration. It was a recording," Lars announced.

"A recording to get us to rush inside."

"Because this guy doesn't want the files. He wants us."

"There!" Sven pointed across the road to what was left of a barn. Outside of it was a black London-issue taxi.

"Quiet and quick. Get in position and stand by. *Ben?*"

"*Yeah?*"

"*Stand by.*"

~

The door to the cellar opened, this time wide.

Light from the outside poured in and silhouetted the Hungarian.

Jax sat in the chair, hands behind her back.

Addison was in her corner, ropes around her ankles.

He started to laugh. "Nice try." He waved a gun at Addison. "Stand up."

They'd just cut the last rope free when they heard noise from above.

It was almost like he was giving them a glimmer of hope . . . only to slam the door shut.

Addison shimmied up the wall.

Jax gave up the pretense of having her hands tied and slowly brought them around to rest in her lap.

"Eh, eh . . . don't move. Or your sister goes night night."

"Her what?" Addison cried.

The Hungarian walked to Addison, pressed the barrel of the gun to her temple.

"You get up from the chair and move to the corner and sit down," he ordered Jax. "Slow."

What was he doing?

There was too much space between them, and bullets moved faster than legs. Left without a choice, Jax did what he said.

He put an arm around Addison's neck and moved backward, with her stumbling to stay on her feet.

"What are you doing?"

"Insurance." He reached behind the door with one hand and brought into view a vest.

A vest that looked entirely too familiar. "No."

He lifted it in front of Addison. "Put out your arm."

"What is that?"

He shoved the gun until she had to move her head. "Put out your arm."

Addison pushed her chin higher and did what he said.

Her eyes locked with Jax's.

Jax's mind scrambled for an out.

Once the vest was over Addison's shoulders, he slid something around her neck and secured it to something inside one of the pockets. He nudged her toward the chair. "Nice and easy. Sudden movements will be painful to all of us. Sit."

"You're going to get what you want," Jax told him.

"Put your hands behind the back of the chair."

He tossed a pair of handcuffs to Jax. "On your knees. Crawl over and put these on her."

Movement was good.

Jax did as he said, put the cuffs on Addison.

"Tighter."

She pushed them in another click.

"Harder."

Two more clicks.

"I'm sorry," Jax whispered to Addison.

A buzzer on his watch sounded, and he reached for a cell phone in his pocket. He kept his gun pointed at the two of them as he made a call. "I don't take ultimatums," he said.

Jax heard someone yelling no before the Hungarian ended the call.

"What are you doing?"

"Wait for it."

He nodded a few times, smiled as he listened to the air. "Your team is good. Patient."

Jax's mind was reaching for answers.

He tossed her another set of handcuffs. "Her foot to the chair."

Jax took her time, noticed him listening toward the door.

He seemed to have lost track of what he asked her to do, his attention focused on whatever was happening outside.

Jax noticed his breathing increase.

He was expecting something.

"What's going on?"

He walked closer to the door. The smile on his face fell.

"Stand up."

The best command yet.

Jax stood and inched herself in front of Addison.

The gun was close.

A dozen ways to get it out of his hands and survive ran a course through her brain.

As every second passed, the Hungarian grew more nervous.

"What are you listening for?"

"Shh!"

She inched closer. "Are you expecting someone?"

"Shut up!" He leveled the gun at her head.

"Oh, God," Addison cried behind her.

Jax looked, saw a timer on her chest flashing red.

There was no time to play.

Distract, disarm, survive.

"C'mon. Please. You don't have to do this. You can have whatever you want." Jax started rambling and shuffling her feet.

"I said, shut up!"

And then it happened.

An explosion not too far away felt like an arrow through Jax's chest.

The Hungarian smiled, his shoulders fell. "Your team was very patient."

"What did you do?" Her heart sunk with what he was implying.

"Just in case someone survived. You come with me."

No, no, no . . . they were smarter than that.

"Move."

Her heart raced.

"Move!"

She reached the door.

Jax stopped quickly, grabbed her stomach, and bent over and started to gag.

The barrel of the gun touched her side and shoved. "Move."

She took one step, pivoted, and grabbed his hand before he could squeeze off the first round.

Searing heat on the side of her leg raced through her, but she wasn't about to stop.

Another three rounds fired into the door and the wall as they struggled for control.

Her ears rang.

She kept her frame crouched, and when he bent with her, she shot up. The back of her head hit his jaw and he stumbled back and fell onto the ground, the gun now in her grip.

He wiped blood off his lips with the back of his hands and started to laugh.

"You won't shoot."

"Don't tempt me."

"Who will disarm the bomb?"

Jax looked over at Addison, who was hyperventilating and watching the numbers tick down.

"Stop it."

He started to stand.

"On your knees," she yelled.

Another glance at Addison. "Don't look at it. We'll get out of here."

"Two minutes."

Addison lifted her head and screamed.

Jax shifted her eyes and saw the Hungarian reaching behind his back.

A slight glimmer of light hit a metal object, and Jax unloaded the weapon.

~

He heard the blast before he realized he was being thrown across the room by the force of the impact. He felt his second weapon slide out from under his fingertips and heard it hit the floor.

Heat filled him and instantly turned cold as his eyes moved to his chest.

Blood pumped out with every beat of his heart.

He lifted a hand and tried to take a breath.

Only it didn't come.

The others he'd taken from the world were there. All of them in their last moments.

The same look on their faces that he knew was on his.

Disbelief.

Jax dropped the gun and rushed to Addison's side.

"Get it off me."

Jax shook her head. "I don't know which wire."

He tried to talk.

Blood spilled from his throat.

With his last ounce of strength, he grasped at his pocket, felt his sticky fingers on her picture, and looked at his Alexandrea one last time.

I'm sorry . . . so sorry.

And the world went dark.

~

"Cut them all."

"It will go off."

Tears streamed down Addison's face.

Jax felt hers rising to the surface.

"Get out of here."

"No."

"We don't both have to die."

This time Jax screamed. "No!"

Think, Jax. Think!

"Jax?" A man's voice from above.

She scrambled to her feet. "Here. We're down here. There's a bomb."

"Where?"

"Strapped to Addison. One minute thirty seconds."

James rushed down the stairs alone and ran to Addison with a pair of wire cutters in his hands. "Get out of here," he told Jax.

"No."

She knelt beside her sister, the woman she didn't know, and placed a hand on her cheek. "Look at me."

"I'm going to die."

"No, you're not. James is good. A little cocky sometimes, but good."

"We're coming down," Neil called from above.

"No. Get back . . . far back!" they yelled.

"Jax?"

It was Andrew's voice.

"Get out of here."

"I love you."

She held back tears. "I love you, too."

James snipped one wire. "Why don't you save that for when we're done here?" Another wire down.

Each cut made her flinch.

The time still ticked away the seconds.

James looked up at her. "Here goes nothing."

Jax held Addison's head in her hands.

James cut the wire and the lights turned off.

~

Neil and Cooper stood to Andrew's side, holding him back.

They heard sirens in the distance.

The first explosion, he'd been expecting. Neil said it was a trap that would go off once Ben shot open the door. He was right. The blast would haunt Andrew for years.

But as he stood watching the empty space of a barn and a stolen taxi, all he prayed for was silence.

Just walk out.

Just walk out.

Neil looked at his watch and closed his eyes.

Andrew held his breath.

Sirens grew closer.

"Jax!" Claire screamed.

He looked up and saw her limping out. Cooper and Neil let go, and Andrew ran to her.

There was blood on her legs, her face. Her eye was starting to swell.

But she was alive.

As soon as he was at her side, James let her go and focused his attention on Addison.

"I thought we lost you," Claire said, pulling Jax into a hug.

"Takes more than one guy to do that."

Jax took a step, lost her balance.

Andrew reached for her and lifted her into his arms.

"Claire?" Neil called out behind them.

Andrew looked over, saw Neil motioning his hand for the others to come.

"I gotta go," she told Jax.

Jax handed Claire something.

"What is this?"

"A picture. He was holding it. When he died."

Claire waved it in the air.

"I'll see you when you officially get here."

Claire kissed her friend's cheek and ran off.

Andrew carried Jax and followed James to one of the vans.

The other one was already on the move and disappearing before anyone could identify them.

"Are you okay?" Jax asked.

He shook his head. "I'm never letting you go."

He felt her arms tighten around his neck.

At the van, he heard Sven on the phone talking to what sounded like the police and telling them they needed an ambulance.

Andrew set Jax down next to Addison as James opened up a first aid kit.

"Damn, Jax, why did you let him get so close?"

She smiled and looked over at Addison. "Are you okay?"

"You saved my life." Her eyes met James's. "You both saved my life."

"You kept your cool. Most would have been a hysterical mess."

Addison blinked away tears. "It was pretty messy toward the end."

Jax reached out and grasped her hand.

James ran a pair of scissors up Jax's pant leg and exposed the gunshot wound. "Bee sting."

Andrew felt his stomach twist. "Jesus. That's more than a scratch."

James nodded toward the barn. "You should see the other guy."

Jax grasped Andrew's hand with her free one. "It's a flesh wound. I'll be fine."

He swallowed . . . hard. "Any chance I can talk you into changing jobs?"

"Good chance this week. Not sure about next."

Andrew sat beside her as James placed a massive bandage on her leg. Andrew pressed his lips close to her ear. "I love you."

She squeezed his hand. "I love you, too."

~

Much as Jax didn't want to bring media attention to any relationship between Addison and herself, it wasn't something she could control.

They both spent the night in the hospital, mainly because of the drugs the Hungarian had given them. A few stitches and antibiotics accompanied by a killer headache rounded out her physical trauma.

That and the image of the man she'd shot.

She'd woken in the night, the sounds of gunshots in her head. Andrew reached over from the chair he was sleeping in and took her hand.

"I'm sorry I woke you up," Jax whispered.

"Bad dreams?"

Much as she hated to admit it. "Yeah."

"We'll use those phone numbers the social worker gave us."

She wasn't going to suggest otherwise. Closing her eyes made her see the man in a pool of blood.

"He wasn't after the files. He wanted to take out the team."

"You don't have to go over this tonight."

She rolled her head to the side and smiled against her pillow. "I know. But . . . I told him he'd be hunted for the rest of his life, and he said he already was. Someone was forcing him. We need to find out who that is."

"You need to get some sleep."

She closed her eyes. "Okay."

~

Jax sat in the wheelchair she would be forced to use when she exited the hospital. Beside her, Addison Philips did the same.

They both asked to have a moment alone before rolling out the door to the media that was waiting.

"My father always knew," Addison told her. "He didn't know who, according to my mother, but . . . he looked the other way. She wanted a baby, and he loved my mother."

"Their secret almost got you killed."

"I could say the same to you. Only it sounds as if your father pushed you away at an early age to avoid anyone finding out."

"It was me looking for the truth that led the Hungarian to you. I'm sorry for that."

"It's not your fault," Addison said.

"What do you want the media to know?"

According to Jax's coworkers and Andrew, the media was spinning it with a story saying, "A millionaire heiress in a battle for her estate and a private investigator who bears a striking resemblance to her were kidnapped and held for ransom. A private security team closely tied to the investigator are working with the London police to determine if the deceased assailant acted alone or with others. Both victims will be under tight security until possible threats can be flushed out and eliminated."

"Secrets are only useful when they're hidden. If I had known I had a sister in your line of work, maybe I would have had an eye over my shoulder. Or at least an alarm on my front door."

Jax smiled. "I've been meaning to talk to you about that."

"You don't have to. Your friend James might have mentioned it."

It was good to laugh. "I'll be sure and get you the family rate."

Addison's gaze moved to the window of the hospital room they were sitting in. Outside, their families were waiting.

"Where do you and I go from here?" Addison asked.

"I'd like the opportunity to know you."

"I'm so happy to hear you say that. I've never had a sister."

Jax thought of Claire. "I have. It's everything it should be."

"And our parents?"

Jax cringed. "I think family reunions will have to wait. My mother just learned of you."

"That has to hurt."

"She's strong."

Addison reached forward, clasped her hand. "Tea next week?"

Jax grinned. "What do you think about martinis?"

EPILOGUE

"I now pronounce you husband and wife. You may kiss your bride."

Jax was all tears when Cooper and Claire sealed the deal with a kiss to end all kisses.

The minister announced the couple, and they turned to walk down the aisle.

They stopped at the first set of chairs, and Claire accepted Neil's soul-touching hug. In all the years Jax had known the man, she'd never seen him shed one tear.

Until now.

Later, after the pictures were taken, the sun had set, and the lights in the courtyard of Neil and Gwen's California estate twinkled above, Jax danced in Andrew's arms.

"Have I told you how much I love this dress?" Andrew's hand slid down her back, his fingers touching the bare skin her dress revealed.

"Months ago."

He whispered in her ear how he wanted to take it off of her later that night.

"Naughty suggestions," she teased.

"Are you going to miss living here?" Andrew asked.

"Considering I've been back three times in the last six months, I'd say it's hard to miss what you're continually doing."

He spun her around. Pulled her back close to his frame.

Jax glanced over at her mother. "You need to dance with my mum."

"I'd be happy to."

They walked off the dance floor, and Andrew extended his hand. "C'mon, Ms. Simon . . . show me what you got."

Jax stood aside and watched the two of them take the floor.

Claire walked over and stood at her side. "She looks like she's having a good time."

"I saw her dancing with Isaac . . . three times."

"I counted four," Claire said.

"That can't happen."

Claire's staccato laugh was contagious. "By the way, how is Fluffy?"

Jax rolled her head back. "Huge. Darn dog takes up half the bed."

"That's what German shepherds do."

"When Andrew talked me into a dog, I thought the London purse variety . . . I wasn't expecting a police dog."

"Andrew's been gun-shy for months," Claire said.

"He's better since we have a lead from Lodovica."

"Only a matter of time before we have what we need."

"Have you figured out where Neil and Sasha stashed the headmistress?"

"Someplace cold. That's all I could find."

Jax sighed. "Probably best that we don't know."

"I hope wherever it is, the accommodations are less than Richter or a German prison," Claire said.

"Agreed."

"How is Addison?"

"She's doing much better since the trial is over. Her brother is a piece of work. But her dad made sure his will covered all the bases."

"Does she want to meet your dad . . . er, her real dad?"

Jax shrugged. "She's not ready. She's happy getting to know me and Harry. Can't wait for you to come back so we can do a weekend in Paris." Addison had become a friend and was fast becoming the sister she'd never known. The trauma with the Hungarian was something they talked about often, and when Addison asked Jax to join her for a session with her therapist, she went without question. After all, it was Jax who'd led the man to her. Although Addison didn't hold it against her.

Still . . . Jax hadn't forgotten.

"Look at that." Claire pointed to Isaac cutting in on Andrew's dance with Jax's mother.

"I'm going to have to have a word with him."

Cooper walked up, slid his arm around his bride. "What are you two huddled over here talking about?"

"Isaac is hitting on Evelyn."

"Go, Mom."

Jax shoved him.

Cooper laughed.

Andrew danced over to her side. "My son-in-law duty is over," he announced.

Jax narrowed her eyes. "Son-in-law duty?"

"You don't like the idea of me being a son-in-law?"

"I didn't say that."

He slid his arm around her waist, started pulling her back on the dance floor. "Then we'll call it what it is. Son-in-law duties."

Jax heard Claire and Cooper laughing as they moved out of range.

"I think there's an important step before we obtain new titles."

Andrew nuzzled his face next to hers. "I'll have to get working on that, then."

Jax couldn't stop smiling. "Do you ever think about how lucky we are?"

"Every day since we met."

"All the things that had to come into place to make this moment happen."

He laughed in her ear as the music slowed down. "I can't believe you thought I was a driver."

She wrapped her arms around him, leaned back, and looked in his eyes. "You still haven't paid me back that tip I gave you."

His smile was contagious. "I'll pay you back on our honeymoon."

"I'll take you up on that."

Behind them, Jax heard her mother laughing.

Isaac was whispering something in her mum's ear, his hand on her hip.

Jax started to pull away.

Andrew stopped her. "Your mother deserves an unexpected distraction."

"Are you ready to have Isaac as your stepdad-in-law if their unexpected matches our unexpected?"

"The best things in life aren't planned."

Jax turned back to him. "You're the best thing in my life."

I love you. He mouthed the words to her.

"I love you, too."

~

"This is your room, Alexandrea. There is a drawer under the bed for your things. I know this is hard, losing your mother and being moved so far from your home."

"Why?"

"Our home for children has benefactors who make sure your needs are met. And when the time comes, you'll go to a beautiful, spacious boarding school where you'll have the finest education money can buy."

"I don't care. I want to go home."

She placed a hand on Alexandrea's cheek and sat beside her on the bed. "There is no one there to go back to, m'dear. We're your family now. We'll take good care of you."

ACKNOWLEDGMENTS

Writing throughout 2020 has been a constant challenge, but that is behind us, and now we have toilet paper, so yeah! Seriously though, it takes a village, and now is the time I thank mine.

Thank you again, Maria Gomez, for your patience and understanding with this crazy year. Your ideas and guidance with every book are always welcome, and the team effort is never overlooked.

Thank you, Amazon Publishing and Montlake and the entire team, for making this book what it is.

My agent, Jane Dystel, who is my kickstand when I need someone to lean on and motivator when I need a kick in the pants . . . thank you.

Lastly, to whom I dedicated this book. Holly Ingraham, my developmental editor and friend I have yet to meet in person thanks to this crazy new world we live in. You've helped shape my last several books, but this one stands out as one where your stamp and enthusiasm were essential. If every reader loves it as much as you do, it is bound to be an overnight success. Thank you for all your hard work and dedication to making every book the best it can be and pushing me each and every time.

Until we meet in person . . . cheers.

Catherine

ABOUT THE AUTHOR

Photo © 2015 Julianne Gentry

New York Times, *Wall Street Journal*, and *USA Today* bestselling author Catherine Bybee has written thirty-five books that have collectively sold more than eight million copies and have been translated into more than twenty languages. Raised in Washington State, Bybee moved to Southern California in the hope of becoming a movie star. After growing bored with waiting tables, she returned to school and became a registered nurse, spending most of her career in urban emergency rooms. She now writes full time and has penned the Not Quite series, the Weekday Brides series, the Most Likely To series, and the First Wives series.